THEIR VIRGIN PRINCESS

Masters of Ménage, Book 4

Shayla Black and Lexi Blake

THEIR VIRGIN PRINCESS
Masters of Ménage, Book 4
Shayla Black and Lexi Blake

Published by Shayla Black and Lexi Blake
Copyright 2013 Black Oak Books LLC
Edited by Chloe Vale and Shayla Black
ISBN: 978-1-939673-01-5

THEIR VIRGIN PRINCESS

Masters of Ménage, Book 4

Shayla Black and Lexi Blake

Bonus material and excerpts at the conclusion of this book.

Prologue

Nothing could cut the heat of the jungle. The fan overhead turned, but sweat still ran down her forehead. She would have wiped it away, but the fuckers had tied her hands to the bedpost the night before. Poor little kidnappers couldn't handle one small escape attempt without getting pissy. Too bad she'd only managed to cut one of them before they had captured her again.

Alea closed her eyes. Sunset had shadowed the little room with increasing darkness. They would be back, and she wasn't sure she could handle another night of watching her abductors use the other women they had caged with her.

They were all in school, the pigs had told her. They were supposed to learn what a woman's real place was.

Before she'd been taken and sent to this hell, she'd been a graduate student at New York University, studying international politics. Now she was majoring in misery, forced to watch her fellow abductees endure all kinds of sexual deviancy from men who abused them.

From the room beside her, she could hear the high-pitched whimper of a woman in pain and the staccato thud of a headboard hitting the wall.

Alea shut her eyes, wishing she could close her ears to block out the sound. When would this nightmare end? The days were bleeding together. She was losing track of time—and her grip on the carefree woman she'd once been.

When she'd first been abducted, she'd kept a careful count, marking out each day in small scratches on the wall. They were still there, all sixty-some odd lines—proof that she'd once hoped someone would find her. The endless cycle of time and pain had marched on, and she'd stopped carving those stupid lines. With no way to fight the drugs they fed her, time had become meaningless. She merely alternated between being dazed and terrified. When she was lucid, the world around her seemed foreign. Rapid-fire Spanish she couldn't quite wrap her brain around and unfamiliar men, not to mention a situation so alien and horrific, she still struggled to comprehend. Coping was out of the question. Did it matter if she was here a day or a lifetime? Hell was hell.

And she was quickly rotting in it.

Lately, her captors had taken to doping her up more. Some days, Alea wasn't sure what was real and what was a hallucination. The worst part was being dependent on that needle. Even now she was sweating, her stomach cramping, because she'd been too long without a fix, but there was no way they would wean her off of it again after her last escape attempt.

Suddenly, the doorknob was turning. Alea frowned, bracing herself. Perhaps this would be the end. Maybe this would be the moment they bound and trussed her up, then shipped her off to some asshole who would rape her and torture her for the rest of her short life. And it would be short, because she had no intention of being some man's plaything. She was Alea Binte al Mussad, descendant of the royal family of Bezakistan. She was a princess. She had pride. And she would go down fighting and try her damnedest to take as many of these bastards with her as she could.

A single moment flashed across her mind. A sweet summer's day at the palace when she'd been a child turning her face up to the sun. The inner garden had been her own private world. Her beloved cousins had been older, but they'd still played hide and seek with her, calling for their little "monkey," a nickname she'd earned because she climbed the trees and made her nannies insane with worry.

But they don't know you, little monkey, Talib would say. *They don't know how strong you are. One small tree can't*

6

take you down. Some days, I'm not even certain a small army can.

The door opened with a small squeaking sound that signaled her torture would now continue. There were no trees to climb in this place, no armies to fight, only suffering.

She turned her gaze to see which pig had come to hurt her. An unfamiliar man in all black slid inside the door with a gun wrapped around his chest. He held it the way she'd seen military men grip their weapons, like a mere extension of their arms.

Was this a new torturer? If so, then her end would likely be very soon because this man was a killer.

"Alea?" The words were whispered, but came through loud and clear as if the man who spoke them expected to be understood and obeyed.

No one had called her by her name in…forever. Here, she was "girl" or "*puta*." For the briefest moment, she considered denying her name and perhaps avoiding her terrible fate, but her name was all she had left. If she died, she would die as Alea.

"Yes."

"I need you to stay as quiet as possible. My name is Cole Lennox. Your cousin sent me."

It took a moment for the words to sink in. Cole Lennox? She'd never heard of the man before. Her cousin? Talib? Or Yasmin? Would Yas even know how to hire a mercenary? It didn't matter. Someone had come for her. Or had her "keepers" found a new, fun way to torment her and extort money from her royal relatives? Would this man get her hopes up, only to show her a new terror?

Cole Lennox towered over her. "You're going to fight me, aren't you? You think you don't know me, but you do. I saw you once at the palace right after I brought Tal back from his ordeal. You invited me into the drawing room and offered me tea. I need you to understand that if I have to, I will knock you out in order to save you."

Tears welled, the first she'd felt in months, and she fought them ferociously. Now that he was closer, she remembered. Lieutenant Lennox had saved her cousin from radicals, and now it appeared he was going to save her.

"They don't allow me clothes. I'm not wearing anything under this sheet." Shame crashed over her like a wave on the beach.

He shrugged out of the black shirt he wore, revealing a T-shirt. He set the shirt aside and produced a knife. Her hands and feet were free in seconds, and he was wrapping the shirt around her, carefully avoiding looking for more than a cursory glance below her neck.

Alea stood, her hands shaking as Cole Lennox began to lead her out, step by creeping step. In the distance, she heard gunfire and shouting.

"That's baby brother doing his job." He winked over his shoulder at her. "Let's get you home."

She followed Cole out, but the girl he'd met all those years ago was long gone. They could take her back to the palace, but a part of her would always be trapped here, forever tainted.

Chapter One

Bezakistan – Two years later

Alea escaped from the glittering lights and laughter of the ballroom. Everything about the evening was lovely and elegant, and she couldn't breathe. It wasn't her dress or the amount of food she'd consumed, but the press of bodies, the expectation, the terror she could never quite shake...

The warm night air caressed her skin as she closed the balcony doors behind her. The terrace overlooked the garden at the center of the palace. Normally, the doors would be open and a bar would have been placed out here, but Dane Mitchell, one of Tal's bodyguards, had decreed it unsafe for the time being. After an episode that had nearly ended in the murder of her cousins' wife a few months ago, Dane had been on a security tear. Everyone had tried to explain to him that the perpetrator, Khalil, was dead and wasn't likely to rise as a zombie to eat Piper's brains. Alea felt a smile cross her face. She'd been the one to use that argument. But Talib, Rafiq, and Kadir, ever vigilant, had signed on to the new "keep the women safe" plan.

To Alea, it felt more like the "never let the women have any fun" plan. Or a minute alone.

"Hello, Landon." She didn't have to turn around to know he stood there, strong and stalwart. She'd heard the briefest squeak of the door opening...then nothing. Landon Nix never made a sound, but sometimes little things like squeaky hinges defeated his silent grace.

"You don't have to talk. I just can't leave you alone. Pretend I'm not here."

Impossible. She turned and stared at the quietest of her

9

three watchmen, all of whom had been hired months after her rescue. By then, she'd recovered, and Alea was beyond glad they had never seen her so weak. They had been apprised of her abduction and given sketchy details, but by the time Tal had hired them, thanks to Cole Lennox's advice, at least her body had recovered. The three guards kept her safe day and night. And had quickly become the bane of her existence.

As well as the center of her every fantasy.

Landon hovered in the corner, shadows clinging to him, making him look even more dangerous than normal. He was six foot three and leaner than the two Mack Trucks he called friends, but there was no way he was any less lethal. Her brain told her that, but something about him put her at ease in a way she wasn't with the other two. Dane was so dark and dominant. Coop was a relentless flirt—both things that scared the crap out of her. But Landon, with his golden hair and face, with his expression so often as placid as an untouched lake, was a calming presence. He never pushed her too hard to talk or demanded her smiles. When he guarded her, he simply followed and made sure she got where she needed to go. Coop and Dane either pretended to flirt with her or downright insisted that she follow their direction, but Landon just quietly did his job.

He was a little like the large, gorgeous Labrador retriever she'd had as a child. Except she had never dreamed about sharing Duke's wet kisses, much less taking on his friends.

She had to stop thinking that way, but Landon made that difficult when he stood so near and the night fell softly all around her. She'd snuck away to escape the crowd, but she was surprised at just how much she liked being out here alone with Lan. "Did Tal make you wear that tux?"

Even in the deep gloom, she saw his telling flush. Maybe Lan's down-to-earth nature was what made her feel so comfortable. He was obviously uneasy with the wealth around him. Ever since she'd returned to Bezakistan and the palace, she had felt the same way. She'd seen real suffering in the real world, and sometimes this opulence chafed.

"I don't know why I have to wear this monkey suit. It was made for me, but it still feels too tight," Lan said with a bit of a Texas drawl.

She couldn't help herself. He was far too endearing to ignore. Months and months of trying had just proven she wasn't capable.

Alea closed the space between them. "The suit fits you perfectly, but the tie is too tight."

He looked up, his eyes flaring briefly as she neared. "I'm not much good with clothes like this. I have to admit, I liked the uniforms in the Army better. Uncle Sam's dress code made it easy."

And she'd bet he'd looked good. Of course, he looked devastatingly handsome in a tux, too.

Dangerous train of thought. Stop now. After hesitating for an instant, she forced herself to buck up and do what she'd crossed the room to accomplish.

"May I?" she asked before reaching for his tie.

Lan nodded, and she quickly undid the black scrap of silk. The Armani tuxedo had been perfectly fitted, but she knew very well that his normal wardrobe choices ran more toward sweat pants and loose fitting T-shirts. It was a crime against women everywhere that the man didn't just walk around shirtless.

Don't go there, Alea. He can't handle your damage. None of them can. And you can't handle them.

Her inner voice was way more practical than she was, but it was also right. Landon Nix was a gorgeous god of a man who wouldn't look at her twice if her cousins weren't paying him to. None of them would. She'd seen a picture of Dane's ex-wife once. She'd been blonde and stacked and gorgeous. She wasn't sure why they'd divorced, but it couldn't have had anything to do with a lack of desire. Any heterosexual man would want that woman.

No one would want Alea if she wasn't tied to the fabulously wealthy, royal al Mussads.

Landon didn't move a muscle as she knotted his tie again, this time much looser. No wonder he'd been uncomfortable. He'd practically strangled himself. She smoothed down the lapels of his jacket, feeling his hard chest beneath. He was so close and he smelled incredible. The heat of his skin penetrated her senses. His gorgeously sculpted lips lingered just above her own. His eyes, which had always seemed so cold, were now a warm blue and focused intently on her. A flash of heat passed through her body.

If he knew what she was thinking, she would undoubtedly make a complete fool of herself because he was her cousins' employee.

Quickly, Alea retreated, needing some distance between them. "There you go. That should be more comfortable."

He nodded, clearing his throat. "Yeah. Thanks. It is. You're really good with that. I mean with men's clothes." His eyes closed briefly. "I didn't mean it like that. And you were putting them on, not taking them off. God, I'm just going to shut up now."

This was another reason she felt more comfortable with Lan. Looks aside, he wasn't anywhere near perfect. In fact, he could be a charmingly inept conversationalist. "It's okay. I only know how to tie a bowtie because Kadir was so bad at it. When Rafiq would try to help him, they would get into fistfights. When I was a girl, they broke my Barbie house. To avoid future disasters, I took care of their ties from that point on."

Right up until they had married Piper, and she'd taken over the duty. Tal, Rafe, and Kade were now happy men.

Alea was still alone. And standing too near Landon wasn't helping. She crossed back to the stone railing and tried to find some peace. This was one of the few places she felt even a vague connection to her life before her abduction. When it was very quiet, she could almost hear her younger self running among the trees, her head thrown back in laughter.

Why had she ever left this place? Why did she feel like she didn't belong here anymore?

Why could she not focus on anything but Landon right now? "Is there any way you could wait inside, even for five minutes?"

No matter how quiet he was, she knew he was there. He was staring, possibly even thinking how boring it was to watch the little downtrodden royal brat.

"No."

She turned, frowning his way. "I'm not going to climb down the trellis and run away."

He shrugged. "You might."

"Landon, don't be ridiculous. It's impossible in this dress. You can stand in front of the door," she tried to bargain with him.

He didn't move, simply stood rooted in place, a mass of muscle in a thousand dollar tux. "No."

"What do you honestly think is going to happen? It's not as if there are assassins hanging out in the palm trees, waiting for that one moment you turn your back."

"You never know. Assassins could lay in wait anywhere. I haven't checked the palm trees, but that wouldn't shock me."

"So you're just going to follow me everywhere?"

"Yes."

"What happens if you have to go to the bathroom?"

He didn't even crack a smile. "I hold it or you get real well acquainted with the men's urinal."

"I'm not going into the men's room."

"Then it's good I didn't drink a bunch earlier."

"This is ridiculous." She rolled her eyes. "I'm going to talk to Tal."

He sent her a single, firm nod. "I'll take you to him."

Because Landon knew damn well that Tal would agree

13

with him. "I scarcely think someone has come to Her Highness's coronation ball to try to kill *me*. If they've come to hurt someone, it's most likely the others in the royal family. Really, Landon, study a little more history."

He stiffened, his whole body tightening. His eyes turned cold again. A sickening feeling slid through her, and she knew that she'd just hurt him. "I wasn't very good at history, Princess. You'll have to forgive me. I'm just a dumb grunt following the orders of my CO. If you have a problem with it, you should take it up with Dane."

Alea winced and looked away. What had she done? An apology sat right on the tip of her tongue. Why? This wasn't her fault….but it wasn't his either. He was just doing his job. But damn it, she was being followed twenty-four seven. The only place she was allowed to be alone was her bedroom, and even then, the minute she opened the door, one of them waited outside. She felt like a prisoner in so many ways, and it was wearing her out.

As he stared a hole right through her, Alea felt her resolve weakening. She yearned for those blue eyes to glow with the warmth they had just minutes ago.

The door to the balcony opened, and a lean figure slid through. This man didn't have a problem with his tuxedo. She was fairly certain that Oliver Thurston-Hughes had been born in a tux. The very noble Brit wouldn't have done anything so common as to have been born naked.

"Alea? Darling, are you out here?" He nearly bumped into Landon. "Bloody hell, who are you?"

"I'm over here, Oliver," she said before Landon could reply.

A broad smile came over the handsome Brit's face, and he stepped around the guard, utterly ignoring him, then walked toward her. "I've been looking all over for you. That receiving line was complete hell. I've never seen so many people."

Oliver had been at the last British royal wedding, so

Alea doubted that, but he was always polite. Oliver would never say a social function wasn't the greatest event he'd ever attended. "I was happy when it was over. My face hurts from smiling. Where's Yasmin?"

He shrugged an elegant shoulder. "Last I saw, she was dancing with the Prime Minister. She's been looking for you, though. Alea, it's so good to see you." He smiled warmly. "You've been a virtual stranger ever since…"

His words trailed off, and she could see the way he paled when he realized what he'd nearly said.

"Since she was taken hostage and forced to endure something most people wouldn't survive?" A sarcastic voice with a low Texas accent cut through the awkward silence. *Now* Landon decided to get chatty? "I'm sure she's sorry she didn't just pause her recovery to call you up the second she got home."

"No one asked you," Oliver shot back. "Why is he here? You're not seeing him, I hope?"

She saw far too much of Lan. And far too little. "He's my bodyguard. I'm sorry I haven't called."

"You don't owe him an apology," Landon ground out.

"Stay out of this." She couldn't handle him getting involved in her personal life. She could barely handle him being her constant watchman. She turned back to Oliver. "I am sorry. It's been hard to get back into the real world."

Oliver was everything that Landon wasn't. He was perfectly charming as he stared at her with a pitying little frown. "Of course it is, darling. I apologize. It's terribly selfish of me. It's simply that Yasmin and I have missed you."

"I've missed you, too."

They hadn't missed her enough to put off their wedding while she'd been kidnapped. She guessed she couldn't really blame them. She'd been gone for months. They'd assumed she'd been killed, her body buried somewhere in an unmarked grave. Yasmin hadn't had any idea that she'd been found until months after the fact. Yas still didn't know about all the rehab she'd had to go through. The last thing Alea wanted the world to know about was her drug addiction.

She wondered if Landon knew, if one of the reasons he, Dane, and Coop were so zealous in their guardianship was that they had been tasked to ensure she didn't hit the streets looking for a fix.

"I think you should come home with us in a few weeks. We're going to spend the winter at the country estate. I know my brothers would love to see you again."

Oliver's brothers were outrageous flirts. She didn't need that. But it did point out a problem. Lately, she been thinking that she couldn't stay in Bezakistan, aimless and lonely, for the rest of her life. She hadn't really left the palace. Instead, she'd been hiding here, taking classes online. Sure, she could get a degree that way, but what would happen when she graduated?

The door opened again. Yasmin glided through the door. She looked gorgeous in her designer gown, her pale hair in a perfect upswept do. "Oliver? Oh, you're out here with Alea. I thought you had gone back to your room, dear."

Yasmin utterly ignored Landon, moving around him like he was just a piece of furniture. Her perfectly manicured hands reached for Alea's.

"Hello, Yas."

Yasmin had been her childhood playmate. Their fathers had both been connected to the Bezakistani royal line maternally. Alea's parents had drowned when she was very young, so her aunt and uncle, the sheikh and *shaykhah*, had taken her in, given her the al Mussad name, and raised her at the palace. But Alea had always looked forward to the weeks when Yasmin would visit. It had been the only time she'd had another female playmate.

Yasmin hugged her briefly. "Alea, it's so nice to see you. I tried calling for ages, but no one would put me through. I rather thought you were ducking my calls, dear."

Alea groaned inwardly. Yasmin seemed to know how to make her feel guilty, even when she didn't mean to. "Sorry. I really haven't felt up to socializing."

"Talib has allowed you to hide away for far too long. You're never going to feel better if you don't get back to normal." Yasmin frowned, her perfect face forming a mask of disapproval.

"Yas, let it be. We talked about this." Oliver reached for his wife's hand.

"I know, but seeing her has made me more certain than ever that she can't recover by languishing here. She hasn't truly smiled once. And what is Tal thinking putting those guards on her?"

"They're here for my protection." Despite her own problems with the guys, she felt an urge to defend them.

"You don't need a constant shadow reminding you of danger, Lea. Come to England with us. You can enroll at university and take up your schooling again. Or you can work with me at the foundation."

Ah, yes. Reaching Across Cultures. One of the surprises she'd been faced with when she'd been rescued was the fact that Yasmin had taken over the European offices of this al Mussad charity, a job that had been earmarked for Alea.

But it wasn't like she could do the job now, endure all those glittering fundraisers and public speaking engagements. How would that work when she could barely manage to leave the palace?

"I just mentioned that myself," Oliver said with a long sigh. "I thought we were going to do this with a little subtlety. I'm sorry about the hard sell, love. I'm afraid Yasmin has done nothing but plot and plan to take you back with us."

Yasmin pouted prettily. "I miss my cousin. I was beside myself when we thought you were gone forever. It was like losing my sister." She sniffled a little, a tear sliding down her face. "Lea, I miss you. Please think about coming back with

17

us. I want you to be there when—"

"You weren't going to tell her that, either," Oliver muttered under his breath.

"I can't keep it from her. She's my closest relative. Oh, Lea. You weren't there when we got married. You have to be there when I have my first baby. Please say you'll come."

Yasmin was pregnant? Silly, superficial Yasmin was married and now having a child. A little kernel of jealousy weighed in her gut. Yas had been the prankster when they were young. She'd nearly dropped out of school. She hadn't even thought of going to university. So how was Yas the one with a husband and a career that should have been Alea's, and a baby on the way?

She struggled to find something to say. She looked down at Yasmin, who was perfectly slender in her Marchesa gown. "You don't look pregnant."

Yasmin's smile lit up the night. She ran a hand down her flat stomach. "I assure you I am. I'm almost three months along. You have to come. It will be just like our childhoods when we spent summers together. And you can start over in England. The palace is too insular. You need to be out in the world."

Yasmin waxed on and on about all the things they could do in London. They would shop, go to the theater, hang out with Oliver's brothers. One was a very famous football player, and Yas was convinced that Alea should go on a date with him.

The idea curdled her stomach. Alea backed up, her hip bumping the ledge of the balcony. Out of the corner of her eye she saw Landon surge toward her. She quickly edged away from the ledge lest Lan decide she meant to escape Yas by jumping to her death or something equally dramatic. He would think of it as his sacred duty to either save her or go down with her, no doubt.

"You're going to love Callum. He's so handsome, and he's just a bit younger than my Oliver."

"Yas, stop. I don't know that I want to leave the palace right now."

When her cousin pursed her lips, preparing an argument, Alea knew she had to come up with some excuse or Yasmin really would set her up with an athlete. The paparazzi already swarmed her on those few occasions she ventured out in public. They called her the "Prisoner Princess." Tal had managed to keep the gritty details of her kidnapping out of the press. The world believed she'd simply been held in a gilded cage until the royal family had coughed up enough cash. If they knew the truth, they would call her the "Prostitute Princess." The very idea made her stomach turn.

Oliver put a hand on his wife's shoulder. "Back off a bit, Yas. You've just thrown a lot of information her way. Give her some time to think."

"You're not happy for me, are you?" Yasmin stared at her, her doe eyes more than a little sad.

"O-of course I am," Alea stuttered. "I'm just surprised."

And a bit annoyed, which made her feel guilty. Yas merely meant to help. But she just wanted peace. Why had she and Oliver sought her on this balcony? Alea had enjoyed the quiet of her and Lan sharing the space alone.

"But I thought you would be happy for me, too. I'm sorry, Lea. Oliver was right. You're still in a dark place, and I didn't realize... This is all my fault."

She turned and fled the balcony, her dress floating around her ankles. Alea winced. Oliver cursed under his breath. Yas had always been on the dramatic side. Pregnancy hormones probably weren't helping. Of course she wanted her cousin to be happy...but it was hard to feel joy about anything when she felt stuck in a rut defined by numbness, terror, and a slow-burning rage.

Oliver dragged a hand over his face. "Forgive her. She's missed you far more than she's let on. I swear she changed the day you went missing. She was quite manic for a while. I was worried we would have to sedate her those first few days. I think the wedding was the only thing that held her together. And now the baby is coming."

He said the last in a sort of resolved tone that led Alea to wonder if Oliver wasn't the one who was unhappy about the baby. "Are you two in trouble?"

Truthfully, Alea was surprised the couple had made it this far. She'd had a bet with Kade that Oliver would bow out of the wedding. Yasmin, a drama diva, didn't seem like the right fit for the level-headed, stiff-upper-lip Brit.

"It isn't the first time she's been pregnant," Oliver admitted, his voice going low. "I'll be honest, Lea. I actually had plans to call off the wedding, but then you went missing, and Yasmin was expecting. I felt I had to honor the commitment. In some ways, I felt I had to honor it in order to honor you."

"Me?"

"Alea, you know I've always had a thing for you, but you went off to New York…and I kind of fell in with Yas. We do all right, the two of us. We muddle through. She had a miscarriage shortly after our honeymoon. She's been obsessive about getting pregnant again ever since. Please take a little time and think about our offer. It really would do you good to get away from all this pomp and circumstance. I've heard a rumor that Yasmin isn't the only one who's pregnant. If it's true, the spotlights will only shine brighter on the palace."

Piper. She wasn't showing yet, either, but she wouldn't be able to keep her condition from the press for long. There didn't seem to be a minute of the day that one of Piper's husbands didn't have a hand on her belly as though they could already feel the child growing there.

Alea wouldn't have children. She would grow old right here and be the pathetic old maid. No one could possibly want a woman as broken as she was. No one knew just how shattered she was on the inside. What man could handle that, even if she could bring herself to get close to him?

"Yes. They're going to make the announcement in a few weeks, when Piper is past the first trimester."

"It will be a madhouse, then. You must know that. The rags in England don't really give a damn about me unless I'm hanging out with Wills. It's Callum they're interested in, and I promise, you don't have to date him. Though I'll warn you, he'll make you crazy about it, and when you relent, I'll likely be a bit jealous. Come on, Lea. I can protect you in England."

"I'll think about it."

But there was no way she belonged there. If she went, Yas and Oliver would mean well, but with a baby coming, as well as ties to both celebrities and royals, Alea knew she'd find no peace. She was starting to think, however, that they were right about getting out of Bezakistan. Maybe a change of scenery would be good. Maybe she needed to be alone for a while, get her head together, weigh what she wanted in life against how brave she felt in pursuing it.

A long, painful moment passed. "I suppose I should go and check on Yasmin."

"Probably so."

With a nod, Oliver turned and walked out. Finally, Alea could breathe again.

"Did you love him?"

She turned, startled. Lan stood, his stern face expressionless. He could be so quiet, she'd almost forgotten he was there. And he rarely asked questions. In fact, Landon could follow her for hours and never say a word.

"No. God, no. I was so young. I didn't love anyone except Robert Pattinson," she answered without thinking.

Oliver had been a pleasant companion, and they had gone on a few dates, but she hadn't even kissed him. She'd been happy when she'd discovered that he and Yasmin were dating. She'd hoped Oliver would be a calming influence on her headstrong cousin.

"I'm glad. Because he's an asshole." One minute Landon was a shadow clinging to the wall, and the next he was in her space, a mountain of lean muscle.

"He is not! What makes you say that?"

Lan gave her an incredulous stare, as if wondering how she could miss the big picture. "He put the moves on you."

"He did no such thing. He's never once tried."

"Persuading you to come home with him and saying he'd be jealous if you dated the soccer player…yeah, his approach is mostly subtle, but he's still hitting on you. Even if he would never do anything about it, he's married, and that makes him a douche nozzle."

"He's just trying to help…in his way. His relationship with Yasmin is a little complicated."

They'd gotten married far too young, and she wasn't sure Yas was really ready to be a mom. "She's his wife. He should never talk to another woman that way. If I was married, I wouldn't." He stared down at her, his expression soft and searching. She'd never seen him look so gentle. "Don't let them sway you from getting what you need to heal. They're trying to use you to buffer their drama. You don't need that, darlin'."

He hovered so close that she felt the heat radiating off his body. All it would take to press her lips to his was one simple lift to her toes. Then she'd be brushing her mouth against his and know what it felt like to kiss a man again. She hadn't kissed anyone in years it seemed. No soft brushing of her mouth against another's. No arms that wound protectively around her. Just pain and terror. Memories flashed through her head of vicious fingers tangling in her hair, forcing her head back until her neck felt like it would break.

"You just went white. Are you all right?" Landon reached out for her, but she wouldn't be able to endure his touch, not when she felt so dirty.

They could put her in a designer gown, but she was still the girl who knew what it meant to be subjugated. She was still the dumb animal who had watched as the women around her were tortured, raped, and snuffed out.

"Don't touch me."

He jerked back. "I won't. I wouldn't hurt you for the world. Take a deep breath. You're here in Bezakistan. You're at the palace. No one will ever hurt you here. Me, Dane, and Coop will make damn sure of it. Take a long breath. I'll do it with you."

He breathed in, his chest filling with air. He was so calm and kind that she found herself following his directions. When he reached for her this time, she let him take her hand. He held it until she stopped shaking.

God, she wanted him to hold her. She wanted what Piper had. She wanted to be surrounded by men who loved her, who accepted her…who could want her even after all that had happened.

Her captors had ensured she would never have any of that.

She gently pulled her hand from his, hating that moment they were no longer connected palm to palm. "Thank you. I'm fine now."

"Talk to me, Alea. Tell me what just went through your head."

She couldn't. It didn't matter how much she wanted to. She was never going to talk about it, especially to the three men she very nearly idolized. She was never going to tell anyone about her shame. "That's 'princess' or 'Your Highness,' please. It isn't seemly for you to call me by my first name."

Alea needed distance before she crumbled. In that panicked second, she didn't know how else to get it.

But when she saw his face in the next moment, she cared very much. Her heart ached as Landon drew back, his shoulders squaring and his eyes icing over. "I apologize, Your Highness. Like I said, I'm just a dumb grunt. Sometimes I forget my place. Perhaps we should go back to the party."

The urge to apologize and tell him everything swamped her. The impulsive need to bring Dane and Cooper in and confess everything, release all her pain to them, tempted her. But the past was her private hell. They were not only protectors, but kind ones, and she couldn't take advantage of that, imagining that her own feelings for them in any way mirrored theirs for her.

She couldn't have them, and they wouldn't want her—even if she was brave enough to try.

Landon opened the door, and music spilled out into the night. Alea followed him back into the ballroom. Instantly, friends and family surrounded her, yet she still felt utterly alone.

* * * *

Dane Mitchell cursed under his breath as Alea walked into the ballroom followed by a sullen Landon. To an outsider, Lan's frown wouldn't look any different than normal, but Dane had been around the Texan long enough to know when he was in a real shit-kicker of a mood. Lan's shoulders were too square and tight, his movements lacking their normal grace, to be anything but pissed off. Dane had little doubt it was something the prickly princess had said.

"Dayum, what do you think happened out there?" Coop's voice came over Dane's earpiece. "Lan's doing his whole 'stony soldier' routine."

"No idea." But something had happened, and it had affected Alea, too. She'd pressed her mouth into a grim line and looked close to tears.

Stopping at the edge of the ballroom, she drew in a breath and collected herself. Oh, it looked to most as if she was merely smoothing her dress down and checking her hair in one of the ornate mirrors that lined the hallway, but Dane knew better. If she'd listen, he'd tell her that she looked stunning. He'd tried to tell her about a hundred times that she was the most gorgeous woman on the face of the fucking planet, but she always demurred. He would have comforted her, but she'd just shut him down and push him away. Same as always.

"You don't think Lan would have suggested that she find the rest of her bodice, do you? Because we all agreed that was likely a damn fine way to lose our balls," Coop joked.

When she'd first walked out of her room earlier in the evening, it had been right there on the tip of his tongue to order her back inside to find a dress that actually covered her breasts. Luckily Coop had known he was about to unleash his inner Dominant on a woman who wasn't ready to handle the demand. Coop had slapped him on the back, shooting him a glance that warned Dane he was about to make an idiot of himself. Into the silence, Coop had loudly proclaimed to Alea that she looked beautiful. She'd taken that to mean her dress, then explained that someone named Narciso had designed it. Dane didn't give a shit. Narciso needed to learn how to sew a proper top into his wretchedly expensive evening gowns.

Lan had just kind of drooled.

Alea had finally cracked a smile as she lifted her gown a fraction and showed off her ridiculously hot shoes. Then all Dane could think about was just how nice those stilettos would look wrapped around his neck as he drove his cock deep. And then she'd utterly shut down as though she'd realized she'd sought their opinions and enjoyed their attention. After that, she'd straightened her gown and dismissed them with a wave of her hand.

He was getting real damn tired of Alea always pushing them away. If he believed for a minute that she didn't want them, he would take a mental step back and protect her from afar. But he'd noticed the way she sometimes watched all three of them when she thought no one was looking.

Now, Lan stood a good ten feet behind her, watching her as she visibly calmed herself. She turned to him and said something, her hands coming up in a little plea.

"Oh, here we go. I've lived this scene before. Allow me. 'Don't follow me, Lan. Please, let me get my gorgeous self horribly murdered by the first psycho who comes along. It's my right.'" Coop sometimes provided offbeat dialogue when they were too far away to hear the object of their affection actually speak.

Landon had moved past Dane, but he could still see the way his friend moved his head in a sharp, unmistakable shake. Coop continued his translation. "And then Lan says, in his too often verbose diatribe against her stubbornness, 'no.' You know, I think the dude should explain himself from time to time. Oh, look, he got the designer shoe stomp."

Sure enough, Princess Alea stomped her right foot, threw her hands up, and stalked off, tossing open the door to the ballroom and flooding the hall briefly with glittering lights. Dane saw the way Lan sighed and opened the door again, his stare following her as he pursued.

Dane's hand twitched, and he made a fist to quell his urge to smack her sexy but rebellious little ass. "I swear to god, Coop, sometimes I want to lay that girl over my knee and not let her up until we've reached an understanding."

"Only sometimes, Dane?"

Nope. Pretty much all the time. From the minute he'd seen Princess Alea Binte al Mussad, his cock had been hard and his heart had taken a nosedive. She'd hit him like a bolt of lightning. He'd stood there staring at her, feeling like a damn fool, but he wasn't going to let that stop him. Then he'd looked at his two best friends, ready to tell them that he'd finally found the one woman he wanted to put a collar on—as crazy as that would have sounded—and realized they were just as head over heels. That quickly, all three of them were fucked.

But they had all backed off, unwilling to step on each others' toes. They had been through too much together. Coop and Lan were the only family Dane had left. Oh, there was a father and three brothers back in Georgia, but he'd come back from the Korengal Valley a different man. Shortly after his second tour, the family drama and his divorce had ended any affection or allegiance they had for him. In their head, Dane was as good as dead. Coop and Lan were his brothers now, and he couldn't fight with them. They had been at an impasse.

Until they had really understood the way relationships worked here in Bezakistan. It was tradition among the wealthy and the landholders in this small country for the brothers of a family to share a wife so they didn't have to divide the family riches or leave any sibling to suffer poverty. After a few weeks, Dane had decided they could adopt the Bezakistani way. He, Lan, and Coop might not truly share blood and they might not be preserving a fortune, but they all wanted Alea and weren't willing to stab a brother in the back to have her.

So after a full month here, he'd decided he liked the idea of sharing. The families in Bezakistan seemed happy, and he wouldn't have to relinquish his backup. He'd spent the majority of his adult life in the military, his whole childhood before that following his dad from base to base. The idea of having a family that functioned as a team really suited him.

And then just as they'd settled everything between the three of them, they realized they had forgotten to talk to the most important member of the team. And Alea didn't want anything to do with them. Or at least that was her story, and she seemed to be sticking to it.

Landon touched his earpiece and suddenly his voice came on the line. "I want you to do a background check on that British fucker, Oliver Thurston-Hughes. Get me everything you can. I want to know it all, right down to what the asshole eats for breakfast so I'll know what to poison."

"Slow down," Coop said. "Why are we going to poison that Brit's oatmeal? Do they even eat oatmeal in England?"

Lan ignored the question, getting right to the point. "He's a little too interested in the princess."

Fuck. If he was calling her "princess," then their conversation had been a clusterfuck. "What's going on, Lan?"

His pal didn't look back. Instead, Lan stared across the ballroom, never taking his eyes off her. "That cousin of hers is trying to get her to go to England. The princess walked out onto the balcony to get some fresh air. First Mr. Small Dick followed her, then Crazy Bitch crashed the party. They laid all kinds of guilt on Her Highness."

"She's not going to England." There was no way Dane would allow it. Especially now that he was pretty sure she was still in potential danger. He would talk Talib into putting her on lockdown if he needed to. And if, for some reason, she left anyway, he would have to quit and follow her because he couldn't leave her unprotected and alone.

"I don't think she really wants to go," Landon replied. "But the British fuckwad sure seemed interested in her being a bit more than a traveling companion."

"I got a shot, boss. I can take him out in one," Coop said, his voice serious.

"I think that's a damn fine idea, Coop," Landon interjected. "Can you aim for his pecker?"

"Don't know, brother. I suspect that is a mighty small target, but I'm a damn fine marksman."

Dane hated it when he had to be the voice of reason. "You can't kill him. Not here anyway. I'll run a check on him, guys, but seriously, we can't go around assassinating every man who looks at her twice."

"I don't see why not. We're good at assassinations. If Tal had let us take out Khalil when we wanted to, we could have avoided a whole lot of heartache." Coop sighed over the line. "Are our 'friends' here yet?"

Lawson and Riley Anders were private investigators with the prestigious Anthony Anders firm. It was made up of the brothers, Lawson and Riley, and a badass named Dominic Anthony. They had come with the highest references from the two PIs who had tracked down Alea when she'd been kidnapped. Burke and Cole Lennox were good, but they also had married a really sweet girl named Jessa and now had one son with another on the way. They couldn't do the kind of twenty-four seven work that Dane had demanded after the death of Khalil al Bashir.

With the prime suspect dead, he had to know once and for all if Khalil had been the one responsible for Alea's abduction. In fact, he prayed that Khalil had been the guilty fucker. That would set his mind at ease. But it didn't add up.

The report the Lennox brothers had filed had stated plainly that Alea had been held for months in a state of "training." She'd been moved from New York to Colombia and housed in a brothel. Yet the physician who had treated her after she'd been returned to Bezakistan had said there was no sexual abuse evident. According to him, Alea remained a virgin.

So he feared the random act of slavery was bullshit. Dane's guess was that someone had paid for her to be taken. Someone had wanted her to disappear and suffer. Money had been on the line. Money and maybe something else. Revenge? Pride? He couldn't be sure until he had more information.

Once, Khalil had seemed like the best suspect, but Dane hadn't been able to connect him yet to the crime either via physical evidence or motive. He prayed that Law and Riley gave him the proof tonight. He would be thrilled to find out that Alea's abduction had been a random act or that the asshole who had sold her out was dead.

But it felt too fucking easy.

Dane shook off his suspicions and brought himself back to reality, answering Coop about Riley and Lawson. "I have confirmation that they landed about half an hour ago. They should be here any minute. It's bad timing, but this is the best window they could give us, given the tight schedule Dominic keeps." Plus, if the perp was still alive, he might well be attending tonight's event and wouldn't notice a few more visitors to the palace that might raise suspicion. "We're going to meet in Tal's office to go over what they've learned."

"Won't someone notice if the sheikh disappears from his wife's coronation ball?" Coop asked.

"Not for a few minutes. We're going to make this short and sweet. Rafe and Kade will keep Piper occupied." In fact, Tal planned to give Rafe the signal, who would then make sure their wife was occupied on the dance floor until the meeting adjourned. The goal was to keep the party rolling as normally as possible so as not to alert Piper—or Alea—that anything potentially dangerous might be going down. If the news was bad, as Dane suspected, they would need a whole new game plan.

"I'll keep an eye on Her Highness," Lan said.

"What the hell did she say to you, buddy?" Coop asked.

"Nothing I didn't already know," Landon grumbled over the radio.

Dane was getting a headache. Nothing was going the way he'd planned. From the moment he and his friends had made a pact to go after Alea as a team, Dane had been sure they would succeed. He'd told himself back then it wouldn't take more than a few months before she was surrounded by them, before they overwhelmed her. Over a year had passed, and he was starting to believe she would never be ready for a romance, much less one that involved three men.

And he was beginning to understand that he might never be complete without her.

The doors from the main hallway opened, and two tall, well-built men walked through. Law and Riley Anders hadn't bothered with tuxedos. They were dressed casually in jeans and T-shirts. One wore a blazer and the other a leather jacket. Even though the palace was in the heart of the desert, it got cold at night.

The brothers nodded to each other and turned toward Dane. He quickly sized them up. Lawson Anders was just a slight bit taller than his younger brother, but there was a coldness to his eyes that Dane recognized. Law had spent time in the military, likely in black ops, though his dossier claimed he'd only been a communications officer. Bullshit. The man in front of him had obviously seen and done too much. "Communications" was code for "too classified to discuss."

Riley Anders had gone the college route. Burke Lennox swore Riley was one of the premier hackers in the United States. It was a skill that would mean the world to an investigator. There was a lighter air to him, but Dane didn't doubt he'd been trained well.

"Lieutenant Mitchell?" Lawson asked.

Dane winced inwardly. How fucking long would it be before he could hear military titles and not have his stomach go south? "It's just Dane. I'm not in the Navy anymore."

Law leaned against the wall. "Yeah, from what I hear, you got a bad fucking rap. But I understand. I got out because I couldn't listen to the brass anymore, either. Now Dominic is the only person who bitches at me. I'm the idiot who gets his ass out of the military, then goes to work for his former CO."

Riley shrugged. "Well, I'm the smart one who didn't go into the military in the first place and I still end up getting my ass chewed out on a regular basis by your former CO."

Dane didn't have time for the Anders brothers comedy hour. "Do you have the information I asked for? I don't understand why Dominic wouldn't just send it to me. I could have saved you a very long flight."

"Dominic never likes to give bad news over the phone." Lawson glanced down at the briefcase his brother carried. "Do you have some place where we can set up?"

A knot formed in his stomach, and Dane wondered if he was really braced for the truth.

"Should I give Tal the signal?" Cooper asked him over the radio.

From the edge of the ballroom, Landon looked back. He stood in the shadows, watching over the woman they all loved. The woman who might still be in danger. Dane gave him a nod, and Landon edged closer to Alea. He would keep an eye on her so Dane and Coop could take this meeting.

"Dane?"

He was procrastinating. "Yeah. Get everyone into Talib's office pronto."

With a nod to the private investigators, Dane began to lead the way to a more private part of the palace. Behind him the brothers chattered on, throwing more annoying digs at one another.

Dane was grim as he unlocked the office and turned on the light. It was past time to find out just how screwed they all were.

Chapter Two

Lan looked out over the ballroom and tried to imagine himself belonging here. It was an impossible task.

Alea held out her hand, greeting some big wig. Schmoozing was probably politically important, but all he gave a shit about was that her smile didn't quite reach her eyes. He hated to see her so withdrawn. When she didn't realize he was watching her, she gave in to pure joy. Then her dark eyes glittered and her pillowy lips curved into a smile that could light up the whole fucking world.

But now she was faking it, flashing that annoyingly bland smile to the crowd, which she often did to people who didn't matter. When she didn't want anyone to look at her too closely. He didn't even mind the little fit she'd thrown earlier because at least when she was pissed off at him, she was being honest. He would take her anger over nonchalance any day of the week.

But she was right about one thing: he was a dumbshit who didn't deserve her. He needed to remember that. He was here to do a job, which meant protecting her, period. No matter how much he wanted to take her in his arms and love her until she couldn't think about anything else, she was a princess. He was pure Texas trailer trash. He was nowhere near Alea's league.

"Does Rafe have the target?" Dane asked over the tiny device in his ear.

Lan quickly found the man they were talking about. Rafe took Piper's hand, kissing it as he started to lead the *shaykhah* to the dance floor. The music had changed from a bouncy song to a long, slow grind. That was baby-making music, and Rafe grinned wolfishly at his wife.

Alea stopped and looked out to the floor, longing plain on her face. God, he wanted to walk over to her, thread his fingers through hers, lead her out there. But he also wanted his two best friends to be there touching her, too. And that made him a fucking freak in most of the world. Bezakistan was different, so in Lan's book, that's what made the country great.

"He's got her." Piper was following Rafe onto the dance floor, her face shining up at him.

"Excellent. Keep an eye on our brat. I'll let you know when we're done. Out." Coop's voice cut off, and Lan knew he was out of the loop for a bit. He'd volunteered for this duty to remove himself from the meeting. He'd rather watch over Alea because he didn't agree with this clandestine shit. Everyone was planning Alea's life without including her. She should be in that fucking meeting, but he'd been outvoted.

Rafe and Piper started a slow dance. Kade walked up behind them, putting his hands on Piper's waist and leaning over to kiss the back of her neck.

Those two had backup. Even if anything ever happened to Rafe or Kade, Piper al Mussad would never be alone. If one of them went down, she would have two more husbands to lean on. They would protect the woman they loved. He'd heard sad stories about some of the widows of guys he'd served with in the Army. Once their husbands were dead, they were often utterly alone. So many became single moms, struggling to make ends meet because they didn't have anyone else in their corner.

"Nix, how you doing?" A deep voice asked behind him.

He turned and saw one of the Lennox brothers holding out his hand. Lan took it and tried to give him a smile. The other man tried to return the gesture, mostly baring his teeth in return.

Cole and Burke were near perfect twins, but Lan had quickly learned that Burke was the one who smiled. It wasn't

34

that Cole was always grim. He could light up when his wife walked in the room, but otherwise, he was a little standoffish. "Going good, Cole. Dane's meeting with your guys right now."

Lennox nodded. "Good. Dominic runs a tight ship. They'll get you what you need. Sorry I couldn't handle it personally, but this pregnancy has been giving Jessa hell for a couple of months."

"She's perfectly good now." A gorgeous redhead threaded her arm through Cole's and turned her face up to his. "I just needed to get through the vomiting-up-my-toenails phase."

There was that smile of Cole's. Lan watched, a knot of jealousy in the pit of his stomach. He hated this envy. He didn't want Jessa or begrudge Cole his happiness. He just wanted a little of his own.

"Jessa!" Alea's smile turned genuine as she approached the auburn beauty. What he wouldn't give to have that smile directed at him...

"I heard you were here," the princess said. "How is baby Caleb?"

Lan supposed it had been inevitable that Alea would become close to her saviors' wife. Alea's friendship with Jessa made her happy. As far as Lan was concerned, that pretty much was all he needed to know about the woman. If Alea loved her, then she had to be good people, as his granny would say.

He watched as Alea talked to her friend, her posture relaxed for once. Cole's brother, Burke sauntered up, sliding his arm around Jessa's waist as they chatted with Alea.

When everyone was occupied, Cole's face turned serious. With an almost imperceptible cock of the head, he motioned Lan to follow him. They stepped out of the conversation, just far enough so they couldn't be overheard.

"What's going on between you and Alea?" Cole asked.

"I'm her bodyguard. That's it." And that was where it

would stay because she had zero interest in him.

"Bullshit. Do you think I don't have eyes? I saw the way you looked at her. Man, I'm not trying to mess with you. I like very few people. Alea is one of them. You're one of them. That girl is still in trouble. Even if Dominic's guys found out that Khalil was the one behind her kidnapping and she's out of danger, she's still in trouble."

Because she hadn't gotten over what had happened during her abduction. How was she supposed to get over that? She wouldn't let them see her fear or pain, so how the fuck were they supposed to help her?

"I don't think there's a damn thing I can do. She doesn't want me."

"Is she into one of your crew?" Cole's face creased as though he was thinking through a problem.

"No. She doesn't like any of us." Would it be better or worse if she wanted Dane or Coop? Maybe. At least someone would be happy.

"Again, I call bullshit. The minute we stepped over here, she started casting glances this way, and she's not staring at me."

Lan let his eyes slide toward her. Sure enough, Alea jerked her gaze back to Jessa Lennox as quickly as she could. In fact, a little crowd had formed around her now, as Jessa and Alea had been joined by a familiar, pretty blonde, Hannah James. Her husbands, the James brothers, ran Black Oak Oil and had long-standing ties with the Bezakistani royal family.

Husbands. It seemed like everyone was getting on the marital bandwagon lately. Everyone except the one woman who had grown up surrounded by plural marriage.

"You were with her those first few days after you rescued her, right?" Lan asked.

"I was." Cole's tone turned grim.

"How bad was she?" He'd read the medical reports, but they were clinical. Sure, he knew the date of her kidnapping, where she'd been held, when she'd been rescued. He knew she'd been tortured. But none of that really explained the ordeal that had shaped the woman he knew now.

"Unimaginable. Look, she should be the one to tell you, but I'm starting to worry that she'll never confide in anyone. She looks healthy now. She's a hundred and eighty degrees from the skinny, drug-addicted girl I carried out of that brothel. In fact, she looks great, until I see her eyes."

"Drugs?" Nowhere in those fucking reports had anyone mentioned drugs. Alea would never have done that of her own free will. She was so proud and seemingly in control. So...fuck. Her captors had drugged her. Hell, just how much of her soul had they taken?

"Shit. I'd hoped Tal would have let you in on that since you're her bodyguard." Cole groaned a little. "I'm going to get my ass kicked, but Tal, Rafe, and Kade are treating her with kid gloves. She's drifting. I know they think they're sheltering her, but someone has to push that girl to open up. Look, I understand the impulse to stay out of things. I really do, but if there's one thing I've learned about getting people to heal...sometimes you gotta give them a shove. You can't just hope people will change all by themselves. If you care about Alea, you have to pry her open, man. She's not made of glass. That woman fought like hell in that brothel. She fought to get off the drugs. Maybe she just needs a little help from someone to help her fight for her future."

Wouldn't he love to be that someone? "Man, she'd just fight me, too."

Lan stared at her openly now, not even trying to disguise his longing. He didn't give a shit what anyone else thought. He was in love with that woman. She would never love him back. They came from different worlds. She was a princess, and he had no idea who his father was.

But maybe sometimes love wasn't about getting what he wanted. Maybe sacrifice was really at the heart of it. If he pushed her, fought for her, maybe she could tear down that tough-girl mask and find a way to be happy—even if it wasn't with him, Dane, and Coop.

"I don't think you'll have to fight her too hard. Just push a little every day. Talk to her. Don't let up and don't let her force you to the side. I know how this goes. Jessa tried her hardest to shove us out of her life. She said some horrible things to me. It hurt, but then I realized she was both lashing out and testing us. Burke and I had hurt her when we'd left her alone. She had to push until she realized we weren't going to disappear again, no matter what. Nothing she could say or do was going to throw us out of her life. Alea might have the same M.O."

"We've never been with Alea."

"We?"

Lan felt himself flush. *Damn it.* "We all have feelings for her, me, Dane, and Coop. We thought we could pursue her together, but she wasn't interested in us, either together or apart."

"Or she's scared that none of you can accept what she's been through."

"She survived. That's the only thing that matters. Why wouldn't we accept that?"

"Survival is a funny thing, man, and you damn well know it. When you're down in the trenches all that matters is living, but it's not so simple once you return to the real world. People judge you. You measure what you did to live against conventional social mores...and suddenly what once seemed like a simple choice is murky and gray."

He knew exactly what Cole was talking about.

"That's when you have to deal with the reality that you lived and some didn't," Cole went on. "That's when you have to accept who the fuck you really are."

He hadn't thought about it that way before. Alea was a survivor, but she had a heart. How guilty did she feel for getting out alive when others hadn't? How ashamed was she by whatever she'd had to do in order to live? She'd been through a war of sorts, and he had no idea how much of herself she'd lost along the way.

The fact that Alea had survived and could function now proved how strong she was. She deserved better than to be treated like some fragile doll who couldn't make a decision about her own life. Despite what all the other guys thought, she could handle the truth. Being in control of her future might even help her heal from the past.

Lan knew what he had to do. "Well, hell."

"What?" Cole asked.

"I'm going to get my ass kicked. I hate getting my ass kicked." He steeled himself. If he was going to start fighting for his princess, he might as well start now.

"No one ever tries to kick my ass anymore," Cole grumbled.

Resolved, Lan stalked back to Alea, his heart chugging. Right here, right now, he was going to change everything. Yeah, he should probably wait. If he wanted to play on a team, he shouldn't make decisions alone. But he wasn't risking that Dane and Coop would hate the plan and try to shut him down. Alea deserved to know what was going on.

"Landon?" Alea's eyes widened as he reached for her hand.

"Come with me, Princess. We've got a meeting to attend."

She began to protest, her words saying one thing, while her fingers said another. Maybe he was going about this all wrong, but as he led her out of the ballroom, Lan could have sworn she squeezed his hand, holding on tight.

* * * *

Cooper held the door open for Sheikh Talib al Mussad and wondered if they were doing the right thing. Alea needed peace and to believe she was safe. He didn't like the idea of worrying her just because they had a gut instinct that could

39

be wrong. If his hunch was on the money, they'd handle it so she could be none the wiser. Right?

Tal strode into the room where Dane and the Anders brothers had already set up. There were seats with a folder in front of each.

The investigation into Alea's abduction. God, he almost didn't want to know what that file said. A part of him wanted to pretend that the past was behind them all, that she was healing even now, and merely playing coy and hard to get.

But he knew better. Alea had been ground under some fucker's boot, and deep down Coop needed to know who he could blame so he'd have someone to kill. He'd finally found the girl who made his heart pound, and she was broken because of this asshole. Or maybe there was more than one asshole. Shooting multiple criminals wouldn't bother him.

The tall dude at the front of the room slipped out of his blazer and took a seat at the head of the table. "If you will all take a seat, we can go over the findings fairly quickly and get the sheikh back to his ball. My name is Riley Anders, and I'm the research expert at Anthony Anders. This is my brother, Lawson. He's pure muscle so don't expect him to actually talk. He prefers to grunt."

Law sat beside him, straddling the back of a chair, and flipped his brother the finger.

"So they're civilized," he muttered as he took a seat next to Dane.

Dane leaned over, talking behind his hand. "No doubt. But according to the Lennox brothers, these guys are the best."

"I just wish we'd done the investigation ourselves."

Dane shook his head. "We wanted the best. Alea deserves it. After they tell us the news, then we take over. We can either give her the good news that Khalil was the one who had her kidnapped or we quietly take down the motherfucker who did. That, my friend, is a job we will do ourselves and relish."

Because they damn straight were the best at killing someone who needed to die.

"If you'll open your folders, you'll see that we've done a very thorough investigation of the princess's abduction. Since we were not allowed to interview Princess Alea, it's incomplete," Riley pointed out with a tight smile.

Tal scowled. "I've explained this. You have everything you need in the reports."

Law's eyes narrowed. "Do we? Those reports seem a bit sanitized. There are no real details about what happened to her while she was held."

"Bad shit," Dane shot back. "What the fuck more do you need to know?"

Riley glared. "Shut the testosterone off and get real. We need to know everything. We're not here to judge the princess. We're here to figure out who plotted her kidnapping. Knowing what she endured during her captivity might provide clues."

Tal leaned forward intently, his jaw tight. "Are you telling me you know this wasn't random? Alea is a beautiful girl. Isn't it possible that she was taken and held for the highest bidder? It makes sense that she'd be targeted because she hid her wealth. The person who nabbed her might have believed she wasn't protected."

Law's head shook, shooting down Tal's earnest hope. "Not a chance."

"What my brother means to say is that we have proof to the contrary. Turn to page five of the file. It's a photocopy of the note that brought Alea to the club that night. It was found amongst her things from New York," Riley said quietly, the very somberness of his voice an answer to the question.

Meet me at 7 at the Jackson Club downtown. Please. I need help.

It was unsigned, but the stationary was unmistakable. It had come from the Bezakistani embassy in New York.

"We've seen and discussed this note." Dane sighed.

"You're right. She must have believed she knew who wrote it. Whoever's behind her abduction knew she would respond to a request from the embassy. It stands to reason this person knew exactly who she was and targeted her. Motherfucker."

"The question is why," Riley said, then turned to Tal. "You never received a ransom note?"

The sheikh shook his head. "No. I would have paid. I would have paid anything."

"Then they weren't after money," Dane concluded.

Riley shrugged a little. "We can't be completely sure of that, but there's one other reason we're convinced this wasn't random. If we were just dealing with slavers filling an order, she would have been raped about ten minutes after her kidnapping. You've read the medical file. You know that didn't happen."

Dane's whole body had stiffened. Coop wasn't any happier. When they had first heard Alea's story, he, Dane, and Lan had sat down and talked. Even if she hadn't been raped, she'd been through a lot. They had backed off physically because of it. Coop had started reading about the psychology of victims, trying to understand.

Law frowned. "From what we've been able to tell, Alea was brutalized in every other way imaginable. They left her virginity intact for a reason."

Tal slapped at the table. "Do we have to talk about this?"

"The information won't leave this room," Coop vowed. "But you asked us to be responsible for Alea's well-being. It's hard to do that if we don't talk about information that might be relevant."

"This is none of anyone's business, even yours. I tasked you with making sure she doesn't get hurt again. That's all." Tal glowered.

Ouch. That hurt like a bitch. But Coop refused to back down. "Knowing what she endured may tell us what happened to her and why, so yeah, I think it's my business. I also happen to think that protecting her life is more important than protecting her modesty. She's not just a job to me. She's a good woman who deserves to close her eyes at night and sleep soundly, knowing that she's safe."

Tal drew in a calming breath. "Sorry. You're right. I know how you all feel about her. I've seen how Alea reacts to you three. I asked you here for a reason, and it wasn't as her security team."

That was news to Coop. The last he'd heard, the sheikh had reminded all three of them of their completely non-royal status. Dane had gone the "I hate authority" route, while Lan had slid into his whole "woe is me/I grew up in a trailer so no woman can love me" pile of shit. Coop...he'd seen the play for what it was at the time.

Back then, Tal had been in a bad place with Piper. He'd been a bear growling at anything that even halfway moved. Dane wasn't known for his subtlety. Lan sometimes stepped in it—when he bothered to speak at all. So they'd made nice, big targets for the sheikh. When Coop had written off Tal's craptastic mood and snarling outburst to not getting any, Dane and Lan had called him an overly optimistic Pollyanna and told him to shut the fuck up.

Coop shrugged. He was realistic, thank you. The other two could be morose morons. But they were his family.

"What are you saying, Your Highness?" Dane asked, his jaw squaring in that comic book, all-American hero way of his.

Tal turned to Dane. Coop's stomach rolled. Here it came, the big emotional "I'm sorry" scene that had been building for six months. *Fuck.* Coop hadn't gone into the Navy so he could have the verbal equivalent of dude hugs. He'd rather cut through the crap and put it behind them. "Let me translate. Tal fucked up and he's sorry. He's cool if we go after Alea because he knows we'll take care of her. Now can we move this along?"

Tal frowned Coop's way. "That's not exactly how I planned to say it, but yes. I had a very long apology planned,

43

too."

"Can't we handle this like men?" Coop asked. "Just punch each other, then share a beer and we're all cool."

Dane's lips curled up. "Sorry, Tal. Coop isn't a big believer in the whole 'emotional sharing' thing. I think it's because he grew up surrounded by cattle."

Coop shrugged. Sometimes he missed his dad's ranch. "I was raised by cowhands who were long on work and short on chatter. Sorry."

A huge smile crossed the sheikh's face. "Well, Cooper was succinct, but correct. Alea needs you. I've talked this over with my brothers, and we've agreed that we will approve the marriage if you can convince her to accept."

"We will." Coop smiled now. "But it's not fair. You had it easier. You got to steal a bride."

"We followed in the tradition of our ancestors. They would whisk a woman away to someplace quiet and fuck her until she finally agreed to marry them," Tal said with a long sigh. "You'll have to be sneaky. I doubt Alea will prove as accommodating or as easily deceived as Piper. Plus, we had the whole language thing on our side. Unfortunately for you, Alea is proficient in five languages. I don't think she knows Swahili. Do any of you?"

Coop rolled his eyes. "I think we can all agree Alea is smarter than any of us. We're going to have to rely on how hot we are."

"That's worked so well for us up to this point." Dane rolled his eyes. "So please stop walking around in your boxers on the off chance that Alea will walk in, see your body, and fall at your feet."

He elbowed Dane. It could have worked.

Law yawned, looking generally bored. "If you guys are done with the huggy portion of the evening, we could move on."

Riley frowned at his brother. "Sorry, he's the emotional equivalent of a lobotomized pit bull. Now for the bad news.

There is no indication that Khalil had anything to do with the kidnapping. In fact, we talked to the private investigators he hired to look for the princess."

"What?" Tal asked, nearly coming out of his seat.

Coop was confused, too. Khalil had been a violent asswipe bent on destroying the whole family. "He hated his cousins."

"He hated everyone in line for the throne. Alea isn't. And there's no doubt he hired a small firm in California to search for her. It was actually a smart play. Those particular investigators have deep ties in South America."

"It had to be a ruse," Tal shot back.

"I don't think so. Yes, he could have used it to point suspicion away from him if you'd thought he had something to do with the kidnapping. But it makes more sense to me that he would look for her so he could get his hands on her before you. That leverage might have been very interesting to a man like Khalil. Unfortunately for him, your investigators got there first," Riley explained. "And the firm he hired doesn't know anything we don't."

So if Khalil hadn't been guilty, and the act hadn't been random, where did that leave them? Screwed. Everything inside Coop tightened. Knowing that the asshole behind Alea's torment was still free to plot against her again would feed his nightmares. Random, they could deal with. It sucked, but the Lennox brothers had taken vengeance out on the men who had actually grabbed Alea from her university. He, Dane, and Lan found comfort in that. Even Khalil as the mastermind made him feel better. That fucker was dead, and Coop knew that he and his buddies would watch over her and make sure nothing ever happened to her again.

But neither of the above wasn't what he wanted to hear.

"So you believe that Khalil was in the dark, too." Tal's fingers splayed across the table as he leaned forward and cursed in Arabic.

Riley continued. "We've made a careful study of the

flow of money of the abductors and the brothel where your cousin was held. It's all a bit of a nightmare. The brothel was owned by a man who had close ties to the Delgado Cartel. The money filtered through there, but when the Lennox brothers took down that cartel and killed the Delgados, it splintered into three different groups. Getting any kind of financials on a criminal organization is difficult. Scraping figures together on one in disarray is nearly impossible."

"So you're saying you've reached a dead end?" Coop was already planning a trip to Colombia in his head. He would cut through all that red tape and just kill a bunch of fuckers until one told him what he needed to know.

"No. I'm saying I'm a genius and the world should really bow at my feet," Riley quipped with an arrogant smile.

Law made a vomiting sound. "He likes to build it all up so he looks good. All he did was play around with his computer."

"Luddite. I can cause more trouble with a few keystrokes than you can with all the guns in your arsenal. Now, I don't have it all figured out, but I do have a very interesting pattern of deposits and withdrawals. If you look on page sixteen, I've documented what I've got." Pages shuffled, and Riley went on. "I've managed to discern that the brothel's business transactions were handled by the owner's wife. It's all routine and in cash until two weeks after Alea's kidnapping. A wire transfer of twenty-five thousand hit a bank account the cartel used strictly for the brothels. Now, we all know they were selling women, but the same account then wires five thousand every ten days until two days before Alea was rescued."

Dane shook his head. "Like…someone was paying for her upkeep?"

"If that's the case, they definitely overpaid. According to Cole, she was kept in horrible conditions," Tal muttered.

"I think someone was paying them simply to keep her alive, Tal," Coop said darkly.

This twisted plot was far worse than he'd imagined. Someone out there had paid to keep Alea tied up and drug addicted. Someone had wanted her held captive. But why?

"Where did that money come from?" he demanded of Riley.

The PI paused. "Directly from a Cayman account, which was closed shortly after Alea was rescued. I'm still looking for the records that indicate where and how the account was funded, but as you can imagine, the banking laws in the Caymans are beyond liberal."

"So what you're saying is that we might never know." Dane scrubbed a hand over his hair. He'd let it grow after he'd left the Navy. Coop kept his in a military cut because it was easy, but that hair of Dane's seemed one way he distanced himself from his past.

Riley squared his big shoulders like he was ready for battle. Though he came across a bit like a geek, he was obviously in good shape and possessed a little badass. "I will figure it out. I won't stop."

"He's serious," Law explained. "He's pissed off now. He'll never quit. It's why Dominic sent us out here. We're going to go through some of the palace records. Some of them are kept on paper."

Riley shuddered. "That's barbaric, but I have to examine those records."

"Are you suggesting someone at the palace was behind the atrocity?" Tal asked, clearly horrified by the prospect.

"We have to rule out every possibility," Riley said without a hint of apology in his voice. "I've already checked on everyone Princess Alea knew in New York, including all the employees at the embassy. I suspect that whoever is behind her abduction is someone she knows."

"Will they try again?" a soft, shaky voice asked from the shadowed doorway.

Fuck. Fuck. Fuck. Alea walked into the light and stood like a gorgeous statue in her gown, her hair caught in a soft chignon that Coop wanted to run his hands through until all that midnight softness flowed around her shoulders. Her face was a tense mask. She had obviously heard far more than they wanted her to.

Dane touched the comm device that rested in his ear. "Lan, you're missing your charge, buddy."

"No, I'm not." Lan stepped up behind her. His face was closed off as though he was just waiting for Dane's brutal judgment to fall down on his head. "It's her life. She has the right to know."

Coop winced. Hell, there was going to be a throw down now. He would be lucky if he managed to keep the ballsy Texan from losing his life, much less his job.

Alea walked into the room, her head held high. "I caught wind of this little meeting and I threatened Landon. He didn't have a choice."

Dane's face had turned a spectacular shade of red. "What exactly did you threaten him with, Princess? Were you going to use your nail file on him? Maybe you were going to throw one of your high heels at him."

"Don't be condescending. I threatened to tell my cousins that he'd made a pass at me and have him fired if he didn't cooperate." Alea stood her ground even as Dane rose and stalked toward her.

Coop stood, too, because this could get out of hand very quickly. "Now, Dane. Hold up. We should listen."

Dane towered over her. Her crazy-hot, four-inch heels were no match for his six and a half feet of pure muscle. Alea tilted her head back to look him in the eyes. "I didn't give him a choice, so if you have a problem with me being here, you really should talk to me."

Lan shook his head, and Coop knew he was about to do something stupid. "She didn't threaten me. Besides, everyone knows I hit on her all the time. I haven't gotten fired yet."

"That's not going to be a problem anymore, Nix. Consider yourself officially fired. You can pack your bags and be out of here by morning." Dane turned to the rest of the room. "Gentlemen, I think we have everything we need. I'm sure the sheikh will cooperate fully with the investigation."

Tal was sitting back in his chair, watching the drama unfold with curious eyes. "Naturally, I will help in any way I can."

Alea wasn't through with Dane. She stomped one of those designer shoes as she followed him. "You can't fire Landon. I won't allow it. Tal, tell him."

The sheikh shrugged negligently. "Dane is in charge of security. He can hire and fire as he likes. But he might want to remember that there are more important things at stake than whether Landon followed orders."

Dane turned and glared at Lan, seemingly trying to intimidate the younger man and waiting for him to break, to ask for forgiveness.

And Alea was now looking through one of the folders, her skin turning pale as she caught sight of the pictures taken of her in the hospital after her rescue. That frail, gaunt creature looked nothing like the stunning beauty standing before him now. Her hand shook as she touched the picture.

Lawson Anders stood up, shoving some file folders into his briefcase. "To answer your question, Princess, yes. My gut tells me that whoever is responsible will come after you again. They had a bleak future all planned for you, and it didn't involve you being rescued and coming home. I don't know why you weren't killed, but if someone wants to wipe you off the face of the Earth, I suspect they won't hesitate to snuff you out next time."

Alea's eyes fluttered, and her shoulders dropped. "And you believe this is someone I know, someone I spend time with?"

There was no hint of emotion in Lawson's eyes. "Yes. No idea who yet, but we'll find out."

Tal cursed and glared at Law. "Did you have to be quite so blunt?" Without waiting for an answer, he turned to Alea.

"Are you all right?"

She nodded, looking drawn and still.

Straightening his tuxedo jacket, the sheikh cleared his throat, hiding a whole lot of pissed off. "Then I'm retiring back to the ballroom. I probably only have a few more hours of peace left. Once Piper finds out about this meeting, there will very likely be hell to pay. The good news is, she's adorable when she's mad. We'll leave the cleanup to you three. After all, you wanted to be responsible for her. Be careful what you wish for."

After Tal had gone, Alea swayed on her feet. Cooper moved across the room in a flash as her eyes closed and her body crumpled. He caught her just before she hit the floor and lifted her weight into his arms as if she was a precious burden. Dane and Lan stood right beside him, wearing matching expressions of concern.

This wasn't how he'd pictured holding her for the first time. But no matter. He held her close now, even as her eyes fluttered open.

"Lea, you're going to be okay." Damn, was that his voice shaking?

"I think I'd like to go to my room, Cooper. Could you please take me?" She wasn't fighting him. He'd expected her to struggle and tell him she could walk, but she let her arm drift up around his shoulders and she laid her head on his chest. She could probably hear his heart pounding.

"Absolutely." He glanced back at his friends. "Someone get my med kit."

Without waiting for Dane and Lan to answer, he started out the door. If someone was still after Alea, it was time to start putting her first.

Chapter Three

Alea dragged in a long breath as Cooper strode toward her private apartments. "I changed my mind. You can let me down now. I need to talk to those investigators and look at that report."

She enjoyed being in his arms far too much. He made her feel delicate and feminine, loved and almost innocent. And it was all a lie.

"Not until I've examined you, Princess. You passed out."

"I got woozy. I never lost consciousness."

No, but that would have been nice. She'd been brutally aware of all of tonight's events. Her cousins, whom she trusted more than anyone in the world, had hired investigators and not bothered to mention it to her. Coop and Dane had gone along with the plan to keep her in the dark. When had they planned to tell her that someone was out there waiting for another chance to send her back to hell?

Cooper used his foot to kick the door open. "You were about to hit the floor."

Alea frowned. "Well, the dress is tight."

She could barely breathe. Her evening gown hadn't been designed for comfort. And now she was a little worried that if she tried to take a deep breath, her breasts might peek or plop out.

"Then maybe you should get out of it, but I'm not leaving here until I know you're all right." His dark eyes were full of glittering determination.

He swept her through the living area and back toward her bedroom. He didn't need to be pointed in the right direction. He, Dane, and Lan knew every square inch of this place because they were always watching over her. They did a sweep of her room every single night before she went to bed. One of them was always somewhere in the shadows, waiting to defend her.

And now it looked like she needed them more than she'd imagined. Some psycho had gone to a lot of trouble and expense to make her life hell and was probably waiting to do it again. God, that someone must truly hate her. The fact that it could be someone she knew boggled her mind. She tried to think of any obvious enemies she might have, but came up terribly blank.

"Alea? You went pale again." He carried her to her bed and settled her on top of the silky, pale-gray comforter. His hand went straight to her forehead. "You're hot."

She wished he'd said that in a way that meant he found her attractive—and that she could believe. Unfortunately, Cooper Evans was an outrageous flirt. She couldn't take anything he said seriously. And he'd only meant the words medically.

"It was stuffy in the ballroom."

Cooper looked behind him. "Where the hell are they? I need my kit."

"I'm not sick," Alea insisted. "You don't need to examine me."

She struggled to sit up. She really did need to talk to those investigators since she'd only gotten a brief glimpse at the reports, and so much of what they'd said had been strained through the filter of her incredulity. Just thinking about what had happened in the past—what might happen again—her heart ratcheted up to a jackhammer's pace.

Oh, god no.

For the last two years, she'd been plagued by panic attacks, though they'd begun to slow down. She'd thought she was getting better, but now she couldn't breathe. Damn it, she needed to breathe.

Alea pushed off the bed and started charging across the room, her blood racing through her veins, her heart roaring in her ears. Blackness swam at the edge of her vision.

"Lea? Baby?"

The "baby" nearly did her in. She needed his arms around her, and it wasn't going to happen. Coop probably called every female under the age of eighty "baby." Even if his voice had been so tender that she wanted to cry, she couldn't take his endearment personally.

Suddenly, Coop raced around her, gripping her shoulders, holding her secure. He towered over her, his golden brown hair shining under the soft recessed lights. His broad shoulders seemed to go on for days. He looked so masculine, so fiercely capable of protecting the woman he loved. Yet Coop regarded her with such soft concern.

She wanted to melt against him—and if she did, she'd make a fool of herself. Time to put space between them. "I'm going to the bathroom. Just go away, Cooper. I'm fine."

Alea charged toward her luxurious bathroom, slamming the door behind her. He would leave now. And damn it, no, that wouldn't disappoint her. Cooper had a job to do, so of course he would retreat outside her bedroom doors, leaving her utterly alone.

Even knowing that's what he should do, she leaned against the back of the door, trying to get a lungful of air, and fought tears. Why cry for what she couldn't change? Angrily, she swiped at the wet paths on her cheeks, then wound her hands to the back of her bodice, pulling at the cinches. In a moment, her breasts broke free and she dragged blessed oxygen into her lungs.

She pushed the whole gown off and got out of the god-awful spandex undies she'd forced her body into because she didn't want anyone to know that she wasn't perfect. God, if they only knew.

Tears streaked down her face as she turned and caught sight of herself in the mirror. She wasn't beautiful. She was supposed to be a princess, but somehow she'd ended up with small breasts and an ass that was a bit too wide. Her stomach wasn't flat.

They had beaten her for that in the brothel. She could still feel the switch they had used on her, still see the faint scars on her belly. She wasn't pretty enough to sell. She wasn't sexy enough to fuck. No one would want her.

But someone hated her enough to have her kidnapped and tortured.

Alea crossed to the sink and turned on the cold water. She had to get control of herself quickly because the coronation ball was still in progress. Piper would expect her there. She needed to get dressed again. And she needed to confront her cousins who had involved everyone in the investigation about her abduction except her.

She'd been so sure when Khalil had died that her ordeal was all over. She'd cried and tried to come to terms with everything. But she'd been safe—or so she had believed. Now she knew it had all been a falsehood.

And her cousins had perpetrated it.

She couldn't face the investigators again wearing that dumbass gown. She'd picked it out for stupid reasons. Piper had told her it was gorgeous, and she'd thought that maybe Dane, Landon, and Cooper would think she was pretty for an evening.

So stupid. She should have just picked a black dress that covered everything and wouldn't potentially embarrass the hell out of her.

"Oh god, you're gorgeous."

Alea started, her heart nearly stopping at Cooper's masculine groan. He was standing in the doorway, staring at her intently, his mouth set in a slightly salacious expression. Slightly? A second glance suggested that maybe she was underestimating him.

Her first instinct was to leap for a robe, a towel—anything that would cover her—but she just stood there, utterly frozen. He was staring at her naked body, and he wasn't running away. In fact, he was moving toward her. She retreated a quick step, but her back met the marbled wall, and there was nowhere else to go.

Alea could hardly catch her breath to speak. "You should go."

"God, you're so fucking beautiful." He sounded like he meant it. He edged closer, towering over her.

"You can't be in here," she protested, but it wasn't the sound of a woman who strongly meant what she was saying. Instead, it sounded breathy, almost like a seduction. What was wrong with her?

"Why not, Lea? Give me one good reason." He braced himself against the wall behind her, his body pressing close.

She could think of about fifty reasons, but only one came out of her mouth. "I'm naked."

"Yes, and that's the best reason I can think of to stay."

He leaned toward her, touching their foreheads together. If he'd been the least bit domineering, she could have pushed him away, but this was a sweet intimacy. How long had it been since she'd touched someone? Felt the heat of another body close to her own quite like this? Never.

"Baby, do you know how many nights I've sat up imagining how beautiful you are? Do you know how off I was? You're a hundred times more gorgeous than I ever dreamed. Tell me you don't want me, too. Tell me, and I'll walk out of this room. I won't try to touch you again, but you should know that I'll never stop wanting you. You're the only woman I've been able to think of since I met you."

He brought one hand to her shoulder, his fingers just barely touching her, making her shiver in the most delicious way possible.

She shook her head, trying to come out from under the spell. "You've dated since you've been here. Don't try to fool me."

His head snapped up, and she found herself staring into

the warmest chocolate brown eyes she'd ever seen. His handsome face settled into a frown that did nothing to detract from his male-model gorgeousness. "Not once."

She bit her bottom lip. She wanted to believe him. God, she was standing here naked with him and she couldn't seem to make herself move. "That's impossible."

"That's the truth." His fingers made their way down her arm. "I'm worried about touching you. I don't want to scare you, baby. You have to know I would never, ever want to hurt you."

He sounded so different from the laughing, sarcastic man she'd come to know. This was the Cooper she'd always suspected hid under his playful exterior. He was so sweet, but it was hard to believe he wasn't sexually active. He was the only one of the three of Tal's guards who regularly took weeks off and left the country. "I thought you had a girl back home. I thought that was why you left every six weeks."

He was staring into her eyes, holding her hostage. "I go to a little hospital in Pakistan. I have an old buddy who runs a clinic there. Baby, I'm not seeing someone. I'm vaccinating babies and running the clinic so he has a little time off. I told you. I haven't wanted anyone since the minute I laid eyes on you." He swallowed hard. "Are you ever going to look at me the way I look at you?"

Alea wanted to. She studied him all the time when she was sure he wasn't looking. Tears sprang to her eyes. "I don't know. I don't know that I can do any of this, Cooper. I…I don't think I function the way other women do. I don't respond to sex."

Except she was kind of responding now. Her breathing was ragged. She wasn't panicked the way she'd been after her rescue. When she'd first come back, she'd pulled away from anyone who tried to touch her. Lately, she'd been wondering if she was missing out. Piper was a hugger. At first it had seemed rude to shove her cousins' wife away, so she'd endured it, but more and more she found herself initiating the hugs. And she definitely thought about being able to touch her men. In her dreams, she opened to them fully, and they took her in every way. She felt such pleasure, such love… What a far-fetched fantasy.

And just the fact that she thought of them as *her* men was proof enough that she'd gone half mad. She should shove Cooper away right this second before he found out how cold she was.

"Baby, your nipples are hard."

He backed up just enough to brush his knuckles over them. Rough, work-callused skin touched her own, lighting a fire deep in her belly. She shivered and gasped, then tried to shrink away. He wrapped an arm loosely around her waist and kept her close.

"You respond just fine." His voice sounded rough. "Let me kiss you."

Alea shook her head. "I-I can't stand too much touch. I can't close my eyes without…"

"Shh, baby. You can't stand being tied down or having someone on top of you. We can work on that. It'll take time and patience, but I've got both."

"It's more than that." But he wouldn't understand, and frustration welled. She needed to grab her robe and run away. She looked around for an escape, but the only way out was through Coop. "I don't know how I would handle hands really…touching me."

"Let me do all the worrying. We'll work it out."

That sounded nice. No, it sounded like a huge relief, letting someone else bear the strain and horror of all she'd endured. God, she was so deeply lonely, but she feared the risk. What if Coop touched her and she panicked? How could she ever look at him or the other two again if she freaked out and made an idiot of herself? They'd know she was frigid. Hell, she'd confessed it. But they didn't know she woke up screaming and fighting some invisible attacker far too often.

Slowly, Cooper slid to his knees, somehow making the

move deeply graceful. "I won't touch you with my hands, baby, but I want to show you that there's not a damn thing wrong with you. You can respond. I can prove it. Let me kiss you."

He wasn't talking about her mouth.

Cooper was right *there*, staring at her. She should be horrified. No one had seen her naked since she'd come home from South America. But there was something heady about the intimacy of being bare and alone with Cooper that she couldn't deny. She felt frozen, hopeful.

And then she felt desperate because Cooper didn't wait for an answer. He leaned in, and she felt the heat of his breath right on her pussy.

Alea braced for the panic to set in. She parted her lips to warn him that, any second, she would kick out and try to fight him. She lifted her hands, ready to push him away.

But everything stopped—time, her heart, her breath—as he kissed her with such aching tenderness, placing little butterfly kisses across the mound of her pussy. Women in her culture waxed their bodies, and now Alea was glad she'd kept up the practice because she could feel every press of his lips against her sensitive skin. Heat flared, but she found herself trembling as she looked down, watching his golden brown hair move as he tilted his head, seemingly determined not to miss tasting an inch of her.

"You see, you could handle a little kiss," he whispered against her thigh, and his words tingled along her flesh. "The key is to go slow so you know you're safe. But we can push the boundaries just a little. Do you know how long I've wanted to taste you, baby?"

She'd been kissed before on the mouth, short, groping attempts at affection when she was younger. Her childhood had been deeply protected. Growing up behind palace walls with three male cousins had ensured she'd gone to college with very little experience, but she'd been kissed a few times. She'd even been touched by two male suitors.

But nothing had ever been like this, a heady, trembling rush of amazing pleasure. *Oh god...* And no one had ever gently drawn his tongue across her swelling folds.

She couldn't stop the cry that fell from her mouth. Suddenly she was glad she was leaning against the wall because she was pretty sure her legs nearly dissolved underneath her. She couldn't quite catch a full breath. His mouth felt so good.

"You taste so sweet, Lea. So fucking sweet." He drew his tongue right up the center of her pussy, stopping at her clitoris to press little circles there.

Alea could feel herself getting soft and wet, her pussy nearly pulsing with desire. Pleasure drummed behind her clit. And she ached everywhere.

He sucked half of her labia into his mouth, pulling gently, tonguing her with wicked purpose before returning to her clitoris. She'd read about this feeling, but she'd never thought her parts actually worked. Apparently, she'd been wrong because every nerve in her body now stood at attention, expectant as he laved affection all over her pussy. He licked her clit with the tip of his tongue, and she moaned, melted, dying for more.

But he seemed intent on making her wait for it, making her crazy. He tapped her clit, then drew it between his teeth, suckling in gentle passes that had her panting for more. A plea sat on the tip of her tongue. Her head fell back against the wall, and her eyes slid shut. Her fingers filtered into his hair.

"Yes..." she moaned.

Oh, god, she was soaking wet. He was eating her up, sucking down everything she gave him. And still, he seemed hungry for more. These foreign sensations he gave her made her feel powerful and sexy and right. She started rolling her hips with every brush of his tongue, pushing toward him, forcing him to tongue her harder as she silently begged for more. He could make her come. He could give her everything she'd secretly craved. And she would thank him because she'd never felt more free.

So close. As he rubbed her clit with his tongue, worrying the perfect spot over and over, she fisted as much of his hair in her hands as she could. Her eyes were going to cross. She held her breath. Soon—in seconds—she was going to scream his name. She was going to find that bliss everyone talked about and shout her pleasure from the heavens.

Suddenly, he gripped her hips, caging her against the wall and stilling her movements. Her brain blanked and readjusted. Memories catapulted her to a different place. Pleasure vanished.

No love. No affection. Just chains and pain and heartache.

Fat bitch. Stay where you are. They were always telling her how ugly she was. How she wasn't worth the food they gave her. How some day they would just slit her throat and leave her to the dogs.

She could hear the sound of that hand coming for her. They slapped at her stomach because the skin was thin there. They caned her feet so she couldn't walk, much less run, for days.

"Lea! Lea, baby, stop!"

She couldn't. They would kill her, rape her. They told her she was nothing. A piece of trash. Worthless. And they would annihilate everything inside they hadn't yet destroyed.

A stupid princess without her own family. She was cursed and useless, and it would be better if she'd died.

The worst part was, those words were her own. It was her own voice in her head, in her sleep...when she considered how much easier it would have been if she'd rotted in that jungle.

"Lea!"

Strong arms caged her, and Alea fought harder. She kicked out, determined to get away. They wouldn't take her this time. She refused to let that happen. No way was she going back to hell. She would rather die. She heard a long, tortured scream, then realized it was her own. She refused to go quietly. Never. She would make them kill her before she'd go back into a cage.

"Please, baby. I won't touch you again. Please come back to me. Please."

"What the fuck is going on here?" A deep voice cut through everything.

Authority dripped from that voice. Authority decided how she was punished, how and where she would hurt that particular day. Authority meted out "justice" swiftly.

"Fuck you!" Alea shouted. She was done. They could kill her, but she wouldn't go meekly. They wouldn't shove that needle in her arm and make her compliant again. They wouldn't make her crave the drug that made her kidnappers' job easy.

Not again. Not again. Please not again.

"Alea!" That voice was insistent, pulling at her. "Alea, you're in Bezakistan. You're safe. You're here. No one is going to hurt you."

Strong arms shook her, forcing her to open her eyes.

Dane? When had Dane come to South America? Had he come for her? He couldn't see her this weak and pathetic. She tried to push at him, but he was a massive brick wall. "Go away."

He refused to budge.

Tears ran down her face as she thrashed violently for freedom.

A sharp shock hit her skin, and the fleshy part of her ass flared with a stinging heat, forcing her into the present.

Then reality hit her harder than any smack to her ass.

She was in the palace, and she wasn't alone. She was surrounded by all three of them. Cooper was on his butt on the floor, staring up at her, guilt carved into his face. Lan had a hand on Coop's shirt as though he'd pulled his friend back. And Dane stood in front of her, his gorgeous face stern and tormented as he stared down at her. His blue eyes were steady as he braced his big hands on her shoulders, seemingly ready to shake her back into reality. He was the one who had slapped at her ass, jarring her long enough to return to the present.

And suddenly, Alea realized that she was naked in every sense of the word. "Get out of here!"

None of them moved.

What had she been thinking? What the hell had she been doing? A sob formed in the back of her throat. She couldn't handle this. Panic was still there, rolling in the pit of her stomach. Those memories were so close to the surface, she could smell the dank sheets and hear the cries of the women around her. She shoved out at Dane, but he was a tower of pure muscle.

He didn't even register her pitiful attempts at freedom. "Calm down, Princess. Do you know where you are?"

Alea hated his perfectly sensible tone. She was past sanity, and he sounded so completely cool. She tried to calm down, but they were all so close. "I need you to back off. Back off!"

It wasn't fair to lash out at them, but she *needed* to be alone so she could regroup. She had to get them out of here before she lost it again. She'd humiliated herself enough. And more panic hovered at the edge of her consciousness, stuck in her throat, threatening to escape in a long scream.

They had all conspired against her, even Landon. He'd known about the investigation. It was the only explanation for how he'd known where and when that meeting about her life had been taking place. All three of them had been complicit.

Broken and ugly. That was all she was.

"Alea, I'm just about ready to put you over my knee and smack that ass until you're in your right head again."

"Nice. Well, go ahead. It's nothing I haven't been through before. You think you're so big and bad? Go ahead, abuse the stupid, weak princess. Maybe that will make you feel like a man." She spewed bile his way because she wasn't about to let him know that she needed them to hold her, to surround her until she was sure no harm could reach her. Eventually, they'd find out she was broken. Then they would leave. She had to erect some really high walls that would protect them all, so their rejection wouldn't hurt so much. "Men only see women as punching bags anyway, right?"

Dane's face went a bright red, his jaw tightening to the point she was sure it would break. He was so righteously pissed that she thought surely he would beat her and prove who was stronger.

Instead, he jerked away from her, then pivoted, giving her his back. He didn't look at her again, merely reached out and grabbed Cooper's shirt, where Lan's hand had been previously. He twisted his fist in the garment and started dragging his friend out behind him.

"Goddamn it, Dane." Cooper struggled, but nothing seemed to faze Dane. "Let me go. We can't leave her like this."

Dane merely stalked out of the room, hauling his partner along.

Alea's hands shook as she felt warm, soft fabric cover her shoulders suddenly. She looked up. Landon. He was settling her robe around her body, covering her nakedness. His face was a careful blank.

"I'll admit that I knew you were all kinds of fucked up, Princess," Lan began in that down-home Texas drawl of his.

She laughed, but there was no humor to the sound. She pulled the robe around her like a coat of armor. "Good for you, Lan. You just proved you have eyes and a brain that halfway works."

He flinched, and his face closed up. Alea fought tears. What was wrong with her? Why did she keep saying such horrible things? Why was she hurting them?

Because they terrified her. Because if she hurt them first,

they might not be able to hurt her back.

"Wow. That's a good one, Princess. You know how to go for the throat. You definitely kicked Dane where it hurts the most. Did you know his ex-wife thought that BDSM was abuse? Did you know that even though he never touched her like that, when he asked her to experiment she called him a wife beater?"

She gasped. How horrible. And how terrible she felt now. Dane would never hurt a woman.

Alea closed her eyes for a moment. Sometimes, she didn't recognize herself anymore. When she lashed out like she just had, the fear and hurt talked, not her. "No. Oh, Lan, I didn't know. He wouldn't have abused her."

"Well, you have great instincts, Princess. Dane feels like he failed everyone, his whole family, definitely his ex-wife. I'm pretty sure I'm the dumbest idiot ever born, so reinforcing that is a surefire way to hurt me. Let me give you some advice on how to hurt Coop because I'm not sure you figured him out yet. He hides his insecurities really well."

"Don't." Alea felt hot tears scalding her face.

Lan thumbed away the tears, but his voice didn't change. It remained a deep, polite monotone. "Coop came from a big ranching family. When he was a little kid, the ranch hit real hard times. His family almost lost everything. Every dime they made went back into the land or to pay the mortgage, so he grew up poor. He was the youngest of seven boys so by the time the hand-me-downs got to him, they were patched up and worn and he was so skinny that the kids in his school called him Scarecrow. Call him that a couple of times and it'll cut him to the quick. Since you're not only fucked up but cruel, that should give you some ammunition. Enjoy it." He shook his head. "The way I see it, either you were always mean or you let them make you mean. Either way, it's a goddamn shame."

Lan brushed away another tear and turned, following after Dane and Coop. They were all leaving, and she'd been the one to shove them away, hurting them and lashing out because she wasn't brave enough to be kind, welcoming. That required a strong heart, and hers was shattered.

More tears fell, but the scream that was always in her throat stuck. "Landon."

He stopped but didn't turn. "What do you need, Your Highness?"

So many things. Nothing she could ask for. "Tell Dane I'm sorry. And Cooper and… I'm very sorry that I hurt you too."

He nodded and left, and she was alone again.

Alea crumbled to the floor. The gorgeous gown she'd picked out in hopes that they would notice her was lying on the tile, trampled by boot prints, ruined. What had she been thinking? She could dress up all she liked, but she was still that girl chained to a bed, waiting to die.

The only trouble now was she seemed determined to take everyone to hell with her.

* * * *

Dane let Cooper drop as soon as he'd hauled him out of the princess's quarters. He didn't trust Coop not to run back in and try to get on top of her again.

And he didn't trust himself not to walk back and have a throw down with her that would very likely end with him getting his ass arrested for laying hands on Her Royal Highness.

"You asshole." Coop was on his feet in a heartbeat. "What the fuck was that about?"

The hallway around them was quiet. He'd been afraid Tal would follow them, but it appeared he had gone back to the ball. He was fine with that because he was just about ready to start throwing punches. Caving in Coop's face might take the edge off the nasty anger building inside him.

Alea had scored a direct hit. He could still hear Kelly

screaming at him that he was a pervert, a freak for what he needed. He could still remember the day his father had told him what an embarrassment he was to the family and that he was no longer welcome in the house he'd grown up in.

He hadn't been invited to his brother's wedding. Of course, that wasn't such a huge surprise since his very vanilla brother had been marrying his ex-wife.

He felt Coop shove at his arm, goading him. "What? Now you can't talk?"

Dane narrowed his eyes, flexed his hands. He'd thought he was going to beat the shit out of Lan for bringing Alea to the meeting, but Cooper had done something much worse. "I can talk, man. I just don't think you're going to like what I have to say."

Cooper pulled back slightly, frowning. "I didn't mean for it to happen."

"Oh, it was an accident then? You tripped and fell on top of her pussy? Did your tongue fall out and land on her clit?"

"She was responding, damn it."

Dane had seen just how she'd responded. "Yeah, you must have done a hell of a job with her, buddy. She was screaming and kicking and fighting you as if she was struggling for her very survival.

He'd heard her from down the hall. He'd been lighting into Lan when they both heard Alea's shout. They'd run, terrified that someone was trying to kill her. Lan had his gun out and he'd just about taken off Coop's head when Dane realized who it was.

Coop's whole body sagged. "It didn't start out like that. I was trying to check up on her. I wanted to make sure her BP was okay. She nearly fainted. When she took a while in the bathroom, I went in to make sure she hadn't fallen or stumbled and hit her head. And I saw her. She was…"

"Beautiful." Yeah, he'd gotten that, too. He'd seen every inch of her golden body, every curve and valley. Even though she'd been screaming, he was just enough of a bastard to get a hard-on because she was so fucking sexy. Shame filled him. She didn't want him and she was probably right. No man with real morals would have gotten an erection when the woman he adored was terrified.

And they damn straight wouldn't have threatened to spank her. The trouble was, she responded to dominance. It was only when he'd used his Dom voice that she'd calmed and come out of her episode. She needed someone to take control when she couldn't, to make sure she didn't hurt herself. To stand by her and give her the safe boundaries and structure she needed.

"Yes, she was so beautiful, and we had this connection, Dane," Coop continued. "She thinks she's frigid, but she's not. She was pressing her pussy against my mouth and wriggling around. That's why I tried to hold her down, so I could finish her off. Damn, I don't think that girl's ever had an orgasm. If I hadn't wrapped my arms around her, we would be in a totally different place."

"Yeah, you would be fucking her, and Dane would be rearranging my face," a laconic voice said from the doorway. Landon stared at Cooper.

Coop rolled his eyes. "God, don't give me that. I wasn't trying to steal her. I was trying to show her how good it can be. And you're a fine one to talk. What the fuck was that move you pulled? Did you sell her on how awful Dane and I are to cut her out of that meeting?"

"Fuck you, Coop." Lan squared off, facing the other man down. They started to circle each other like two pit bulls waiting to take a chunk out. "She deserved to be in that meeting. It was about her. She's not a child."

"She sure knows how to throw a temper tantrum," Dane said, frowning. "That shit she just pulled is exactly why I left her out. Alea isn't ready for that much reality. We all agreed on this plan, and you took it into your own hands to reverse our decision."

He'd been trying so hard to get them all on the same

page. Alea needed all three of them. She'd grown up in a country where she was practically expected to marry two or three men, maybe more. Being kidnapped had torn her world apart, but eventually she would find comfort in her custom of plural marriage. But in order to offer her what she needed, they had to stick together, and his asshole, idiot partners were being selfish pricks.

Lan's face flushed an angry red. "Look, I talked to Cole. He's been in this place before."

"Oh, Cole Lennox is now your best friend?" Coop shot at Lan, rounding on him. "Or is he the guy giving you advice on how to get her all to yourself?"

"What are you talking about? He shares his wife with his brother." Lan growled a little, a sure sign that this situation was about to get ugly. "And you're a fine fucking one to talk, Coop. I made a decision to bring her into something that involved us all. I thought we'd sit down and hash this out with her. I thought that maybe if she understood the situation, she would be a little easier on us. Let us closer. What's your excuse? Are you going to try to convince me that you were just warming her up so Dane and I could come in behind you and show her a good time? I didn't see you leaving a whole lot of room in her pussy for us."

Coop's right fist flew out, catching Lan's jaw. There was a thud, and a nasty, happy little smile crept across Lan's face because he was a man who appreciated violence, and Coop had just made the enormous mistake of giving it to him.

Lan's fist popped up almost faster than Dane could see it, and a nice splash of blood came from Coop's face. His lip, it looked like. He'd shifted just enough that Lan hadn't broken his nose.

They started to wail on each other, but Dane had lost the desire to fight.

Because he was pretty sure they had just lost Alea. Or maybe she'd already been lost, and tonight had simply forced him to face facts. The woman spitting the cruel barbs just wasn't his princess.

He heaved a long sigh. She needed him, but she would never acknowledge it, never give him the chance to prove it to her. And, hell, maybe he was wrong. It wouldn't be the first time. Maybe he should just join a fucking club and spend his time with the subs there who came out for a good time. He'd wrecked his marriage. He'd fucked up his career.

"I should have expected this." Tal stood beside him, watching the fight and shaking his head.

Dane turned, and it looked like Tal had brought out the whole fucking gang. Rafe and Kade were with him, along with the three James brothers—Gavin, Slade, and Dex—as well as the Lennox twins, Cole and Burke.

"Brothers shouldn't fight like that, man," Dex said, shaking his head.

Gavin James sent his youngest brother a scorching look. "Really? My nose is crooked because of you two fuckers."

Slade shook his head. "That was all on you, brother. Ouch, that's going to hurt. They're not big believers in rules, are they?"

Dane winced because Coop had just landed a kidney shot. "He was my team's medic. I don't think he takes the Hippocratic Oath very seriously. And we're not really brothers."

"That's where you're making your mistake," Rafe said. "If you want Alea, you better behave like brothers. Blood or no, be a cohesive unit. You have to take care of each other and work together."

"Yeah, you've got to do that if you're going to survive your wife. Trust me, Cole's the dumbass. He's always hiding behind me when he says something stupid." The Lennox twin on the right pointed to his other half.

Yeah, Dane would like a word with Cole. "He might want to hide behind you now."

A single eyebrow arched on Cole's face. "You're pissed that I talked to Landon? Well, someone had to. You guys are fucking this up and hard."

The urge to kill flared up again. "Is that right?"

Tal held up a hand. "Before you kill Mr. Lennox, perhaps you should understand a few things."

"Like he could kill me." Cole rolled his eyes.

Burke shrugged. "Dude, we've spent the last year hauling our son around, not training for battle. He would probably take you down."

"Please. I could take him down with Caleb strapped into his baby Snugli across my chest."

"The fact that you just used the word Snugli proves how out of the game we are."

The Lennox brothers continued to argue, but Dane looked to Tal. "What do you mean?"

"I mean what you've tried hasn't worked. You've all come at her in different ways, and she is going to require a coordinated assault where you leave her absolutely no way out. It's imperative the three of you work together. And be smart for a fucking change. I believe she'll respond to how gentle Landon can be, to Cooper's playfulness, and I absolutely believe she needs you most of all." Tal looked pointedly at Dane. "But you're the one who's holding back the most."

Tal could accuse him of a lot of things, but not that he'd been holding back. Something crashed in the background, and Dane looked over his shoulder. Landon had Cooper pinned to the ground, getting ready to bash his head in with what was probably a priceless vase. *Idiots.*

Cooper kicked up and Lan groaned as his balls met with a steel-toed boot. Every man in the hallway moaned, and Lan started a long fall to the floor.

Yeah, this was fucking helping.

Dane moved in to avoid utter catastrophe. The last thing he needed was to get billed for damaging historical art or some shit. He caught the vase just before Lan hit the floor.

Cooper and Landon were both on the carpet, chests

heaving and blood dripping. They had done numbers on one another.

"You two, stay the fuck down or I will get involved in this," Dane promised. Maybe Rafe was right and they should start considering themselves brothers. If they did that, Coop and Lan better understand that Dane was the big brother, and they were going to have to fall in line.

For now, they seemed content to lie there and focus on breathing.

"Sorry." He handed the vase back to Tal. "I'll talk to them."

Tal nodded. "That was a start."

"How the hell can you say I haven't been trying with her? I've been on walks with her almost every day. I try talking to her, coaxing her out of her shell. I've brought her treats, complimented her… Everything I should."

"Everything a vanilla man should. Alea requires more, and you know it."

Fuck. "She's fragile."

"She's also submissive without a firm Dominant. She's in free fall without a safety net. Rafe, Kade, and I have stood back, hoping you three would get your act together, but…" Tal shook his head.

Damn and hell. Tal wasn't telling him anything about Alea he hadn't already known. Every instinct in his body told him to top her, but she just kept shoving back. He didn't want to push her too hard. He'd been down that road with Kelly, and it had only ended in divorce.

"I can't force her to see what she needs," Dane argued.

"I've watched you with Alea," Kade said, stepping up. "You're at your best when you tell it like it is. But you've been very careful with her. Hell, we all have. My brothers and I have resolved to stop now. You have to do the same. I'm not telling you to force her to your will, but you should be open and honest about everything you can do for her. What the three of you give her."

"We've tried so many things," Rafe added. "We've brought in therapists, given her charity work to take her mind off things, surrounded her with family and friends from her past who can help her remember happier times. None of it has worked. She pretends to be content, but she doesn't connect with people anymore."

Coop pushed himself off the floor. "She's got a terrible self-image. She thinks she's ugly and frigid. We can't work on that from a distance."

Lan got to his feet as well, wiping blood from his mouth. "I hate to admit it, but I agree with Cooper. What we've been doing so far hasn't worked. We've been treating her like she's too fragile. We've almost convinced her that she is, too. But she won't break. She just needs to know that we're strong enough to handle her."

Dane looked at his two best friends. They had beaten each other stupid, but now they were standing together. Maybe that's what real brothers were like. And maybe it was time to start following his instincts. Alea was floundering. Her world had been broken in a way that she couldn't put back together all alone. She didn't know how to ask for help and was afraid to need it. She was damn straight terrified to open her heart.

He'd worked plenty of operations where he couldn't just walk through the door, guns blazing. The key was strategy. Find a sneaky way in. He could manage that. A two-pronged approach would work. He could start doing exactly what Tal had suggested, tell Alea everything she was missing, everything they could give her in the filthiest language possible. He wouldn't hold back. He wouldn't be polite. And he wouldn't let her get away with anything.

And then, when she couldn't stand another second, they would deliver on their promises. They would show her just how beautiful they thought she was, how hot they could make her, how high they could send her soaring. Once her body belonged to him and his brothers, her heart wouldn't be

72

far behind.

"Go get cleaned up," Dane said to Landon and Cooper. "We have a lot to talk about. Tal, please have the investigators send me the report. We'll will regroup in the morning and figure out exactly where to go from here. In the meantime, were going to figure out new protocols for the princess."

Tal held out his hand, shaking Dane's firmly. "The backup security team can handle the rest of the evening. It's winding down anyway. Consider your team reassigned. You're completely in charge of Alea's security from now on. Good luck."

Tal and his brothers, along with their friends, filed down the stairs, heading back to the ballroom, leaving Dane alone with the two men who had watched his back for the last two years. There wasn't anyone else he would rather go into battle with.

This was the mission of a lifetime, and Dane didn't intend to fail.

Chapter Four

Alea nearly cursed when she heard the soft knock on her door. The last thing she wanted was more conflict. At least she was dressed this time, having donned silk pajamas after a punishingly hot shower. "Please, Dane, can we talk about it in the morning? I'm so tired."

Dane would be the one they sent. He always delivered bad news or a lengthy lecture on how stupidly she was behaving. She knew putting him off wasn't right, but she couldn't handle another confrontation tonight.

The door opened, and a pretty brunette in a designer gown floated in. Piper al Mussad stood halfway in the room, her hands raised in a silent gesture that pleaded for peace. "It's just me. Don't blame me because my husbands are nitwits."

Alea couldn't help but smile. Despite the terror, uncertainty, and shame of the last hour, Piper was a breath of fresh air. Her cousin-in-law was one of those people who lit up the room simply by walking into it. "You really should have had their IQs checked before you decided to marry them."

Piper shrugged. "Give a girl a break. I was blinded by their hotness."

"Okay, as a girl who remembers them during their prepubescent years—ewww." But Alea smiled. Piper had been so good for her cousins. She'd become the sun they all orbited around. It reminded Alea of the joy her aunt and uncles had once shared and how happy the palace had been during her youth.

Piper closed the door behind her, her radiant face

suddenly serious. "Are you all right?"

Alea was so far from all right that it was ridiculous, but she didn't need to drag Piper any farther into this mess. And she wasn't about to cause problems in Piper's marriage. "I'm perfectly fine. My cousins have always been protective. I'm positive they would've told me in the morning."

"You're taking this way better than I would have. I have to confess, when Talib admitted what had happened, I thought about shoving something up his backside."

"Piper!"

She shrugged. "It's his favorite form of discipline. We should see how he likes it."

Alea felt her face flush. She shook her head as she sat on the couch in the living area of her apartment. "I don't understand how you can talk about things like that."

Piper eased down beside her. "Because it's nothing to be ashamed of. Tell me something. Was your aunt very proper? I know when she was the *shaykhah* she was every inch a lady in public, but was she reserved in private? I've only known her in private and she's so open. I'm wondering how she dealt with the public side of this life."

Alea laughed. Her aunt had been the same whether cameras were on her or not. "She used to tell us that she wouldn't hide how much she loved my uncles. She's very British, my aunt, but that stiff upper lip completely softened around her husbands and children. She is a lovely woman. She was the perfect queen in her day. You actually remind me a lot of her."

"Thank you." Piper smiled. "I've heard enough stories about when their fathers were alive to know that my husbands weren't raised in a household that lacked warmth. When they were children, their parents often displayed their affection and told my husbands that they were loved. So were you. She still loves you."

"My aunt and uncles created a wonderful environment to grow up in, though I missed not really knowing my own parents."

"Do I offend you when I talk about my intimate life with Tal, Rafe, and Kade? It's not my intention. You're my closest friend here. I'm afraid I like to talk about everything. It helps me process all that's happened. The last few months have been full of change for me." She laid a hand over her still-flat stomach.

"Oh, god, Piper, you don't offend me at all. I just can't understand." And Piper was such a sneaky woman. Now Alea understood why she'd been asking about the family. Piper had been backing her into a corner, and it was easier to simply answer the question she knew would eventually come. "Yes, I grew up in an open household, and yet I'm very reserved about sex. I'm sure it's because of what happened to me in South America. I've been to several of the world's best therapists. I know what my problems are."

Shrewd eyes stared back at her. "But you don't seem interested in fixing them."

Alea stood up every time she talked about it, she got restless, uneasy in her own skin. "I don't like who I am right now. It's weird because I can remember the girl I used to be, the one who didn't blow up at everyone, the one who wasn't isolated. But it feels like all of that was a dream and I had to wake up. Believe me, if I could forget what happened, I would."

"You'll never forget, Alea. Forgetting shouldn't be your goal. But it's up to you whether or not you allow them to win. Though I admit, watching you continually give in to your captors is painful."

"I'm not letting anyone win, damn it."

Piper sent her a skeptical stare. "Tell me you don't want those men who guard you, Lea."

Everything always came back to Dane, Cooper, and Landon. Since the moment she'd seen them, it seemed as if her thoughts had started to revolve around them, if not her world. If she'd been the same exuberant girl who'd left for

New York, she would have had all the confidence in the world to try a relationship with them. But this was now.

"I don't want them."

Piper sighed. "You can lie to yourself, but I know the truth. I think they know it, too."

Tears welled, unbidden, unwanted because she wasn't that girl anymore. "It doesn't matter."

She didn't see how she could possibly be pretty enough, sensual enough, or healed enough for them—ever.

Piper leaned forward. "What happened? Did you get mad because they tried to keep that meeting secret? I don't think you should blame them. Tal said it was his call."

Because Tal always shouldered the responsibility. "No. This whole plot reeks of Dane, too. I can see him arguing that they needed to get the whole story before they talked to me. He wouldn't want to worry me until they had a plan in place. He would have taken all the data and come to me with a detailed 'op,' as he would say."

Piper's eyes went wide. "It sounds like you know Dane pretty well."

Alea shrugged. "Cooper and Landon would have argued, but Cooper can be swayed. Landon is the one who would fight him. Cooper would hesitate to tell me bad news, but Lan would just shove it all out there because he doesn't know how to be dishonest." She sighed. "Not that they were intentionally unkind, but, damn it, Piper. It's my life on the line. I have a right to know."

"I agree," Piper said calmly. "Obviously Landon did, too. I heard he nearly got his balls kicked in. But you can be very difficult to talk to about this subject. You were the one who asked Tal to keep huge, deeply relevant portions of what happened to you in Colombia out of the reports. You understand how that hampers the investigation?"

God, she didn't want anyone to know. She hadn't even told the therapists everything. "They have all the information they need."

Piper sat back with a long sigh. "No, they don't, but you're not going to believe or admit that. You did nothing to be ashamed of, Alea. What happened was a crime perpetrated against you. You didn't cause it, but only you can give yourself permission to heal from it. Only you can let go of the pain and really beat the bastards who hurt you."

"There are no winners here, Piper. Just a whole lot of losers." Alea crossed her arms over her chest.

"Ah, there's the bitter girl." Piper smiled tightly. "You've been almost happy lately. I've been wondering if she'd finally left the building, but no. She's in full force tonight."

Bitter. Yes, that described her. She sat down again. The surroundings were so familiar. She'd been happy here at the palace long ago. Now she just felt stuck.

Alea let a long moment pass before asking the question that had plagued her for months. "Do you think it would be best if I left the palace?"

"What?" Piper leaned closer. "How can you think that?"

"Because you're having a baby. I'm not the nicest person. I don't mean to lash out, but I can't seem to help it. I'm wondering if...maybe it might be best if I went away. This should be a happy time for you."

Piper sighed and shook her head. "You see everything in the worst possible light. I'm not pointing out bitter girl to blame you. I'm simply saying that you've seemed more relaxed these last couple of months. You've even been smiling when you walk the grounds with Dane or sit in the garden with Lan and Cooper."

Yes, she'd enjoyed all those times, but they were over now. She would likely be assigned new guards. She'd ruined everything. Maybe they'd all just give up on her now, even Tal. He could ask her to leave because she was like a wounded animal and no one knew when she would kick or bray and hurt someone around her.

"Well, I rather thought the whole sordid kidnapping

mess was over. I found out tonight that it's not. So forgive me if I can't quite find my charm."

"No. That's not it. I'd hoped you were healing, but you've just gotten more adept at hiding your feelings. Alea, no one wants you to leave. You're more like a sister to my husbands than a cousin. You'll be my baby's aunt, and I want him or her to know you. We love you for the strong woman you are. You say this isn't a game, but in many ways it is. You didn't mean to play, but you're holding the cards now and you have to decide whether or not you want to win or let the bastard behind your kidnapping crush you."

Alea shook her head. "I can't win. I wouldn't even know how."

"You win the minute you decide to become a survivor instead of a victim. The minute you accept that you can't go back and you elect to move forward. You win when you allow the fact that you've survived to strengthen you, to make you a better human being than you were before. When you take all the horrible things that happened to you and make something good out of it—that's a moment of triumph. And you win the minute you let yourself love those three men." Piper stood and placed a hand on Alea's shoulder. "I hope you decide to win, because the rest us of love you and want to feel close to you, like family should. We hate that you've isolated yourself. We're all here for you. You just have to decide to join us in the love and laughter. In the light. This is your home. I hope you start acting like we're your family, too."

Piper brushed a kiss across her cheek, and it took everything inside Alea not to pull away. Piper must have felt or sensed it because she had the saddest look on her face as she turned away.

And she'd screwed up again. Alea sank to the couch. It seemed like the only thing she was capable of lately. The doors closed behind Piper ,and Alea suddenly felt how very alone she was. Piper's words rustled around in her brain.

"Lea?" a soft voice called out.

She should lock her doors.

Alea sighed. "Yes, Yas?"

Yasmin walked in, still in her perfectly tailored gown. "I heard there was trouble."

"It's nothing." She didn't want to bring her cousin in on all the problems of the evening. She really just wanted to shut out the world and go to bed.

"I doubt that." She spoke with an upper crust British accent, no hint of her Bezakistani roots at all. Yas had worked for years to fit into the English ideal of perfection. She'd bleached her hair a platinum blonde and maintained a slender figure. She wore the right clothes and the right makeup. She was everything Alea wasn't. Somehow picking out the perfect outfit for the season didn't matter so much anymore.

Find the good. That's what Piper had recommended. There was no good. She was wrong.

"Lea? Are you still with me?"

Alea shook her head. "Sorry. I'm really tired."

"I heard about what Tal and those horrible guards of yours did. Is it true that he gave them complete control over your security?"

"What?"

Yas leaned in, sympathy softening her face. "Tal released those brutes from his service tonight and dedicated them to your protection full time."

It was the absolute worst outcome. Dane, Cooper, and Landon would be on her case twenty-four hours a day, seven days a week. And now they had no reason to be nice about it. They would watch and hover, silent and unsmiling, a constant reminder of how awful she'd been. "Are you sure?"

"Oliver overheard them. You know he's always been dreadfully concerned about your welfare. It's very difficult for me to forget that he was interested in you before he was interested in me."

And this was why she didn't spend much time with Yas anymore. Her cousin was never content to merely talk. She had to find a way to turn the conversation to herself, usually about how terribly she was being treated. It wasn't that Yasmin was a bad person. She'd simply always felt like a lesser relation because her parents hadn't lived in the palace.

"We're just friends, Yas. He married you."

"I know." Her eyes turned down. "I just always wonder if he regrets not marrying the real princess."

Not that again. "Yas, I only have the title because our uncles legally adopted me, and they only did that to protect me. They were still my aunt and uncles. That's what I called them, not mom and dad. They made certain I didn't forget my real parents."

"Still, you're referred to as a princess and you have the trust fund to go with it. Most men would be interested in marrying into that."

"Well, it's Bezakistan. Even as a 'princess' who isn't in line to ascend, if I marry, I'll be expected to take at least three husbands. Our country is modern compared to some of its neighbors, but it's still steeped in tradition. Be grateful you got a choice to marry exactly who you want and love."

Three husbands. Big and broad men who could protect her and care for her if she would only let them. Dane, Coop, and Landon's faces swam through her thoughts.

Yasmin frowned, turning away slightly. "You might be surprised. Sometimes I think Oliver and his brothers would have been happier with the Bezakistani way of life. But that is neither here nor there. I didn't come here to talk about my problems. I came to help solve one of yours."

Alea wasn't sure how any of her problems could be solved, but Piper's advice was still fresh in her mind. If she was ever going to have a life, she had to at least try not to shut her loved ones out. "Which problem are you talking about?"

"You need a vacation. I can't imagine how stressful it is

for you here."

It would be just as stressful in London, and now, thanks to Tal, a big chunk of the problems she was trying to escape—three big ones—would be on her heels. "I don't think I want to go to London right now, Yasmin. I appreciate the offer, but I don't think I would make great company."

"Oliver and I were talking. He's always the voice of reason. I think you're right. The last thing you need is to be surrounded by people. But what if you could get away on your own, all alone for a while? Oliver and I were supposed to leave tomorrow morning in our plane for Sydney." Yas shrugged. "A little alone time before the baby comes."

"That sounds lovely." But she wasn't sure what it had to do with her. She didn't want to intrude on their babymoon.

A weary look crossed Yasmin's face. "But the thought of getting on another plane makes me sick. I'd already decided to tell Oliver that I would rather stay here at the palace for a few weeks when he suggested a change of plans. Everything is ready to go at the apartment in Sydney. It's private. It's well protected. And no one would know who or where you are. Oliver's brother already hired security for us. They can just protect you instead."

No one would know? Not Tal? Not Dane or any of the others? If she could pull that off, she would be totally alone, without anyone's expectations weighing her down. Despite what the press suggested, she wasn't a prisoner at the palace. For just for a few days, she could pretend she was normal and maybe she could sort out her thoughts, find a little peace. With that much tranquility, maybe she could figure out what to do next. It sounded heavenly, but… "I don't know. Tal would be furious."

"Oh, it's only for a short while. Oliver and I won't say anything. So Tal won't have any idea where you've gone. If anyone asks about the plane, I'll simply tell them that we sent it along with notes and supplies for the Reaching Across Cultures' Sydney office. We'd planned a vacation, but I was hoping to squeeze in just a little bit of work. I really do need to send some things there, so it's not a total lie. You wouldn't mind dropping them off, would you?"

If it meant she got to escape all the censure and pressure here, if she truly got to be alone to sift through the rubble of her life, she wouldn't mind. "Just leave me instructions, and I'll take whatever you need. Oh, Yas, do you really think it could work?"

A bright smile curved up her cousin's lips. "Oliver is very smart. Trust my husband. He always tries to do the right thing for his family."

Alea nodded, and they started to make plans. By this time tomorrow, she would be far, far away.

* * * *

Landon couldn't sleep. The events of the evening kept playing out in his head over and over again. He shouldn't have risen to Alea's bait and been so hard on her. His first instinct had been to reach out to her, to hold her and try to coddle her back to reality.

But he'd been doing a version of that for over a year and it simply didn't work. She was farther from them than ever before.

He stepped out of the quarters he shared with the full-time guards. Tal had offered all three of them rooms in the palace, but Lan had turned him down. He wouldn't know what to do with the space. Dane and Coop had made their apartments look something like homes, but Lan felt more comfortable out here with the help. He looked up at the palace, and his stare inevitably drifted to her room.

What was it about this one female that made him so fucking crazy? He'd seen more beautiful women before, but none of them moved him the way Alea did. It wasn't just her tragic past. He wasn't chasing her for the challenge. It was like…his heart recognized her. God, that sounded dumb and girly. Maybe he was a masochist who only craved what he couldn't have.

The trouble was, he'd seen the soft woman under all that armor. He caught glimpses of her when she was working with children or visiting the hospital. He loved to go on those duties with her because somehow she managed to shove aside her own pain to help others. And that's when he saw her most genuine smiles.

"Lan? Is that you?"

Landon sighed and touched his right side. Cooper had done a number on his kidney. He would be lucky if he wasn't pissing blood for a week. "Yeah, Coop, it's me."

Cooper rounded the corner, and Landon noticed he was carrying his medical kit. "Hey, I was just coming to see you. I thought I should probably check you out since I was the one who damaged you."

"You barely managed to hit me." Lan rolled his eyes.

Cooper laughed a little. "Well, I'll feel better if I check you out. Amuse me."

"Fine." Lan looked up at the palace one last time before turning and leading Coop back into the barracks.

Cooper looked around at the large, mostly antiseptic building. There were twenty small rooms, each with a single bed, closet space, and a desk unit. Cooper followed Landon into the room that belonged to him. "You know you left the Army, right?"

Lan was deeply aware of the fact that his room had no personal elements. Cooper had pictures of his brothers and his parents on his walls. Dane had decorated his apartment with paintings and books and other things he picked up in his travels. Lan had only had his grandmother, and she'd never let him forget that his mother had dropped him on her doorstep on her way out to her next party and never come back. There were no pictures of his childhood, no family photos with smiling faces. "I like to keep things simple."

"You keep things spartan." Cooper set his kit on the bed

and opened it with a flick of his wrist. "Are all your parts still working?"

"I don't know. Strangely enough, I haven't had a chance to use my balls since you decided to shove them halfway up my ass."

Cooper chuckled. "Well, you were trying to kill me at the time. How about we just call it even?"

That was fine by him. "I guess we all made mistakes tonight."

A calculated expression crossed Cooper's face. "Or we all did the right thing, and we were just wrong because we didn't do it together. I think I was onto something tonight. She was interested. Maybe not in me in particular, but she was curious about sex. She needs to experiment. We need to set ourselves up in some intimate situations with her."

"What? Like walking in on her while she's buck naked?"

"Hey, I didn't plan that. I really was trying to check on her."

Lan shrugged. "Maybe I'm just jealous. So she really did respond? I was a little surprised she let you see her naked. Did she fight you?"

Coop shook his head as he pulled out a couple of bottles and some washcloths. "Not really. She gave me a weak 'go away' before things got really heated. I know what a woman looks like when she's aroused. She wasn't afraid. She was inquisitive and hot. And she enjoyed having her pussy loved on."

God, he really was jealous of Cooper now. "So she responded."

"Yes, she was moaning and shoving her cunt at me. She wasn't scared, not until I wrapped my arms around her. That's when she screamed. I wasn't hurting her, Lan. I was trying to get closer."

Damn it. He hated being a reasonable man. He slapped at Coop's arm, a brotherly show of affection. "You probably didn't do anything I wouldn't have in your situation. If I had the chance to get my mouth on her, I would. It just makes me worry that she's never going to be ready for what we want to give her. And if she can't handle one man, what about three? If you holding her was too much, how the hell will she ever handle Dane?"

A part of the submission Dane needed fell squarely into the bondage category. Lan had watched Dane with more than one submissive. He took their needs very seriously, but those women had always needed what Dane had to offer. Alea would be terrified.

"I think the key is to experiment," Coop went on. "We need to retrain her. Her captors did a number on her. But she can never have a normal life if she can't accept love and affection, or enjoy sex. Are you willing to let her live that way just because you're squeamish?"

Put like that, it seemed like a cowardly thing to do. "I get what you're saying, man. I just don't know that she wants me."

Cooper groaned, his eyes rolling. "You have got to get over the insecurity thing. She wants all of us. She wants the whole ménage thing, or at least she did when she was a kid. I was doing a sweep of the palace the other day and I wound up in the library. Did you know Talib still keeps everything the way his fathers left it? Including the pictures taped to the wall. One of them is Alea's. I would bet she was about eight or nine when she drew it. It's of a woman with dark hair and three men. And the title of the picture is 'my three husbands.' I think we could be those men for her."

"I'm in." Lan didn't hesitate.

Cooper was right. If they loved Alea, they had to be willing to risk everything to make sure she could enjoy life again, even whatever shot they had at a relationship with her. "So how do we get ourselves into...what did you call it? Intimate situations?"

It would be damn near impossible here. The palace was filled to the brim with people and would be for weeks to come because of the coronation. Between family, friends, and visiting dignitaries, Lan wasn't sure when they would get more than two moments alone with her.

There was a short knock on the door, then it opened. Dane's large frame filled the doorway. "Hey, I came to check on Lan."

"Jeez, guys, my balls still work." He hadn't gotten hit that hard. Not that he'd admit, anyway.

The corners of Dane's mouth curled up wryly. It was good to see him smile for once.

"I'm glad because, unfortunately, your balls are important to my plan. But once we put the plan in motion, we all need to watch our balls, guys."

Thank god he was joking. After what happened earlier, Lan had been worried Dane would turn into a morose asshole, and there was only room for one of those on the team. He'd taken that place a long time ago and he wasn't giving it up. "Does this mean I'm not fired?"

Dane nodded. "You know I hate paperwork, man."

"Excellent. Now, when can I use my still fully functional balls on our girl? Because the way I see it, it's going to be a long while before we can get her alone."

Dane held up the folder he'd been carrying. "That's where you might be wrong. This is the flight list for tomorrow out of the palace's private airstrip. I get a daily update and something odd happened."

"Shit," Coop said. "How many more people do we have to vet? Tell Tal to stop with all the coronation celebrations. Slap a tiara on Piper's head and call her a queen, damn it."

Lan didn't understand the need for all the ceremony, either. Spending a ton of money didn't make Piper any more official. It just created more work for them. He hated running background checks. He would rather just shoot people. "How many are there?"

"It isn't the people coming in who caught my eye. It's the people leaving, or rather the person leaving. Oliver and

Yasmin Thurston-Hughes changed their plans. They've decided to stay in Bezakistan for the next few weeks. They were planning on heading for Sydney tomorrow, but now they're only sending their personal assistant."

And that affected them how? "So?"

"So? You guys need to pay more attention to palace gossip. Their assistant is that little brunette who's been fucking the hell out of Tal's valet, who told me tonight that he was very happy because she isn't leaving tomorrow after all. This is a small craft. The weight on the plane is delicate and has to be fairly precise. So when they changed the flight plans, in addition to the flight crew, they listed a single female passenger, weighing approximately one hundred forty pounds."

"But that chick might weigh ninety pounds when she's soaking wet." As far as Lan was concerned, that assistant needed to eat a cheeseburger.

"Yes. She would likely hyperventilate if her scale said that, yet she's the one who filled out the change-of-flight form," Dane finished.

"Son of a bitch, she's running," Cooper cursed.

"I don't think she can run in those heels. Yas's assistant seems really puny and unhealthy." Lan was pretty sure she wasn't a runner.

Dane laughed. "He's talking about Alea, buddy. She's the one who's the right weight. They're trying to pass it off as the other girl. They're giving her the means to leave on her own and away from all these people, including us."

Damn, he should have caught on. That sounded like the kind of play Alea would pull. "I saw that Thurston Hugs-a-Lot fucker listening in on you and Tal. The slimy bastard told Alea that we're taking over, and she's running."

"You have a way with words, Lan," Coop said, then he turned to Dane. "So what are we going to do? Stop the plane?"

Lan didn't think that was a good idea. Alea was going

somewhere private. They wanted to be really damn private with her. "I think we should get on that plane."

"I'm ahead of you," Dane said. "I've already revised the flight plan to include the three of us. I met the woman who's going to be serving on the plane and I talked to her. She's willing to help us out. We'll sneak on and be in the air before Alea can do a damn thing about it. Pack up, boys. We're headed for Australia. We're going to spend some time all alone with our girl."

It could go crazy well. It could be the apocalypse. Either way, he was ready.

Lan smiled. "I'm in."

Chapter Five

Alea cast a cautious glance behind her as she stepped onto the airstairs that would take her up to Oliver's private Boeing. She half expected to see Dane, Coop, and Landon running across the darkened tarmac to stop her, but the world was quiet now. And she hadn't seen them at all this morning.

Of course it was five thirty a.m., and they were likely sleeping. Even knowing that, a little kernel of completely perverse disappointment weighed down her stomach. She took a deep breath and ascended the steps.

"Good morning, Princess," the flight attendant Oliver had hired said in her crisp British accent, a jaunty blue and yellow scarf tied at her neck that matched her smile and the navy blazer she wore. "It's a pleasure to have you here. I hope you find everything to your liking."

"I'm sure it's lovely. Thank you." Alea handed the young woman her suitcase, then looked around the cozy cabin.

But what the small, yet well-appointed interior looked like to her was lonely. She was the only passenger. The pilot was in the cockpit, and a door between them was closed. Another door separated her from the rear of the plane, which included the kitchen and the hostess's quarters. Once again, Alea was separated from everyone else.

The flight attendant also offered to take her rolling carry-on, but Alea demurred since it held most of her entertainment for the long flight.

As she made her way deeper into the cabin, she felt vaguely guilty for running off when Tal had hired investigators to dig into her kidnapping. But last night had proven that she was near a breaking point, lashing out at everyone. She felt more than vaguely ashamed by the things she'd said to Dane, Lan, and Coop. So Yas and Oliver's offer had come at the perfect time. This holiday alone would help her think, clear her head. No one would know where she was, especially the asshole behind her abduction. She didn't want to worry her family, so she'd text Piper and tell her cousins' wife to assure everyone that she was perfectly safe.

Two weeks. She was giving herself fourteen days to decide what she wanted to do next in life. She had the investigators' report in her bag. She was going to read up on her case and decide on a course of action. Maybe she would just take her trust fund and disappear. Then no one would have to deal with her anymore. But the thought of never seeing her family again, of never seeing her men…

"Princess? If you'll take your seat, we'll be taxiing in just a moment." The hostess gestured to one of the eight executive-style seats. "The pilot has brought you a bottle of wine from his homeland. He is so very proud to be flying for you today."

Alea sighed inwardly. She wasn't much of a drinker, but she would have to try the wine to be polite. It was expected as part of the Bezakistani royal family. Then once she hit Sydney, she could just blend in, be anyone, while she thought things through.

She picked a seat near the window and glanced out. She could see the palace from here. It looked like home, and something inside told her not to leave. But if she went back, she would be forced to deal with *them*—and she wasn't thinking about her cousins. She just couldn't face her gorgeous guards again so soon after making a complete ass of herself.

"Thank you and I would love to thank the pilot personally."

A little jolt told her the aircraft was moving. She would have to thank the pilot later.

"I'm sure he'd like that after we're in flight. I'll serve the wine with lunch, if that's to your liking, Your Highness." At Alea's nod, she smiled. "I had to scramble, but I think I have enough food for everyone. This is a very long flight. We'll be in the air for almost fifteen hours. Those men look like they'll eat a lot, but I'll ensure you have all you need." The hostess patted her arm. "I will serve coffee and tea as soon as we're level. Please don't hesitate to ask for me if you need anything. Gentlemen, you really must take your seats now."

As the flight attendant found her own jump seat in the back, a chill iced Alea's body. Gentlemen? Large men who needed a lot of food? Oliver better have found a small rugby team to send to Sydney because it couldn't be who she feared. They couldn't know about this trip. She'd been careful and kept her mouth completely shut. She'd gotten up at an unholy hour and packed fairly light. *No.* She closed her eyes and drew in a long breath. She was supposed to be alone. Please let these be a few hangers-on who wouldn't be anything like…

"Do you think she's going to keep her eyes closed the whole trip, Dane?" Cooper asked from the back of the plane.

Fuck. Fuck. Fuck! She shook her head, praying that she was just having a dream. No, a nightmare.

"I think eventually she'll come to the conclusion that this is reality, and she'll open those gorgeous brown eyes. Then she'll probably start spewing more bile at us. Or at the very least objecting that we're crashing her clandestine solo holiday. Either way, she's going to be pissed off. So just sit back, relax, and wait for it. After the pointless argument is over, we'll have hours to hash out how everything between us is going to work from now on." Dane's voice reeked of self-satisfied authority. And sex. After last night and coming so close to discovering firsthand the whole big deal about consensual sex for pleasure, she really didn't know how to cope with how hot he sounded.

Alea gritted her teeth. It didn't matter. In theory, she was the princess, and they were paid employees. She'd be well served to remind them of that and establish firm boundaries.

The seats beside, behind, and in front of her all jostled. She opened her eyes, and sure enough, she was surrounded by miles of gorgeous man flesh. Sure, all three of them were wearing clothes, but she could guess what sort of hard muscle was under those T-shirts. Still, that didn't mean a thing because they weren't welcome on her vacation.

"Get off this plane."

Landon's clear blue eyes widened innocently. "How—jump? Gosh, Lea. It's moving. I don't think now is a good time to do that."

"Here comes the bile-spewing portion of the day, my brothers," Dane said with a smirk that really should have crawled under her skin. But his almost obnoxious confidence was somehow sexy. "Watch. She's going to go through a bunch of steps of the grieving process. She's already been through denial."

Two weeks of this—of them—and she'd be no closer to finding peace than she had been last night.

"You have to get off this plane," Alea said, her voice tight. "Please. I need time alone to think, so you can't go with me. After last night, you shouldn't want to be with me. Just tell Tal I skipped out on you. I promise I'll come back safely if you'll just give me some space."

"I think she's a little bit afraid, Dane," Cooper suggested.

Dane shrugged. "She's bargaining now. Only because she doesn't understand yet and doesn't trust that we mean business. She will soon enough."

"Lea, we're not going to hurt you," Lan vowed. "We're here to protect you."

"Among other things." Dane smiled smugly. "Just wait, man. This is the pain and fear talking. She'll calm down soon." He settled back into his chair like he was enjoying the show and waiting to see the next act.

Oh, she was so done with him. Dane thought he understood her? That he could read her mind and guess how she was going to react? *Bullshit.*

Despite the plane still rolling along the runway, Alea yanked her seat belt off and stood, then grabbed Dane's hand in hers. She would throw his ass off the plane herself if she had to. She could do it. She'd read about women who got great bursts of strength when they really needed it during a panic. Surely this qualified.

"How far out are we, Coop?" Dane asked as she pulled fruitlessly on his arm.

He glanced out the window. "Looks like there's another plane ahead of us. I think that's the prime minister heading home. She's got three-to-five minutes to try to haul you out of here."

If that concerned Coop, he didn't show it. Instead, he leaned his head against the headrest and closed his eyes like he didn't have a care in the world.

"Damn you, get off this plane!" She tugged even harder, putting her weight into the effort. Instead of staring at her like he was bored, this time Dane stood. His massive frame towered over her. He wasn't smiling.

"Sit down, Alea. We're going to cut through the rest of this crap and get straight to acceptance. We're going wherever you're going. If you would like to stay in Bezakistan, we can do that. As it happens, I think a little time away would be good for all of us."

"No," she nearly shouted. "I need time away from everything that distracts and confuses me. That definitely includes you three."

"Does it now?" he asked, his voice going dangerously low.

He didn't touch her, but she could feel the heat of his body reaching her, wrapping around her. He was so close. Like Cooper had been close the night before. Alea took a long breath, trying to calm herself, but what she got was a nose full of the delicious, masculine scent of soap and something else uniquely Dane.

"Answer me, Alea. Do you really want to be away from us? Because I think you're lying. I can see your nipples. They're hard."

Damn it, she should have worn a sweater. She crossed her arms over her chest. "It's because I'm mad. They're not aroused nipples. They're angry nipples."

"I'm going to teach you not to lie, Alea. Those are lonely nipples. Those are aching nipples. Do you want to know what I've got planned for them?" His voice had gone husky.

A hot denial sprung up inside her, settling between her legs, and she wondered if she was fending him off or just baiting the bear. "You're my guards. You're supposed to keep my body safe, not touch me. No, wait. You aren't my guards. I'm firing you right now. You can't talk to me like that."

"We are your guards, according to Tal. He signs our paychecks. And I'm going to talk to you this way a lot from now on. We're not going to let you dismiss us anymore. There's something between all of us. Chemistry like this doesn't happen often, and I'll be damned if I let you keep shoving that aside just because you're too scared to see where it leads, Princess." Dane's voice sizzled over her skin, an unavoidable reminder of the heat scorching through her.

"He's right. I've never felt anything like this." Landon was suddenly behind her, his voice a hot whisper on the nape of her neck. "I can't just walk away from it. I want to be around you. With you. Inside you. I want you to work with us to make this whole thing good."

Alea stifled a moan bubbling in her throat at the feel of them so close. "There's no 'thing.'"

She'd meant for that statement to come out in a firm voice, but it just sounded breathy and sensual. They weren't touching her, but for the first time, she wanted them to. She'd

lost it last night when Coop had grabbed her just before...
But what if he hadn't? What if she'd kept her head? What if
they took everything really slowly? Maybe she wasn't totally
broken and her body could actually respond if they told her
what they planned to do, prepared her mentally first. Maybe.

"There's more than a little something between us, baby,"
Coop said, sitting up now, his previous laziness shoved aside.
"It's real, and we've all been dodging it. I'm done with that."

"I am, too." Dane's words sounded like a vow. "So now
I'm going to tell you exactly what I want to do."

The desire shimmering from those blue eyes made
something in her belly jump and tighten. If what he had to
say was half as hot as his face suggested, she wouldn't be
able to handle it. "Don't. Please. I'll sit back down."

"Ah, we're back to bargaining." Dane's hair was just the
slightest bit shaggy, and she loved the way it curled around
his ears as he looked down at her. "I think we have another
couple of minutes before takeoff, so I'll elaborate. First, I
want to look at your breasts, Alea. I want you to take your
shirt off and show them to me. I want you to cup them with
your hands and offer them up."

She shook her head even as the heat inside her surged. "I
can't do that."

"He'll tell you how beautiful they are," Landon
continued. "We all will. We'll sit and watch them for a
minute because none of us will be able to take our eyes off
you and your gorgeous, full breasts."

"They aren't. They're small." Why was she talking
about herself? She should be shoving them away and firming
up boundaries. But no, she was standing there and arguing
over the size of her breasts. And practically feeling Dane's
hands on her, even though he wasn't touching her.

"No. They're the perfect size, baby. They'll fit right in
the palm of my hand. I don't think I've ever seen breasts as
beautiful as yours. Tell me something, Princess. Did Cooper
get his mouth on those nipples last night?"

She shivered, remembering everywhere Cooper had put his mouth. "No."

"I barely touched her breasts. I just ate that pussy like it was the tastiest treat I've ever had." Cooper edged closer to her. "You tasted so good, baby. I've had a hard-on ever since, and no amount of masturbation satisfies my cock. I want *you*."

The idea of Cooper touching himself while he thought of her sent another wave of arousal through Alea. She actually wanted to touch him, to see and feel him all over. Their words were turning her into a woman she didn't know, one who ached to do and feel everything they murmured in her ear. Would they let her explore without asking for anything in return? Likely not. Men seemed geared to take from women. These three had proven they could be polite and kind, but she was sure in the bedroom, Dane, Lan, and Coop would be like other men.

But…what if, like Coop's mouth on her, that could actually feel good?

"I want to suck your nipples, Alea." Lan's voice was softer than she could ever remember. "I'll be so gentle. I'll lick, play, and kiss on them until you forget there was a time when they weren't in my mouth."

"He's got a breast obsession," Dane admitted with a chuckle. "Now, as for me, I really want to touch your ass. God, Alea, do you know what that round ass does to me?"

She tried to back away, but only bumped into Landon. "Now I know you're joking. My ass is huge."

Instantly, Dane tensed. Cooper shot a placating stare to his pal. "No. Go easy on her, man."

Dane's jaw tightened. "We're going to establish a few rules, baby, some for your protection, some for our sanity. Rule number one, you don't *ever* talk badly about yourself."

Why did what she thought or said about her ass matter? No clue. In fact, she couldn't think about anything except the fact that they still loomed so close—and seemed to be moving in. "I am going to talk to Tal. You can't treat me like this."

"Poor baby. Who do you think gave us his stamp of approval?" Dane leaned closer until his lips were almost touching hers.

She tried to move, but Landon wasn't willing to let her retreat from them. The minute she backed up, something thick and hard poked at her bottom. His erection. That didn't scare her the way it should. Still she tried to move forward. When she did, another erection poked at her belly. Dane. Her knees went weak.

"Sorry, Princess." Dane didn't sound sorry at all. "I'm afraid that's my permanent state around you, and I just don't have the inclination to masturbate like Coop there."

"God, you smell so good." Landon groaned against her neck.

"Are you sniffing my hair?" She brushed it in front of her shoulders, away from Lan's nose. What rabbit hole had she fallen down?

"That's not all he's smelling, Princess," Dane replied. "I know because I smell it, too. If you're going to tell me your pussy is angry like your nipples, I'm going to call bullshit. You're aroused. Do you want me to take care of that for you? Cooper didn't quite make it. I promise you we won't have that problem this time. I'll touch that pussy until you find heaven. We'll go so slow, and you'll be in charge—for now. We'll only do this your way and for your pleasure until you can handle more."

"Come on, Lea," Lan groaned in her ear. He wasn't pressing his erection into her, but it was big enough that she couldn't miss it. "Let us taste your pussy. I'll be so gentle. I'll just lick and love it until you come all over my mouth. I want that so bad. I want to touch you, but I won't until you're comfortable with it. Just my mouth and your sweet pussy. Don't you want to come? Don't you want to feel good?"

Landon's words were drugging her, pulling her into a

place where all she wanted to say to him was yes.

"Such a pretty flush on your cheeks," Cooper murmured. "We'd persuade you to pull up your skirt. We'd take off your panties and have you sit back in one of those big chairs. We would spread your legs wide and take turns eating at your pussy. I'm dying to get my mouth on you again."

Now that she'd opened herself up to the possibility of pleasure, Alea could see that vision so clearly in her head. And heat pulsed between her legs. Landon and Cooper would jostle for position between her legs. Their tongues would run all over her, and she would find that magical moment other women talked about. And Dane. She would do what he demanded. She would lift her shirt and unhook her bra and let his lips and teeth touch her not-so-angry nipples.

That all sounded...fantastic. Sexy. Maybe she could do it. Maybe she could have them.

The plane jolted forward as it started to move again, slinging Alea back against Landon. His big arms came around her, keeping her upright. That was all it took to incite panic. She screamed and tried to shove away from him, thrashing and kicking.

"Alea, no. You will calm down now." Dane's deep voice cut through the sheer terror.

His command drummed in her head. She was on the plane, and Lan was just trying to steady her. Finally, she dragged in deep breaths and stilled, even managing to brace herself against Landon's hard chest. He froze as she regained her balance.

"I want to hug you, Lea," he whispered, lightly brushing her arms. "But I won't. I just want you to know that if I could do anything in the world right now, I would hug you and try to make you feel safe."

Tears sprang to her eyes. His words were a far cry from anything any man in Colombia had said to her. God, how could she turn that away? Lan sounded so vulnerable. He was making himself that way. It couldn't be easy on him, but he

99

was doing it for her.

Very slowly, she turned and put her arms around Landon, her body shaking as she did.

He didn't wrap her up, didn't jump on her. He just stroked her hair gently, his voice achingly tender. "Thank you, Lea."

She nodded and let herself sink into him a bit more. It wasn't bad. Actually, it was sort of nice. But it proved she was still fucked up because it had taken all her courage and mental focus just to allow herself to hug the man trying to protect her.

Alea shuddered and pulled away. God, she was so damaged and she wasn't sure if or how she could be fixed.

Dane sighed. "We're about to take off, baby. Sit down. I think we've reached the depression phase of this mourning."

Sure enough, they were gaining speed. Soon, they'd be in the air to Australia. With these three along, no telling what that would bring. But she didn't see a peaceful holiday in her future.

Alea eased back into her seat and buckled her belt. Her voice was still shaky. "What exactly do you think I'm mourning?"

"The days of wallowing, Princess. They're over."

"Jerk." She turned her chair away from him, but that sent her looking straight at Cooper, who smiled at her and didn't try to hide his erection.

She turned toward the window as the plane touched off the runway, and she stared out into the big, dark sky just beginning to lighten with the coming day. It was vast, expansive, right in front of her. But all that open freedom may as well have been a million miles away.

Why couldn't they understand that this was never going to work? She was never going to be able to handle a man on top of her much less three.

"I believe our princess has gone into the inner-journey phase," Dane whispered as though she couldn't hear him.

"By the time we get to Australia, she'll be in acceptance."

"If you think I'm accepting that you took it upon yourself to crash my vacation without asking what I wanted, you're wrong."

"You can thank us for our stellar company later," Coop teased.

"God, I wish I had something to throw at you." But her lips were turning up.

And what the hell had happened to Dane? When had he gone from super polite to this ridiculously charming asshole? And why did she like him so much more this way?

Because he was finally being himself. They all were. Instead of being what they thought she wanted or wearing their professional masks, they had dropped all pretenses to just be themselves. They had been so gentle because they were worried she would break at any moment, but the whole "poking fun at her" thing meant that she really couldn't stay angry. And she couldn't take herself too seriously. It was so much more dangerous because it made her feel almost normal again.

And she had to remember that she wasn't. They might be comfortable showing their real selves, but she didn't have that luxury. The minute they knew the Alea who lived deep inside her, they would run as fast as they could.

She looked through the tiny window and watched as the world she knew fell away.

* * * *

About six hours later, Cooper watched as Alea started to drift off. She'd probably been up half the night packing and plotting her escape, only to discover they had her cornered. Now she was exhausted. There was nothing more he wanted to do than to cuddle close to her and let her sleep on his chest.

Instead, he cursed under his breath. Besides the fact that

she wasn't ready for any man to hold her close, he sounded like some sort of rom-com loving freak. If he didn't watch himself, he was going to burst into song, and that would be bad for everyone because he was tone deaf.

"Do you think she's okay?" Lan asked quietly.

"She handled being accidently touched today a hell of a lot better than she did last night," Dane whispered.

Well, she hadn't tried to deball any of them, so Cooper was calling it a win. She'd held it together and honed in on Dane's voice when panic had threatened, so that was progress. And she'd actually managed to put her arms around Landon.

Funny, that. Coop knew damn well he'd had more of an intimate connection with Alea than the others, but he'd felt a twinge of jealousy when she'd haltingly placed her arms around Lan's chest and stood there in his arms. The moment had felt deeply tender, and she'd pushed herself to extend the gesture rather than just stand there and accept it because she'd known that Landon needed the contact. Lan's yearning had compelled her to give him the comforting balm of her hug in return. That compassionate, loving woman—that's who Alea was deep down, when she let herself be.

Building a relationship with her that included compromise and trust would not be easy. But with time and open communication, Cooper had hope that they would work it all out. If nothing else, she hadn't found a way to throw them off the plane, and that had to count for something. She'd responded to Dane's dominance way better than Coop had expected. When she'd started to lose control, Dane's commands had snapped her attention right back. And he hadn't missed the way she'd smiled and turned yielding in the face of Dane's sexually-laced arrogance.

Lan was the gentle one. He was the one she'd bend for because she hated to hurt or upset him. Dane was the Dom who could give her the firm foundation she needed.

Where the hell did he fit in?

Dane stood up and gestured toward the seats grouped together in the back. He and Lan followed. The cabin of the plane was small but luxurious. Alea was sitting close to the front, so they migrated away to let her sleep.

They'd all eaten breakfast together. The lovely but bland flight attendant had served croissants and Danishes, along with smooth, rich coffee, but it was the conversation that had really surprised him. He and Dane had started talking about activities they could potentially do in Sydney. Alea had joined in, discussing her favorite places in Australia. Lan had listened with an excited smile. Within minutes, they had all been laughing and teasing, especially after Lan had threatened to find a crocodile to wrestle because he was certain that no Aussie could be tougher than a Texan.

It felt natural and right to be with these people. In those moments of flowing laughter, they had felt like a family.

Then Alea suddenly seemed to realize she was this close to being happy. She'd excused herself, turned away, and fallen asleep.

"I wanted to talk to you guys about the investigators' report." Dane had a familiar folder in his hand. "I set up a conference call with the guys at Anthony Anders for the day after tomorrow. I refuse to be out of the loop just because we're on a different continent. And we need to discuss her security protocols."

"She should never, ever be left alone," Landon said, frowning.

Coop didn't even want to think about it, but he had to. "If her abduction wasn't a random act and this is someone who knows Alea, then the question becomes who and why would anyone want to do this to her?"

This. God, he couldn't verbalize the idea of someone torturing Alea or selling her into sexual slavery, sending her into a hell most people couldn't imagine. It made him somewhere between panicked and violent.

But she hadn't actually been raped, not in the most

technical sense of the word. She'd been horrifically abused, and he didn't know the full extent of what she'd been forced to witness or endure. It made no sense that her virginity had been left intact. That had been a deliberate choice on someone's part. But why?

"I can't imagine forcing this on anyone," Lan said, looking through the file. "Much less someone like Alea. She was just going to school."

"And she was working with a charity organization that helped battered women," Dane murmured. "Why didn't I know that?"

Cooper wasn't sure either. From the beginning of the investigation, she'd very likely kept lots of information to herself. "She sure hadn't let her cousins in on it."

"Why would she keep something as kind as charity work a secret?" Lan asked.

"If I hadn't, my cousins would have come in and made a big production of it," Alea said, startling them all. "I just wanted to do something good. I had some free time, and I like charity work. I've done it all my life. If word had reached the palace that I was working at a women's shelter, someone would have decided to use it as good press." She was still sitting in her chair, but she'd turned it. She clutched the blanket he'd settled over her close. "I want to talk to you guys about whatever danger is still lurking out there. Don't leave me out of the conversation when it's my life. I get that you thought you were protecting me, but I have to know."

Dane nodded slowly. "All right. From now on, I'll include you. We have a conference call in a few days, baby. I'll try to be better."

"Good. Will you stop calling me baby?" she asked hopefully.

"Not on your life, baby," Dane shot back without a hint of guilt. "Now according to the Anders brothers, you started working at the shelter the same week you moved to Manhattan. Why did you pick a shelter in the Bronx?"

Alea huffed a little. "Because that's where the most help was needed. My roommate's mom was a social worker there. I got very close to her."

"To your roommate?" Dane asked.

Alea laughed, a bitter little sound. "No. Heather was a righteous bitch. She couldn't be bothered to help anyone. She was far too busy trying to set herself up as the queen of NYU. She was furious when I wouldn't put on a tiara and go to parties with her. So self-centered... But her mother was quite lovely. She invited me to come down and visit the shelter when she found out I was interested in social work. I met some of the women, heard their stories. My heart broke for them. I knew I had to go back."

That was his Alea. She couldn't turn away a person in need. Now she could completely reject her own needs, but when she was faced with someone else's, her natural compassion shined through.

"Did you have any run-ins with anyone there?" Dane asked.

"We helped women and their children escape abusive partners, so there were always threats. They kept their address a secret, but even so, the determined jerks found the place and showed up to rant. But no single incident stands out."

They should have included her in on the case sooner. Cooper saw that now. Some information only Alea could give.

Dane stared down at the folder. "You called the police on the fifteenth of October about a man who threatened to shoot you."

Cooper felt his blood start to boil. "Shoot you?"

Alea shrugged, an animated grin crossing her face. "It's the Bronx. I could have gotten shot just walking down the street. I disarmed him and called the police. He was crying and telling me his tale of woe by the time they got there. I don't think he had me kidnapped. He had no idea who I was or that I was a student at NYU, much less a princess from Bezakistan. How would he have had access to stationary from the embassy? To him, I was a random 'bitch' keeping him from his punching bag."

"But there were potentially a whole bunch of men who came to that shelter with a reason to hate you," Lan argued.

She shrugged slightly. "I guess that's one way to look at it. But, guys, I dealt almost exclusively with very poor people. Didn't I read something about the person behind my abduction paying for my upkeep? Like five grand every ten days? By the way, that was not five grand worth of upkeep. The accommodations sucked ass, as they would have said back in New York."

He was actually taking her sarcasm as a positive sign. "She's got a point, Dane. I don't think it was a person she encountered during her charity work. Seriously, if it had been one of those douchebags, he would have either fucked her himself to show Alea that he was all big and bad, or he'd have made sure she was 'learning her place.'"

"Nice way to put it," Alea said.

He held his hands up. "Baby, I'm just telling you the way that kind of man would think."

Alea's eyes narrowed on him, and it was all he could do not to shrink back. She had a damn fine evil eye. "Not you, too."

It was his turn to shrug. He wouldn't take it back. "Yeah, you're my baby. Deal with it."

Her gorgeous eyes rolled. "I have a name, you know."

"I'm going to call you darlin'," Lan offered.

"That's not better," Alea said, shaking her head.

"Okay, how about snuggle bear?" Lan returned. "Or puddin'? That's another real popular choice down South."

Alea sighed. "Darlin' it is, then."

Lan just smiled.

Score one for the guys. It was good to know she could be cornered. Why hadn't they tried this tactic earlier? Now that they had her alone and were establishing rules, everything seemed so much simpler. It was as if her stress level had plummeted, and she seemed more willing to compromise. Maybe being away from her cousins and the pomp of the palace would be a good thing.

"Could we sort out the endearments later?" Dane asked, obviously annoyed. "Just to be sure, I want you to write down the names of every man you came in contact with at that shelter. I want Anthony Anders to check them all out."

Alea groaned. "Dane, I didn't catch most of their names. I tended to call them things like 'Overly Hairy Guy' and 'Dude Who Needs Deodorant.' I had a very fluid role there. I doubt that most of those men knew my name, either. It wasn't like I wore a nametag or distributed my bio. I'm not trying to be difficult. I'm just telling you all the reasons I'm pretty sure this is a dead end."

The curtain to the back of the cabin opened, and a heavenly smell wafted through. Coop's stomach rumbled. The rich really did know how to travel.

The hostess walked out with a smile on her face, like she was genuinely happy to be serving them. "May I serve the first course of lunch now? It's a lovely French onion soup, which will be followed with an herb salad with goat cheese croustades. The main course, a beef burgundy, should pair perfectly with the wine from the captain."

"Please," Alea said, sitting up. "It smells wonderful. I hope you try it yourself."

The hostess inclined her head in a show of deference. Staff tended to love Alea. "I would be thrilled to try it, Your Highness. You're so kind. If you would gather around the table, I will serve."

Dane frowned and closed the folder. "We're going to get back to this. I'm not going to stop until we know who did this to you."

"I'm sure you won't," Alea conceded. "But it can wait until after lunch. Poor Landon is practically fainting."

Lan did look a little piqued. He stood up. "There was no meat with breakfast. It was all bread and stuff. I'm a carnivore."

The hostess returned and set glasses before them, each filled with a deep, ruby red wine. "The pilot says that this vintage comes from the region of France in which he was born. Enjoy."

Cooper took a long sip of the wine. It was rich and tasted just slightly sweet, with a hint of tartness. Like Alea. But he wasn't much of a wine drinker. Give him a good beer any day. But so far, the flight attendant hadn't given them water or anything else to drink. So he took another sip.

They sat down around the table, getting ready to partake of their first full meal as a family—whether Alea wanted to acknowledge that fact or not. They drank and talked, the minutes speeding by.

The first course was served, and Cooper felt his every muscle relax. He laughed at something Dane said, but suddenly sounds were strangely far away. So was everyone in his field of vision. Even his muscles felt heavy. In fact, he couldn't quite lift the spoon.

Alea looked so happy, relaxed. And he felt so...weird.

He tried to push the glass away because something was so wrong, but his hands wouldn't work. They kind of flopped around like fish out of water.

What the hell was happening?

"Sir? Sir? Are you all right?" He could halfway hear the hostess. She sounded like she was talking through a funnel.

Cooper tried to get up. His vision was narrowing, focusing in on one thing. Alea was asleep again. She looked so sweet, but...hadn't she just napped? Why was her head at that unnatural angle?

He tried to fight, tried to stay awake, but he failed.

The last thing he saw as he fell asleep was an unfamiliar man in a white shirt standing over them, wearing a triumphant smile.

Chapter Six

Dane fought the darkness in his head as though his subconscious knew his sleep was unnatural.

He heard a low groan to his left before something rolled closer and closer, but he couldn't open his eyes to see or move in time to prevent it from smacking his head. Pain flared.

What the hell had happened?

Using all his concentration, Dane shoved his lethargy aside and forced himself upright. His head throbbed as he reached up and wiped away a trickle of blood. He looked down at the wine bottle that had spun down the aisle and struck him. And now his head pounded. His tongue felt double its normal size and a bit furry.

Fuck, they'd been drugged. How long had he been out? He held up the bottle before it rolled down and hit anyone else. And he stared at it. Someone—the flight attendant?— had drugged them with this wine. The hostess had served the soup, but none of them had eaten a single bite of it before passing out. The good news was, Dane didn't think any of them had imbibed more than a half a glass. He glanced at his watch. About an hour since he'd last looked. What the hell was going on?

"What the hell?" Lan moaned. "Did someone run me over?"

"Where's Alea?" Coop asked, his words slurring.

Alea. Panic threatened to take over. They were on a fucking plane. Who would abduct her on a goddamn plane? And how?

They all looked around, groaning as they rose to their

feet and stumbled around the cabin, searching for her. Shit, he felt like he was in a fun house that wasn't a whole lot of fun. His vision was like looking through a tunnel, and the floor seemed to tilt down just slightly. He lurched forward and saw Alea, grabbing onto her seat for balance. Relief flooded his system, and his heart started beating again.

"Huh? I need to sleep," she protested, all cuddled up in her chair, safe and sound and still in the drug's happy place.

Dane started to relax. She was safe. Then, as his own head cleared, he realized something was really wrong. It wasn't just his perception leading him to think the floor was tilting a bit downward. It actually was. The whole nose of the plane was, in fact. He had to get her—and all of them—out of here fucking fast.

"No sleep for you, baby." He turned to Coop and Lan, who staggered behind him. "We've got to get her up. We've all been drugged. I don't think we got much of it, but I have no idea how she'll react to it. She weighs less than we do, so she won't metabolize it as fast. I need you two to figure out how fucked we are. There's no way we aren't. So find out how far we're about to take it up the ass."

Coop shuddered, obviously feeling the effects, but he rallied. "It had to be the pilot or the flight attendant."

Since one had brought the wine and the other had served it… "Yeah. Where the hell are they? I think the plane is diving, and if someone's going to try to kill us before we deal with that, I'd like to know."

He looked around the cabin, but he encountered nothing but the eerie white noise made by the engines.

Lan staggered, then forced himself to stand tall. He looked out the window. "Diving? Is the pilot trying to crash the plane? There's nothing but ocean. Where the hell are we?"

Coop ran a hand over his head. "It's been a while since I've flown and I'm not familiar with planes like this, but I'll figure it out. If the pilot doesn't shoot me first."

"Both of you gear up," Dane said, looking down at Alea. Her color was good, her lips curving up in sleep.

"My gun is still in its holster," Lan said, pulling his SIG Sauer from underneath his jacket. "Why would the person who drugged us leave us with guns? Why wouldn't they just kill us in our sleep?"

It didn't make a lick of sense. If whoever had poisoned the wine wanted them unconscious, why wouldn't they have used that time to disarm the three big bad soldiers? Or kill everyone since there'd be hell to pay once the drug wore off. What the fuck was going on here?

Coop took out his piece and started for the cockpit, his feet moving silently across the floor while Lan went in the opposite direction, gun drawn, in search of the hostess. Alone, he stood over Alea.

"Come on, Princess. Get up and don't freak out on me. I'm going to have to touch you," Dane explained.

Her eyes fluttered open. They had almost a dreamy quality to them. God, she was so beautiful. Even in the midst of life or death, he couldn't *not* notice how fucking gorgeous she was. Especially when she looked so soft and sleepy. Welcoming. That was how she would look after they made love to her, when she'd taken them all and they surrounded her. She'd look happy and exhausted and satisfied.

"You have to touch me? Oh, what a shame. Which part are you going to touch, babe?"

He felt his eyebrows rise. "Babe?"

"You call me baby. I get to call you babe. Or maybe I should go with sweetie pie." Her voice was low and languid. Seductive.

Wow, she was high. Apparently a little wine and some sedatives did wonders for her disposition. "You can call me anything you like, Princess, but right now you're getting on your feet."

She shook her head, her lips pursing in a sweet pout. "No. Need sleep. But you can touch me. You like my

111

breasts? Touch mine. Second base." She giggled before sleep overtook her again.

Oh, what he would do to her if they weren't potentially in a fight for their lives.

"Yes, Princess, we'll get to second base eventually—and way beyond—but right now I need you to stand. Up we go." He lifted her, forcing her to her feet.

Alea groaned and tried to wiggle away from him. "This is mean. I'm having a good dream. Go away."

He needed to get some coffee in her, but even if the hostess suddenly appeared and offered some, he wouldn't trust that it hadn't been drugged either. But damn, where had the flight crew gone? Had they managed to get off the plane somehow? They couldn't have opened the door. Despite what happened in movies, the pressure from the outside would keep the door closed, no matter how hard someone tried to push. They would have to blow the door. If that had happened, there would be nothing between the pressurized cabin and the great outdoors now, and they would all have been sucked out of the plane already.

Since he, Alea, and the guys were still in the plane, it followed that whoever had drugged them was still on board, too.

"You feel nice. So much muscle." Alea sighed as she leaned against him, her fingers running over his torso as if she wanted to touch him all over.

Adrenaline had already given him a hard-on. He did not need her making it worse. "Baby, I need you to focus."

Lan pushed the curtains aside that separated the main cabin from the back. He had his backpack in his hands and tossed it on one of the chairs, rifling through it as he spoke. "The hostess is dead. Someone whacked her over the head with something heavy, maybe a pan. It's not pretty back there. Lots of blood. I doubt she's the one who drugged us. Since I don't think we have a stowaway, that leaves the pilot. He hit her a couple of times. I checked the whole back, but couldn't find the fucker.

Fuck. "Where is he? We need to find him."

"He's in there." Cooper hitched a thumb back toward the cockpit. "He's dead."

That was bad news. Could Cooper fly the plane? He'd only handled small aircraft with propellers before.

"Who's dead?" Alea asked, her head coming up from Dane's chest. "Dead is sad. No one should be dead. Except for Khalil. He was an asshole."

"What's wrong with her?" Lan asked. "Coop, maybe you should have a look at her."

"She's just a lightweight," Dane shot back. "Coop needs to fly the plane."

Alea gasped and tried to step back. "Am I on drugs again? Did I take drugs?"

"It's fine." Dane pulled her closer, unwilling to let her get very far. She raised her arms and gave him an ineffectual push, trying to put distance between them. But the struggle was short-lived, and she finally let him hold her. "Someone drugged the wine. You didn't have much."

"I can't relapse. Can't go back there. Can't." Tears streamed down her face.

She was talking about the shit her captors had addicted her to. "We'll take care of you, baby. Don't worry."

"Dane, we have bigger problems," Cooper said. "The pilot poisoned himself, but not before he also killed the radio and all the electrical equipment, then dumped most of the fuel."

Cooper's words landed like a bomb in the cabin, diving toward the earth even now.

"Are you telling me that we're over the Indian Ocean and we don't have any fuel?" Dane asked.

"I don't know where the fuck we are. I don't know how long we've been in flight. I don't have a fucking longitude or latitude. I don't have a goddamn radio to call for help because that dead fucker made sure that we're going to go down without any hope of sending out a distress signal," Cooper said between clenched teeth.

Dane pushed down his burst of panic. He had to take things in hand or the others might fall the fuck apart. "Cooper, we're not in trouble because you're going to fly the plane."

"You know I've never flown anything like this," Cooper replied. "And it's not really flying since we're going to be completely out of fuel in about five minutes."

"Then you'll glide us down." Landon seemed to have picked up on Dane's calm vibe. "We have a couple of minutes. What are our options? Do you see any land where we can set down? Should I look for parachutes?"

"Parachutes won't work," Dane replied, settling Alea into a chair. He didn't want to leave her alone, but this was getting damn fucking serious. This plane and everyone in it was going down. He had ten minutes tops to formulate the best plan for their survival. "The pressure against the door will make it impossible to open until we get closer to the water. Our best bet is to try to find a place to put the plane down. Coop, I need you in that cockpit. If we're lucky, maybe we're not far off the coast of Indonesia or one of its islands. Go look."

Cooper nodded and disappeared again.

"I don't even have a cell signal," Lan said, looking down at his phone.

"Cell towers don't cover great swaths of water, man. But we all have apps on our phones that could be helpful. Everyone try to waterproof your phones. And save as much battery life as you can. Lan, get every bit of food you can find in back in case we aren't rescued immediately. We're going to need water. And see if there's a life raft."

"What's happening?" Alea asked a bit more lucidly, pushing her hair back with trembling hands.

His first instinct was to coddle and protect her, tell her not to worry and to go back to sleep, but she was more than a pretty doll. She was a brave woman, and he was going to need every available hand and resource if they had any hope of getting out of this alive.

Dane sank to one knee and took her hands in his. "Our plane has been sabotaged, and we're crashing. We need to do everything possible to mitigate the damage and find a way to survive. I need you to focus."

She nodded, genuine tears running down her face, but he watched as she visibly straightened her spine and gathered her strength. "Okay. The cushions are floatation devices. There should be an inflatable raft."

"The pilot took a knife to it," Lan said, tossing a big yellow thing into the cabin. "It's useless as a raft, but we could build a desalination unit with it. If we can find some land. I tossed the clothes out of this case. I think it was the hostess's. It's now holding water bottles and a bunch of snacks. Hope you like crackers, peanuts, and pâté. What the fuck is pâté made of?"

He didn't have time to teach Landon about the art of fine cuisine. "Anything we can use to fish?"

"I've got land!" Cooper shouted.

Dane shoved down his relief. It wasn't over yet.

"I'll find something." Lan moved quicker, running to the back of the plane again.

Alea stood just as the plane jerked and the engines died. She staggered, and the truth hit him. No more fuel. They were coasting now, and that could be very bad because they were dependent on a lot of factors they couldn't control, like the wind, the current, and their speed.

Alea lurched toward the cockpit just as the plane started to take a nosedive. It almost immediately corrected with a jerk, then tilted the opposite direction. She tumbled, but Dane threw an arm around her waist, hauling her close. She stiffened but calmed, then stepped through the door with a gasp.

Damn it. The body. Cooper had shoved the pilot to the

floor and now occupied his seat, his hand on the yoke. The pilot had definitely poisoned himself, as evidenced by his blue lips and the empty cup he clutched in his hand. Dead eyes stared up into nothingness.

Why the fuck would the pilot kill the hostess and himself, then sabotage the plane and leave him and the others alive?

"Alea, come on. You don't need to be here." Dane urged her toward the door. The last thing he needed was for her to freak out.

"I'm fine." She pulled out her phone, all business. "This isn't my first dead body. Cooper, how can I help? Do you need latitude and longitude?"

"Yes," Cooper said. "Can you get that?"

"Alea, baby, there's no signal," Dane pointed out. She wasn't thinking.

"I don't need a signal," Alea insisted. "The magnetic poles work just fine without a satellite signal. Zero-seven and thirty degrees north by one hundred thirty-four and thirty east. I think we've crossed past the Indian Ocean and into the western Pacific. We're *way* off course, probably somewhere near the Philippines. It looks like there are lots of little islands out there." She seemed to notice everyone staring at her. She shrugged a little. "What? I liked taking geography and I'm really good at memorization."

Damn. She sounded competent. Dane looked out over the horizon. Sure enough he could see little tiny dots of green and gold in an endless sea of blue.

"I don't know how far away that is." Cooper wiped away the sweat dotting his forehead. "We started at about thirty-five thousand feet. Damn, it's been so long. My father made us all learn how to fly cropdusters, but they were little prop planes. I had a little training in the Navy, but..."

"What's the wind like, tail or head?" Alea asked. "I'm sorry. I should be able to feel it, but I'm still a bit woozy."

Coop visibly calmed as Alea spoke, as though focusing

and doing his level best to save her. "It's a tail wind, baby. It's at our back. Do you know anything about flying?"

She nodded. "I do. I took lessons when I was a teenager and I studied hard. I always did. In a glide, we'll lose four to five thousand feet a minute. We're light and have a tail wind. We've got around six or seven minutes. We're going to go past those patches of land, but like I said, there should be other islands in the region. Get us close, Coop. Even if we hit the water, we'll swim. At least I hope I can swim."

Damn, his girl was smart even when she'd been drugged. A ridiculous pride surged in his chest. "She's right, Coop. You can do this. And Lea, don't you worry. Even if you're still weak, we'll get you to safety. I can swim with you on my back if I have to."

It would be rough, but if Coop could get them close to land, they could survive. Because they damn straight wouldn't last in the open ocean. This was warm water. *Sharks.* Every Navy man knew the story of the USS *Indianapolis.* She went down in the Central Pacific during World War II, and three hundred were lost in the sinking. The remaining nine hundred or so went into the water. During the next four days, almost six hundred men were consumed by sharks.

These were the waters below. No fucking shark was going to take his crew. They were going to live, goddamn it.

First, he had to hope that Coop could actually land the plane and keep it from breaking apart. Even if he set down on the water, they could all survive if the crash was controlled and they got to land fast.

Six minutes. He had six minutes.

Dane put a hand on Alea's shoulder. "I'm going to help Lan. You keep Coop on the right path. I'll be back in a minute."

Her face turned up, and he saw a strength there that blew him away. "We'll be good. Get my suitcase. I'm ridiculously organized and I pack for everything. I have a first aid kit and some other helpful things, including a box of protein bars. I wasn't sure I could find them in Australia. It's the Louis Vuitton roller case."

Well, of course. She would stave off Armageddon while wearing designer heels. "Will do, baby."

He jogged back, determined to find that bag. Even if they dumped it in the ocean, if it was close enough, he could dive and find it.

Toward the back, he discovered that Lan had made a little mountain of crap on the floor. He'd pulled out wires, blankets, a small tool kit. *Yes.* He'd filled a backpack with extra water bottles and found enough odds and ends to build a desalinization port if they ran out of water.

The wire they could fashion into hooks and weapons. The sea would provide protein if they had the tools to get it. He knew enough about plants and herbs to know what to eat and what to avoid. They had the tools. They just needed the chance to survive.

He walked through the curtain and toward the back. Lan had decimated the food station. He'd taken everything except the ceramic mugs. *Mistake.* Ceramic made great knives. They all had a few, but it never hurt to bring more. And he'd left a pot. They would need that. The heavy plastic of the useless life raft would mean nothing if they didn't have a damn container. Potable water would be their first goal. The bottled stuff wouldn't last.

Lan walked through, carrying the luggage. He had all of their cases, including Alea's Louis Vuitton bag. "I shoved some extra blankets and pillows into those."

"Good. Did you find the flare guns?"

Lan nodded. "I wrapped them in plastic. They should be safe from the water."

The plane dipped, now at a steeper angle, nearly sending him careening forward. *Closer to the ocean.* The phantom of the *Indianapolis* played through his head. He couldn't let his men die. God, he couldn't let Alea die.

"No matches," Lan said, bracing himself against the wall.

The plane lurched again, the sensation causing Dane's stomach to roll. Faster and faster, they were going down.

"Suit up," Dane barked.

If Coop set them down flat, keeping the nose up, they would float for a brief time. They could get the door open and get to land.

Dane could feel the force of the descent pulling them down, threatening to tear the plane apart. The whole aircraft shuddered. But Coop managed to bring the nose up again as he and Lan gathered all the stuff and shoved them into whatever packs and suitcases they could find.

"Get ready," Dane shouted.

He grabbed the nearest backpack. All military guys carried them, big, weighty duffels with arm holes. He tossed one to Lan. "I'm going to try to pry the door open. When the water's two feet below, we start tossing out whatever we can't carry. It should float and if it doesn't, well, we know how to dive."

"Damn straight, brother, but we shouldn't have to. I found some rope. I was able to tie most of the luggage together. I'll haul it in." Lan's previous nerves had morphed into pure, grade-A special ops arrogance.

That was exactly what they needed because they didn't have anything left except for the stubborn belief that nothing and no one could take them down.

Dane stood at the door, braced himself, and threw it open. He stared down into the blue void below and prayed their stubborn arrogance was enough.

* * * *

Alea felt her stomach roll, but forced the bile back down. She'd never particularly loved flying, even when she'd learned how to do it. She'd taken the lessons for the same reason she did everything; it had been expected of her. Her cousins had learned, so she had, too, even when her hands had shaken. Even when everything in her body had screamed at her to stay on the ground. She'd conquered her fear and learned to fly.

Now she was going to learn how to crash.

Cooper's concentration was absolute. After the first couple of minutes, he'd settled in and was now nothing but cocky confidence. "Brace yourself, baby. We're going to hit the water hard."

She settled into the seat beside him and strapped herself down. On the horizon, she saw a tiny piece of land, yet another green jewel in a sea of blue. They would land as close to that little patch as possible.

Her hands shook. Nerves. Stress. God, she'd been given some kind of drug. She hated drugs. She'd fought so hard to get off them. She wanted to shove her fingers down her throat just to purge the rest out of her system. Now wasn't the time. Everything was still a little hazy, but she could remember plastering herself all over Dane. But she'd deal with that humiliation later.

Dumb slut. No one wants you. When the money runs out, we'll just kill you and no one will miss you. You're worthless.

God, she hated those voices, but they were always in her head, just waiting for the perfect time to start replaying and take her down. When she heard them, she just went to bed with her iPod on and her ear buds firmly in place. And she tried to forget. She couldn't do that now. She had to stay in the present.

No, more than that. She had to be useful. Alea refused to be another piece of luggage they had to haul around. They would do it. They would really put her on their backs and swim so they didn't leave her behind.

God, these men of steel with iron will and big hearts, would never leave her behind. Would they if they knew the things she'd survived? Probably. They would save her if only because they were good to their cores. And they would feel sorry for her.

They couldn't know the whole truth. She wouldn't be able to stand their pity.

Cooper fought with the yoke, trying to angle the plane to ensure their best chance at survival.

A loud bang shot through the little plane.

"Dane? Lan?" She started to tear off her seat belt. She had to help them.

Cooper didn't look away from the horizon. "Stop right there, Princess. They're fine. I bet Dane just blew the door. That shit-ass island doesn't come equipped with a runway. I can't put us down on land. The trees are too thick. Unless… Baby, go back and sit with Dane."

Her jaw dropped. Alea knew damn well what he was planning, and it wasn't happening. "Yeah, sure. I'll leave this seat when you land. In the water."

His jaw tightened. The plane jerked again. "It would be best if I set us down on land. That way you'll have the plane to take refuge in, and the metal can be seen from above."

"I'm not stupid, Cooper. The chance of the cockpit not folding in and killing everyone inside is miniscule if you take us into those trees. I'm staying where I am." He wouldn't play the martyr if it meant killing her, too. No way. No how.

Yes, they would lose the plane, but they would *all* have a shot at living.

And suddenly she knew deep down how significant that was. The question had floated through her head for a long time, since the moment she'd been taken…was living really important? She'd fought to survive in Colombia, but mostly because instinct had urged her. The human animal fought for its life, for the right to continue breathing from one moment to the next. But Alea had wondered in the darkest recesses of her soul whether she actually wanted to live. Because living was more than taking her next breath. Living meant being brave. Living meant taking chances.

Yes. She wanted to live.

She wanted a chance to be like the woman she'd once been, a little bold, mostly unafraid. She couldn't go back in time, but she could move forward. In some ways, she'd never really left the dank, filthy cell of her captivity. Piper had been right.

It was time to shed the pathetic Alea who had hidden in her room, burying her head in the sand and building walls around herself to keep out everyone who tried to help her. She needed the Alea she'd been before, the one who strove to be the best, studied the hardest, helped those around her. That Alea had been in a coma, but it was time for her to wake the fuck up. She might not deserve a shot at happiness, but she wanted one.

"I'm not moving, Coop." She wouldn't leave any one of them to die the way she'd left that girl. Gritting her teeth, she shoved the image away. "So you better set us down easy."

"Damn it, Lea. One of these days—soon—I'm going to spank your ass bright red." Cooper pulled the yoke and the nose came up again.

The plane shuddered. She braced herself. He would let the tail touch to slow them down. That's what she would do in his place. They wanted the plane to float for as long as possible.

Time seemed to speed up as the island loomed closer and closer. Distance and time meshed together in a horrifying carnival ride. The sound of the plane screamed against her ears, blocking out the rest of the world. The skyline tilted, a brief flash of greens and browns. Then she was thrown back. Alea's head slammed against the headrest as the plane went almost vertical. It stood there for one terrifying moment and then belly flopped, striking the water with bone-jarring force.

"Let's move, Princess." Cooper had hit his head at some point. A thin trickle of blood streamed down his face, but he moved with surety, unbuckling his belt, then her own. "We'll have to swim for it."

Yes, but they were alive.

She nodded and jumped up. The plane was bobbing in the waves, white foam cresting up the window.

"You're hurt." As soon as they reached land, she needed to dress and clean that wound, stop the bleeding. Infection was their enemy, so she had to prevent it. She had antibiotic ointment in her first aid kit.

"Coop? You two okay?" Dane staggered to the doorway, his big body taking up all the space. Alea wanted nothing more than to throw herself into those strong arms and hold him, but they had to hit the water and swim for land.

"We're good, but we won't float forever. If we're getting stuff off this plane, we need to do it now. Come on, Lea. We've got to move." Cooper turned her, pressing her toward Dane.

She nearly tripped over the body of the pilot. She forced her gaze away from the dead man and allowed Dane to pull her into the cabin. The door was open, and Landon was already in the water, surrounded by pieces of luggage and bags he'd tied together forming a long train of survival gear.

"It's a good five hundred yards to the beach," Lan shouted up. "I swam out a little. There's a beast of an undertow."

She wasn't the greatest swimmer in the world and she was still hazier than she'd like. Dane had one of the cushions in his hand and he'd used some rope to tie it around her, placing the cushion on her back. "Swim as long as you can. When you get tired, flip over on your back and I'll drag you in. Just keep your head up and lose the shoes, baby. There's no need for Prada here."

Alea slipped out of the shoes, her hands shaking despite the heat she felt shimmering outside. Dane dove into the water, then she stepped forward. Landon was starting for shore, dragging the train of luggage behind him. It looked like he'd tied the rope around his waist. His body moved swiftly despite the undertow, showing no signs that the added weight held him back at all.

Dane surfaced, slicking his hair back and holding a hand up for her to join him. Despite the horrors of the last few minutes, he paused to encourage her. "Come on in. The water's warm."

The water was also a clear, crystal blue. As she stood in the doorway, she could see down into the water, despite its depth. A coral reef lurked below. She couldn't tell how far down it was, but it was farther than Dane's kicking feet. That had to be good enough.

"Go on, Lea," Cooper said. "The water is about to start coming in the door. Once that happens, the plane will sink fast. Go!"

Alea sucked in a deep breath and jumped. In seconds, warm water surrounded her. Almost immediately she felt the floatation device around her waist yank her to the surface as surely as Dane's hands. He helped her right her body and pushed the wet hair from her face.

Deep blue eyes stared into her own, silently demanding her focus. "Stay with us. I'm going to tether us together so you can't drift off."

In the distance, Landon was almost to the shore. Cooper splashed in behind her, then came to her side. Dane swam to the other, and together, they started for the shore. Alea kept pace, not wanting to fall behind or drag them down. She looked back, but only briefly saw as the plane that was supposed to take her to freedom began to sink to its watery grave.

She stared forward resolutely. She'd brought them into her nightmare. She wasn't going to let them down.

Chapter Seven

As the sun started to sink over the horizon, Cooper thought about running from Alea. And then he thought about it again. But the truth of the matter was, she would only find him. And she'd only be more pissed off.

"Don't move. I just want to clean it." She walked up to him with a small red kit in her hands.

According to Cooper's watch, two hours had passed since the plane had sunk below the surface and into the ocean. In two hours they'd managed to build a fire, gather palm fronds and bamboo for an eventual shelter, and scout around what was now their base camp. The island was tiny. It had taken Landon a whole twenty minutes to jog the circumference.

But in that two hours, the one thing he'd managed not to do was give in to Alea's sudden desire to play nurse. It looked like that time had come to an end.

"I'm fine. Really, I used to be a medic. This little cut is nothing. Just hand me a bandage and it will be fine." Cooper went back to sorting through the food and water.

"It's only a little cut until bacteria gets inside. Then it becomes a flaming septic pus-filled wound that kills you within forty-eight hours," Alea explained, wielding her first aid kit like a sword. "I won't even go into all the bugs that would just love to burrow under your skin and make a nice home for themselves."

Cooper shrugged. "I got saltwater all in it. Salt can be very purifying."

Alea looked over his shoulder to where Dane was digging a pit. "Can't you command him or something?"

"I tried to command *you* to get out of those wet clothes," Dane said. "It didn't do me any good. He's a damn fine medic, as well as the absolute worst patient who ever walked the earth. He's a complete pansy when it comes to stuff like this. Oh, you can shoot him and he won't complain, but try taking off the band aid and he'll howl."

"It's a different kind of pain," Cooper grumbled.

He hadn't really had a choice the couple of times he'd been shot. The assholes who'd shot him hadn't brought him in for a consult on the situation. He looked up at Alea, his brain processing what Dane had said and finding something he might be willing to endure that sting to get. She was still in clothes. Despite the heat of the day, it was humid. They stood under the shade of the trees. She was still soaking wet.

The rest of them had immediately stripped down to their boxers and laid their clothes out to dry. Though Alea had unpacked some of the clothes they'd salvaged, they were wet, along with everything that hadn't been wrapped in plastic. She'd fashioned a clothesline by tying some rope between two palm trees and hung their garments to dry. But she was still in her skirt and top.

"Cooper Evans, you are going to let me clean and dress that wound," she said, her mouth firming.

Somehow, after years of fighting with his older brothers and dealing with Special Forces commanding officers, the gorgeous set of curves in front of him just wasn't very scary. Sexy? Hell, yeah. And it was about to get a hell of a lot sexier. "Negotiate with me."

"What?" Her mocha-colored eyes narrowed.

"Life is a negotiation, Princess. You took all those political science courses. You should know plenty about that." Yeah, he liked this idea. It had been a crapfuckingtastic day. This could make it all a little nicer. "So let's negotiate."

Her bare foot tapped on the sand. "Fine. I want to save your life."

"I want to save yours in return. Take off the clothes,

Princess."

Her eyes rolled. "Don't be ridiculous."

"You're cold, Lea. You've got goose bumps all over your skin. It's going to get worse as that sun goes down." He and Dane had already talked about the fact that, after sunset, the temperature would drop. The blankets wouldn't have had time to dry out. Alea needed to sleep close to the fire, and she would need body heat. But none of that would help much if she wasn't dry first.

She frowned. "I'm not walking around here naked."

Just a little give. That was all he needed. "Your panties and bra will dry a lot faster if you strip out of everything else."

She turned around, and for a moment he thought he was going to lose. Then she tossed the first aid kit his way. "All right, damn it. Don't expect me to be gentle."

With jerky, slightly nervous motions, she tore into the buttons of her shirt. Once she'd undone them all, she shrugged the garment off and settled the heavy fabric over the clothesline before she shoved at the waistband of her skirt. She was wearing a plain white cotton underwire bra and panties, but plain didn't begin to cover just how gorgeous she was.

Fuck. She had curves for miles. She was built to please a man, and he damn straight wanted to be that man. Well, one of three. Somehow the whole near-death experience was making it way easier to realize that they might not have time to waste. Tomorrow might be now. If they wanted her, they were going to have to find just the right way to take her.

And they'd do it together. Coop knew he wouldn't have survived without his brothers. Without the three of them, Alea would have died or she would have been stranded alone. They wouldn't have the bounty of supplies they'd gathered without Dane and Lan. And god bless him, Lan had fought that vicious current to bring all of those necessities to the island. They could survive quite nicely for a while because everyone had done their part, including his sweet Alea. She'd calmed quickly and figured out their coordinates, then settled into the cockpit to help him land, and he was in awe. She seemed to soak up and retain most everything that anyone had ever taught her.

The four of them made a damn good team. If they were lucky, they could make a fine family.

Alea turned, a blush high in her cheeks. "Fine. Now I'm almost naked."

"It covers more than most bikinis."

"I don't wear bikinis," Alea said.

Dane was suddenly at his side. There was a happy, hungry look on the big guy's face that only happened when he got around Alea. "I just thought I should help."

Yeah, right. Dane wanted to get as close to the candy as he could. Not that Cooper blamed the guy, but he'd been the one to unwrap the treat.

"Your help isn't required, but thanks for playing." Coop made a sound like a rude game show host's buzzer. Then he turned back to Alea. "Did you learn to swim as a kid?"

She frowned. "Yes."

"Did you swim as a teenager?"

"Sure. I was as rambunctious as any other kid. Bezakistan gets too hot in the summer to play outside much, and I didn't like being trapped indoors all day. My aunt and uncles took us to the shore at least once a year, so swimming was a necessity."

"But you don't swim now?"

Alea got on her knees in front of him and opened the little kit. With an air of "whatever," she started digging out the instruments of his torture—little cotton balls and packs of antiseptic. "Not much anymore."

"It's good exercise, and you're right about the summers in Bezakistan. So why did you stop?" Cooper asked.

"I don't know." She seemed to want to look everywhere except at him. She focused intently on dabbing the cleaner on a cotton ball.

"When exactly did you stop?" Dane asked in that deep voice, his Dom voice. Cooper knew his buddy meant business. "No lying."

Alea shrugged. "A couple of years ago. Hold still."

She pressed the cotton ball to his cut, and he nearly came out of his seat. Damn it, that burned. He cursed, and Alea's lips turned up.

"Really, you big baby?" she mocked. "You're a SEAL?"

Yeah, he got that a lot. He touched the tat on his left arm. It was a SEAL tattoo of an eagle clutching a rifle, anchor, and trident. "I even have the tat, baby. But I'm out of the Navy now. I don't have to suck it up anymore."

Dane huffed. "You didn't suck it up then. I was with you in Kandahar. You took one measly knife to the gut and whined about it for hours."

Alea gasped. "Someone stabbed you in the stomach?"

He pointed to the nice little scar on his right side. "Yep. And I was very heroic. I saved three kids and stitched up some soldiers before I finally lost consciousness in a very manly fashion."

"He face-planted on the street," Dane clarified, then turned his attention back to Alea. "So you stopped swimming after the abduction. Why? The warm water and solitude should have been relaxing. Did you quit so you could avoid bathing suits and hide your body?"

Crap! Cooper bit back a protest. He'd just gotten Alea to strip down to her skivvies and he'd been trying to make her nice and comfortable. Did Dane really have to push her now?

She paused, hesitated, then very cautiously continued to clean his wound. "I suppose so."

"Why?" Dane's voice was softer as though she'd pleased him by answering. "Baby, whatever they told you, they were lying."

Had the fuckwads who'd taken her told her she wasn't pretty? He reached up and caressed her hair, pushing one side away from her face. It had dried into sexy waves, rather than that stick-straight mane she unmercifully flat ironed every day. "Unless they said you're the most beautiful woman on the planet, they were lying. Lea, baby, they would have said anything to break you."

She took a long breath, studying her handiwork on the side of his face, seemingly happy. Then she started looking through the kit again. "They might be liars, but I've always had issues with my weight."

"What issues?" Cooper asked, truly astounded at the thought. "Is it hard to be perfect?"

She snorted slightly. "Yes, it's so difficult."

"Alea, I would seriously consider what you say about yourself in the next few minutes," Dane warned. "I'm willing to listen to concerns, but don't degrade yourself."

Her hands balled into fists on her lap. "I'm not a size two. God, Dane, I'm not even a size eight. It wasn't just my captors. The press hasn't always been kind."

Cooper had no idea what dress sizes meant. "Uh, if those are smaller than you, then I'm glad because I want a woman with curves. I want a woman who looks like a woman. Ask most guys. They do, too."

"Lea, you should damn well know that most women modeling in magazines are far too thin. They might photograph well, but it's actually unhealthy," Dane said. "Who idolizes models? Do you think it's men? No, baby. Mostly women. Porn is a better example of what men like. Those women have hips and boobs."

Cooper sniffed with disdain. "I only watch the amateur stuff now because the pros have gotten too thin. And I like *real* boobs." Alea had real boobs. They were encased in a sturdy bra, but they were totally getting his attention. Soft and round. They would be a sweet handful. And last night, with her distraught…and then his mouth on her pussy, he hadn't really gotten a good look at her ass. But what he'd seen in the past always looked so damn good. "Not to mention a juicy ass. Love that."

"Juicy is good," Dane agreed.

Alea squirted ointment onto her finger and quickly wiped it across his cut. "You don't have to try to make me feel better. Growing up, I always wanted to look more like Yasmin. Taller. More graceful…"

Dane made gagging noises.

Coop joined in. "No girl looks good with her head that far up her own ass. A bony-looking ass, I might add."

Alea shook her head and giggled. "You two are so juvenile. Really? She's blonde and willowy, and she doesn't have to have her dresses custom made. I had to pay through the nose to get that Narciso Rodriguez gown. They don't normally make my size."

"Then they suck. And you look gorgeous in anything you wear." Coop frowned.

He didn't normally notice Alea's clothes. He noticed how her boobs and butt looked in them. And he loved her toes right now. It was kind of freaky, but he wanted to suck on them and rub them. They were a pretty pink.

She slapped a butterfly-style bandage over his cheek and stood. "I think that should prevent infection from setting in. Keep it covered until it closes. And you two don't have to be nice. I appreciate it. I really do, but I own a mirror."

"Then it must be your eyesight that's suffering." Dane stood beside her. "Cooper is never just nice."

She shrugged as if she was a bit uncomfortable with their compliments. Or maybe it was the way they stared. Because he couldn't seem to stop. Her nipples clung to the thin white cotton of her bra. God, he wanted to get those nipples in his mouth. He could suck on them and bite them just the tiniest bit until she squirmed. And begged. He'd really like to hear her begging.

"Of course Cooper is nice. He's not really interested," Alea said, then blushed. "You don't have to try to convince me."

"I'm pretty sure that was *my* mouth on your pussy last night," he pointed out.

And Dane just rolled his eyes. "You really are blind, Lea. His cock is poking out of his boxers. Dude, shove that thing back in."

Cooper readjusted, but not before he noticed that Alea's eyes widened at the sight. Her breath hitched. Yes, she was at least a little intrigued.

And they were on a deserted island with absolutely nothing to do and nowhere to be. Sure, they were having to fight for their lives, but Cooper believed in the power of positive thinking. Anything could happen. In fact, he was damn sure hoping everything did happen soon.

"Are they angry with us again?" Dane asked with a grin as he ran one finger over her hard nipple.

She immediately crossed her arms over her chest, blocking him…though he could see some great cleavage. "I'm just cold."

Cooper opened his arms wide. "Come here, baby. We can warm you up."

Another blush stole across her face. "I liked it better when you were all moody and standoffish."

Dane shook his head. "That didn't work out for us, so we're trying something new."

"Shouldn't we be worried about survival?" Alea asked, turning away.

"Baby, you won the lottery. You went down with three former Special Forces soldiers." Cooper stood. It was completely reasonable that she was scared and wondering about the basic necessities. What did a princess know about survival training? He wanted to hold her, but she might be scared that his dingus would likely make another appearance. "We've done this before."

"Hell, yeah," Dane added. "And we've done this in far worse circumstances. This is practically the Ritz compared to that time we got stranded in the Dashti Margo. We were tracking some Taliban scum. We took care of them, but our Humvee got blown to smithereens."

Cooper shook his head. "Taken out by an RPG. Damn, we moved fast to get away from that one. Good times, man."

"It sounds horrible." Alea had turned to face them again, still valiantly trying to cover up.

"It was absolutely awful," Cooper admitted. "We spent ten days in the desert until we were located and someone sent transport. We survived with virtually no supplies while hostiles were shooting at us. We'll survive this, baby. Living here will be a cakewalk. A little vacation." He caressed her arm in what he hoped was a reassuring gesture, trying not to think about how soft she was and how good all that would feel up against him. "We left word with your cousins that we were traveling with you. We didn't bother to mention the whole sneaking away part, but they know when to expect the plane to land. They'll send out search and rescue."

She sniffled a little. "It's a big ocean."

"In water this clear, the plane might well be visible." Dane said. "And they're patient men."

Tears formed in her eyes, and she looked down at her bare feet. "I did this to us."

Oh, damn, she couldn't think that. "No, you didn't." He couldn't restrain himself a minute more. He walked up to her. "I want to hold you. Can I, please? Can Dane and I give you a little comfort? It's been a hard day. Let us reassure you that it's going to be all right." When she hesitated, he joked, "I promise to keep the beast in my boxers."

She rewarded him with a little laugh, then nodded. "I'd like that. For the most part, it's been a long time since I let anyone hold me. I want to try."

He eased forward cautiously, letting her observe his every move, giving her plenty of time to object. She was a little like a wild deer he wanted to feed from his hand. One wrong move and he could spook her.

"My hand is going to touch your waist, Lea," Dane said

before settling in behind her. "You can lean back against me any time. You're cold. You need to get warm. We'll settle you by the fire, then have a nice dinner. Relax and know that we're going to take care of you."

Cooper slowly wrapped his arms around her. She trembled for a moment, then sighed as though she appreciated the heat their bodies generated.

Once again, he appreciated how soft her skin was and how sweetly she fit against him. "Consider this a break from civilization. You wanted one, right? Here you go. No reporters. No one who needs your attention. Well, besides us. No one is going to ask you to make appearances or to go to balls."

"No curious people who look at me with pity," Alea continued.

Coop wanted to take exception to that, but now wasn't the time to argue with her. Making her laugh seemed to work so much better. "Nope. You just have to worry about us ogling you. All the time. Every day. Every hour."

Sure enough, she laughed. "You guys are crazy."

Dane had his cheek against her hair. "My main goal in life is to convince you that we're not. At least not completely."

"How can you not be mad at me? I'm the reason you're here," she admitted in a whisper.

"I think I speak for all three of us when I say we wouldn't want to be anywhere else," Cooper replied. "If I wasn't with you here, I'd be going out of my damn mind with worry. But cuddled up with you... It's all good. Alea, this wasn't your fault."

"But when we get home, and we *will* get home, I intend to find out whose fault it is," Dane said, sending Cooper a dark look. "Someone planned this."

Someone meant to kill her. Cooper knew exactly what Dane's expression meant. He was asking Coop to join him in hunting and taking down this fucker. He nodded to Dane. Oh, yeah. They would make sure this asshole couldn't ever hurt her again.

"I thought the pilot was just crazy and hated my family." Alea's arms slowly wound around his waist. "You're both so warm."

Cooper cuddled a little closer. "We'll always keep you warm, safe...whatever you need. We'll take care of you. We can survive here indefinitely. Landon is scouting the island for more food right now."

"What happens if he doesn't find any? What happens when the food we took from the plane runs out?" Alea asked, then bit her lip for a moment. "We got all we could, but we can't survive on crackers, pâté, and peanuts for very long."

Dane chuckled softly. "There's an ocean of food right out there. This place has bananas and all kinds of fruit. We were all trained to know what kind of plants we can and can't eat. Lea, we've got this. We survived the crash. That was the hard part. The rest is easy, especially now that you've convinced Coop to make sure he doesn't die of gangrene. I won't say it will be like hanging around the palace, but if we take care of each other, keep the fire going, find a safe place to wait out any storms that might come, we'll be golden."

She nodded against his chest. "I want to help. Just tell me what to do."

"Really?" Dane asked.

"Yes. Of course."

"What we need most now is your trust. You have to rely on us. Take this time to get to know us better. Let us have an actual chance to please you and make you happy." Dane laid a small kiss on her temple.

She shivered a little, her head coming up off Cooper's chest. He wished Dane hadn't pushed yet, but everything his buddy described...yeah, he wanted that, too. "Just a chance, Lea. You don't hate this, right?"

"I'm getting used to it," she admitted, swallowing hard. She was tense, but not rejecting. It was a step. "Can we agree to go slow? I don't know what I want and I don't have any idea what I'll be able to handle. It's going to take a while to get used to the idea that you guys could actually want me. That someone touching me isn't doing it to hurt me."

There was a low shout as Landon marched through the foliage and back into camp. He was carrying Alea's mesh laundry bag, which he'd appropriated earlier when he'd left on his quest to gather coconuts. But it was dripping wet.

"Hey, I found a bunch of conches!" Lan held up the bag and looked at it proudly. "That's some good eating and—holy shit."

Lan had obviously caught sight of Alea's half-naked state because it put a truly sizzling stare on his face. Then he lost his usual athletic grace as he walked closer, jaw hanging around his knees, stumbling over the log he'd dragged into camp earlier. He tripped in an epic pratfall. That would make some popular shit on *YouTube*.

Alea broke free and started running for Landon.

"I'm okay!" Lan shouted, but Alea was right there, crouching beside him, and there was no mistaking the way Lan took advantage to stare right at her boobs.

Dane slapped Coop on the back. "Let's shore up for the night. We're all tired. We can cook up those conches and talk about making base camp more comfy. Tomorrow we put our plan into action. It's time to claim our girl."

Coop nodded. "Amen, brother."

Dane strode over to give Landon a hand with the conches, whistling as he walked.

It was the happiest he'd seen Dane in a long time. As Alea turned to glance at him over her shoulder and shot a smile his way, he had to admit, it might be the happiest any of them had been in a good, long while.

* * * *

Alea shivered a little and wished that her clothes had

dried during dinner. But they hadn't yet. The fire Dane had built was roaring, but she still trembled. Even so, the stars awed her. They wove a brilliant canvas across the dark sky. She'd never seen so many twinkling so brightly.

"Beautiful, huh?" Lan sat beside her, his shoulders rubbing against hers.

She wasn't alone. She might be on one of the remotest islands in the world, but these three men had gone out of their way to show her that everything would be all right.

"It is." The fire crackled in front of her. Cooper and Dane were talking quietly on the other side of the fire pit they'd dug. "Do you think someone will find us?"

"Sure." There was no hesitation in his voice. "I think your cousins will move heaven and earth. But it's a damn big ocean, Lea. It could take some time. Be prepared to settle in and get comfortable waiting."

Her cousins. They would be worried by now. She'd intended to text…and now that wasn't possible. They would know the plane hadn't landed in Sydney. Piper would be so worried. They would be forced to call all of Dane, Cooper, and Landon's relatives to tell them their sons were missing. She knew Dane had a father he didn't talk to anymore. Cooper had a big family scattered all over southern Colorado. What about Landon? "Is there anyone back in the States who's going to be upset? You have to know Talib is going to call your parents."

Lan turned to the fire. "Don't have any."

His parents were gone? "I'm so sorry."

A bitter smile crossed his face. "Don't be. They aren't dead, darlin'. At least I don't think they are. I don't know. My mom ditched me about five minutes after I was born. As for my dad, I don't even know who he is. I'm not even sure my mom did. She got around."

She knew he came from a small Texas town. How hard had it been to be abandoned by the woman who should have loved him above all others? "How old was she?"

"She was all of seventeen when she had me. The way my grandma told it, she tried really hard to get rid of me, but I was dug into that womb."

"Get rid of you?"

Lan turned to her, his face a careful blank. "She tried a homemade abortion. I wasn't part of her plan."

"Oh, Lan." She reached for him, feeling sick, and yet an urge to comfort him all at once.

Then she stopped her hand in midair as she realized that she'd been about to hug him. The sympathetic gesture had come almost instinctively.

Lan turned back to the fire as though he couldn't stand to watch her choose to not touch him. Like other women in his life had rejected him. "It's no big deal. My grandma raised me. We didn't have much, but she made sure I got fed and had clothes."

He'd said absolutely nothing about anyone loving him. "Do you miss her? Is that who Tal will call?"

"She died a couple years back. She wouldn't have really cared. She was a mean old lady. There was a reason my momma wanted to get the hell out of that trailer. My grandma ran off everyone who ever loved her. She never let a day go by where she didn't tell me what a whore my momma turned out to be and that I was an embarrassment. She kept me because righteous women take care of their mistakes."

How hard had it been for his sole guardian to consider him a burden? Lan was so competent. In the course of one day, he'd scouted the perimeter of the island, found food, and set up a desalinization station that was gathering water so they could stock up. He was amazing and he'd always been so deeply kind. She didn't stop this time. If nothing else, he was her friend.

Alea scooted closer to him and placed a hand on his back, leaning her face against his strong upper arm. His skin was warm and smooth, so much softer than she'd imagined, though it covered rock-hard muscle. "You weren't a mistake.

I can't imagine any mother not being so proud of you."

He turned slightly, forcing her head up and looking on her with a curious gaze. Slowly, he reached down and brushed away tears she hadn't known she was shedding. "Are those for me?"

She shrugged, then nodded. He wrapped a bulky arm around her and hauled her in close. For a moment, she stiffened, then sank against the heat of his body. And the safety. She felt safe with all of them.

"Don't you cry for me, Princess."

Sometimes when he called her that she could almost believe it was a term of endearment and not merely a title. "Someone should. And I'm not really crying for you. It's not pity. You came from so little and you've turned into a wonderful man."

"Sometimes," he began, staring down at her, "bad things happen to good people, and they still find a way to turn it around. They find a way to be brave. I know you're brave, too. I want you to kiss me, Lea."

So much for his lack of smarts. He was a manipulative bastard. But if she wanted to heal, wanted to move forward and not let the kidnappers beat her, as Piper had pointed out, she had to be willing to take chances. Get out of her comfort zone. Try to be a whole woman. Believe that she could trust them.

Alea closed her eyes and tilted her head up. She could handle this. Landon would never hurt her.

She waited, but nothing happened.

Alea opened her eyes, and found Lan staring down at her. Cooper had moved behind, and she could feel his heat. Dane had edged closer, too. His gaze was fixed on her, smoldering like the nearby fire, as he leaned back against a tree.

"He said he wanted you to kiss him, baby," Dane pointed out. "You have to listen to instructions or there might be consequences."

She stiffened a little. "I don't think I like the sound of that."

Cooper leaned in. "Come on, Lea. Don't be scared. You know Dane likes to play. It's just who he is. He needs to feel like he's in control." His voice dropped to a whisper. "If he thinks you're afraid, he'll pull away. His ex-wife told him he was a pervert, and I don't think he can handle it if you feel the same way."

Talib liked to "play," too. Oh, her cousins had tried to hide that fact from her, but she'd snuck into Tal's "dungeon" when she was a teenager. The locked door had always intrigued her, and they'd never let her in or explained. Unfortunately when she'd finally figured out how to sneak in, Tal had been playing at the time. She'd hidden, of course, but she'd heard the moans, the slaps of leather on skin, the gasps—the sounds of satisfaction.

And she'd heard the tenderness he'd shown his submissive afterward. The praise he'd given her. The woman's sighs of contentment. They had both enjoyed themselves. There hadn't been anything wrong with it. She'd heard that the dungeon was open again and her cousins played with Piper, teasing her and loving her. Tal needed the control after what had happened to him.

What had happened to Dane?

She sat up and stared at him, illuminated by the fire. He had a bland, somewhat expectant look on his face, but she was starting to really know him. His anxiety revealed itself in the hard line of his shoulders, in the stiff way he held himself. "What if I'm not submissive?"

And just like that, his body relaxed, and the teasing Dom was back. "Oh, you are."

"Maybe I want to be in control. Maybe I need it after what happened to me." How would he handle that?

A smile softened his face. "You'll always be in control. That's the great misunderstanding about the lifestyle. The submissive can stop the scene at any time. Any play is meant for your pleasure. Any rule is meant to protect you, build trust between us, and lift you up. It's why I won't listen to you talk badly about yourself. I'm willing to spank you over that so you'll remember. Even if you hate me, I need you to believe how amazing you are."

She didn't necessarily understand, but she was pretty sure she couldn't hate him. Ever. "We have to go slow with the whole play thing, Dane. I might never be able to handle it, especially the bondage. Being unable to move…it scares me."

Which meant she might never be able to please him.

"Hey, it's going to be okay. We'll go as slow as you need," Dane assured her. "Trust isn't an overnight process. We'll take it one baby step at a time, if that's how it's got to be. For now, I want you to kiss Lan slow and deep. He's going to sit back and let you have your way with him."

Lan smiled at her, placing his hands behind him and using them for leverage as he tilted back. The move left his big chest on display. "I'll keep my hands to myself, darlin'."

She rose to her knees. Her having control while she had her way with Lan confused her. "That doesn't sound terribly submissive, Dane."

"There are as many ways to play as there are players," Dane shot back. "We don't have to follow any rules except our own. Now kiss him. I want to watch."

The idea of Dane watching her as she kissed Landon made her heart pound in a sultry rhythm. She'd been kissed before by men, yes. But she'd never been the aggressor.

Men? Hah. She'd dated boys. Not a single one of her few boyfriends had been as masculine as Landon or Cooper or, oh god, Dane. They were big and broad and hard. They oozed testosterone. They had protected her today. They had made sure she was comfortable and safe and warm. They always would.

No, she'd never dated even one man before. Those rich boys had been cultured, some even really intelligent and interesting. And she would bet they would have panicked and screamed like girls the second they realized the plane was going down. They wouldn't have put that much time, energy, or thought into making sure she lived. Hell, Coop had all but volunteered to commit suicide by palm tree just to put the plane down in a visible location that might give the rest of them a better chance at being rescued.

And Landon... She stared up at his stony face, his gorgeous, sculpted mouth. His lips were thick and perfectly curved. His cheeks already had a sexy growth of beard. And his blue eyes were so hopeful.

Kiss him. She wanted to. She could even feel blood rushing to her nipples as she thought about it.

With a little smile, she leaned in and brushed her lips against his, getting just a hint of his warmth and the firmness of his lips before she pulled away.

She'd done it! She'd kissed him. And she wasn't stressed or traumatized. He hadn't pounced on her or...

"You can do better than that, Princess," Lan challenged.

"Yeah, you aren't going to make him crazy with that little kiss." Cooper was watching, too, over her shoulder. He'd gotten to his knees behind her. She could feel him almost touching her. What would it be like to have his hands on her hips? Or her breasts, teasing her nipples as she kissed Lan?

Her whole body flushed with heat at the thought.

Alea leaned toward Lan again, determined to make him—and the others—a little crazy. She could do it. She'd survived a damn plane crash. She could survive being touched and touching in return.

Lan's eyes drifted down to her breasts. He liked them. There was no mistaking the way his cock got hard because he was only wearing his boxer briefs and the fire illuminated his thick length. Yeah, she was already getting to him.

Alea brushed her lips against his again. But this time, instead of backing away, she pressed in, allowing her hands to cup his face. She loved the rough feel of his whiskers against her palm as she inhaled his scent, tested the firm softness of his mouth, acquainted herself with her body being so close to his.

This was nice. So nice. She was getting warm and relaxed.

"Use your tongue, Lea." Dane's command guided her from somewhere near the fire.

Her tongue. Heat surged through her belly…and arrowed lower. No denying that she wanted to know how he tasted.

Alea ran her tongue across his bottom lip and felt his whole body shiver as his lips parted. Then she curled her tongue around his shyly and drank in his flavor for a heady second. Oh, she felt lightheaded, but as she eased away, she realized that she had power over him. Dane was right. She wasn't out of control. Quite the opposite.

"Hey, it's my turn," Cooper said. "I want a good-night kiss, too."

"Go on or he'll whine all night long," Lan whispered against her lips.

Good-night kisses. If she started allowing them, would they want them every night? Would they want more? The thought made her shiver.

She turned to Cooper. He held himself just a bit apart, giving her space, the same way Lan had. She moved closer to him and cupped his face, too. His hair was so short, but when she ran her hand across it, she was surprised at how soft it felt. She bumped her nose against his before finding his lips.

As they touched, a little spark sizzled over her lips. As she opened her mouth and his followed suit, their breaths meshed, their tongues tangled. Coop wasn't quite as good at being passive and patient as Lan. He surged in, wrapping a hand around her shoulder, as he tilted his head and went deeper. Alea stiffened for a moment, then relaxed. A big zing followed. He was potent. And she couldn't deny that it was nice to be close to them.

She sucked his bottom lip into her mouth and loved the groan that came from deep in his chest. Then she nipped at him again before pulling away with a teasing grin.

Alea stood up, perfectly satisfied with this little experiment so far. But she had one more man to go. *Dane.*

Gulping down nerves, she walked to the fire, her feet sinking deliciously into the sand. It was funny how much more aware she was of everything now. The night suddenly wasn't cold, but rasped a nice cool breeze over her skin.

Dane watched her, his gaze warm as she halted beside him. "Is it my turn, baby?"

She nodded, putting a hand on his chest. He was perfectly ripped, every muscle gloriously hard. His face had no give. And somehow, without a word, he demanded that she try her best, give as much as she could. For some reason, she found herself wanting to please him.

"Go ahead." He spread his arms wide, giving her full access.

Alea had a suspicion that he wouldn't give her this much leash often. She'd better enjoy exploring and setting the pace while she could.

Searching up into Dane's blue eyes and finding a gentle understanding under his hunger, she leaned against him and kissed him, not waiting this time. She drew her tongue along his plump bottom lip, and he remained still beneath her, letting her control everything. How far would he allow her to go?

She pressed harder, but his lips stayed closed.

"Open your mouth," she whispered.

He obliged when she kissed him again, giving her access. She hoped she was doing it right. She rubbed her tongue against his, curling and sliding. He played along, but he was largely still beneath her.

Alea stopped and backed away.

"What is it, Princess?" Dane asked.

"I want you to kiss me back."

"I moved with you."

She shook her head. "No, you—"

But he had. Yes, it was reassuring to have all the control, but she wanted him to respond. She wanted him to truly want her and to prove it in his kiss. Even twenty-four hours ago, she wouldn't have been able to imagine needing him to kiss her. Now she ached for what he held just beyond her reach.

"What I mean is, I think I'd like it more if you kissed me."

"Do you really want me to kiss you?" Dane asked. "Because I won't keep my hands off you. I'll take control. Just a kiss, Lea. It won't go any further than that. I'll kiss you and hold you. And then we'll go to sleep."

He was baiting a trap. She sensed that he'd push a bit beyond that…but she was alive after a harrowing day. And she realized that for the first time since Cole Lennox had pulled her out of that brothel, she wasn't terrified. Somehow, kissing them made her feel like she was taking control of her life again. Doing what *she* wanted, not what fear allowed her. No way would she stop Dane now. She wanted to know what it would be like to kiss him.

"All right," she murmured.

He sat in the sand and leaned against the tree, then patted his lap. "Sit here."

If she did, so much of her would have to touch so much of him. He'd maneuver them into a position that ensured he was in control. But she knew Dane would honor his promise. Just a kiss.

"It's all right, Lea," he said, that hard tone to his voice disappearing. "Let's just get some rest. You sleep between Cooper and Lan. They'll keep you warm."

She'd been such a coward and she was through with it. They had been nothing but kind to her. She didn't have to be afraid of them. They were all alone on an island. No pressures, no reporters, no threats. Right now, they didn't know everything in her past. Maybe they never would. This was her clean slate.

Someone would eventually rescue them, but maybe she could take this time and enjoy it. She could be their Lea just for a little while.

She scooted on to his lap and felt his erection right against her hip. Dane Mitchell wanted her. That was all that mattered tonight.

Dane's expression changed, turning hard and dominant. He reached up and touched her face, brushing across it with his fingertips as though trying to memorize the feel of her skin. Alea had to swallow down a gasp as his hand trailed down her neck to her chest.

"I'm going to touch your nipples."

She nodded and felt them tighten before his fingers even got close. They strained against the cotton of her bra, trying to meet him halfway. While his right hand traced the hard points and a soft sigh escaped her, his left wound around her waist, clutching her hip.

And she wasn't freaking out because this was Dane, the man who had risked his own life to save hers.

He cupped the nape of her neck, pulling her forward. "Put your hands on me, Lea."

There was something about his deep, rich voice that had her fingers moving to his chest and stroking him. She rubbed her palms over his muscled shoulders as he brought her closer and pressed his lips to hers.

His hand slowly fisted in her hair, every movement precise and slow. She wasn't startled. Once she reminded herself that he wouldn't hurt her, she let go of the fear. Then he was drugging her with long, slow kisses, leading her closer and deeper. God, he smelled like a man, musky, potent. She couldn't stop herself from melting.

When his tongue licked along the bottom of her lip and she opened for him, he invaded, sliding against her. Over and over, he dipped inside her mouth, taking possession, as his fingers toyed with her nipples. Heat pooled low in her gut. She gave herself over to the moment, moaning softly, arching her breast into his hand.

Then suddenly, Dane leaned away. He dropped one last, chaste kiss on her lips. "Time for bed, Princess. Lay down on your belly, and let Lan and Cooper touch you for a while."

"What?" It was over? And she was supposed to do what?

Dane moved, shifting her off his lap and standing up. He held a hand out to help her up. "It's part of your training. Or rather it's part of your retraining."

"I'm being trained?" She was a little unsteady on her feet as Dane led her back to Lan and Cooper.

"Yes, you're being trained to accept love and affection. Lay down. They're not going to do anything except stroke and rub you until you relax."

Landon and Cooper had made a place for her between them. She was the only one with a "bed." They had saved the cushions from the plane and laid them out so she would be comfortable. They would sleep on the sand. She had argued with them, but to no avail. They wanted to know she was comfortable.

And now they wanted to touch her. To retrain her. To teach her to accept their hands on her body.

Alea settled down, aching to be with these brave, honorable, sexy men, too. She wanted to leave her fears behind and just give herself over to these men she was falling for.

Cooper took a foot in his hand, cradling it in his own, warming her. "I give a damn fine foot massage."

He started to rub, and Alea couldn't stop the groan that came from her throat.

Landon's fingers found her scalp and started to rub. "Go on and get some sleep, baby. We'll protect you all night long."

Her body relaxed, and Alea gave over to the heavenly contentment, reveling in the fact that she didn't feel a bit of fear.

Her last thought as she closed her eyes and drifted away was a sweet one. She'd held the title of 'princess' for years, but this was the first time she'd really felt like one.

Chapter Eight

Four days later, Alea watched Landon emerge from the jungle with a huge branch of green bananas slung over his rippling shoulder and realized she was in lust.

The guys kissed, cuddled, and touched her at every turn. They murmured endearments in her ear. They whispered enticements against her lips. Every night, they stroked her and curled protectively around her until she went to sleep. It was like a fantasy.

And they were slowly killing her. Death by sexual frustration.

She often awakened with one's hand cradling a breast as he buried his face in her neck. Another would have his hand cupping her mound as he pressed his hard cock against her backside. But no one fondled her long enough to release the orgasm now constantly bubbling inside her. They'd primed her body repeatedly, and she felt ready to explode. Just being near them—even looking at them—aroused her. Yes, she'd made them promise to take it slow. But "slow" had become its own form of torture.

Alea sighed, watching the way Lan's body moved. He was all strength and masculine grace, from his bulky shoulders to those legs that had been chiseled by hard work and pure grit. His hair was growing out already, though he took care of his beard every day during what she now called "Hot Guy Beach Bathing."

All three of them would get in the shallows and wash themselves, their strong hands coasting all over those muscles with the soap they'd made here on the island by straining boiling water through ashes and collecting the lye, then mixing it with the melted fat from a pig Lan had caught. They'd tossed in a collection of clean-scented herbs from the island, and it wasn't bad. In fact, the process had fascinated her, but not as much as watching them shave themselves and shove each other around in the surf. For some reason, men seemed to show their affection for each other with curses and punches.

But they showed their affection for her with toe-curling kisses and slow strokes of their hands. She was so ready to show them her affection in return.

"Hey, darlin'," Lan said with a big grin as he entered camp. "You won't believe what I found."

Bananas, obviously. Alea had no trouble believing he'd found those. Lan had become the provider. He'd managed to fashion a spear from bamboo and his wicked hunting knife. Besides yesterday's wild pig, he brought home bags full of fish every day.

Part of the pig was now roasting over the fire. It was going to be a nice dinner. She'd already gathered wild tubers to cook, too. Food was not a problem here with these men around.

Sex was, though. Or the frustrating lack of it.

God, she wanted them.

"Earth to Alea?" Lan shoved the bananas into the small storage shed Dane and Cooper had built.

They were rapidly turning into the *Swiss Family Robinson*. Dane, it turned out, had a true talent for tropical architecture. He'd built a little shelter with a bamboo floor and a roof made of palm fronds he'd woven tightly together, then secured to hold against the wind. It was the rainy season in this part of the world, and Dane had known it. He'd made certain she stayed safe and dry. Now, he was busy building a smoker since a small population of wild boars inhabited the island and her men seemed eager to put as many as possible in their bellies.

"Sorry. My mind is drifting," she confessed. "What did

you find?"

He shook his head. "Can't tell you. You just have to see it. Come on. Cooper is waiting there."

She looked out at the beach where Dane was busy gathering rocks and shells for his SOS message. Four days, and they hadn't seen a single contrail stream from a plane. Alea knew that should probably worry her…but right now being here with them was like the best vacation ever. No outside pressures. No worries. No expectations. They had plenty of food and water, a great shelter, and each other. She was seriously beginning to question what more she needed.

"I'll go tell him where we're going. Hang tight." Landon jogged out to Dane.

He'd taken to just wearing his boxers and his sneakers. It was too hot during the day to wear much else. Alea had gotten used to just wearing her bathing suit or panties and a bra. She wasn't embarrassed anymore. The whole experience had been oddly freeing.

Lan clapped Dane on the shoulder with a nod, then ran back up the beach. He reached for her hand. "He's going to join us when he's done. Come on, darlin'. We've been working our asses off. It's time to take an afternoon for some fun."

She followed him into the jungle, the sun disappearing under the heavy foliage. The men had been exploring and only yesterday had declared it safe enough for her to walk around. Even so, she hadn't been allowed to leave the beach alone. Now, she turned her face up and was mesmerized by the way the beams of sun streamed in. It was a gorgeous matrix of dewy light and green canopy. She could hear monkeys rustling and sending out calls to each other. The jungle was alive. Everything here seemed magical.

Her first night on the island, the sounds had been terribly familiar, and she'd dreamed she was back in Colombia. When she'd awakened, sweating and shaking, she'd been surrounded by her three men, all eager to soothe and reassure. To protect. And they had, every minute of every hour since.

They'd put her at ease, and now she saw the jungle like a playground. She was Eve with three glorious Adams.

"You're going to love this," Lan assured. "I've spent a lot of time mapping the perimeters. This is the first time I've gotten to the center."

He'd also made a sort of trail. Alea noticed he'd cut back the foliage so she could move easily.

Up ahead she heard splashing. The island must be much smaller than she'd thought. "Is the ocean close?"

Lan shook his head, a huge grin on his face. "No. It's a lagoon. Cooper says this whole island must be a volcano, so I assumed the pond we found would be heated by the lava underneath. Except I can't remember the right word."

"Magma?" she supplied.

His face fell a little. "Yeah, that was it. I'm not great with information like that."

She pulled on his hand, forcing him to stop and face her. "I should get to spank you now."

"What?" He glowered at her. His blue eyes had turned serious in a heartbeat.

Just like her, gorgeous Lan had his own insecurities to work through. In the last few days, she'd seen that they all had their own demons. Knowing that made it so much easier to relax and be herself around them. "I want you to stop telling yourself that you're dumb."

He frowned at her. "Lea, I'm pathetic if I can't be honest with myself."

"The same way I've always been 'honest' about my fat ass?"

"No, that's just gorgeous, darlin'."

"Well, I think you're smart." She went up on her toes, pressing a quick kiss to his lips. "But you need retraining, too."

"C'mon... I'm not as smart as Cooper and Dane."

"That's crap. You may not have read as much, but you can fix that over time. Just don't say you're not smart. In fact, I happen to know you can be a manipulative bastard."

"Really? You think so?" A smile broke out on his ridiculously handsome face.

"Absolutely." She ran a hand across his chiseled cheek. It was so much easier to touch them now.

"Fine. I'll try not to talk about it again." He leaned over and kissed her swiftly before they started back through the foliage.

And then Alea saw the reason he'd made her trek through the jungle. Before her was a gorgeous pool of clear water. Cooper stood on a rock fifteen feet above the water, not wearing a single stitch of clothing. He put his hands over his head, every gorgeous muscle in his body on display. He was a thing of beauty. His cock hung out, long and thick even relaxed, his testicles heavy.

From where she stood, Alea watched as he executed a perfect dive and disappeared beneath the blue surface with a splash.

"You'll love it, darlin'. The water's fresh and so warm." Landon toed out of his sneakers and scrambled up toward the rock from which Cooper had dived. "Come on. Let's have some fun."

She watched as he shoved off his boxers and dived in.

As Lan surfaced, she looked around in awe. This was paradise. Beams of golden sunlight shone down on the crystal water. Black volcanic rock formed the edges of the pool, but the water looked inviting and deep. A soft bed of grass surrounded the lagoon, and flowers made a colorful landscape just beyond. This little nugget of paradise was utterly perfect.

Cooper surfaced, his big hand slicking back his dark hair. He let out a long, joyful howl. Alea laughed. Despite everything they had been through, Cooper had kept a smile on his face. It made frowning in his presence damn hard.

In fact, everything was different here. *She* was different. Relaxed and positive. Happy. And she was ready to shed fear and embrace change.

Her hands went to the back of her bra. Was she really about to bare herself, cast caution aside and see where the moment led? *Yes.* Her fingers shook, but she managed to unhook the clasp.

Lan sprang up from the water next to Coop. They were waiting for her patiently. But her patience was at an end. She wanted them. But more, she was coming to need them. They'd taught her to be this Alea she'd discovered on the island. This woman cooked, cleaned, and did laundry. She had purpose. This Alea had shed her past here and now refused to let the past rule her life anymore. This Alea knew what she wanted.

Her men.

This island was her haven. Being here with Lan, Dane, and Coop had opened her soul. With a deep breath, she pulled her bra off.

A big smile broke across Landon's face. "You coming in, darlin'?"

"Join us, Lea!" Cooper shouted.

She let her bra drop, and as quickly as she could, she shoved her panties down her hips, then off her legs. God, she was naked. She was completely naked. Alea shivered but not in fear.

"Hey now, gorgeous." Cooper made his way to the side of the pool with a leer and pulled himself up to reveal his chest. "You're a damn beautiful sight."

Landon edged toward her, too, with a hot stare. "Holy shit." Then he frowned. "Sorry. I lose my head when I see something that beautiful."

They genuinely thought she was beautiful? They'd spent days telling her so. They'd shown her with their hands and their kisses. They seemed determined to make her believe she was gorgeous. It wasn't easy after her captors had told her repeatedly how ugly she was and how little she was worth. But those pigs had been criminals, horrible human beings. Dane, Cooper, and Landon were heroes. Why should she listen to assholes more than true men?

That rationale made logical sense, but sometimes emotions—fears—weren't logical at all. She was realizing that it was going to take time and patience to break through those barriers.

She forced her hands to her sides and walked to the edge of the pool. Without clothes—even the little bit she'd been wearing—made her feel *so* naked. She was more aware of the air on her skin, the cool grass at her feet, the perfume of the flowers, of just how alive she could be.

All she had to do to let herself truly be a part of everything was take one simple step.

Alea closed her eyes and turned her face up to the sun, letting it warm her skin. Then she stepped off into the void.

Water enveloped her, surrounding her utterly in warmth. She opened her eyes, shocked that she could see everything in the crystal water. Life surrounded her. Fish swam all over the pond, both alone and in small schools. A turtle with its eyes open observed the humans as it swam by. Alea watched, drinking in the sight of nature teeming. That was what she wanted—to be wide awake and alive. Unafraid.

With a smile, she broke the surface, and tropical air caressed her skin. She smoothed her hair back and sank into the moment. She'd been missing this, a deep awareness of every moment. Life would always be filled with hope and sorrow, thrill and pain, fear and bliss. And love. It was impossible to truly understand love without knowing those other emotions, without enduring loss. Everything seemed so clear now.

As she'd grown up, she'd been focused on the future. Since Colombia, she'd almost drowned in the fear and self-pity of her past. She'd damn near let it kill her. Now, she wanted to be in this moment, to forget yesterday and tomorrow, just live for now.

Landon and Cooper both dove under the surface, making their way to her. She knew exactly where they were headed and smiled. They wouldn't leave her alone. Never.

Then one of them wrapped a hand around her ankle. A joyous little scream left her mouth before they pulled her under with them. How long had it been since she'd trusted someone enough to play? To just laugh and be? She kept her eyes open, and Cooper floated in front of her, his mouth looming closer to her own. They kissed in a sweet, if wet tangle of lips while the fish swam around them, and Lan's arms circled her from behind.

They let her go and bobbed to the surface. Landon smiled as he waded around her. "Hey, I want one, too."

Of course he did. She had to treat them all equally or jealousies arose. Her aunt had taught her that. Her aunt had juggled four husbands, and she'd talked to Alea about her marriage in order to prepare her niece for the future. Her aunt had always preached loving all husbands equally because each possessed different traits that completed her. Being the center of her husbands' world had been an honor and a blessing, according to her. Alea understood now.

She put her arms around Lan. How had she ever shunned them? She'd wanted them from the moment they had walked into her life. At one time, she'd been too afraid to take them. Here, fear was no longer a necessity. It wasn't even an option. Right here and now was heaven.

His lips parted hers, and Alea allowed his tongue to invade and seduce. He made her melt. Once, she'd been frightened of an embrace that pressed her breasts against his chest. Now she reveled in the sensations, their closeness. He clutched her hard in return. Every day, her men wrapped her up a little bit tighter, a little bit longer. Each moment, each embrace, slowly coaxing her trust.

When Landon released her, he laughed, the sound deep with joy. "I fucking love it here."

Then he disappeared under the surface. Cooper winked at her and disappeared, too.

And the game was on. She couldn't help the giggle that bubbled up inside her like champagne. She swam, the water flowing around her, caressing every inch of her skin. She felt in harmony with nature as she played with her men and worshipped the sun that gave life to them all. For the first time in years—maybe ever—she was brilliantly, vibrantly alive.

Finally, she made her way to the far end of the pool and pulled herself onto the grass. Smiling in contentment, she lay flat, the air and the sun caressing her skin. She watched birds fly overhead as if they didn't have a care in the world.

"Are you tired?" Landon asked, now standing over her.

Somehow it felt right to be naked here with him, seeing every inch of his body glistening and wet. Alea propped herself up on her elbows. "No. I feel great."

Landon sank to his knees beside her as Cooper continued splashing in the pool. "Are you hungry, darlin'? If you are, I can find you some food. Just give me a minute."

He would do it. He would figure out a way to fish without a pole or just catch the little creatures with his hands. Or he would grab the turtles and make soup. Landon always found a way to fill her belly. But that wasn't what she wanted him to fill right now. "I'm not hungry. Or thirsty, before you ask." She took in a deep breath, paused…and let the rightness of the moment slide over her. "Landon, I want you."

He flushed, his skin going the sweetest pink. His cock immediately stood and saluted. "I want you, too, baby. Are you sure?"

Even swimming with them among nature had made her realize how much she longed to do everything that felt natural to her now. "I'm past ready."

Landon glanced over his shoulder, looking back to the pond as if looking for Cooper. "Uhm, well… This isn't the way we planned it."

Of course they had a plan. But she was tired of following other peoples' plans. She got to her feet. Lan's hesitation suddenly made her feel her nudity. They'd spent so much time praising her beauty and telling her that they wanted her. Why was Lan hesitating now?

Those nasty voices from her nightmare in Colombia started circling in her head again, vultures eager to gnaw on her confidence. Still, she refused to jump to conclusions. Maybe Lan hesitated because Dane hadn't arrived yet?

"Why does this have to be planned? I want to be spontaneous. I want to enjoy being with you"

Lan sighed and looked up, like he was trying to gather his thoughts or his patience. "Are you really sure? I think we should talk about this."

She'd thought they would just fall on her the minute she said yes, that sex would be easy. Alea had mentally prepared herself not to freak out if she found herself underneath one of their big, hard bodies. They claimed to want her. They were together in paradise. So what was the problem?

At times, she'd behaved wretchedly to them. And they'd been so patient. She would bet these men didn't take crap off anyone, but they'd taken it from her. They claimed to be crazy about her, and she'd begun to believe it, but…Landon wasn't exactly jumping on her offer.

Alea wrapped her arms around her middle. "What is there to say?"

Lan hesitated, like he had something to confess that he'd rather keep to himself. Her heart twisted. Maybe it had nothing to do with a lack of desire for her.

But what else could it be?

She turned away to find the bra and panties she'd discarded earlier when she'd been sure this afternoon would be idyllic and perfect. "Never mind. Forget I said anything. I'll find my way back to the beach."

Landon grabbed her arm, and when she flinched and jerked away, he held up his hands. "Alea…"

She needed to get her clothes on and she needed to do it now. But Landon had scooped them up first and was holding them to his chest.

"I need my clothes, Landon. Could I have them, please?" She was fighting off that horrible panic that came from knowing just how foolish she looked.

Cooper surfaced in the pool, his gaze bouncing between her and Lan. "Lea? What's going on?"

"Nothing." She took a deep breath as the truth of that statement hit her. There was nothing going on at all. It appeared that nothing ever would. And she'd made a mistake hoping otherwise.

* * * *

"Dude, what the hell happened?" Cooper barked as he climbed out of the pool and stood expectantly.

If anyone had told Lan years back that he'd be comfortable standing naked with other naked dudes, he would have told them they were crazy, but there wasn't a whole bunch of privacy in the Army. And nudity was even easier here in paradise. He'd become pretty comfortable seeing everyone walking around with their junk hanging out.

"Alea said that she's ready." To move forward. To accept them. *Thank God.*

Cooper's eyes widened. "Are you shitting me?"

"Nope. But there are a few problems with that scenario."

Coop looked down the empty trail leading from the beach. "Besides...the plan?"

"Yeah. I need to tell Alea something, and she didn't let me get it out before she decided...I don't know. That she was ugly or I didn't want her or some other bullshit."

Lan kept his eyes on Alea. She was so fucking gorgeous. The sun kissed her skin, and he could just about swear she glowed.

Cooper frowned. "Not want you? Lea, his cock is so

hard it's, like, halfway up his nose. Mine's not any softer. How can you say that? What are you thinking?"

Okay, halfway up his nose was an exaggeration, but not by much. It sure wanted to crawl toward her and work its way inside her. "Of course I want you."

In fact, he really wanted to jump on her and spread her legs and get inside her before she could have a second thought. When she'd said she wanted him, his whole body had flashed hot. All he'd been able to imagine was her naked and under him as he fucked her until they were both sated, spent, and he had emptied everything he had inside her.

Then the big problem had whacked him in the face with a two-by-four of *duh!*

"Fine. Tell me what the problem is." Alea stared at him, arms crossed over those luscious breasts.

When she turned that arrogant frown on him, he totally understood why Dane wanted to lay her out and smack her ass until she begged for mercy. Then he would let her suck his cock in apology. Lan smiled at the image.

"I only lost one piece of luggage during my swim from the plane to the shore. I've dived out there twenty times looking for it." He scrubbed a hand down his face. "I think the current swept it away."

Cooper's jaw dropped. "No. Tell me you didn't lose the condoms, man."

He should have mentioned it before now. "Our stash of condoms is probably growing algae on the bottom of the sea floor. Darlin', I have no way to protect you. None of us do."

And that didn't make a damn bit of difference to him. He still wanted her. Actually, the idea of fucking her with no latex between them made him crazy, primal. He could mark her. He could fill her up and know that something of him lingered inside her. He stared at her and his heart stopped a little when the sweetest smile stretched across her face.

She flushed a pretty pink. A gorgeous light glowed in her eyes. God, he loved her eyes. They were a mystery to him always, but he never loved them more than when he saw them lit as though she had a fire deep inside. It was banked most of the time, but Lan got the feeling that if he could just crack that shell of hers, she could warm them all for a lifetime. "So you still want me?"

The question nearly brought him to his knees. "Always."

She stepped toward him. "Then don't go. I still want you, too."

"Good." He swallowed, trying to hold it together. "I'm not worried about disease. Not at all. We've all had physicals and none of us have touched a woman since we hired on at the palace, but you could get pregnant, Lea. We could try to pull out, but…" This was probably a dumb move, but he wanted her to understand what she meant to him. "When the time was right, we were going to ask you to marry us anyway. I have no hesitation making love to you without birth control. I can't wait for a future with you, if you'll have us. I would love to look at your rounding belly and feel the life underneath kick my palm. Fuck, I'd love that."

"Really?" Her lips parted in surprise. Her eyes softened.

Cooper scrubbed a hand through his hair. "We all feel that way, baby. We're committed to this, to you."

A pink flush crept up her cheeks. "I… That's so sweet."

She walked toward Lan then, arms outstretched, and he let himself look at her glorious body. First, the curves of her breasts. A heartbeat later, his gaze dropped to her nipples. So fucking pretty. Her curvy waist. Her oh-so-fuckable hips and that mound he couldn't stop staring at. Her pussy. He wanted to taste it. Coop had licked at that pussy. He'd rubbed it across his face, and Lan was pretty sure he hadn't washed his fucking face for days so he could still smell her.

God, his cock was killing him. His heart ached, too. He started toward her, determined to meet her halfway.

"This isn't just sex for you?" she whispered.

Lan took her in his arms. "I love you."

"I second that." Cooper kissed her temple and caressed

her back.

Tears spilled down her face as she planted her hands on the sides of his face. "Be sure. I'm trouble. I'm difficult. I don't want to be, and the three of you make me want to heal and be better. So I need you to be sure."

"*You* be sure. If we do this, we don't know what the future will bring…but we know the possibilities. I'll never be as smart as Dane and Coop, but—"

"You're wrong." She shook her head, more tears flowing. "You're wonderful. The future used to scare me, but not now. I see it with you and me, Dane, and Coop. I don't care about the condoms. I don't care about anything right now except you. Kiss me. Love me. I need you."

Amazing that he could give her what she needed. A real princess and an illegitimate punk from Texas should have nothing in common, but his heart had damn sure spoken. He needed her, too.

Lan swooped her against his chest and devoured her lips. With her was where he'd wanted to be for fucking months. Years. All his goddamn life. He hadn't always known her, but he'd been looking for Alea, for the woman who could make him whole.

He fastened his hands on her hips, loving the way her velvety skin felt under his fingertips. He gripped her tighter, pulling her into the cradle of his body as he eased her lips open under his and his tongue invaded. She'd given him permission. She didn't care about condoms? Fuck. He could fill her up about a hundred times over. Everything he had belonged to her, especially his heart.

As his hands caressed their way down, he cupped that gloriously juicy ass. It was so fucking sexy. When she'd turned earlier and flashed those cheeks to him, he'd thought he might die. Again, he slanted his mouth over hers, going as deep as he could. This was heaven. His cock was nestled against her belly, the heat of her threatening to make him blow before his time, but it wouldn't matter. He'd just get hard again. She was the one. She made his heart soft.

Alea was goddamn everything to him.

Along with Dane and Coop, he'd worked for days to make her comfortable with his flesh against hers. Now, he pulled her even closer. She didn't shrink back. In fact, she melted right into him, and Lan smiled. Her arms wound around his neck and she kissed him back, her tongue tangling with his. *So good. So right.* His cock pulsed against her belly. He could feel her nipples brushing against his chest.

He rubbed his tongue against her, showing her what he wanted to do with his cock. In and out. In and out. The way she clung to him, giving him breathy little moans, was so fucking perfect. She pressed those breasts close, and he knew damn well that this was the time. And he was her man.

"Tell me you want me," she whispered.

That was an easy request. "More than I want my next breath."

"I want you, Landon. Be my first. Cooper, will you help us?" Her head turned slightly, looking at his friend.

"Do I get a turn?" Cooper sounded tight, like he was damn close to the end of his rope.

A brilliant smile broke across her face. "Yes, I want to make love with you, too. We're going to have to work on your sweet nothings, Coop. I want all my men. But you guys do all the camp work tomorrow because I have a feeling I'm going to be sore."

"Deal!" Coop assured.

Lan laughed. He'd just carry her wherever she needed to go. In fact, he would prefer it that way.

He bent and thrust his right arm under her knees, hauling her to his chest. He wanted to make love to Lea in the soft grass. He wanted to watch every moment. He wanted to memorize it.

She wrapped her arm around his shoulders and smiled into his eyes, making him feel like the fucking king of the world. He carried her to the grass. It was buttery soft and would suit his purpose.

When he set her on her feet, Lan immediately shoved his nose in her hair. She smelled clean and tangy and sweet. Heavenly. Like the home he'd been looking for all of his life. She might wake up someday and decide that he was all wrong for her, and he would need these memories to get him through the next fifty years or so. But right now, she wanted him and was embracing the idea of their tomorrows.

With a coy smile, she wrapped her hands around the sides of his chest. He struggled not to shiver as she caressed her way lower. He kissed her again, then backed off as he felt Cooper moving in behind Alea, his arms around her waist.

"Is this okay?" Cooper asked, pushing her hair to the side so he could kiss her neck.

"It's wonderful." One of Alea's hands trailed back and found Cooper's hip.

She was no longer the woman who flinched every time one of them touched her. Landon had started to think that crashing and finding this island was the best thing that could have happened to them. If they had been in Sydney, they would never have made this much progress with her so quickly. Tal and the others would have found her, and she would have had a million and one distractions. Even though she'd meant this trip to be a vacation, she would have had responsibilities and pressure.

Here, they had nothing to do except focus on each other.

Lan watched as Cooper turned her head slightly and covered her lips with his own. It was hot to watch his buddy kiss their girl. Cooper's hands cupped her breasts and offered them up to Lan. Yeah, he would take those. He got to his knees and licked at one nipple. Firm and ripe, he traced the areola with the tip of his tongue. Alea whimpered a little and thrust her breasts out, begging for more.

A succulent scent wafted up. Her arousal. Sweet and exotically spicy. She wanted him. Them.

He sucked at her nipples, drawing the first one into his

mouth before moving to the second and suckling with abandon.

He let his fingers drift lower, slipping across her mound and splitting her labia. She was wet, a soft, sweet heat he couldn't wait to sink into, but he would have to because she wasn't a quick lay. No. He was going to let her take all the time she needed.

He bent over and stuck his nose right into her pussy.

"Doesn't she smell good?" Cooper murmured.

Lan looked up, and Cooper was twisting Alea's nipples. She was writhing in his hold, but it was a sweet little torture. There was no fear at all in her eyes.

"She smells perfect. I bet she tastes even better."

Alea's hips rolled and a gaspy little moan came out of her mouth. "Oh, god. Please. Please touch me, Lan."

He didn't think for a second that she wanted him to touch her with his fingers. No way. He ran the flat of his tongue right between her swollen folds, gathering the cream of her arousal. Oh, he'd been so right. She tasted sweet and tangy. He sucked her into his mouth and then licked a line up to her clit. That little pink jewel was pouting and begging for attention.

"Lan, please," Alea said.

She'd been interrupted with Cooper and hadn't gotten to come. In fact, she'd very likely never really orgasmed. She'd known violence, but she didn't know how much ecstasy another's touch could bring. Landon intended to show her. It was the most important thing he'd ever done. He leaned in, set his mouth on her again, and focused on showing her pleasure.

Chapter Nine

Alea's legs were disintegrating under her as pleasure seeped in and made her boneless. She would have fallen to the ground while Landon feasted on her pussy if not for Cooper wrapping her in his strong arms. Just days ago she would have felt caged and utterly terrified. But he embraced her, rather than trapped her. His touch was filled with affection. Cooper wouldn't hurt her.

If she needed him to, he would release her instantly.

But that was the last thing she wanted now. Cooper held her to allow Landon to have his sweet way with her pussy. Alea glanced down her body at his sandy blond head moving between her legs, tilting to get deeper as he licked, sucked, and laved until she felt like she was in a pleasure-induced haze.

"Lay her down," Landon commanded.

Cooper positioned her in the grass before she could protest. *No!* She wasn't ready for this part to be over yet.

"Spread those legs, baby," Cooper whispered into her ear as he sat and cradled her head against his chest. "Lan wants more of you. Give him your pussy."

Lan didn't wait for her to comply. He grabbed her ankles and forced her legs wide, then slithered to his belly between them. Alea sighed with relief that he simply wanted her in a different position. The minute she felt his tongue push through her slick, sensitive folds again, she understood why. He speared his tongue inside her, and the velvety hot invasion had her squirming, arching, crying out.

"Be still, Lea," Coop warned. "Let him have his way."

Cooper squeezed her nipples again, pinching and

plucking. A hot flare darted down her body, straight to her clit. She pushed her hips up at Lan.

Alea couldn't find the breath to tell Coop that his "punishment" only aroused her more. They made her feel so alive and aware of her body. With every moment, every intimacy, they pushed her closer to the edge of the cliff. God, she wanted to fall blissfully over it.

Landon continued to worship her with his tongue, not leaving a single slick inch of her untouched. He held her open while Cooper held her down. And it didn't frighten her in the least. Alea relaxed because they wouldn't hurt her. She belonged with these men and she felt that all the way to her soul.

Alea wriggled to get closer and panted. Desire rushed through her blood, need escalating, coalescing. Her head fell back against Cooper's chest as his palms cupped her breasts, fingers still plucking and teasing, driving her mad.

"I think our girl likes having her pussy eaten. Don't you, baby? You like having a mouth on your cunt. Does it feel good? I can tell you, it tastes so fucking good. You're the sweetest thing I've ever had on my tongue."

The blunt words coming out of Cooper's mouth probably should have shocked her, but it merely sent more desire shivering through her body. Every word he uttered in her ear sounded low, sexy, and seductive.

"Come on. Tell us you like it. Tell us how much you like having his tongue on your pussy." He punctuated the command with a sharp pinch to her nipples.

With a frantic nod, she cried out. "Yes! It feels *so* good."

Good? A ridiculous understatement. This was heaven. Lan's tongue was dedicated and strong, thorough and unerring. He settled his thumb over her clit and rubbed circles that magnified the ache. She couldn't help arching closer, shoving against him with a moan.

This time Cooper encouraged her. "Oh, you're close, aren't you? Ride his tongue. Let him take you all the way, baby. I can't wait to watch you come."

His fingers pulled at her nipples, matching up with the rhythm of Lan's tongue. Over and over, they sent her higher with a tangle of sharp sensations—the slide of Lan's tongue as he circled her clit, Cooper pulling on her nipples and whispering filthy hot suggestions. Alea held her breath. Who needed air now with this epic wave of pleasure swelling inside her? She stiffened in anticipation, keening, almost praying to finally feel the release she'd been denied all her life.

Finally, with another slide of Lan's tongue, the crest broke through her body. Ecstasy unlike anything she'd ever felt or imagined burned the blood in her veins. She felt dizzy, light, euphoric.

Oh god! This was the incredible, mind-altering experience other women whispered and moaned about. This was what made Piper smile all day as she hummed through the palace. The amazing burst of need seemed to take her up, send her soaring until she swore she could almost feel heaven. Her heart roared. Her pussy felt electric.

Alea came down slowly, panting for precious air. An almost divine peace flooded her mind as satisfaction relaxed her body. She let herself sag in Cooper's arms, knowing she was warm and safe here.

Lan kissed her pussy one last time, then crawled up her body, planting his lips on hers.

Now he would take her. Alea swallowed, steeling herself. But she could handle it. He'd proven that he knew how to give nothing but joy and love. If she opened her body to him, it would be all right. She might never enjoy this part, but she would focus on delighting in the pleasure she gave him. Likely, she'd have to remind herself that having a man on top of her wouldn't be scary or awful. But she wanted to give this to him. She wanted to be completely connected to them all.

Alea wondered where Dane was. He was supposed to

join them. Yes, Coop and Lan made her feel incredible, but she wanted Dane, too. When it came to her men, she suspected she would be greedy.

Lan's tongue invaded her mouth with a hard press of his lips and a barely contained breath. She tasted herself on his tongue. The way he shared the flavor of her pleasure with her felt deeply intimate. Alea tangled with him—tongues, fingers, bodies. His cock throbbed against her belly. She might be perfectly happy and sated, but Lan needed more. She wanted to give to him as he'd given to her.

"Make love to me," she whispered.

"Not like this." Lan brushed her lips one last time, then he spread his big body on the ground beside her, letting his head rest in the soft grass. "I think you should make love to me."

Then Cooper was helping her up and taking her place on the plush earth next to Landon. "Go on. We want you to explore."

She dragged in a breath as they displayed themselves for her, all rippling muscles, freshly bronzed from the island sun. Landon was lean like a swimmer, his every muscle perfectly chiseled. He had a cut torso that flowed into long, powerful legs. His cock was long and thick, standing out from a nest of blond hair. His eyes could be like ice chips, but now they glowed with a brilliant blue warmth. Cooper was built more like a quarterback, tall and buff, with broad shoulders that went on for days. His brown eyes blazed nearly black, searing her.

So beautiful and so different. And both hers.

"Go at your own pace, darlin'. When you're ready, you take us. Take as long as you want." Landon offered her his body.

"But please say it won't be too long." Cooper's hand was on his cock. A mischievous smirk lit his eyes. "We've wanted this for so damn long, baby."

With an unblinking stare, she watched his hand move up

and down. Cooper was thicker than Lan, but not by much. Both men had long, massive cocks. Cooper's hand roughed up and down his own, from the tip to the base, just above his balls, then back again. It should have been dirty or she should have felt like a voyeur. But no, this sharing felt natural. They didn't need modesty in paradise. Arbitrary boundaries just closed them off from one another. Here, now, they were connected and complete. Well, almost.

Soon.

Alea let herself sink to her knees in the velvety grass. They'd left space for her between them, and she took advantage of it. She settled a hand on both of them, reveling in the catch of Lan's breath and Coop's groan. She drew her palm up their stomachs slowly, her touch skating up to their muscled chests. They controlled so much strength for her benefit. Both men were deadly, trained to kill, but they used it to protect, not to vanquish or take.

Explore. That was the word Cooper had used. And she did.

Alea leaned over and kissed Landon's chest, right above his heart. She let her cheek lie against his skin and she could hear his heart pounding. He wrapped his arms around her, and Alea knew he could have held her tighter, but he merely clasped her lightly so that she could escape if she panicked. A sweet but unnecessary gesture. She nuzzled him instead, gratified to hear him groan as he filtered his fingers through her hair.

With a bye-for-now kiss, she left Lan and shifted to Cooper, spreading her lips across his chest. As she pressed her cheek to him, Alea listened to the rhythm of his heart for a moment before sitting up again. She wanted to explore them, but more than anything, she wanted to please them.

"Tell me what you like." Alea rubbed the flat of her palm against their chests, letting her fingers prowl down their ridged abdomens, gratified when Coop sucked in a breath and Lan seemed to get harder.

"Everything," Landon croaked.

"As long as it's you, baby. Touch me. You'll see the power you have," Cooper groaned.

That invitation was too good to pass up. Alea shivered at the thought of holding him in her hand both literally and figuratively. How long would it take to give him the kind of pleasure they'd given her?

As she reached tentatively for Cooper's cock, he grabbed her wrist. "Go on. You can be rough with me. Just…please. Goddamn it, touch me."

Her breath catching, Alea gripped his erect flesh and gasped. So hard…and yet so buttery soft, like the finest silk. Cooper's cock twitched in her hand. The head was almost like a purple plum, swollen and blood-filled. She swiped her thumb across it curiously, gratified by his guttural groan of pleasure.

"That's it. Fuck, I want to watch." Landon turned on his side, propping his head on his hand. "Go on, darlin'."

"Wow, that's amazing." Then she realized that sounded silly and blushed. "Sorry. I've never touched a cock before."

"Really?" Landon sounded stunned.

She knew exactly why. "My captors beat me silly, but they never raped me, Lan. They didn't actually force me to do anything except watch the horrible things they did to others."

"Lea?" There was so much sympathy in his voice, but she understood that it wasn't pity. He cared about her, loved her. He would empathize. Once she'd realized that, she'd felt more equipped to deal with it. And it felt all right to talk to them about those dark days. She was safe now.

Cooper clapped a hand over hers, stopping the rhythm of her strokes. "Do you need to talk about it first?"

She shook her head and eased his hand away from hers to resume stroking him. She fell into a sensual, measured rhythm. "No, I'm not letting those ghosts haunt me anymore. I just want to move past it. I want to be able to be with you all."

Lan kissed her shoulder, rubbing his cheek against hers. "We want to be with you, too, but you have to tell me if something scares you."

"Yeah," Cooper practically purred the word. He was all tawny and golden, his eyes intent and filled with delicious need.

The idea of pleasing them aroused her. Already wet from Lan's mouth and her orgasm, she felt her folds grow even slicker.

"Am I doing this right?" she whispered.

Coop just groaned.

"Grip him harder." Lan murmured the words against her skin. "He wants it. Look."

A little pearly drop of liquid formed at the slit. Acting purely on instinct, she swiped at it with her thumb and brought it to her mouth. Salty and rich. A little decadent. So very intimate.

"Fuck," Cooper moaned and another drop welled.

Alea hesitated. "Was I not supposed to do that?"

Lan chuckled. "He liked it, darlin'. It was sexy as hell. Stroke him good and hard. Keep running your thumb over the top. Soon, he's going to come all over your hand."

"Really?" She blinked down at Coop. "You want that?"

He was panting now. "Fuck, yes. Please. Damn it…"

The slit of his dick was already wet again, cream coating the head. Alea touched him there, getting her palm coated in the liquid silk. It was easier to stroke Coop now with the lubrication. He seemed to grow even larger as she increased the friction of her fingers over his flesh. She watched, utterly fascinated, as Cooper closed his eyes in concentration.

Was he trying to block her out? Thinking of someone sexier? Alea bit her lip, hating the anxiety plaguing her again. They'd done everything to reassure her…but she didn't know how to curb the terrible insecurity.

"He's just trying to make it last," Lan explained as if he

could read her mind.

"It's hard because she feels so good," Cooper growled as his hips rolled, shoving deeper into her palm. "And he's wrong about why I closed my eyes. Fuck, baby, I'm pretending that you're riding me. In my head, I can feel you all over my cock. You're drenching me in your hot cunt and… Damn it."

He was panting now, his rough breaths sawing out of his chest like he was at the end of a marathon.

"Faster," Lan urged.

Alea picked up the pace, watching each move his body made, feeling every twitch of his cock. He opened and closed his eyes again as if he was utterly lost in the pleasure. God, he swelled again in her hand. Her shoulder burned with effort, but she pressed on, determined to make every stroke throb against her palm and give him ecstasy.

Cooper moaned, and she watched as his heavy balls drew up. An agonized groan tore from him as his body jerked, his hips arched. Then pearly fluid spat from the head of his cock, coating her hand as he came with a roar.

"Fuck, baby!" He kept thrusting into her grip.

The violence of his release calmed. The satisfaction in his moan made her smile gladly, especially when he settled back into the grass, peace settling over his face.

Lan kissed her shoulder, then fell back to the ground, tugging her around to face him. "Damn, watching that has me hot. Touch me, darlin'. Now."

That was a demand she wasn't about to ignore. Quickly, she leapt to the pool and rinsed her hands, then hustled back to her men, flushing at the way their gazes sizzled her. When she crouched between them again, Alea leaned over Cooper, kissing his mouth in a soft meeting of breaths and lips before turning back to Landon.

With an expectant stare, he silently urged her closer. Alea smiled. Where to start? She let her fingers trace the sharp line of his jaw and felt those perfectly sculpted lips before she moved to the dimple on his chin. His late-afternoon whiskers tickled the pads of her fingers.

He grew restless as she explored his shoulders and chest, running her palms all over. Alea watched him fight for patience. He placated himself by fondling her breast, the curve of her waist—and pulling her in for quick, demanding kisses, each more urgent than the last. Lan was slowly unraveling. Alea loved it.

Drunk on the intimacy, her head still buzzing from her orgasm, she got brave. "Turn over."

He lifted a brow at her, then winked before turning onto his belly, revealing what had to be the most beautiful male backside she'd ever seen. She grinned as she contemplated all the ways she might touch him.

Alea started by gliding her hand down the long length of his spine. His shoulders clenched. The tendons in his neck stood out. *Hmm…* So much strength right under her hand. She cupped his ass, then, feeling really daring, she bent and pressed a kiss on one cheek before gently sinking her teeth into the other.

Cooper, now rolled to his side and watching, laughed. "Are you trying to make him crazy, baby?"

"Maybe…" Her response was probably rash and a bit reckless. Bringing Cooper to orgasm had reignited her body. Having license to touch Lan wherever and however she wanted had thrown kindling on the flame. Her body sizzled with new arousal. When she'd said yes, she'd thought she would just lie back and let him take her. But she liked being an active participant so much more.

"It's working." He sounded strained, then he groaned. "But it's the best kind of crazy."

She touched him everywhere, reveling in the way his muscles tightened, and he closed his eyes. She loved every groan and gasp that tore from his chest. "Turn over again. I want to kiss you."

He rolled over on cue, but he had a gleam in his eye.

"You're in charge today, darlin', but don't think this is how it's always going to be."

Because he would want to control the sex eventually. They all would. They were too alpha to let her have the power for long, but today was proof of Lan's amazing tenderness. He was willing to grit his teeth to be with her however she needed this first time. And she planned to enjoy it.

"Thank you." She leaned over and kissed him, a sweet brushing of their lips.

But that wasn't enough for him. He sank his hands into her hair, fisting the strands, tilting her head. He might be on the bottom, but he had absolute authority over the kiss. He ran his tongue over her bottom lip, demanding entrance. She let him in and melted against him, chest to chest, belly to belly. Warmth encased her, a blanket of soft skin and his hard will. He wrapped his arms around her and dove deep into her mouth. Alea lost herself to him.

A low thrum started in her belly, a wanting she couldn't deny. Her blood pounded through her veins. Her heart punched her chest. She wriggled restlessly, trying to ease the burn gathering heat inside her pussy.

"You aching, darlin'? You ready to come again?"

"Yes…" Alea didn't know how it was possible. She'd gone her entire adult life without an orgasm, and suddenly she didn't think she could wait another five minutes.

Lan gave her a long, slow grin. "Take me inside you, Lea." He snatched her from the grass and brought her body over his to straddle his hips. "Ride me."

Beneath her, his cock was straining. Lan took himself in hand, forcing it upright and placing it against her pussy, the head slipping in. The feel of his hard flesh against her yielding folds was foreign and a little scary. She'd been told that this would hurt. He was obviously big.

But she'd come too far in life and with her men to be deterred by a little pain or fear.

"Go slow, baby." Cooper had gotten to his knees and now sat beside her, reaching for her arm. He steadied her. "It's okay. Just sink onto him. You can take him."

Alea followed Coop's advice, easing the head of Lan's cock past her folds. She felt herself clench around the intrusion as her body instinctively welcomed him, hugged him.

"Oh, darlin', you feel so damn good." He gripped her hips, tightening on her but not forcing her down.

Inch by unhurried inch, Alea lowered herself. The moment seemed to slow as his cock filled her tight passage. She felt no pain yet, just an amazing fullness.

Until the head of his cock bumped the barrier of her virginity.

Lan swallowed, his muscles already trembling with restraint. Sweat beaded on his forehead. "Take it slow."

She could, but sort of like removing a bandage, she figured that slow would only prolong whatever pain she felt.

With one long breath, she closed her eyes, then shoved her hips down, forcing his cock deep.

Pain flared, sparking between her legs. She gasped in a protesting breath. He was too big, too thick. *God!* Tears blurred her vision. She was just about to scramble off of Lan, but he held her in place and hauled her forward, bringing her close, soothing her with a touch. Even as he did, he lifted his hips and his cock filled her to the point of bursting.

Alea cried out. "Don't. I can't—"

"Shh, darlin'," Lan soothed. "Am I scaring you?"

She shook her head, trying to separate the sensations. "It hurts. It's too much. You don't fit."

"I do. Give it a minute. Coop, help me out here." Lan glided comforting palms up her back as he raised his head, brushing her lips with his own. "Open for me."

He didn't give her an opportunity to protest, just took her mouth and drugged her with long, toe-curling kisses. Then Cooper settled behind her, and his hand found its way between their joined bodies. His fingers unerringly settled on her clit, and he traced slow circles over her sensitive flesh. Tingles leapt back to life. A slow ribbon of pleasure unfurled just under her clit. Between Landon's slow, desperate kisses and the stimulation from Cooper's touch, she relaxed, sinking deeper until she'd taken his cock inside her all the way to the root.

"That's it," Cooper praised in a low voice as he pressed kisses along her shoulder and up her neck. "You're pussy is so soft, baby. Lan and I can make you feel good. Just close your eyes and let us."

Her body came back to life, and Lan's cock inside her seemed to throb, as if she could feel his very heartbeat. With Cooper at her back, she felt surrounded, treasured. Making love with them both would be like this, their breaths over her skin, both their big male bodies enveloping her in heat and straining to pleasure her. She worried for a moment that accommodating one in her pussy and the other in her ass would be somewhere between agonizing and impossible. But Piper never seemed distressed or frustrated. Her aunt never had either. Alea took another deep breath, giving herself over to Coop and Lan. They would make it work when the time was right. She trusted them.

As if trust were the magical key, she was able to unclench on Lan's cock and ease her body up a fraction. The pain was gone. Only pleasure flared through her as she sank back onto him.

"That's it, darlin'," Lan encouraged. "Take me."

"You're so sexy, Lea," Cooper whispered. "Fuck, I'm already hard again."

Alea tossed her head back and rocked her hips again with a whimpering moan. Now that the pain was gone, the sensations of Lan inside her weren't merely okay. They were incredible. The friction of his thick, hard flesh sliding against her nerve endings, scraping gently at the sensitive end of her channel, then dragging pleasure from her as she rose back up… *Wow.* Lan gripped her and moaned. Coop whispered dirty little encouragements in her ear. It should have overwhelmed her, but no. They made her feel beautiful and free. All her anxiety melted away as she let go of everything except how good they felt. Why had she been so scared of them? They were perfect, and she needed this. She needed them.

"Tilt your hips, Lea," Cooper instructed, positioning her just the way he wanted her. "Let his cock drag over the front wall of your cunt."

Beneath her, Lan tensed and thrust up, brushing over some insane pleasure button buried deep in her pussy. She nearly screamed out his name.

"Exactly like that, baby." Cooper let his teeth sink gently into her shoulder as he continued to rub gentle circles around her clit.

Her pussy was on fire. Orgasm bubbled and brewed, sharper than before. Deeper. She tightened on Lan and wailed, trying to absorb all the ecstasy about to crash over her. So close…

"Yes, Lea, yes." Lan's hips thrust up over and over again, a measured, insistent rhythm that got progressively faster.

The burn of his friction ignited her pleasure. Orgasm exploded inside her like a bomb, and she screamed, tossing her head back as she dug her nails into his shoulders. Lan's whole body bucked under her, tensing as he came inside her. She felt the warm flood of his seed jet against her sensitive flesh, making her heart race and her body arch as pleasure rolled over her body once more.

Finally, their movements and heartbeats slowed. A deep sense of peace filled her as she cuddled against his chest, her ear right over the steady, strong rhythm of his heart. Tears of joy pricked at her eyes. She was almost grateful for them following her on this impromptu trip, for the plane crash. Without those events, she'd still be lost in her darkness, dreadfully unhappy with no idea how to pull herself out of her shell. Being isolated with them in a life-or-death struggle had forced her to examine what was truly important…think about what she genuinely wanted in life. Because the answer was simple.

Them.

"I love you, Lea," Lan said, brushing her heavy hair away from her face and looking up at her with a soft smile of adoration.

Coop leaned around her and curled a finger around her chin, bringing her lips to his. "I do, too, Lea. That was incredible, baby."

She let their beautiful words sink into her. For once, she believed them. Happiness was so bright inside her, she must be glowing with it. For this one perfect second, she felt worthy of them all.

"Well, this gives a whole new meaning to 'showing her the pool.'" Dane's voice cut through her languor. "Looks to me like you showed her every inch of your dick, too—right up her pussy."

Dane. She hadn't thought about the fact that he wasn't here while the guys had drowned her in pleasure. But when she looked up, ready to hold out a hand and bring Dane close, the nasty fury on his face and the ice in his blue eyes stopped her cold.

"Dane, come on, man. What is your problem?" Cooper scowled.

"That fucker." He pointed at Lan. "I'm going to rip you limb from limb."

Lan sat up and lifted her off his cock, rolling to his feet in front of her as though determined to protect her. "Lea, why don't you get dressed and go back to camp while we talk this out."

"You didn't wear a fucking condom?" Dane's scream echoed through the trees. Startled birds flew from the treetops. Dane's face went red. He clenched his fists.

Alea looked down and saw remnants of his semen and traces of her blood on his cock and her thighs. The sight of it seemed to enrage Dane, and suddenly she thought maybe she should be the one protecting Lan.

"No. They were in the pack the current took during my swim to shore, so we don't have any," Lan said calmly. "I explained that to Alea."

"He was carrying so much…" she added.

"Let me get this straight, Lan. You 'lost' them," Dane made air quotes, "so that you can knock her up and cut the rest of us out? Or is Cooper in on your plan, too, and I'm the only schmuck still standing here with his dick in his hand?"

Clearly, she should have waited until Dane was with them, but it had been spontaneous.

Cooper held up a hand and gave an awkward little smile. "Dude, if you'll ratchet down the drama, we're all going to get a turn at knocking her up. She knows we want to marry her and have a family. We're just making sure it will be a shotgun wedding."

"I don't need your jokes right now, asshole." Dane glowered, then turned that nasty stare on Lan. "So when were you going to tell me about this new plan? I'm betting never. Because, oh, you didn't want the big bad Dom touching your pretty princess and scaring her away, right? That's why you waited to fuck her until I was busy."

Alea flinched at the ugly accusation. "It just happened. I—"

Lan held up his hand to her, and Coop pulled her back with a shake of his head.

"What are you saying to me?" Lan challenged, his voice going low and guttural.

She was a little surprised they didn't start beating their chests like aggressive apes. Only minutes ago, she'd felt so languid, sated. Happy. Now all she felt was the weight of the moment. Everything she wanted, everything they all *needed* could be in jeopardy if she couldn't pull them together.

"I'm saying you had no fucking right to deviate from the plan." Dane was a good two inches taller than Lan and he seemed intent on proving it by looming over him. "We were *all* supposed to be here with her the first time. But I shouldn't be surprised. You broke from the plan to bring her to the meeting with the Anders brothers, too. Think you're the big smart man making all the decisions now?"

The last of her sated peace dissipated and fury replaced it. "Don't talk to him like that! I belonged in that meeting, so he took me. I wanted him, and he gave me what I desired."

Dane pinned her under an icy stare. He raked that cold gaze up and down her body until she shivered. "I'll bet he did. Did he fuck you good? Is Coop going to back him up now?"

God, his snide tone made her feel cheap. She'd wanted to make love, and they had given her a special memory to treasure. She'd felt special. Now, she just felt like a bone the gentle lab and the rabid hound would fight over. And she felt more than vaguely guilty for something that wasn't her fault.

"It wasn't like that!" she insisted, feeling sick to her stomach. "You're being a bully."

"Shut the fuck up, Dane. Are you even thinking about her?" Cooper rose and dove into the fray.

"All I've done is think about her," Dane shot back. "I'm the only goddamn one of us who thinks with his head at all. You two have done nothing but think with your dicks since the moment you saw her. You tongue-fucked her in a bathroom and couldn't get the job done," he sneered at Cooper, then shifted to Lan. "You took a virgin *and* a princess on the ground like any ol' hook-up because your cock got hard. You were supposed to treat her right, but no. You just chucked her on the ground and sank your cock in, spewing all your swimmers in her unprotected womb. That's a great first time for her."

"I enjoyed it. It was a great first experience." Or it had been until Dane had stomped in and made it sound crude with his destructive accusations.

"You weren't here, so you don't know shit." Landon ignored her, too. "I took care of her."

"Dane, you need to calm down, brother." Cooper got in between the other two men, obviously ready to stop them if they threw down.

Lan took a step away, his gaze tangling with hers and now full of regret. "Lea, I'm sorry. Darlin', let's wash up. If Dane is determined to fight, he can do it with himself. But he's right about one thing; I'm not taking care of you the way I should right now."

When he tried to lead her away to the pool, Alea dug in her heels. It was obvious Dane had a serious problem with what they'd done. Maybe she hadn't understood the "plan" well enough. Maybe they should have talked more first. They were damn sure going to talk now. "Dane, stop being a hothead. I'll get dressed, and we can discuss this like rational adults."

Dane looked down at her, his eyes cold. "I wouldn't dream of interrupting your little party. I'll just take myself off, so you can get back to fucking my friends."

If he'd slapped her across the face, he couldn't have hurt her more. Shame coursed through her, shoving out all the happiness she'd felt just minutes ago. Then Dane pivoted away and stalked back toward the beach like she didn't mean a damn thing to him.

"I'm going to kill him." Landon started to stomp after him.

Cooper put a hand on his friend's shoulder. "You want to go and beat the shit out of Dane with your junk hanging out? Don't, my brother. Dane fights dirty. He will not have a problem trying to pull your dick off."

"You stay here. *I'm* going." She looked around for the nearest garment and found Cooper's shirt, then dragged it over her head. It wasn't much but it would cover her long enough to give him a piece of her mind. "I am not letting him get away with that."

Dane had talked and talked about taking it slow and easy. He'd assured her that the choice was hers, that when she was ready, they would all be here for her. Yeah. He'd really meant that bullshit.

"I am glad I'm not the one she's mad at," Lan said under his breath.

"She's really pissed off." Coop sounded proud.

Furious, actually. She didn't have a thing to be ashamed of. Dane did. He wasn't allowed to make her feel like a whore, then walk away. He'd tried so hard to convince her this relationship would work, but the first time he got angry, he pouted and threw a tantrum.

She took off after Dane, anger thrumming though her veins. She took a deep breath. He wanted a fight? He'd better brace himself for what he'd claimed to want all along—the real Alea al Mussad.

Chapter Ten

The minute Dane's feet hit the beach he knew he should go back and apologize. Hadn't the fight at the palace and Tal's dressing down taught him anything? Everyone with a successful plural marriage had told him they had to behave like brothers. Brothers didn't normally walk away from brothers. Well, his biological ones had, and he'd resented the fuck out of it.

Hadn't he just done the same to Landon and Cooper? Yes, but they'd taken Alea without him. And he hadn't really listened to what they'd said. He'd just lost his temper and his fucking mind.

Now he was arguing with himself. *Awesome.*

Dane planted his hands on his hips and forced himself to suck in a breath, clear his head. What exactly had happened? The whole way up the trail to the lagoon, he'd been hoping that this would be the day. Once he got to wherever Lan and Coop had claimed was paradise, that maybe they would kiss her a little, maybe seduce her out of her clothes. They'd talked about all being there, going slow with her. But he'd wanted to get inside her. He'd wanted to make love to her.

Then he'd discovered that Landon had beaten him to the punch.

When he'd crashed into the clearing to find her, so fucking gorgeous with her head thrown back, taking pleasure from Lan and Cooper, he'd felt dizzy with shock. He'd stood there and watched as she'd given herself to them, and his blood had boiled with betrayal. Terrible accusations had spewed from his mouth. On the way back to base camp, he'd cursed. This wasn't her fault, or Coop and Lan's.

It was his own.

While on top of him, Lan had allowed Alea the control she'd undoubtedly needed. His buddies could be gentle with Alea. They could treat her right. They didn't have perverse needs.

They were better for her than he was.

Cooper and Landon hadn't been kicked out of the military. Oh, Dane had been allowed to leave of his own accord, but everyone knew he'd been a hairsbreadth away from a court martial. Alea deserved an honorable lover, and he wasn't that.

He didn't have a family anymore. They'd all turned their backs on him. He didn't have wealth or even much of a future. When he really thought about it, he didn't have a whole fucking lot to offer her. He scrubbed a hand through his hair. He should have kept it together, but no, he'd said some terrible things because he'd felt so damn inadequate in that moment. He'd just known that she'd waited until he was gone and she was alone with Lan and Coop to make love.

He sank down into the sand, his head in his hands. He'd walked into that little piece of paradise and he'd turned into a kid again. He'd been eight fucking years old and his brothers had been taking what he wanted just because they could, so he'd lashed out. How pathetic was he?

"Dane?" A soft voice pulled him out of his misery.

Alea stood looking at him. She was wearing Cooper's T-shirt, her golden legs bare and her feet sinking into the sand. He'd expected to see rage on that gorgeous face, but she was looking down at him with doe eyes.

And all he could do was beg for forgiveness. "I am so sorry."

She sniffled a little before sinking into the sand next to him. "At first I was going to throw things at you like a warrior princess. I think I'd better leave the battling to you guys because all the enemy has to do is look sad and I give up."

Her heart would always be too soft for real war. She proved it by sliding her arm against his. He was willing to take any warmth she would give.

"I jumped to conclusions and said things…" Dane sighed. "I was a complete ass."

She nodded slowly. "You were. We weren't trying to shut you out. I know that's what you think. But for once in my life, I was in the moment. So much of my life is planned out for me—schedules, appearances, even my meals. I didn't want this to be planned, too, Dane. I was swimming with nature, basking in the sun…and I felt so free. I wanted to keep that feeling. I wanted to share it."

She hadn't done anything wrong. He kissed the top of her head, loving how she opened up to him. He'd been the one to fuck up, yet she was still here with him, offering his dumb ass comfort. "I want that for you, too, Lea."

She pulled back slightly so she could look up at him. Her gorgeous face was so grave, he would have done just about anything to get the softness back. "Are you sure you want this kind of relationship?"

He hadn't in the beginning. At all. "I wasn't taught to share, Alea. But, yes, I want this. I screwed up today. I can only say I'm sorry and it won't happen again."

"How can you be sure? Dane, I know about your wife."

"She's not my wife." He couldn't even stand to think about her now.

"Your ex-wife. She left you for your brother, right?"

"My brother turned out to be the better bet. And he didn't need to tie her up to get off."

"You needed to tie her up?" Alea frowned. "I mean, like always?"

She sounded daunted by the prospect. "No. Not always, but toward the end I realized I wasn't in love with her, so sex became a game. There was no making love in that relationship. There was an exchange of goods and services.

When I got cut off from the family money, she found another way to tap into it."

"I can't make up for what she did to you. But this is the kind of relationship where jealousy just can't have a place."

"I wasn't asking you to make up for what happened to me." Was he?

"I can't fix what she did, either. Dane, I believe this relationship can work, but not if you're going to make me choose. I grew up differently than you. I know this will require a shift in your thinking, but I'm crazy about all three of you. My aunt and uncles were so happy, and I want that for myself. I want that for us. But it can't work if you don't believe that I'll care for you all wholly and equally."

"I've done everything I know to make this work." The accusation stung. He'd been the one to bring them all together. He'd been the one to pull Lan out of his damn shell and to soothe Coop's doubts. He'd been the one to get Alea talking. Sure she didn't like discussing her abduction, but she at least opened up about how she felt now.

For his effort, he should have had her first.

Goddamn it. She was right. Dane cursed. He wasn't looking at this from a "family" point of view. He'd been selfish and dumb and he'd ruined it for her. He'd been the one to tell her to go with the fucking flow. He'd just been sure the flow would bring her straight to him.

He had forced all of them to try to face their demons, but he hadn't even started to face his own.

There was a part of him that wanted to slink away. He could go to the other side of the island and not have to deal with any of this shit. He could be alone. It was what he deserved, but was it what she deserved?

What she deserved was a man who was fucking brave enough to tell her the truth. He hid behind his Dom role so often that he forgot she needed a place in this family, too and not just the one on her back. She wasn't a blow up doll they were going to pass around. If he wanted to know her, really know her, he had to let her know him, too.

Families were so fucking scary. His own had let him down. He would rather face down ten guns than risk heartache again. Unfortunately, when he forced himself to acknowledge the truth, he couldn't deny that he yearned for a family more than anything. He wanted *this* family—Alea and these brothers.

"You have," she agreed. "But…"

"But I'm having a hard time trusting it."

"Explain that. Make me understand." She turned her face up, those dark eyes full of sympathy.

Dane knew a whole lot of his friends would have backed off then and there, sympathy equaling pity in their heads, but Dane took it for what it was, an offering from a deeply kind and loving woman. He hadn't known a hell of a lot of love and kindness in his life. He latched on to it now, taking her hand in his and holding on for dear life. The man his father had created wanted to pick up his shit and run to the other side of the island and let bitterness be his only friend, but Dane knew that would make him miserable. Instead, he was going to be the man Alea needed, the kind who embraced happiness. It was a gamble, and if he lost, well…at least he'd have the consolation of knowing he'd given it his all.

"The whole family thing. I think that's why I tried to be the one in control of all of it. If you all needed me, then you wouldn't get rid of me."

She leaned closer, her skin warm against his, and he felt all the ice in his chest starting to melt. He'd tried to put her in this very position, to need him, but fuck, he needed her.

"I would never get rid of you, Dane. Why would you think that?"

At her sweet words, he relaxed a little, shocked by just how nice it was to talk. "Besides the fact that you've been trying to fire me since I got hired?"

"I'm awfully glad I didn't succeed." She pressed against him, their hips touching, her arm through his, then she looked up at him for a long moment. "Tell me. It's about more than just your ex, isn't it?"

Her perceptive question stunned him, but the beauty of this place and the intimacy of sitting beside her settled him. He'd sat with lots of women, had plenty of lovers, but somehow Alea made him breathe easy. Something about sitting with limbs entwined, the sound of the surf rolling on, brought up a deep well of peace in him. And that made it so much easier for him to talk. He'd thought he would never discuss Kelly with Alea, but she needed to understand. And he was shocked at how good it felt to let go and tell her about his damage.

"It's not just her, baby. It's my whole life. My dad was a military man. He believed in running his household like a war camp. He was a Darwinist of the highest order."

"Survival of the fittest?"

"Yep. He thought getting the shit kicked out of me on a regular basis would make me a man. He didn't hit me himself, just didn't really stop it when my older brothers did. And yet I still tried to please him, tried to keep up with my brothers. I got married because she was beautiful and my dad liked her. Said she'd make a fine military wife. I didn't love her. I thought I did, but I didn't even know who the hell I was. How could I love her? And then the long deployments started, and my team was shipped to Afghanistan."

"They kicked you out because of what happened in the Korengal Valley, didn't they?"

He turned to her, a little startled. "How do you know about that? It's supposed to be classified."

There was not an ounce of shame on her face. "I snuck into Tal's office and read your files. He has a very good relationship with the US. They sent him over a lot of stuff on the three of you that no one should know. You did the right thing, Dane. That CIA agent was an asshole."

"He was covering his own ass. Things didn't go down the way they should have. We were working on faulty intel, but make no mistake, Lea. I knew what I was doing and I knew I would be out. I made the decision to get those civilians out of the line of fire thereby blowing an undercover op."

"You saved them," Alea said, her cheek against his arm. "I think it makes you a hero."

"And I blew a multi-million dollar op. When I flew home, I expected my wife to be waiting to drive me home from the airport. I knew it was going to be a rough conversation, but I didn't even get to say a word. She wasn't there. I got served with divorce papers the minute I stepped off the plane. They were right there in an envelope with a note from my father disowning me and a key to the storage place where they'd shoved all my worldly possessions."

Cooper had been standing next to him. He'd been ready to board a plane for Denver to get back home, but he'd stayed with Dane. And eventually they had found Landon, then made it to Bezakistan, to Alea.

To this island where he just might finally get the family he deserved if he wasn't an insecure prick.

"I want this so badly, but I'm afraid I can't be what you need." There it was, all out there for the world to see.

She moved, shifting away from him. He thought for a moment that she would leave, but she cupped his face as she moved, positioning herself between his legs. "Take it easy on me. Let's go slow and see where it's heading, Sir."

Sir? The word caused his cock to tighten. "No, Lea. It's okay. I'm going to shelve that shit."

He could do it for her. He wasn't sure if he could be as passive as Lan had been, but he could try.

"It's not shit, Dane. It's what you need. You were out of control all your life. I can see that. Even when you were grown, you were still at the mercy of everyone else. You need one place where you have complete and utter control, and I trust you to take care of me."

"And you need control, too." That was the problem with

their relationship, the basic, never ending, no-solution-at-all problem. They were both damaged, and he wasn't sure how to fix it.

She frowned at him. "Not like you mean. It's different for me. I didn't grow up scared the way you did. I had a great family. The sex stuff is hard for me, but being here has given me a lot of time to think. You said that how I eventually dealt with this would be the measure of what kind of woman I am."

He remembered it like it was yesterday. He'd been standing in the background watching Alea with Piper on the evening she became the future queen. Alea had thrown a bunch of bile his way, and Piper hadn't understood. "I said those things to Piper. You had stomped off in a blaze of rage and sequins."

A little smile curled her mouth up. "I didn't stomp very far. I listened."

"You eavesdropped." *Little minx.*

"Another lesson from my childhood. Dane, I listened in on a lot of things. Why do you think I was always in the garden or the hall or wherever the three of you happened to be? Because I couldn't let myself believe you wanted me and I couldn't really convince myself that I didn't want you. I didn't choose Landon. I went with the flow and made love with my men. This is the way of life in my world. I can't set up a schedule. I can only promise that I need each of you."

He didn't want a schedule. God, not at all. "I guess I'm wondering why you need me. Landon is like your knight in shining armor. Cooper makes you laugh. I just seem to make you mad."

"You make me think. You make me get off my ass and fight. I'm not dumb, Dane. You've been topping me from the minute we landed on this island. Oh, you put it in questions and circle it all back around so it sounds like it's my idea, but I know what you're doing and I need it. I think it's what I've been missing for a very long time. I know I've pushed a lot of people away and made it hard to help me, but you've found a way to do it. If you want something to shelve, make it the jealousy."

His cock stirred because that last line had been said with a tone of perfectly intended brattiness. She knew exactly how to provoke him.

"I'll always be possessive." It was his nature. No amount of beat downs by his brothers had taken that away from him. He'd just gotten good at hiding what he wanted to keep and he'd gotten really fucking good at fighting dirty. But he didn't have to with Lan and Coop. "Did they send you here?"

"I came myself. To fight the good fight, so to speak. Do you understand what we could be?"

Dane nodded. He understood and deeply desired it. "I was an ass. Forgive me."

"Make me."

He felt his whole body go on alert. "Do you know what you're asking for?

"I know what I'm willing to try. Go easy on me, Sir. Landon was really big and I'm a little sore, but I want you. I want to…play."

A haze of lust seemed to envelope him. Yeah, he could play. He could play hard and rough, but he had to be careful. "I can handle it, Lea. I'll get the lube. I'll go easy on you."

She stopped, frowned. "We have lube?"

Of course. He was a Boy Scout. He'd had plans that had involved a metric shit ton of lubricant. "Yeah, baby. I'm prepared."

Her eyes narrowed. "The waves took the condoms but not the lube?"

Fuck. He was the one who had to explain this? "Baby, the waves only took one bag. The lube was in a different duffel." And thank god Lan had made the right call. The lube was way more important. "If it makes you feel better, he also sacrificed my favorite pair of nipple clamps which are now at the bottom of the sea."

Her whole face flushed, but the sweetest smile came over her lips. "We have to talk about your priorities, Dane. Condoms are more important than lubricant."

"You're wrong." She'd just given him an all-access pass, and he was fucking taking it. "I want you pregnant. I want to fill you up because you're my female and I want the family only you can give me."

He dreamed about her round and soft and full of their baby. His children would have such a different experience. They would know love and peace and joy. They would have four parents to protect them. He wanted this life. He wanted to know that if anything happened to him, his precious wife and their offspring would still be loved and protected by his brothers—brothers who would never take from him, but simply enhance his life, be by his side no matter what. He'd been dealt a shitty hand in the past, but this time he'd come up aces.

"I want that, too," Alea said quietly. "I thought I would be married by now. I thought I would already have my husbands and I would have kids. I never wanted to wait. I wanted my happy ending"

"Your husbands are right here, Alea."

Tears pooled in her eyes. "You don't know everything."

He shook his head. "I know everything I need to know, baby. I love you."

"Right here and right now, I believe it. I don't know that I want to leave this island. It feels like a dream. I don't want to wake up."

They would get rescued. He knew it deep down inside or he wouldn't risk getting her pregnant. He had faith. But nothing had to change. "You're safe with us." The "us" came easy now. And so did something else. "Take off that shirt. Show me your breasts."

She hesitated, but just for a moment, then her hands went to the edge of Cooper's navy-blue shirt and she started to pull it up, revealing inch after inch of gloriously golden flesh. Her knees. Her thighs. He held his fucking breath as he caught sight of her pussy. She was smooth and golden there, too, with just a flush of pink to show that she'd recently taken a cock. She'd given up her virginity and moved forward, taking another step in her healing.

"Keep going. I want to see everything."

She pulled the shirt up, her belly button coming into view. He loved her roundness and the way her belly sloped into her hips. So graceful. That was Alea. The bottoms of her breasts showed beneath the hem of the shirt, and his cock sprang up long and thick, tenting his sweats. The fucker seemed to be pointing her way.

Nipples. Hers were sun-kissed brown, and he couldn't wait to get his mouth on them. But he had control. He needed to have control. For her. For him.

He sat back, aware of every cell in his body coming to life for her as she held the shirt in her hand. "Toss it away and tell me about it."

"It?"

Like she didn't know what he meant. "I want to know how it felt to be with my brothers."

He loved the way she blushed. "It was nice."

"Oh, that won't do. Tell me how it felt and I don't want you to use the word nice. Landon isn't exactly a small boy." He shrugged a little, moving his hips to give his cock more room. This was right where he wanted to be. In control. "You live with a guy long enough, you end up seeing more than you'd think or want. It's not like Coop's tiny, either. Tell me what you did to them."

She sat back on her heels, her knees together. "I don't know if I can talk about this. Can't you just kiss me?"

He felt his eyebrow arch. She didn't understand the word submission, but she would. "I could spank you. It's your choice."

He loved the way she flushed and her mouth made that perfect little *O*. "You want to spank me?"

It was said with a breathy little huff that lifted his hopes. She wasn't disinterested. "I would kill to spank that ass. I dream about it. I want to get that skin just the perfect shade of pink. Come on, baby, give me a reason to put the flat of my hand on your ass."

"I gave Cooper a hand job. I don't know why they call it that. It didn't feel like a job." She spoke way too fast, her words tripping over each other as she flushed.

"Did you like it, you little vixen?" He hoped she did because he wanted to feel her hand and her mouth on his own cock as soon as possible.

The sweetest smile crossed her face. Fuck, she was beautiful. "I wasn't sure I would, but I liked the way he pulsed in my hand."

His cock twitched, his whole body relaxing as he realized she was going to give him everything he needed. She wasn't running away. She'd come after him, despite his idiotic outbreak. She was smart, his girl. She'd fought for what they all needed, and they needed that kind of courage in a wife. "Did he fill you up?"

"Yes. I could barely get my hand all the way around it."

Alea's voice went husky, and he could tell the moment she became comfortable. Besides the deepening of her tone, her body relaxed, her knees spreading wide as though she didn't realize that she opened her pussy wide and lovely. Damn, he needed a camera because that sight needed to be preserved.

"You must have done it right. He looked happy."

"I tried to make sure he enjoyed it, but I had never done it before."

He reached out for her because the insecurity that slipped into her words hit his heart as hard as it hit his cock. He got to his knees and brushed his lips across hers. "I'm sure you were perfect, Lea. You couldn't be anything but. I have no doubt Cooper loved it."

"I did," a masculine voice said.

His brother was here. A feeling of deep rightness flowed over him, and he knew that not only could he handle this—he wanted it. He glanced behind him and saw Coop and Landon waiting there. Cooper had gotten dressed again, but Lea had stolen his shirt. Lan was in his boxers. Damn. If they were here much longer, they would all be nudists.

Alea looked over and her hand almost went for the shirt. "Maybe you guys should go."

Dane reached out and grabbed the garment, dragging it away from her. No way was he giving this up. "Cooper, tell her how much you liked her hand on your cock. Lan, could you please grab the lube? I think we need to start preparing our woman to take all of us."

Lan practically ran toward the luggage.

And Cooper sank into the sand beside him, his eyes on their very naked woman. "I loved it. I can't stop thinking about it. You were amazing, baby. And I think you should suck Dane's cock while Lan and I start your prep."

Oh, his brothers knew just what to do.

"Come here, Lea." His voice had gone super deep. Dom voice. *Fuck.* He wasn't ever going to use that voice on any woman but her again. She was the end, the final win. He relaxed back against the log they'd dragged into camp that first night. He spread his legs wide so she had a place to plant that gorgeous body.

She crawled forward. Every sensuous move made his cock jerk. His body felt deliciously heavy.

"Yes, Sir?" Her breasts swayed as she moved on all fours. *Fuck. Fuck!* He was lucky he wasn't coming just from the sight of her. Her nipples were hard and pointing down. She looked toward him, those full lips of hers glistening wet as her tongue darted out, sliding across her bee-stung lips.

"Take my cock out." He could barely speak. His dick ached to jump out of his pants and lurch toward her.

She got to her knees, those breasts settling in and looking so fine he couldn't help but smile. He spread his legs out as her hands moved to his waistband. He was damn happy he'd gone commando. It left one less layer between them. He pushed his hips up as she dragged his pants down. His cock bobbed free, a sense of deep relief flowing through him.

"Kiss it." He didn't measure his voice. She could handle it. He would need to go slow when it came to holding her down, but she didn't have a problem with commands. His girl would just refuse any order she wasn't ready for. Everything else was play, just fun and relaxation. Anything serious they would work through, and that gave him comfort.

It was funny. He'd topped women for a long time, the trust seeming to flow one way, and now he realized what he'd been missing. Trust should flow both ways. He trusted Alea to tell him what didn't work for her. He trusted her to know what she needed when it came to sex so he didn't have to worry if this was all weighted toward him. He was a service top, a Dom who needed to give pleasure and satisfaction to his submissive. Alea would never accept less. She was his perfect partner.

A little grin lit her face as she leaned forward, letting him know she wanted to play as much as he did. And then her lips connected with the head of his cock, and he stopped thinking about anything at all. Well, beyond how hot her mouth was. Her little pink tongue darted out, laving the sensitive head.

"Lick me." Today would be just a small taste. Eventually he'd give her a full meal, but not this time. He wanted to get inside her. Needed it like he needed his next fucking breath.

She leaned back down, showing him the graceful arc of her spine and the way the sun kissed her silky skin and brought out the shades of her hair. She fascinated him. And she had him moaning as she ran her tongue over the slit.

Her tongue moved over his cock, rubbing and nuzzling and lighting him up. She explored freely, trying to map his every hill and valley, line and groove. There was nothing fast and hard about the way she sucked a cock. It wasn't done to get him off in the quickest way possible. Alea loved his cock, lavished it with affection, took her time as she licked around the head and ran her lips across the vein on the underside. He watched her, giving up control for a moment because seeing her find her power was a magical thing.

"God, that is beautiful." Landon was watching intently on his knees in the sand beside them. Cooper stared, too.

It *was* beautiful. Dane closed his eyes, letting the moment roll over him. He wanted to memorize every second. The breeze from the ocean, the softness of the blanket under them, a barrier to the ever-present sand, the way her hair tickled across his thighs. The soft sound of her mouth suckling him.

The knowledge that he wasn't alone, would never be alone again, filled him. He had his wife and his brothers.

He opened his eyes, and Alea stared up him with languid, dark eyes, even as her tongue ran his length.

"You are so perfect." He reached out and stroked her hair, worshipping her as she worshipped him.

Landon watched, but his gaze met with Dane's, a question lurking there. He was asking if he could join in.

"Let's start getting our girl ready for us."

A smile split Lan's face, making him look happier than Dane could remember.

"I'll help with that, too," Cooper promised with a laugh as they positioned themselves around Alea.

Her head came up. "Prepare me for what?"

He narrowed his eyes and pointed back to his erection. "We'll prepare you for a spanking if you don't get that sweet mouth back where it's supposed to be."

She frowned, but it was a flirty thing. "Bossy."

"That's right, baby," he groaned as she put her mouth all over him again. He was the boss and that was just how he wanted this to be. Dane relaxed and shifted his hips up. "Play with my balls, Lea. And get that gorgeous ass in the air."

It was time to get her ready. It was time to share with his brothers.

Chapter Eleven

Alea loved the way Dane tasted. She loved the soft velvet of his cock under her tongue. She definitely loved the way he moaned. Oh, it was a completely controlled, utterly masculine moan, but it came from deep in his chest, a definite sign that he loved this, too.

He was giving her orders, but she felt her power.

"I told you to play with my balls, baby. Do we need to have a discussion about the word obedience?" The question came out on a sexy growl.

She looked up his perfectly cut body, and he stared down at her with those blue eyes. So often they reminded her of a frigid lake, but there was nothing cold about them now. Though his voice was perfectly controlled, his eyes told a different tale. They were hot, a little desperate.

He wanted her. She could feel it. And it wasn't that he wanted any woman. He wanted *her*. He'd waited for her.

Alea didn't understand it, but she wasn't about to turn him down. And she wasn't going to push him to spank her when she was more than curious to play with his balls. She let her hand run down the length of his cock, skimming the bulbous head. *Fascinating.* She loved watching the way it twitched and moved as though following her fingers as she felt her way down to the heavy sac that rested below his cock.

Big and round, the globes had been groomed at some point. The men had managed to find razors and though Dane was letting a sexy beard shape his face, he'd taken care of himself down under. His balls were smooth, like twin plums hanging from the hottest tree. As she watched, they tightened, pulling up closer to his body.

There was a neat line of flesh dividing the two sacs, and Alea outlined it with her fingertip, watching the way he reacted. He gave a sharp intake of breath, and his thighs tightened as though he was holding himself in rigid check.

"Does that hurt?" Alea asked.

"Hell, no." Dane's face was rock hard, his jaw a sharp line as he ground the words out. "It's perfect."

She cupped them, secure that it was all right to continue. She could hear Landon moving behind her and Cooper was suddenly at her side, his hand smoothing up her back. Her men were with her.

Alea rolled his testicles. They were so big, they couldn't quite fit in the palm of her hand, but she caressed them, closing her hand gently, squeezing just a little. She palmed them and leaned back to take the head of his cock back in her mouth again. It slid in just behind her teeth, and she sucked him, loving the salty taste on her tongue.

"God, that's so good, baby." Dane's hand found her hair, an encouraging gesture. He settled his fingers in the strands and helped her keep the rhythm.

Over and over. Around with her tongue. There was a peace and serenity in serving him in this fashion, a music they were making together. It wasn't dirty. She wanted to give, and he gratefully accepted. The act was beautiful. Oh, it could be made dirty. She'd seen that up close and personal, but it didn't have to be. Sex, Alea realized, was different for everyone. It could only be judged by the motivations and emotions behind it. She wanted to please her partners, and her men were careful about pleasing her.

They were in love.

A hand cupped the cheeks of her ass, and Landon's voice rumbled along her skin. "Our girl seems to like the hell out of sucking cock, Dane."

"She does it beautifully," Cooper responded.

"Peace to that, brother." Dane let out a long breath.

"She's the best head of my life."

Alea felt her skin practically glowing. She knew they merely said all this to infuse her with confidence, but it worked anyway.

"I think we should challenge her a little bit," Dane said. "She's damn straight perfect at sucking a cock when she doesn't have a distraction."

"I can give her a distraction or two." Landon chuckled.

"I can help." Cooper's voice was filled with sexy male arrogance.

Alea wasn't sure what they meant by distractions, but refused to worry. Instead, she settled back to her task. She wanted to see if she could make him lose that vaunted control of his and fill her mouth.

Then she felt Cooper plucking at her nipples, pulling a hard gasp from her throat. Coop's fingers rolled the nubs with practiced ease, then pinched down. The sharp pain sent pure sensation through her body. Her nipples seemed to have a direct line to her pussy. Yes. That was very distracting.

"Landon, she's stopped. Could you please help me?" Dane asked, his hand tightening on her hair.

She heard the smack to her backside before she actually felt it. The slap cracked through the air, an oddly sultry sound, before her skin flared as she felt the sensation sink in. Lan kept his hand where it was as though trying to soothe the place he'd just hit.

Her breath hitched because that had not been what she was expecting at all. *Wow.* Yes, there had been pain, but then it flared to a shimmering heat. The sensations were deeply erotic.

"Again, Lan. She hasn't gotten the message," Dane said.

Quicker than she could prepare herself, the slap found her other cheek, and Cooper pinched down hard on her nipples as though this was a symphony he and Lan had practiced and perfected. Alea moaned.

"I don't think she cares about the message," Lan said in

a Texas drawl. "I think our girl likes to be spanked. Her pussy is wet as hell. I can see it glistening, and damn, she smells good."

"Lea, love," Dane said in a deeply patient voice. "You need to take care of me. If you don't, we'll stop and have a full spanking. But if you manage to continue, Cooper and Lan here are going to play with you. They want to give you orgasms, but they'll only do it while you're sucking me."

Orgasms. She'd kind of thought they were a myth until she'd given herself over to these men. Now she was greedy for them, her whole body softening at the prospect of another.

She leaned over once more and sucked Dane's cock into her mouth, pulling him inside inch by delicious inch. She had to work to take him all, forcing her jaw wide so she could fit him deep. She loved working her lips open, pushing down on him as she tried to get his whole hot shaft in her mouth, the pressure threatening to make her blink. Then the deep breath of relief as she worked back up his cock, her jaw loosening and her tongue swirling all around him. Over and over. Catch and release.

She settled back into her rhythm, the hands on her breasts just another part of the music she made.

Then Lan's fingers slipped inside her pussy. One, at first, and then two. He didn't linger inside, but scissored and stretched her, as though massaging the nagging little ache that had taken up residence after his possession.

She wasn't thinking about anything like soreness now, just about how she was going to get him to give her a third finger. She wasn't full enough. Her mouth was lovingly full of Dane, but her pussy wasn't. Landon had given her his big cock, and now she couldn't handle anything less.

Cooper's fingers continued to pluck the sensitive tips of her breasts, squeezing and nipping her in perfect time.

She sucked at Dane, trying to keep her attention on his cock as Lan pulled out. She could feel Dane's cock swell in her mouth, his hips starting to move.

"Stop." Dane pulled gently on her hair.

Alea didn't want to stop. She wanted to keep going until he'd filled her mouth, but he was insistent.

"I'm too close," he explained. "And I want to be in your pussy the first time I come with you. I want to feel that tight cunt of yours gripping me as I get off."

He moved back, getting to his knees and moving away. "Landon, let's get started."

Started? It felt like they'd finished, and she couldn't stand the thought. Even though she'd made love with Landon and Cooper not thirty minutes before, she needed Dane to fill her.

"This is going to be a little cold, baby," Dane warned.

Something liquid and chilly slid between her ass cheeks. She couldn't help the gasp that came from her chest. "What are you doing?"

She had a suspicion.

"I told you. We're preparing you," Dane said, as someone pulled her cheeks apart.

"Preparing me?" She'd known deep down they would want this, but already? Now?

Dane's chuckle played along her spine as he kissed her right at the small of her back. "Yes, Lea. I'm prepping you to take all of us. I won't accept less, and you shouldn't either. One of us will fill your pussy, another one your mouth. Then the last one will squeeze into your sinful ass. We'll share you. Eventually, you'll take all of us in every way. Do you understand what the word sharing means, baby?"

If she hadn't before, she did now. Dane's words painted her a vivid mental picture. Now she understood what Piper meant when she talked about being sore in triplicate.

"Maybe we should talk about this," Alea said, trying to turn back to see them.

A loud smack cracked through the air, and she was gasping. Two smacks. Three. Dane kept it up, smacking her ass over and over until she'd counted to ten. Tears pricked her eyes, but by the fourth slap of his hand against her, she felt the sweet heat sinking in and making her shiver with need.

"We're not talking, Lea," Dane said, a deep command in his voice. "We're preparing."

Cooper leaned close to her ear, his tongue sliding over the shell. "You can always say stop, but god, your skin is so pretty all pink. I like watching you get spanked and I'm going to like watching you get plugged."

"Plugged?"

Cooper smiled, his gorgeous face coming into view. He took Dane's place, but leaned toward her, pressing their lips together. "It's a nice little plug. Pink. We bought it for you."

"Landon saved the anal plug, but not the condoms?" They needed to talk about Lan's priorities.

A hand slid up her spine as she felt a firm pressure against her anus. Oh, god. They were touching her there. She'd never been touched there. She shivered at the forbidden feeling. Pressure built, a jangly pleasure-pain shocking her system.

"The plug set was in another case, along with the lube and the whip. But the nipple clamps are gone. I mourn them." Cooper kissed her again. "We bought everything special for you. Tal has this guy."

She could just bet. Her cousin was a pervert of the first order. She could imagine that Tal had a Royal Toy Maker on staff. It had likely been very easy for her boys to make an appointment. "You brought all this stuff with you?"

Dane sent her a low chuckle. "We had to hurry. We thought we'd have weeks to start to get you into the right mode of thinking, but then we found out about your little getaway and we hauled ass to kit up."

The pressure was starting to get to her. No pain. Not at all. Just an oddly intimate sensation as someone pressed something against the rosette of her ass. She tried to concentrate on their words. Kit up. Most people would just pack things like clothes and toiletries, but not her guys. No. They had to make sure they had all the finest sexual aids. "So you picked out a butt plug for me?"

Not exactly the gift she'd thought she'd get.

"Not just one. We picked out a whole set," Cooper explained. "And right now they're not using the plug. Landon is using his finger. He lubed up his finger and he's stretching you."

"You're so fucking gorgeous, Lea," Lan ground out.

He was rimming her, pressing in and circling her untried hole, tempting her to open up for him.

"Lea, we want to share you. Totally. Without reservations. We want to be inside you, all of us at the same time." Dane's voice was a dark seduction. She felt a strong palm run down her spine. "Relax. Let us in. We're going to get in. We're going to take this ass the same way we take your pussy and your mouth—thoroughly and completely. We'll prep you, baby. You'll be ready for us."

All three of them at the same time. She would be totally surrounded, utterly protected by her men.

She closed her eyes and eased back as Landon's finger pressed in. Her eyes watered, the pressure just on the edge of pain, but so erotic. She could feel herself clenching. She could feel their stares on her, caressing every inch of her exposed skin.

A smack to her ass made her moan.

"Don't you try to keep him out," Dane growled. "You let him inside."

"Relax." Cooper kissed her again, his tongue playing against hers. "Open for him. You'll like it in the end. Take a deep breath and flatten your back."

The pressure was killing her, and not from pain. She was so aware of everything. They were forcing her out of a place where she thought and worried and into a place where she simply felt.

She breathed in, the sweetly salty air filling her lungs as she obeyed. She flattened her back, forcing her spine down. She felt the moment Lan's finger slipped inside her ass.

Now that was an intimate sensation.

"Fuck, darlin'. You are so tight. Damn, you can barely take my pinkie, but one day, this gorgeous ass is going to be split wide by my cock."

She had to concentrate on breathing, the sensation was a little shocking, and she whimpered, trying to get used to the invasion.

"You're doing good, baby," Cooper encouraged her, his lips on the nape of her neck.

"She's doing perfectly," Dane agreed. "Alea, are you in pain, baby? This isn't supposed to be painful. There will be a little discomfort until you're used to it."

"How would you know?" She snapped the question at him.

And he slapped her ass again—with Lan's finger in there. She gasped at the sensation.

Dane was suddenly right next to her, his body towering overs her even though he was on his knees. "I know because I trained for this. Dominance and submission is serious, Lea. Sex isn't something I do and then forget about. I won't ever put you in danger."

The sharp set of his face left her no doubt that he was being honest. He was also making himself vulnerable, even as he looked at her with those dark eyes. He was waiting for her judgment, for her to accept him—or not—as he was. A sudden joy hit her system. He was offering her his truth, and there was something beautiful about that.

She couldn't turn them away. They were in paradise. Nothing bad could happen now because she was surrounded by them. "Yes, Sir. I'll try to keep the sarcasm to a minimum, but it's very difficult to be serious when Lan is giving me a colon exam."

Dane growled, but he was smiling as he did it. "That's

another ten. Damn it, you're going to kill me."

His cock, already hard, had tightened even further as he'd promised her discipline. He was gone in a flash, proving that he really did enjoy the whole spanking thing.

"You keep up what you're doing, Lan. No need to stop because our submissive has a bratty mouth." Dane's voice was right back to smooth and deep, and she was starting to recognize that this was his Dom voice. He'd used it on her more than once when he snapped an order her way. Those orders almost always had to do with her safety. Then his tone was hard, unrelenting, but the same unmistakable air of command was there. But this was sexy Dom, whose rough edges softened marginally as if he lived for this type of command.

She groaned as the pressure in her ass increased. Another finger. God, he was stretching her, opening her up, and all she could do was try to stay on her knees.

It soon became harder because Dane's hand found her cheek, connecting and making her howl.

Shit. It hurt and it made her eyes water, but she wanted more. She could feel Cooper's hand soothing over the skin of her back, a perfect contrast to the sharp sting of the smacks. Dane settled in and Landon kept up the pressure, scissoring his fingers deep inside, pulling out and pushing in while Dane lit her up from the outside. Over and over. It seemed to take forever, yet it was over before she'd really drawn a deep breath. Tears squeezed from her eyes, but they felt good, clean, uncompromised. She laughed a little on a breath as she steadied herself.

"Hey, you okay?" Cooper asked, reaching up and touching those tears.

She smiled at him, feeling so strong even as her knees were weak. "I can take it."

The words were a revelation. She could take it. She could take them. She didn't want to go hide somewhere or just get through the next few minutes so maybe someone would hold her. She wanted to take that dumb plug and then she wanted Dane to mount her and give her the orgasm she needed.

She felt more feminine and powerful than she'd ever felt before. Kneeling in the sand, submitting to these men showed her strength.

"I know you can." Dane's voice floated over her, the anchor she needed to keep herself grounded. "I've always known you could. You're my girl."

"You're our girl," Lan corrected.

"Ours." She could practically hear the smile in Dane's voice. "And it's time for her to take this plug because I don't want to wait weeks to share her. I want to get in her ass as soon as possible."

There was her dirty Dom.

Alea winced a little as she felt Lan's fingers leaving her and he moved out from behind her. She clenched as though trying to get that feeling back, but there was already something pressing at her. Dane had taken Lan's place, and he pushed the plug right against her tight hole.

"I'm going to get cleaned up. I get the feeling this is going to be a nice long day." Lan got on his knees and leaned over, his lips touching her head sweetly. "Be right back, baby. You take everything he gives you. I want to watch."

"Fuck, I'm already watching." She turned and saw Cooper had gotten rid of those confining shorts of his. She'd never thought a cock could be gorgeous, but her men had lovely ones. Cooper ran his hand along his thick stalk as his eyes trailed back. "You know how beautiful you are?"

She felt beautiful when they were around. "I want to watch, too."

She wanted to watch Cooper stroke himself while she submitted to Dane.

"Watch all you like, baby." He sat back and spread his legs wide, stroking himself, his cock growing bigger and harder with every pass of his hand.

"There we go," Dane said as the plug slid home, invading and stretching, taking up all the space. "You're going to wear that for a while. And you're going to wear me, too."

She felt Dane's big hands on her hips, pulling her back, and then he was fondling her breasts as she felt his cock rooting at her pussy.

Yes, this was what she'd needed from the moment their fight had begun. She'd needed to take him inside, to know he was with her. She felt him pulling at her nipples as though trying to get her ready, but the minute his cock had touched her, she'd softened. "Please, Sir. Dane. Please."

His hands seemed to be everywhere, running along her every curve, worshipping her. She wanted to be able to see him as he filled her up, but even as she thought about it, she knew she wasn't ready to lie underneath him. He was giving her what she needed, how she needed it, and he was sharing the experience with his brother.

Cooper smiled her way even as he moved closer, his hand never letting up on the slow stroke of his cock. "Do you know how happy you make us?"

"All of us," Dane added. "I've waited my whole fucking life for this."

She gasped as he drove his cock inside her.

So full. Oh, she was so damn full. She clenched around the plug and Dane's cock. He was so big and he'd forced himself in to the hilt, sparing her not a moment of his hard possession.

Because that was Dane. He would fight for her, die to protect her, but he needed to be in control of this moment. For the first time, she saw that it was a fair trade. The love between them didn't have to be fifty-fifty every minute of the day. There would be times when he let her have her way…and other times when he would conquer and take her however he pleased. The thought made her moan.

He held himself still for a heartbeat, his hands on her

hips, tightening as though he was afraid of losing her. "Are you all right?"

Alea winced. She'd done a number on him.

She smiled at Cooper. "Will you tell him, please?"

A brilliant grin crossed his face. "She can take you. She can take me. We already know she can take Lan. Our girl's made of strong stuff."

"Damn, what a woman." He smacked her ass, making her cry out because every nerve lit up. "You'll take me when I say. How I say. For as long as I say. Isn't that right, my pretty sub?"

Why had she ever been afraid of him? Now that she really knew this man, she heard what he meant. *You'll take me, and I'll take care of you.* "Yes, Sir. I'll take you anyway you want."

She would try anything with them.

Dane moved behind her, dragging his cock back out, just keeping the tip in before diving back deep. "Move with me."

He was letting her off the leash, and she gave him everything she had. She slammed back toward him, fighting to keep him inside, then shifted to start the process again. Over and over, she slammed against him, his cock pushing up, filling her until she thought she would burst, but she fought for her pleasure, fought for this feeling of oneness with him. She lost herself in the sun and the sand and her men.

She heard Dane groaning as he shifted up and hit that miraculous place deep inside her and sent her flying. Her vision seemed to dim briefly as the orgasm propelled her into a white-hot realm of pleasure.

Dane pulled her body up, her length against his as he groaned and pumped his orgasm into her body. "Our woman."

He turned her head to his as his cock slipped out of her, his lips taking hers, each moment progressively more gentle than the last. Her body hummed, her blood pumping through her system. She kissed Dane again. Then she caught sight of Cooper still and watchful, his back against the log, his legs stretched in front of him. His cock strained, long and thick, just begging for her.

The old Alea would have wondered if he simply didn't want her, even in the face of massive evidence to the contrary, but the dark doubt that had been with her since the day she'd been taken had finally begun to fade. The very act of loving her men seemed to have turned down the volume on those voices in her head. She heard different voices all of the sudden, *their* voices telling her that she was beautiful and sexy and worthy.

She didn't hesitate, didn't feel self-conscious. She felt…new, free. She moved to Cooper, her body sensuous and alive.

Cooper shook his head. "Lea, baby, you've got to be sore."

Even as he said the words, she could see how his cock pulsed with need, the purple head weeping.

She was sore, but it was a delicious ache. "I need you, too."

Dane and Lan were suddenly on either side of her, helping to settle her on Cooper's lap.

"We have to face facts," Lan said with a smile. "We've created a monster."

For once, Cooper didn't get the joke. He tensed under her, his cock beneath her pussy, still long and thick and begging. "Please, Lea. I'm dying to be inside you."

She groaned with pleasure as she lowered herself, and Cooper's cock began to penetrate. Each of her men were so different, and all so good. Cooper's cock was thick and seemed to almost immediately find that special place deep inside her. She'd been so sure she couldn't possibly come again, but as Cooper gripped her hips and thrust up, she felt the stir of orgasm teasing along her skin.

"Lea," Cooper's voice was breathless. His hips never

stopped their rolling movement. "You're so beautiful, baby. It's feels so good."

She stared at his gorgeous, masculine face, the strong jaw, the chiseled cheeks. She looked into those deep dark eyes, and the connection leapt between them, so much more than merely physical. She moved with him, their bodies finding a rhythm that was uniquely their own. Comfort and desire. She found a lovely blend with Cooper.

"You feel incredible. I'm so happy." She had to say the words because they were true. How long had it been since she'd felt this sense of joy? Perhaps never. Perhaps this was the kind of happiness that only happened when everything fell into place, when a person's puzzle was complete.

"Me, too. So happy. Oh, god, Lea." Cooper picked up the pace, his face tightening.

One deep thrust sent her over the edge, and this orgasm was the cherry on top. He called out her name again as he clutched her to him. Pleasure flooded her system as she felt Cooper's cock deep inside her. Then he came, filling her with everything he had.

Lea let her body fall against Cooper's, their chests cuddling together.

She forgot about the past. She didn't think about the future. She just let herself drift in this sweetest of moments.

* * * *

Cooper forced his head up as he watched Alea come out of the surf, her naked body revealing itself to him with every footstep she took. She brushed her hair back with a scrub of her hand and turned her face up to the sun. Just like that his cock went to full mast, come-on-baby, take-me erection.

Damn, he liked paradise.

Four weeks and five days. They had been on the island for all that time without a hint of rescue, and he was beginning to wonder if he even wanted to see a plane.

Alea looked so relaxed, so fucking full of joy. Her shoulders weren't up around her ears, and she'd just stopped wearing clothes around day fourteen. That was fine with him.

She took a long breath and looked around the beach. As she caught sight of him, a bright smile lit her face. She looked so carefree, so uninhibited. He wished he could take a picture, but the batteries on their phones had died weeks ago. But he wanted to capture her like this. He never wanted to see worry in her eyes again.

"Hey, did you check the traps?" Alea asked as she stood in the shallows, wringing out the water in her hair.

This island was like a fucking protein basket. They all looked a bit leaner, but everything here was so fresh and healthy. He felt great.

"Yep. We'll have fish for lunch and some nice roast pork for dinner. Dane's been roasting that last pig real slow for two days. When I saw him earlier, he was shoveling pineapple into the pit for flavor."

His stomach growled a little. He was pretty sure that a month into being stranded he should be begging for food, not wondering if Dane wasn't overcooking their dinner. He'd gotten picky about his wild boar.

Alea laughed and threw herself onto the sand beside him. Yep. They would be getting right back in the ocean before they headed to camp. She sighed happily and put her head on his shoulder. "I see Mr. Happy is making an appearance."

She'd named his penis, and she'd done it real damn well. His penis was happy. Fucking thrilled, in fact. "Baby, that's his permanent state around you."

He moved his arm so he could get it under her neck, cradling her properly. He had to admit, he loved the nights when all three of his brothers loved her, but he also enjoyed these long afternoons when he had her to himself. They'd taken to splitting up alone time with their girl. Nights were for the family, but afternoons were split shifts, and mornings

were all up to Alea. Whatever she wanted. If she wanted to
be alone, they allowed her the illusion that she was. One of
them was always watching her because she was the most
precious thing in the world and they weren't about to let her
drown or fall or have anything bad happen to her, but they let
her be.

Afternoons were all about relaxing, and nights were for
exploring.

Yeah, he was in no hurry to go to back to civilization.
He kind of loved island life.

She giggled, actually giggled, and turned her body into
his, one leg tangling between his, the intimacy doing strange
things to his heart. "I think you're all just permanently
aroused, but I love it."

He was glad because they were all on her at least twice a
day. He kissed her, relaxing because eventually Mr. Happy
would get what he wanted, and Cooper was damn straight
content to just lay with her for a minute or two. "I think Dane
wants to play with his flogger tonight."

Dane had built a Tropical Dungeon. He'd been busy,
using their knives and his constructed weapons to build their
shelters. Shelters. Because Dane wasn't happy with some
craptastic *Survivor* hut. No. Only the best for his former CO.
He'd managed to put together a sleeping shelter with
luxurious pillows and blankets they'd saved from the plane, a
shed for food and water storage. And he'd found a cave in
the inland that he'd tricked up so they would be comfortable
during storms. He was the MacGyver of island living.

And Lan was the provider. The dude could kill shit. He
had a freaking sixth sense when it came to hunting and
fishing. Their bellies were full every night thanks to him.

Cooper was proud to be the workhorse and the medic
and the all-around Alea whisperer. He'd once wondered what
role he could play in this family, but he'd discovered that he
was the peacekeeper. When the other two didn't know how
to talk to their woman, he was the one they turned to. They

were all way better now, but there were still points of contention.

She still wasn't ready to handle them being on top of her, and there were still plenty of acts that set her mind spinning back to her captivity.

Alea rose up to one elbow, looking down on him. Damn, but she was sweeter though. "What do you think the flogger is like? I don't know much about it. I've heard the word, but I don't really know what it means. I know sailors used to get flogged on occasion."

He had to smile. "It's not quite the same, baby."

"Is it like getting whipped?"

He didn't want her to worry. They were trying to move her slowly into the BDSM fun. "Not at all. There are a lot of different kinds of floggers, but my personal favorite is deerskin. It's soft. We can have another one made at some point. But before we would ever play around with it, we would let you touch it, get to know it. It wouldn't hurt. It's more like a massage, but it can get you into subspace."

Her gorgeous dark eyes rolled slightly. "Yeah, you guys like me there."

"Do you like it there?"

Her head came back down, resting on his chest, the sun shining down on their bodies. "You know I do. It's very relaxing. Who knew that I would find a spanking ultimately relaxing?"

But spanking hadn't exactly achieved what they wanted it to. They'd been trying to get her to open up, to talk about what had happened during her captivity. It wasn't some perverse curiosity. Until she talked about it, she couldn't really heal, couldn't move on.

Cooper wasn't dumb. This idyll in paradise was a complete break with everything she knew, everything that weighed on her and dragged her down. It was easy to throw off stress about tomorrow here because she didn't have to worry about being a princess or the press or family obligations. She could be their island lover. He got that, but they had to think about the future.

They had to think about what happened when they were back in Bezakistan. If they got back to Bezakistan.

She nuzzled his chest. "If I relax anymore I might die. You guys won't let me do anything."

"Because we love to take care of you." He rubbed his hand along her back, down to her ass. He loved her ass. She'd been wearing the plug for a couple of hours every day, going up to a bigger plug twice now. She was almost ready to take them. God, he couldn't wait. No matter how many times he'd gotten inside her, every damn time seemed like the first.

"I think it's because I ruined the conch that second night. No one will let me near the fire. I can learn, you know."

She was a horrible cook. Seriously bad. Like had a curse on her bad. "Baby, I like to cook. Don't take that away from me. Here, come give me a kiss."

She'd gotten good at fishing with Lan. He was even teaching her to throw a spear, and she'd become the freaking queen of weaving together palm fronds for their ever evolving roof, but he wasn't letting her near their food.

"Fine, but we're going to talk about this," she said, getting to her elbows and bringing her mouth close to his. He loved the husky quality of her voice. She gave in to pleasure so easily now.

But he hated the boundaries that were still between them.

He lay back, letting her take the lead when every cell in his body wanted her flat on her back with her ankles around his neck, screaming out his name.

She leaned over and kissed him, her tongue running along his bottom lip as she reached for his cock. Her small hand played with his balls, cupping them and rolling them before she stroked up his length and let her thumb swipe across the head of his cock.

Fuck, she was getting so good at that.

He brought his hands to her hair, tangling them in her damp strands and holding her mouth to his so he could settle his tongue in. This was what he loved. She softened beside him. He started to roll her on to her back. Little bits at a time. Ease her into it.

She pushed back. "No. Not like that."

Frustration started to well. It wasn't that he wouldn't take her any way she would have him. It was that she wasn't even trying to push past her fears. "Lea, baby, can we just try?"

She wrinkled her nose. "I don't like it. But you like this."

She kissed his throat, an obvious attempt to deflect the problem.

"I want to talk about it." He really did, but he adored the way her mouth was covering his skin, her hands running across his muscles.

"I want to make love."

"Lea, how are you going to take all three of us if you won't let anyone on top of you?" He forced himself to sit up, his erection complaining mightily, but this was an issue they needed to address.

She frowned, sitting up and back on her heels, that 'imperious princess' look on her face. He wondered if she'd been taught that look, the one that let everyone know she was royal and they were not. "If you aren't interested, I'll go find Lan."

"Lan wants to be on top of you, too. We all do."

She frowned, her eyes turning down. "I don't understand why."

"Because it will mean you trust us."

She softened slightly. "I do trust you."

"To a point. Talk to me. Give me part of this burden, baby. You don't have to keep everything rattling around inside you. Just start talking and let it out. It's a poison in your system until you do."

Her fists clenched and for the first time in weeks, he saw that icy persona she used to wear like armor. "You don't know what you're talking about, and I would thank you to leave it be. I don't ask you to bare your soul to me, and I would appreciate it if you would stop trying to delve into mine."

He lay back, hating that cold tone that crept into her voice. They'd made some progress with her body but not her soul. "All right, Lea. You're right. Go find Lan. I'm going to stay here for a little while, soak up some sun."

He knew when he'd hit a brick wall. He closed his eyes because he couldn't watch her walk away.

And yet she didn't move. Her hand crept back to his chest, her palm over his heart. Her voice was soft, almost a whisper. "I'm scared to talk about it."

There was a crack in that brick wall. Finally. Maybe they'd done more good than he'd thought. He didn't open his eyes, giving her some cover, but he put his hand over hers. "There's nothing to be scared of."

She was quiet for a moment. "Why can't things stay like this? I like it like this."

Now he opened his eyes, focused on her. "Things change, Lea. We can't stop them from changing, but if we really know and love each other, then maybe we can change together. Lots of people start out in love and they really mean it, but that love dies because a couple of years down the road, they're not the same people anymore. And it doesn't work anymore because they never really knew one another. I want to know you. I want to know your past and the you right now. I want to grow with the Alea of the future. But I don't know how we do that if you keep all the doors closed between us."

A sad smile curled her lips up. "We've opened a whole lot of doors, Coop."

He sat back up because she really had been trying. He caught her mouth with his, a sweet affection. "I know, baby, but this is a damn important door."

She took a long breath and her shoulders shuddered slightly. "It was hell."

Oh, crap. He'd kind of thought Dane would be around when she opened up, but he wasn't going to shut her down. "I know, baby, but it can't hurt you now."

"What if some of those doors you want me to open lead to bad places? What if they show you things you might not want to see?"

He didn't want to see any of it, wished it had never happened, but those months were so important to who Alea was now that if they didn't talk about it, those memories would become landmines that eventually exploded. "There is nothing you can tell me that will make me love you less, Alea."

"Sometimes I feel like I should have done more," she began quietly. "Lots of women died in that place. Why was I kept alive? Why didn't they rape me? I know that sounds horrible. I'm happy they didn't, but there's this piece of me that wonders…"

He stayed perfectly still. She was like a deer he didn't want to scare off. So beautiful and fragile and ready to bolt at the slightest sign of danger. He kept his voice quiet, tender. "Wonder what, baby?"

"If they had used me the way they did the other girls, maybe it would have been easier on them. Maybe some of them wouldn't have died. The girl in the room next to me…" Her voice cracked a little, and her hand found his, linking them together. "I could hear her. She was forced to service so many men. So many. They used her until she died. I'm not sure of what, but I know she was dead in her bed one morning a few days before I was rescued. What if I had taken some of her burden?"

Tears made his vision a blurry mess, and he tightened his hand around hers, willing his love and comfort into her. She didn't need his strength. She was so damn strong. This guilt had to be a heavy burden to bear. "Baby, you didn't get to make that choice." And he was so happy she hadn't been forced to make the sacrifice. "And you have no idea whether it would have helped or not. You didn't force those men on her."

"I felt so helpless. So small and meaningless."

That was the true horror of what those bastards had done to her, Cooper realized. She'd had her identity and her whole worldview torn apart and ground into the dirt. Alea was a woman who had been taught to reach out to people. It had been bred into her bones. Royalty in Bezakistan worked for the country and for their people. Tal, Rafe, and Kade were constantly in the oil fields and scoping out the work at the site of the new green project. Alea's aunt still visited hospitals, her days filled with charity work. Alea had been born to do the same. Then she'd been forced into a situation where she could do nothing but watch the women around her suffer.

He sat up and forced her to look at him, gently tilting her head up. Tears streaked down her face. "You did everything you could. But you aren't there anymore…"

Alea turned suddenly, her gaze taking in the ocean. "Cooper, I…What is that?"

A sound like a buzzing, and then a loud splash, followed by another. Cooper looked out over the water and felt his eyes widen. There in the sun and surf was a mirage. It had to be. It couldn't be a boat coming their way. No. Not a boat because he wasn't ready. They weren't ready. He'd just started making real progress with Alea.

"It's a boat. Oh my god. Someone's found us." Alea stood up, wiping the tears from her eyes. "I have to get dressed. We have to find Lan and Dane. I don't know what to do."

Now it was getting closer, and he could see two men in the body of the boat, their figures still in the distance. He stood with Alea and hugged her because she was close to panic. He could feel it, see it in the way her body stiffened and her eyes became tight.

She looked up at him. "Make them go away, Coop. Make them go away."

He held her close, but his heart sank. He couldn't hold her for long, couldn't make the moment last because every second brought the boat closer and closer to shore. Reality was encroaching, and they couldn't meet it like this. They had to find their clothes and get ready for what came next.

Their time in paradise was over.

Chapter Twelve

"This is Nix. Talk to me." Lan picked up the phone with absolutely no regard to the fact that the person on the other end of the line had probably called to talk to Dane. He wasn't willing to let Dominic Anthony wait until Dane got out of what seemed like the longest shower of all time.

Of course, Dane and Cooper were in the shower with Alea, so it could still be a while.

A deep voice came over the satellite phone. "Nice to know you're alive, Nix. Have you talked to the sheikh yet, or am I your first call now that you're back from the dead?"

Back from the dead? If that had been death, he didn't want to be alive again. All he could think about was how closed off Alea had become, as though she was shutting down a little more with every mile that stupid boat had put between them and paradise. He'd been surprised she'd allowed Dane and Cooper to usher her into the bathroom of their hotel on Koror, an island in the Palau chain. "Her Highness has already spoken with her cousins."

"I assume the plane crash was an attempt on the princess's life." There was no uncertainty in Dominic Anthony's voice.

Why question an undeniable truth? "Oh, yes. There's no doubt about that."

"I've already worked up a profile on the pilot. He was being treated for chronic back pain. It wasn't life threatening, but several members of his family had heard him talk about not wanting to live with it anymore. Surprisingly enough, his wife said she found twenty thousand in euros in a safe at their house the night he died."

That had been the payoff. Cheap. Twenty thousand for six lives. Of course, the pilot had only actually managed to take out himself and the hostess. "Well, it was smart to pull cash."

"Yeah," Dominic agreed. "Hard to follow that trail. I have a few ideas. I've been pulling all the CCTV feeds from around the palace and in the surrounding city for the days before the crash. The wife claims the money wasn't in the safe when she looked two days before her husband died, and we got his day planner. He was supposed to have a meeting with someone, no name, of course, the day before the crash. All I have is the time the meeting supposedly took place in the al Mussad marketplace."

Which about twenty thousand people walked through each day, so it would be damn hard to find the culprit, even if they knew who they were looking for. "Damn it."

"Riley's got some hotshot facial recognition software. Let's give him some time."

Lan didn't have a choice on that front. "Let me know if you find anything. In the meantime, we want you to look into everyone who knew she would be on that plane, starting with that British asshole who let her take his place."

"Thurston-Hughes? Absolutely. I started that investigation the minute I heard the plane hadn't made it to Sydney. The funny thing is, ol' Oliver claims that his brother received an e-mail the day the plane went down, claiming responsibility for killing him and his wife. Anti-monarchists, supposedly. I thought it was rather convenient, especially since we can't really trace the e-mail. Best we've managed so far is to determine it was sent from somewhere in the Middle East."

Where Oliver was currently spending his time.

"And why would the pilot go through with the job once he was in the air? I get that he might not have gotten an updated passenger list. He's not the one who loads the fuel and takes care of meals and drinks, but the hostess would have informed him." It didn't make a lick of sense to Lan. He'd been involved in a lot of operations, and rule number one was to take out your intended target.

A long sigh came over the line. "Yeah. I thought about that, too. This pilot routinely flew to London, so he could have connections there, but it doesn't make sense to continue that job if the targets aren't on board. People who hire assassins tend to want their money's worth, and they wouldn't have a problem coming after a pilot's wife to get their dough back."

"Do you have anything incriminating on Oliver? If he's lying about this so-called threat, he's probably doing it to cover his own ass."

Lan was thinking about offing the guy any way he sliced it, but having an actual case might help at his eventual trial if he got caught. He hadn't liked the way the Brit had been sniffing around Alea. If the asshole had really wanted her, maybe he'd been the one to have her kidnapped and kept for him. Perhaps he'd decided, since the first plan had failed, that if he couldn't have her no one could. He'd made it perfectly plain that he didn't appreciate her guards. Maybe he'd known she had a thing for him, Coop, and Dane, so he'd decided to kill her.

"We've had this case on hold for a few weeks while Law and Riley aided in the search for the princess. Riley can do some amazing things with other people's satellites. The wreckage wasn't deep and the water is fairly clear in that part of the world. He narrowed the search to a hundred possible sites, and we've been checking every single one of them, combing all those little islands. Law was going to take the plane up and go over that particular chain, but the government of Palau told us it's some sort of eco-sanctuary, and today was the day their scientists came out to check on birds and shit. They were not happy to see you. Apparently, you four are a plight on the delicate ecosystem. How many fucking pigs did you have to kill?"

He'd been hungry. He would fucking do it again. "I want you back on the case."

"Already on it. And I'm on my way out to the palace right now. Lawson is on Koror attempting to keep the press in line, but you should know they are all over this story, and some of it isn't good, man."

He moved away from the shower. "What do you mean? People are really that upset that I killed some pigs to survive?"

"No." Dominic hesitated. Lan hated those nasty little pauses because he knew that whatever came next would be shitastic. "It's about Her Highness."

He felt himself go cold. "What about Alea?"

"Ah, there it is. I thought you were going to keep up the professional pretense forever, but I was pretty sure something was going on there. So you three finally got the princess to come around. Good. She's going to need you." Dominic sounded satisfied, as though he'd thrown out a bit of bait that had gotten a nice-sized bite.

"Tell me." Lan didn't have the patience to play games.

"The press started out good. I mean, good as in everyone was worried about the princess, but somewhere along the way some asshole reporter picked up the story of her kidnapping and found three of the other girls that the Lennox brothers saved from the same brothel. Two of them wouldn't talk, but one has been all over the fucking media spilling about how the princess would watch them be tortured and do nothing to help."

"She couldn't help." Lan found the words hard to grind out of his mouth. His vision was starting to go red. "She was a *victim*."

"Yeah, well, the press loves a juicy story, whether it's the truth or not, and they seem to want to make the princess the villain of this piece. Sells more copies of their rags. You know how it goes. No one loves the one percenters these days. And you three won't be kept out of it, you know."

"What do you mean?" What did the press want with them?

"They know your names. They've been all over your family members. You don't have a family, but they've been to the town where you grew up. Nix, you should know that they're asking all kinds of intrusive questions, making nasty assumptions."

He couldn't care less what they said about him. Alea was a different story. "We'll cross that bridge when we come to it." There was a knock on the door. Law Anders. "Your boy is here. I'll catch you at the palace. We'll do a debrief there."

"Good. And you should know I'm investigating the girl who's singing to the press. I hate to put a bunch of heat on a victim, but I don't buy her story and I don't like how much she seems to be enjoying her fifteen minutes. Riley's running some reports on her as we speak."

Lan opened the door to let Law Anders in, and it looked like the man had gotten what they needed. He was carrying a case that had to contain a nice shiny new set of guns. They'd tried to save their own, but after getting wet and being exposed to the elements, Lan had preferred new ones. Not that they'd needed them on the island. There it had felt better to have a spear in his hand. Now that they were back to reality, Lan couldn't wait to armor up because someone was still coming after his girl.

Law stalked in, setting the case on the bed as Lan finished up with Dominic. He hung up the phone and went straight for the SIG.

Law Anders took a step back. His suit jacket came open, and Lan noticed he was already armed to the teeth with two semis in shoulder holsters. "Hopefully they're adequate. It wasn't easy getting handguns on this godforsaken island. I had to have them imported. Can we get back to concrete and shit soon? All this tropical crap bugs me."

Yeah, he was a peach, but he had good taste in guns. Lan felt the weight in his hand, a welcome friend. "When's the plane getting here? And who's the pilot? You can't expect me to put her on another plane with some random asshat."

He didn't want to put her on a plane at all, but the revelation about the press made it impossible to stay here. They needed to get her back to the palace where they could shelter her and start the damage control. No doubt, Tal would get his PR people on it soon, but the longer they hid from the press without floating a story of their own, the longer those reporters would repeat whatever the hell that stupid snitch told them.

Law gave him a sarcastic salute. "I'll be flying that baby. The sheikh is having his private plane sent. It should be here in a couple of hours, and it's been under guard twenty-four seven. I'll check it out myself and take the controls. I'm licensed to fly just about anything. We'll be back at the palace tomorrow morning, then Riley and Dominic will want a full report on everything that happened. Well, all the non-naked stuff. So, you going to give this whole sharing thing an actual go?"

Lan heard the shower cut off and the sounds of Cooper and Dane talking softly to Alea. He thought about telling Law to mind his own fucking business, but there was something about the way he asked the question. And he remembered how close the guy had seemed with his brother. Even despite their dumbass fighting, he would bet those two boys had shared their toys a time or two.

"Yeah. We haven't made anything formal yet, but we're going to marry her."

Law stepped up to the window and looked outside. "Weird little country, Bezakistan. Back where I come from, me and Riley are kind of freaks. Throw Dominic in and we're just a parade of crazy. Women like it for a night, but they will jump right off the train when you try to make it permanent."

"You looking?" He was a little surprised at that. Law Anders looked to be a tough guy, the kind who wouldn't want to settle down.

Massive shoulders shrugged up and down. "I want what everyone else has. I just can't have it on my own. I got wired wrong, I guess. Anyway, the plane should be here in a couple of hours. I'm trying to find some extra security, but this place is full of like divers and shit. If I wanted to go swim with a fucking dolphin we would be set, but finding someone who knows how to keep the crowds back is a different prospect. The way I heard it, the press is on their way as we speak. Some of them were already set up here because it got leaked that the princess is staying here."

The door to the bathroom opened, and Alea emerged looking soft and sweet and vulnerable all wrapped up in her fluffy robe. Dane and Cooper came out after her. Dane wore a towel, but Coop had changed into the sweatpants the concierge had hustled up.

It was weird not being naked with her.

Lan watched as Alea moved into the suite. She was bundled up, but there was a hint of a smile on her face. She reached for Dane's hand as he walked up to her. Lan watched as their fingers tangled together and was surprised that he didn't feel a hint of jealousy. All of that emotion had burned off on the island as they had found their unique roles in her life and she'd settled into her place as the sun in their sky. She was theirs, and they had to do everything they could to protect her. Including shielding her from the press.

Law softened around Alea, proving he wasn't as much of an asshole as he seemed. "Princess, your cousins are really happy you're alive. The queen has been beside herself."

Alea nodded, pulling the lapels of her robe together tightly. "It was very good to talk to her. Thank you for everything you've done in searching for us."

"But you didn't want to be found, did you?" Law asked the question almost sadly as though he understood.

Alea paused and sighed, her hand squeezing Dane's. "I will only say that the island wasn't so bad. If you're ever going to have a plane go down, I would highly recommend the accommodations."

"Most women would have gone crazy out there," Law said. "But you look like you bloomed."

"Hey, look at her less, buddy," Cooper said, crowding her other side.

But Lan realized that Lawson Anders wasn't hitting on their woman. He was longing for what she represented. Warmth. Love. Acceptance. "You do look gorgeous, darlin'."

She flushed beautifully. "I'm glad you think so. Could someone order tea?"

He'd already done that. "It should be here any minute. I ordered tea and some snacks. It'll be good to get some carbs, you know? And Law here promises me that Tal is sending us the big bus. It's going to be first class all the way home."

Alea nodded, but he could see the strain on her face. She could probably still remember how it felt to have the plane plunge and to wonder if they were going to make it. Hell, he didn't want to get on the plane and he used to jump off the fuckers.

There was a knock at the door. The tea service. He hoped they had gotten the order right, and there were some Cokes, too. Because he didn't do dainty teacups and cucumber sandwiches.

Alea moved for the door.

"Hey, I'll get it," Lan said, blocking her.

"I can get a door, Lan," she said with a smile.

"No. Not this one." He moved to the door but she stayed right behind him. As he pulled the door back, there was a flash and the quick sound of a camera shutter going off at high speed.

"Princess! Princess, is it true you have three lovers? What happened on the island?"

"Would you like to comment on the accusation that you aided your kidnappers in torturing young girls in Colombia?"

"Princess, the world would love to know what you were

wearing when the plane went down."

There was a mob of them with cameras and video equipment, the light coming from the hall nearly blinding him. They were vultures, every single one of them. Rage popped through his system, adrenaline flooding his veins. They had no right to be here.

A microphone was shoved into his face. "Are you the guard? What are you getting paid to be the princess's lover? How many of you are there? How does it work?"

"Are you bisexual?"

The questions peppered against him like rapid gunfire. He reached for the first camera he saw, blocking the doorway to keep the fuckers off Alea. He could make damn sure these reporters didn't get at her again. They would have to get through him, and he was going to let them know that wouldn't be an easy task. He reared back a fist, anger nearly choking him as they shouted crap about the woman he loved.

Before he could connect, something jerked him back into the room.

"Shut that fucking door," Dane snarled, still grabbing his biceps.

Law jogged to the door. "I'll take care of this. You don't open this to anyone but me."

Cooper moved in and locked the deadbolt. Lan saw red. His heart pounded. His fists clenched. Fuck, he had to get control of himself. He would check on Alea, then he was going to take apart some reporters. He would rip a couple of heads off and mount them at the end of the hallway, and maybe the next set of vultures wouldn't be so eager to knock on their door.

"Don't." Dane pulled him back.

"I'll do it quietly."

"You can't. They're *reporters*. Do you forget who we are? I don't just mean our names. Now we're both the princess's guards and her lovers. You can't beat the shit out of people anymore. Everything we do reflects on her.

Ultimately, we represent the sheikh and his family. Let Law handle it."

Fuck. He hadn't thought about that. He forced himself to calm down. Never once during his pursuit of Alea had he thought about the dark side of royalty being his problem if he actually caught her. This was her life, and if he wanted her, it had to be his, too. He would have to put up with all the questions, the reporters, and the constant speculation. *Oh fuck...* Dane was smart; he could handle it. Cooper was charming enough to slide by. But he'd just about walked out into the hallway and started tearing reporters up. It would have all been caught on camera for the world to see. *Shit!*

Lan looked up, and Alea was staring right at him, her dark eyes burning a hole through him as though she knew exactly what he was thinking. "Lea?"

"That's the way it's always going to be now." She wouldn't look him in the eyes. Her face had flushed, her hands trembling slightly. "You won't be able to have a normal life if you're with me."

His stomach sank. God, why hadn't he just slammed the door? "I don't want a normal life."

"That's just the start, Lan. They will come at you every day. They'll drag you down with me," she said, her voice tight.

"Lea, come on. Let's dry your hair." Cooper reached for her hand and started to lead her back to the bathroom.

She walked with him, her head held at that regal angle she used for state appearances.

Damn it. He started to go after her. He had to explain...what? That he was sorry he'd nearly started a new scandal for the entire royal family and made things much worse for her?

"Don't." Dane stood in his way. "Let Coop handle her right now. You need to decide."

He hated the fact that Cooper was with her and not him. "I nearly fucked everything up."

"You should have known this was going to happen. You've been guarding this family for over a year. You know how the press can be."

He did, but he'd never been in the middle of it. He'd never had all that attention focused on him.

Dane frowned. "What did you think would happen? What do you think is going to happen when we marry her?"

"I think I'm going to have to get a grip on my temper. But they said some horrible things about our girl. How can I not defend her?" He needed to get a fucking grip and wrap his head around it all.

Dane took a long breath and held his hands up, backing away slightly. "We have to find new ways to defend her because lashing out will only make things worse. Sorry, man. I think we're all on edge. We need to back off and reconvene after we've gotten her safely back to Bezakistan."

Lan nodded. He could still hear the reporters clamoring outside the door, and over it all, Law's shouts. "I wish they'd never found us."

Dane's shoulders slumped. "Me, too, man. Me, too."

* * * *

Alea felt numb as she was led into Tal's office. She'd pretended to sleep all the way home, keeping her eyes closed and ignoring the conversations around her.

But all she could hear in her head was those reporters and all she could see was the look of horror on Lan's face as he'd realized what he'd really gotten mixed up in.

She'd managed to read some of the press surrounding her disappearance, despite Dane and Cooper's attempts to prevent it.

They were calling her all sorts of names. And despite the fact that it had been tradition in Bezakistan for hundreds of years for brothers to share a wife, her men weren't being considered brothers. Because they shared no blood, the press seemed to think they could deem their relationship kinky rather than traditional and savage it.

And who had even told them they had a relationship in the first place? Who the hell was this palace source they kept talking to?

And the worst part was the girl from the brothel recounting all the ways Alea had failed. According to Brittany Hahn, she was worse than a coward. The girl was telling the world that Alea had actually participated in the other women's torture to spare herself. It was a lie, but she still saw those women in her nightmares, their eyes pleading with her to help. She hadn't tortured them, but she hadn't been able to save them either. Had she tried hard enough?

"Lea!" Piper nearly ran across the space that separated them, throwing her arms around Alea, tears streaming down her face. "Lea, I thought you were dead."

She returned the hug, but Alea felt like she was on autopilot. She'd tried to think of any way to spare her men the pain of the hell they were all about to endure, the constant exposure to the vicious side of the press. But every road led back to one conclusion. They were better off without her.

Her cousins were standing around Tal's desk, all of them showing signs of the strain the last month must have placed on them. Rafe and Kade looked like they hadn't slept, and Tal had a grimness about him she hadn't seen since he'd married his Piper.

Piper stepped back, smiling at the men who had filed in behind Alea. "Dane, Landon, Cooper. Thank you so much for taking care of her. I heard how you managed to land the plane and get her to safety. You're heroes."

They were her heroes. How could she drag them into her world? It had been so simple on the island, but this was reality, and she feared that none of them were really ready for what it would mean to be married to her. Perhaps if she'd never been kidnapped, they would only have to deal with reporters taking pictures and asking intrusive questions about their love life. But now, these "journalists" were out for blood and called her very morality into question. How long could the press ask these questions before Dane, Cooper, and Lan would get tired of comforting or defending her? How long before they wondered if the reports were true? She had no doubt they would stand by her, but they would get hurt. How long before they resented her for their loss of privacy?

Tal walked around shaking hands with her men. "They are indeed heroes. The royal family cannot repay this debt to you, gentlemen. I will only promise this, no matter what happens in the future, you will always find aid and shelter in this house. I consider you family now."

Alea let her eyes close briefly because she was about to blow everyone out of the water. *Damn. Damn. Damn.* She didn't want to do it, but she didn't see another way to ensure their happiness. She hadn't been able to help the women she'd been trapped with, but she could help the men she loved.

She'd known the minute they'd been rescued, seen the speculative looks on the scientists' faces, that it wouldn't work. Not here. The island had been different. She'd been able to let go. There was no pushing away the past here.

The men began talking among themselves, and Piper started ordering food, talking to the staff about a fine welcome home dinner. Alea drifted to the window, staring at the gardens.

But all she could see was that young woman's face. She'd managed to pull up one of the many TV interviews Brittany Hahn had given to various media outlets. Apparently she'd been taken to the same brothel Alea had been held in. Brittany had been on a spring break trip to Mexico when she'd been taken for her youthful blonde beauty and sold into prostitution.

Alea didn't remember her. She'd been one of a hundred girls Alea had been forced to watch be raped and beaten as part of her "training." In the beginning, Alea had fought and

screamed, but she'd quickly learned that they took her
defiance out on the girls she was watching and not her. Oh,
they would slap her, beat her silly, but the real pain happened
to those young women.

Though she didn't remember Brittany, the girl
remembered her. And hated her. She'd blamed Alea for her
rape, claimed Alea loved watching others be hurt. She'd
called the Princess of Bezakistan nothing but a sadist and
hinted that other girls had claimed Alea herself helped hurt
them.

Why was she spreading lies? Why was this happening?
Pain ripped through Alea. She needed...god, she didn't even
know what she needed, but she couldn't stand the waiting
anymore. And she knew damn well, she wasn't going to
bring these men into her hell.

Piper was right. Dane, Landon, and Cooper were heroes.
They had saved her, and what did they get in return?
Cameras shoved in their faces and their lives ripped apart in
the press.

She'd seen that, too. The press had been busy,
interviewing their families and the people in their
hometowns, asking all kinds of intrusive questions.

Dane's BDSM leanings had been splashed across the
papers, his military career coming into question again. His
family had publically disowned him, even when they thought
he'd been lost in the crash. He'd been labeled perverse by his
ex-wife, who seemed to have taken special delight in
detailing all his flaws.

Cooper's family had been inundated. As far as she could
tell, they had been busy trying to keep reporters off the ranch.

Only Landon had been spared since he didn't have
family, but that wouldn't last. The hotel had proven that.
They would be all over him, and he wouldn't be able to
handle the unrelenting pressure.

None of them should have to.

"How was the flight back?" Piper asked, walking up

beside her. "I was worried that it would be hard on you."

Her men had done everything they could to make it safe. They really were the best. "It was fine. Mr. Anders is an excellent pilot."

Alea turned slightly and saw that all three of them were watching her even as they talked to her cousins. This was going to be so hard, but she had to do it. Their time on the island was over, and Brittany Hahn had been right about one thing. She really hadn't done anything to help those other girls. She should have fought harder, found a way out, but no, she'd given into the drugs they'd put her on. She'd closed her eyes and just prayed to die.

She didn't deserve the heroes who claimed to love her, and they definitely didn't deserve this pain. But it seemed like pain and heartache was all she was capable of giving them.

"Tal, can I speak with you privately?"

Piper frowned, obviously upset, but Alea was resolute. After this was done, she was going to lock herself away and just try to stay out of the public eye.

Tal's eyes narrowed. "Of course. Brothers, Piper, if you wouldn't mind."

"I'll go and get everything ready in the board room," Rafe said. "Dominic Anthony is scheduled to arrive in the next hour."

"I'll help," Kade offered. They took Piper's hands and led her out.

Dane, Lan, and Cooper stayed right where they were.

"I would really like to speak to Tal alone, please." She would explain her position to Talib. He would understand. He, more than the others, knew what it meant to be in the public spotlight.

"Lan, Coop," Dane began. "Why don't you go and find the Anders brothers and get things set up. I want to get a full update as soon as Dominic lands."

They nodded reluctantly and left. Then she stood alone

with Tal and Dane.

"Please, Talib. Completely alone."

Tal shook his head. "No, Lea. At least for now, you won't be alone. At least one of your guards must be with you, even in your locked rooms."

"That won't be a problem, sheikh." Dane stepped forward, his expression a bit grim as though he knew he was about to go into battle. "We'll be moving into the princess's suite this evening. She won't ever be alone."

"Excellent," Tal said, and there was no way to mask his sigh of relief. "I'll call the contractors tomorrow. Her suite is too small for all four of you. We'll start the expansion plans as soon as possible."

She was rapidly losing control. "No, Tal. They can't move in with me."

The room got very quiet as both men turned to her. It was obvious she had their full attention.

"Alea, where did you think we would stay?" Dane asked quietly, his voice icy cold. "Did you think we would go back to our own rooms? Just meet in the middle for a little rendezvous?"

"Explain yourself, cousin. The way I heard it, you've settled your relationship with your men. Are you telling me you haven't?" Tal asked.

"They're not moving in with me. It's not a good idea." She couldn't quite meet Dane's eyes.

"Really? So yesterday in the shower was good-bye, was it, Lea?" Dane asked.

"Could you be a little more discreet?" She couldn't help how her face flushed.

Dane towered over her. "Not a chance, and it's going to get uglier. If you had wanted to keep this between the four of us, you shouldn't have brought your cousin into it."

"He's the head of my family." And she was counting on the way things worked here in Bezakistan. They might be modern, but when it came right down to it, Tal made the decisions. If she could get him on her side, she would be home free and there was nothing any of the guys could do.

Dane seemed to grow a couple of inches as he watched her, his whole body going into battle mode. "Is he? Let me tell you something, Alea, because I apparently wasn't clear. I am the head of this family since you seem determined to go old school with this. I've been extremely patient so far, but you need to think about what you're doing and stop. Nothing has changed. We're together, and we will get through all of this together. As a family. Making decisions together. If you continue down the path I think you're taking, you're going to put me in a corner and you won't like how I fight my way out of it."

Tal had stepped back, frowning as he watched them.

She felt her anger starting to simmer. "Everything has changed, Dane. You know it. You can't be so naïve as to think that anything is the same. You were in the hotel room when the press arrived. The island was just a little vacation, a dream. It's time to wake up now."

His face opened up, pure surprise hitting him. "What are you talking about?"

Dane wouldn't understand. She knew exactly how this would go down if she tried to explain herself. He would never admit that this relationship wouldn't work. He would force the issue, and they would all be torn up and miserable. "I don't want to have a relationship with you in the real world."

"What the fuck are you talking about? The real world? Because the island felt pretty fucking real to me."

"It wasn't. We had all been through something frightening, and we bonded over our shared survival. That was all it really meant," she lied. "Dane, you couldn't expect me to marry my guards."

Alea held in her tears. It had been everything to her. It had been the best time of her life. She would hold those memories to her heart forever.

Dane stepped up, not respecting anything so civilized as personal space. "Shared survival? We're just your guards? Yeah, that doesn't fly with me, baby. There's nothing on the books that states you have to marry another royal."

She steeled herself. God, she hated this. "I don't want to marry anyone, but if I do, I will marry someone who's lived in my world and understands it better."

"Like Piper understood this world when your cousins married her? She was a research assistant from Texas. She wasn't royal and she definitely wasn't rich. What the fuck is this *really* about, Alea?"

How could she make him understand? "Did you see what happened with Lan? He's going to get hurt. Do you know what's going on back in America? They're going after your families, Dane. We need to be realistic. We had a wonderful time. I will never forget it, but it can't be more than a fling."

"Are you talking about all that sex, Alea? Is that the fling you mean? Should I remind you just how many ways we had you? And I don't have that family anymore, Lea. I have you, Lan, and Coop, and we will get through this together." He took a long breath. "Baby, calm down. I know being back here and being hounded by reporters is a shock."

It was more than a shock. Tears clouded her vision. She turned to Talib because talking to Dane would get her nowhere. "Would you please listen to me, cousin? I would like to make a formal request to have my security duty turned over to other guards. I will submit to any security detail you deem fit. I will cooperate with the investigators and I will live a quiet life that will bring no further scrutiny to our family."

The press's accusations could hurt her cousins. They had kept everything so quiet, and now all the ugliness was out in the open. What would her people think? There would be some who would view her as sullied. Some parts of the country were still quite backwards.

She turned back to Dane, her head held regally. "Dane, you have to understand that my cousin's throne and our entire family is judged based on our actions. Any scandal hurts us. Our traditions might seem odd to the outside world, but in many ways our people are very conservative. The very fact that I was abused will make some people view me differently."

Tal ran a hand across his scalp, ruining his perfect hair. "Lea, you can't think about them. They're the mountain people. The citizens in our cities won't see you differently. It's one region of the country. Everyone knows they're out of touch with modern ideals."

"But they're not completely out of touch with the media. They will hear the story and they can cause trouble. It will be worse when they find out about my affair. If I cut it off now and go into seclusion, I can mitigate the damage to all of us."

"There won't be damage if you make it legal," Tal drawled. "I rather assumed there would be another wedding. Did you plan to live with my cousin, in my palace, without offering her your name, Dane?"

"Of course not," Dane shot back. "None of us would do that, and you know it. It has always been our plan to properly marry her with full Bezakistani rites. We talked about marriage on the island, in fact. We respect this family and would never do a damn thing to dishonor it."

"I can't marry them." She knew what Tal wanted, but couldn't he see how wrong it was to bring the men she loved into their world, especially now when the press seemed intent on ripping her apart? "Tal, please try to understand. You would try to protect Piper."

A small smile crossed Tal's face. "Piper is strong, Alea. And so are your men."

Dane tried to reach for her. "Lea, we don't need protection."

Which just went to prove that he could be naïve. What if Brittany Hahn wasn't the only one who had resented Alea's "privileged" treatment? What if more women came out and accused her of cowardice or outright collusion? How could they build a family when she was covered in scandal? "I won't marry anyone."

Dane proved he knew their customs way better than she'd given him credit for. "Your Highness, I would like to make a formal declaration of intent to marry your cousin. I meant to do this later and with proper pomp and circumstance, but she's not giving me room for that."

A single eyebrow arched over Tal's right eye. "Really? You want to put her in a corner like that?"

Alea turned to Dane, her eyes widening. "You're trying to force me to marry you?"

According to strict law, because she'd been formally adopted into the royal family and bore their name, she was actually considered to be Talib's property. It was an old law, but still a valid one. Dane wasn't asking her to marry him. He was petitioning Talib to force the marriage.

"I believe I mentioned you wouldn't like how I fought. And don't think I'm alone in this. I have no doubt Landon and Cooper are ready to sign the paperwork, too. We're not going to let your fear rip us apart." He took a long breath and reached for her. "Lea, I don't want to do it this way. Let's go somewhere quiet and talk this out, you, me, Lan, and Coop. We'll hash this out."

So calm. So reasonable. And he'd just threatened to treat her like property. "I am trying to do what's right for all of us. You can't think for a second that my cousin is going to force me to marry you."

"I will admit, I would prefer not to," Tal commented.

"But he will because I haven't played my best card yet, baby. I'm begging you not to make me do this." Dane spoke to him, but never took those predatory eyes off her.

His best card? What the hell? Her blood was pounding through her body. She'd been treated like a sack of meat before, and she wasn't about to let anyone curtail her freedom. She'd been willing to offer it up. She'd meant what she said to Tal. She was willing to hire another guard and to submit to all of their security protocols. She would do it because it helped her family and it protected her men, but she would be damned if Dane and Tal decided her fate.

"Alea, what is this really about?" Tal asked, his voice softening marginally. "I don't understand what's going on here. This is between you and your men, truly, but you've forced me into this situation. I believe Dane when he says he doesn't want to push the marriage rites on you, but I also think he will do it. Don't put me in a position where I have to choose between my family and my very good friends. Tell me what's going on."

"I won't marry them. After this, I won't even talk to them again." The words sounded stupid and stubborn, but she couldn't give in. They deserved good lives with someone less broken, with someone who wouldn't always have a horde of reporters trailing after her, intent on ruining her life—and everyone around her.

"Did you or did you not sleep with these men?" Tal asked, though she was certain he knew the answer.

Alea knew immediately that her sweet cousin had left the building. This was the Royal Sheikh of Bezakistan addressing her as the head of her family, and she felt like she was five years old all over again.

"I don't see that it matters."

"It matters, cousin. I will not ask again."

She felt her fists clench. "This isn't fair. It's not like you, Rafe, and Kade were pure on your marriage bed. No one expected you to marry that first girl the three of you shared."

"This isn't about us, cousin. This is about you. You gave your body and, I believe, your heart to Dane, and yet you will not do him the courtesy of talking to him. It is a disgrace and not worthy of the woman I know you to be."

"I guess you don't know me as well as you thought." It was nothing less than the truth, but her heart broke at the thought.

Tal sighed, a weary sound. "Please, Lea. Don't make me turn them out."

"It's for the best." God, she felt the burn of Dane's furious stare all over her and wanted this to be over so she could lock herself in her rooms and scream and cry and start to mourn them.

Tal turned to Dane. "I am sorry, old friend. I cannot force her to my will. This scandal will pass. The family will survive. The press will turn around when the new baby is born."

Dane had gone cold as ice, his whole body perfectly still. His voice was frigid. "Are you talking about your child, sheikh, or mine?"

Alea felt like someone had punched her in the gut. She turned to Dane, her feet unsteady. Oh, god, she'd thought about it, but it was like a little whisper in the back of her mind. She'd known that she could become pregnant. How many weeks had gone by? She'd lost count. Time seemed to flow differently on the island, but now it was speeding up like a carnival ride. It was making her sick.

Talib had gone an angry red. "My cousin is pregnant?"

Alea shook her head. "No. I'm not."

Was she?

Dane's smile was that of a man who had just tossed down the winning hand when everyone had thought he was played out. "We were on the island for over a month. She never had her period."

Oh god. She hadn't even thought of that until now.

"Perhaps you didn't notice," Tal tried.

"I was inside her every day, sheikh. I would have noticed. We didn't use protection. She's pregnant by one of us, but I assure you, we will all claim the child. We believed she loved us and had pure intentions. We always intended to marry her with full respect to her culture. I understand that you shouldn't have been placed in this position, sheikh, but you should understand that I have no intention of allowing my child to grow up without his fathers. If you choose not to honor my rights as the man who impregnated her, then Cooper, Landon, and I will be forced to petition your courts to have our rights recognized. Since she was in a relationship with the three of us, according to your laws, we all have rights to the child."

Alea felt sick. She managed to stay on her feet.

Tal was still talking, his voice rough. "If the doctors confirm a pregnancy, then the marriage will take place as soon as possible. We'll keep it private, but afterward, we will announce the union to the press. In a few months, we'll publicize the princess's pregnancy." Tal turned to her. "I have no choice. You were right about our people. We could handle an affair. The heat would be on us for a few months, but we would survive the scandal. We cannot handle a princess with an illegitimate child. This isn't England or America where people just accept royalty and celebrities as human. If you don't marry, they will blame me for not protecting my family. It will weaken my position. Did they rape you?"

Honesty would be her death knell. Alea knew it. Yet she couldn't lie. "Of course not."

"Then you made your bed, cousin, and you will lie in it. I know it's not fair, but there are conservative factions in this country that would do anything to topple my throne and set us all back a thousand years. I cannot allow that to happen. In this, I must be the sheikh and not your cousin. I have to keep my throne stable for everyone in Bezakistan. You will marry them if you're pregnant. I would offer to allow you to marry someone of your choice and pay off these men, but I have a feeling they cannot be bought."

"Not for anything, sheikh," Dane confirmed, his face grim but resolute. "We will not back down and we are united in this."

"As brothers should be." Tal reached out and shook

Dane's hand. "We'll sit down and talk about all the details this evening after dinner. Alea, I'll send the doctor up to you in a bit. You should rest until then."

"You can't do this to me, Talib. You can't do this to them." Her voice sounded small and lost.

"You chose to sleep with them, knowing how they felt. You chose to not use protection. And now you're throwing a fit because there were consequences to your actions. I have to take charge because you're acting like a child and not a woman about to become a mother. You're still clinging to the pain and the guilt like they're security blankets. I know because I did the same thing, but I cannot allow it now. I'm not stupid, Alea. I know your refusal has something to do with what happened to you, and I am so sorry it is being dragged up again, but your time to hide is over. You have to face what happened and decide if you are going to allow it to defeat you or if you will grow beyond it and move on. I love you, my cousin. I pray you can heal and embrace the future." He walked away, pulling out his chair and sitting behind that big desk where his fathers once worked.

"Tal?" She'd just lost something precious and she hadn't meant to. Tears threatened.

He didn't bother to look up. "You're dismissed, Alea. I have to prepare for the meeting with the investigators and then I must start the paperwork for your marriage. It's a matter of state, after all."

She felt tired. So weary. She'd been trying to protect them, but it had blown up in her face.

Dane wouldn't look at her. He kept his attention on Tal. "I will see you in the meeting, sheikh."

"Cousin, please. You're family now, Dane. Address me as Tal or cousin as is your right and my privilege. Let Cooper and Landon know I expect the same from them."

Well, it was great that they were getting along. She felt more on the outside than she'd ever felt in her life.

"Alea, we'll see you in our room. I believe you'll find

one of Talib's personal guards waiting outside to escort you. Obey him. And I wouldn't attempt to lock us out if I were you. I will kick the door in. This wasn't the way I wanted to start our marriage." Dane walked away without looking back.

Alea watched him go and then went to join her guard, her heart heavier than ever. She placed a hand on her belly. She could pretend all she liked, but she knew the truth. She could tell herself that she had been trying to protect them, but she'd really been protecting herself. It had been easy on the island because she didn't have to deal with reality. She could simply be. No future. No past.

But the future was knocking at her door, and she couldn't lock it out.

"I understand the impulse to push them away, Alea," Tal said from his desk. "I really do. I thought it would be best to push Piper away. I thought I was too damaged for her, too dark. She was far smarter than I was. I wasn't too dark for her. That broken part of me was no match for her love. Her love was far stronger than any torture I'd ever endured."

"You weren't getting savaged by the press when you married Piper. Would you put her through this, Tal?"

Her cousin's eyes grew misty, and he took a long breath. "Yes. I wouldn't have said it at the time, but now I know the truth. If you love those men, if you want to share a life with them, then you owe them the chance to stand by you. Would you walk out if one of them was in trouble this way?"

God no. She wouldn't. Couldn't. But she hadn't given them a chance. "No. I love them."

"Then honor them by sharing all of your life. This is marriage, Alea. It's good and bad and everything in between, and it only works if you're in it together. Learn from my mistakes. Don't waste a minute of your time. Go upstairs and see the doctor and wait for your men. Talk to them. Be honest."

She nodded, but couldn't seem to make her feet move.

"Alea?" Tal was softer now. "Alea, do you need help?"

They had been asking for over a year. *Do you need help?* She'd seen it as pity then, viewed her silence as strength. But all she'd done was shut out the people who loved her and closed herself off. "Yes, Talib. I believe I do. I would very much like to see the counselor again. If you could make the appointments, I would appreciate it."

"Absolutely. I can have her here this evening." He got to his feet. "Lea, I love you. I know where you are. I don't want this life for you."

This life she'd been living could hardly be called a life at all because it allowed for no love, no future, just an endless stream of meaningless todays with no tomorrows. The past was an anchor that never allowed her to move on.

This was the life of a victim. But Piper's words of wisdom came back to her again. Suddenly she realized that her cousins' wife was right. She could choose. She could move from victim to survivor. Her choice. Her rules. She could defeat the bastards who had stolen her innocence by refusing to allow them to steal her future.

"I don't want it either." How long had it been since she'd asked herself what she wanted? She wanted her men. She wanted this baby, and suddenly she began counting days and was almost sure that she was pregnant. What they had found on that island couldn't possibly have been left there. No. The love they had made had purpose and meaning, and she was full.

Alea rushed to her cousin and threw her arms around him like she had when she'd been a child.

"Welcome home, Alea." Tal held on to her, his arms tightening and his voice shaking. "I know I call you cousin, but you're my sister. Welcome home."

Alea cried because she'd been gone for so, so long.

Chapter Thirteen

Dane forced his feet to move, but he couldn't really feel them. He couldn't feel anything but this horrible aching knot in his gut. The scene with Alea played through his brain like a horror movie. Yeah, he'd gotten what he wanted, but he didn't like the price he'd been forced to pay.

He'd hated the look in her eyes when he'd shown her how far he would go. He was going to have to start his marriage by forcing his bride to a wedding. God, he'd never imagined it would play out this way.

He stalked across the marbled floors of the palace, well aware that everyone was giving him a wide berth. It was a damn good thing because he really wanted to take someone's head off.

He'd realized a few days ago that Alea was very likely pregnant, but he'd wanted to give it time, to be sure, before they had to deal with the fact that they were on an island with no medical care. He'd been standing by the fresh water pool Lan had discovered, watching her smile and swim and kiss his partners and he'd just…known. She was carrying a child.

When they'd been rescued, he'd planned to keep his mouth shut until she figured it out. It was a woman's right to tell her men that she was pregnant, giving them the gift of a family.

He'd been so happy. Something deep inside him had settled as though he'd found a piece to his puzzle that had been wrenched out of place and had finally been made right. His child. His, Lan, and Coop's with Alea. And she'd looked perfectly horrified at the idea of being pregnant. Like it was her worst nightmare.

What the hell was wrong with his eyes? He stopped, the room turning blurry.

Fuck all. He was not going to cry. He didn't cry.

"Dane? Is Lea coming to the meeting?" Cooper asked, his voice drifting up from behind Dane.

Dane took a long breath and banished the unwanted emotion. He should have stayed calm, should have given her more time, but the idea that she thought they would be better apart had made him insane. Dane turned. "No. She's gone to her rooms. We can fill her in afterward."

"I thought she would want to come." Lan joined them in the vestibule that led from the residences to the section of the palace that held staff offices and conference rooms. The early evening air filled the vestibule, and he could smell the scent of jasmine from the gardens where he'd wanted to take Alea and propose when the time was right. They'd talked about it, the three of them. It was traditional for the royal family to become engaged in view of the gardens. The gardens were blessed once a year and had been for the last two hundred years. They were said to be a lucky place for love and peace.

Coop stopped, his eyes widening. "What the hell happened to put that look on your face?"

He'd lost his temper, and now he had to tell his brothers how screwed they were. "We had an argument."

Lan's jaw became a harsh line, his arms going over his chest. "She changed her mind about us. We're back here now, and she doesn't want to be with a bunch of broken down old soldiers, right?"

His brain had gone there at first, too. He couldn't blame Lan. "I don't think that's the problem, but she did ask to have us removed as her guard and basically told Talib that it would be best if she didn't see us again."

Cooper shook his head. "That's going to be hard since she's pregnant."

When had Cooper figured that out?

Lan's jaw dropped. His eyes bugged out. "Lea's

pregnant? How the fuck did that happen?"

Cooper shook his head. "Okay, let's talk about eggs and sperm. When three boys love a girl very much…"

Dane stopped Cooper in his tracks. "This is serious, Coop. She really was trying to send us away."

Cooper shook his head. "She hasn't changed her mind. The press is just freaking her out."

Lan's calm broke, and a hopeless look filled his eyes. "I caused this, didn't I? I don't know anything about this royal shit. I'll just screw everything up. I almost did in Koror. I love her, man. I never loved anyone before, but I love her so damn much. I don't want to wreck her life. And I don't see what we can do. If she won't marry us, we can't force her."

Cooper's eyes narrowed. "No, but the sheikh can. I read up a little on their laws, and I bet Dane did, too. The sheikh can force members of his family to marry if he deems it critical to either state or familial relations. Alea being pregnant and unwed in this part of the world would be a huge scandal that could rock this palace. Shit, Dane. Did you pull him into this?"

Yeah, that was where he'd probably screwed up. "She didn't leave me a choice since she went to Tal without talking to us first. I'm not going to be eliminated from our child's life. And she needs us, too."

Lan stood a little taller. "Damn straight she does. I can learn the press stuff. I'll take a class or something. 'Learning How to Not Pound a Fuckwad 101.' Sign me up."

"I can't wait to see your notes from that class, Lan." Cooper turned back to Dane. "You were right to bring Tal into this. She's stubborn as hell. This way she can't refuse and tell herself she's doing it all for us. I think she would have fought to protect us, even if it hurt her."

Knowing Cooper and Lan were standing beside him gave him great strength. "I couldn't let her go into this alone, but I'm worried that she won't accept us now. We can force her to marry us, but we can't make her like it. Damn it, Coop, she's had all her choices taken away before. I hate to be the man who does that to her again. How the hell did she find out about how bad the press has gotten? I tried to protect her from it. I didn't want her to know what was going on with our families. How are your folks faring in all this?"

Cooper was the one with something to lose. Dane couldn't care less if the press inconvenienced his father, but Cooper was still close to his family, and he'd heard the press had been harassing them.

A low laugh escaped Cooper's throat. "Are you kidding? Have you met Colorado ranchers before? My momma met those reporters at the gate with a shotgun in her hands, and my brothers decided it would be fun to drive the herd their way. Said they'd never seen a bunch of city folks run so fast. And they want to be invited to the wedding so the guest list could get big, but I can't let Momma down. Not just because she's already bought a dress, but also because she still scares me a little."

There was a long laugh, and Dane looked back at Tal, who was walking toward them. He'd been so grim before, but now there was a light in his eyes. "Rest assured, Cooper, that your family is more than welcome here. I can't wait to meet them."

Cooper reached out and shook Tal's hand. "I thank you for that. And when the time comes, I'll consult with the kitchen staff because my parents don't eat anything that hasn't been fried and smothered in gravy. Now, do you happen to know if you have a battering ram handy because I suspect our fiancée is currently barricading herself in her suite as we speak."

"I have some climbing equipment. I can scale the balcony. The doors into her room are about half glass. I can cut through it and be in the room in about a minute and a half," Lan said with utter confidence. He shrugged a little when he noticed everyone was staring at him. "I think about things at night. Do you really think she's going to lock us out?"

"I do not believe so," Tal said. "I think the possibility of her pregnancy has made Alea rethink her position."

So she knew she needed a father for her baby. It wasn't all he wanted from her, but a step in the right direction. He still had to wonder if she would always resent him for forcing the marriage. Would he always be just another man who bent her to his will?

"She asked to start seeing the counselor again." Tal was practically beaming.

"She wants to talk about her captivity?" Dane had tried every sneaky trick in the book to get her to open up. He wanted it to be him she talked to. He was a selfish bastard, but he was also deeply in love. He would take what he could get.

Fuck. He would take her any way he could and pray that he could make her love him. He'd started their relationship with the firm belief that she'd have to take him as he was because he couldn't change. But now he realized that he would. He refused to be another man who controlled her. All his life he'd needed that control, craved it, but he needed her more. He needed to be a husband and father more than he needed to be a Dom.

"If you gentlemen would care to join us? We've got everything set up and we've found some interesting information," Riley said.

Dane joined his partners and walked into the conference room, the knot still in his gut.

* * * *

Alea sat on the sofa in her living room, looking out the window as night began to fall. Pinks and oranges lit up the sky, and she took it in, feeling more settled than she had in years. All the time she'd been held in that horrible brothel, she'd wanted to come back to this place, to this room. When she'd made it home, she locked herself in for days at a time, refusing all company. She'd sat in this room time and time again, looking for safety and peace and finding none because rooms themselves didn't bring such gifts.

People did. Love did. She'd been looking for something around her that could fix her when, all along, the power to heal had been deep inside her. Asking Tal to call the counselor had been a decision that only she could make. A decision to really live. A decision to be brave. She could be hurt again. Or her men could be hurt. The people she loved could die. Life had no guarantees.

But she could control allowing herself to love, to build a future and to fight for it. She could choose to face whatever future came with Dane, Cooper, and Landon, as well as the babies they had. She could choose to love them and be the best wife and mother possible.

And it was certain now. The doctor had just left. She was pregnant.

She took a long breath and waited. How long would their meeting take? She knew she could probably walk in and take part, but she didn't want to sit across the table from Dane with all that nastiness between them unresolved, and the last thing she wanted to do was have the discussion in front of her cousins and the investigators. She had already put Dane in that position once. She wouldn't do it again.

She would be patient and wait until she could close them off from the world and tell them—all three of them—how she felt. She would share how scared she was. She would tell them how wrong she'd been to try to cut them out because now she knew that a family faced things together even when it hurt. Her job wasn't to shield them. It was to stand beside them, to hold hands and weather all the storms.

She would tell them she loved them so much.

"Princess?" Her temporary guard had opened the door to her living area. He stepped through, looking young and so very serious.

"Yes?"

The guard bowed slightly in deference to her. He seemed deeply solicitous toward females. As they had moved through the palace, he had been courteous to every female they had encountered. It had endeared the young man to her.

"There's a man here to see you. He's your cousin's husband, Oliver Thurston-Hughes. I've made sure he doesn't have any weapons. Should I tell him to go?"

Oliver was here? She winced a little. She was going to have to apologize for destroying his plane. She doubted it would have crashed if she hadn't been in it. Oliver's family was ridiculously wealthy, but they would miss a plane. "No, not at all. Please show him in."

"Should I stay with you?" the guard asked.

Alea shook her head. Her rooms were the only place she was going to be allowed any privacy for a while. She wasn't going to give it up. "No, I'm fine. He's family."

Oliver walked through, his face a dull red. He was a little disheveled, his normally perfect suit lacking a tie and his dress shirt slightly wrinkled. "Lea, thank goodness you're all right."

She tried to give him her best smile, but he wasn't the man she really wanted to see. "It's good to see you, Oliver."

"Is everything all right? The guard was rather thorough in his pat down." Oliver smoothed down his shirt.

She didn't want to explain that there was very likely still some crazy person out there who seemed to want her dead. "Everything's fine. I think Tal is just a little touchy right now. Now why are you here? Have you been here the whole time?"

"We went back home for a bit, but Talib asked Yasmin to come back to the palace once the horrible news reports began. I don't know what that terrible girl thinks she's going to get out of this."

She led him back to the sitting area. "Brittany? I'm sure she thinks she'll either get some closure or some money for her side of the story."

"I think we should sue her. Yasmin has been representing the family on some news channels. I'll be honest, I'm rather worried she enjoys the fame a bit much."

Yas had always enjoyed attention. She'd done some crazy things to get it. Alea had hoped she was over that.

Oliver was suddenly invading her space, hugging her close. "God, I can't tell you how happy I am. I was heartbroken. Lea, you were on my plane when it crashed. That was supposed to be me and Yasmin. I can't tell you how hard it's been knowing I caused this."

Alea tried to politely put some distance between them while reassuring him. "Oliver, this was about me. I'm the one they're trying to kill."

He shook his head, stepping back. "No. I don't think so. We've been working with your investigators. It's why we came back here a few days ago. My brother got an e-mail after the plane went down. It said they wanted to take down all of the aristocracy, that our time was done. Yasmin was so upset by it that my brother gave her half a million pounds to upgrade security in all the homes and at the building where the charity is housed. How can we ever make it up to you? I shouldn't have allowed you to traipse off like that."

Allowed it? Something was tickling at the back of her mind. "I'm fine, Oliver. And I think it worked out for the best. If you and Yas had been on that plane, I doubt you would have survived."

"I doubt it, too. How exactly did you manage to escape? When I heard the plane went down over a remote part of the Pacific, I was sure you would drown. Or if you managed to survive the crash, you would likely die of exposure."

She shivered a little knowing how close she'd come. It was funny, even afterward she hadn't had bad dreams about the crash. She'd trusted her men implicitly. She'd never really thought she would die. "We got on quite well, actually."

"You don't know how many nights I sat up thinking about all the ways you could have died. I dreamed about sharks a lot. It's a bloody miracle you're alive." His voice shook a bit.

"Well, I had three former special ops guys in my corner. They're kind of amazing." They had been calm and cool, thinking only of saving her. "They weren't about to let me die."

"One of them had to have known how to fly a plane, thank goodness. According to the news, the pilot killed himself and poisoned you."

"I think we were lucky. The pilot wasn't counting on four of us splitting the wine. The sedative wasn't as effective as it could have been if it had just been me."

"Or me and Yasmin." He turned his face to her, a grim expression darkening his eyes. "You have to know how much I've always cared for you."

She was not going there. "I've always liked you too, Oliver. But I certainly know that I'm never going to drink that particular brand of wine again. What was the name? *Vallee d'Harmonie*. I did not find it harmonious."

Of course, she wouldn't be drinking anything for a while. At least nine months. And breast feeding time. She would want that. She would want to hold her baby, rocking and feeding the precious bundle of joy. She could imagine one of her men would bring the baby to her and they would talk quietly while she nursed. That would be harmonious.

"What?"

Alea looked up, pulled from her thoughts. "I'm sorry?"

"What was the wine?" Oliver leaned forward, his body a study in tension. "What did you call the wine?"

What had she said? "I might not remember it right. It was a red. I just briefly looked at the bottle, but it translated to 'Harmony Valley.' I've never heard of the vineyard before."

His face went white. "Oh, god."

257

"What? Oliver, are you all right?" His hands started to shake.

"You haven't heard of the vineyard because the wine isn't on the market yet. It's one of my family's new ventures. We had the first batch brought in the week before the crash. I had it shipped out here because we were going to gift it to your cousins for Piper's coronation."

"Maybe she put it on the plane as a surprise for you and the pilot used it because it was convenient." That had to be it. Except the hostess had said that the pilot had brought it on board.

Oliver put a hand over his face, nearly moaning his words. "It was in our room that night. I joked with Yas that she wouldn't be able to drink it for another eight months. She wasn't in bed early that morning. I thought she'd gone to say good-bye to you, but she didn't, did she?"

Nausea washed over her. "No. Oliver, was it your idea for me to take the plane and go to Australia?"

"No. The idea never even occurred to me. I actually argued against it when Yas brought it up. I didn't think you should go off on your own, but she was so insistent. She's been...unstable lately, very emotional and angry. I haven't quite known what to do with her."

"Is that why you cheat on me with my whore bitch cousin?"

Alea gasped and whirled to the sound of that voice, completely startled as Yasmin entered the room, lifted a gun, and fired.

Chapter Fourteen

Cooper sat down and wished he could think of a damn thing to say to get that dark look off Dane's face. He'd done the right thing. It was what Coop would have done himself. Alea needed to know they would never leave her. They would fight for her, even if she was the one they had to fight.

A massive man in a three-piece, charcoal-gray Armani suit stood at the front of the room. He was impressive from head to toe, every inch of his six foot seven inch muscled frame encased in what had to be a couple thousand dollars' worth of designer handmade wool. Cooper had to give it to him. Dominic Anthony made an impression. If he hadn't known what the man's profession was, he would have immediately thought gangster, and not the kind who followed orders. Oh, no, Dominic Anthony would be the one tasking his soldiers to kill. He had pitch-black hair and some of the darkest eyes Cooper had ever seen—and he didn't just mean their color.

"Thanks for coming on such short notice, gentlemen." Dominic had a deep authoritative voice to go along with his intimidating physique. "I know you just got off the plane, but I think it's important we go over some of the things Riley has uncovered in the last couple of hours."

"By all means. Tell us," Talib insisted, taking his seat between his brothers. "I want my cousin to feel safe as soon as possible. She's getting married in the next few weeks. I would like to have some confidence that her wedding will be peaceful. We'll need added security."

"I'll handle it," Dane said, frowning. He was such a control freak. He wasn't thinking at all.

"No, we'll need to handle Lea," Coop shot back.

Dane had been married. Did he not remember everything that went into a wedding? Coop had been in the wedding party of three of his brothers' weddings, and they had all been nearly comatose by the end of it. This was a damn royal wedding to boot, one they had to throw together in a few weeks. Cooper could foresee all kinds of trouble. Alea was being forced to the altar. They'd have to spend long hours convincing her that they could handle being her husbands. He had no doubt about how they would accomplish that. In bed. At least that made him smile.

"I think we can handle security for our own wedding," Lan said.

"Are you planning on standing at the altar covered in handguns?" Coop asked.

Lan shrugged. "Not just handguns. I was going to add a P-90 and some knives, too. I feel naked without them."

"You can't be covered in firearms in our wedding pictures," Dane said, his lips curving up in the first smile Coop had seen on him all day. "What is wrong with you?"

Dominic sighed, those dark eyes rolling slightly. It was obvious the man was not impressed with their banter. "If the three of you are done making wedding plans?" He turned to his two partners. "This shit is so not happening with us. If we find a chick, it's going to be no muss, no fuss. It's Vegas or nothing. Now, let's move on. Sheikh, we've hit a brick wall with the whole Caymans account thing. I sent Law and Riley to the island where they canvassed the banks, and no one was talking. I tried bribes, but those are well-trained employees. Or they're terrified of the people they work for. Even if the clients are criminals, if something came out about secret accounts, the mob and the cartels would not be pleased."

"You told us you had some good news," Dane said, his jaw tight.

"I have some news about the girl who's on the news right now." He looked down at his file. "Brittany Hahn."

She's a twenty-two year old from San Bernadino. She was partying in Tijuana during spring break a couple of years ago when she was taken by the same group that was hired to acquire Alea. I've done a little more background on these thugs. They're tied to a cartel in Colombia. Real entrepreneurs, those guys. They're diversifying. This particular cartel has its hands in cocaine, slavery, and kidnap for fun and profit. It's a new enterprise that's starting to become more popular. They take high value targets like celebrities and upper-level businessmen, then they ransom them back to their families or businesses. Let me tell you, if you've got money, you don't walk around parts of South America without ransom insurance."

"But my cousin wasn't taken from South America," Kade said.

"No. But I believe this was a kidnap for hire all the same," Dominic said.

"We've gone over and over everything, and it's the only thing that makes sense," Riley explained, taking over. "If she'd been taken for use in the brothel, then she would have been raped."

"Alea was raped," Cooper stated grimly. "Maybe not physically, but she was violated all the same."

If Burke and Cole Lennox hadn't already killed the motherfuckers and burned down that house, Cooper would be on his way to Colombia.

"Agreed." Riley nodded. "But nevertheless if the purpose of her kidnapping was to use her as a prostitute, she would not have been discovered fully intact, so to speak. So the question then is, why was she taken at all? And who was paying for her upkeep?"

"I assume someone was going to buy her," Dane surmised, his hands tightening into fists. "And they were holding her for this asshole."

"I don't know about that," Dominic said. "Put yourself into the head of a man who would purchase a female for his own use. We're not talking about D/s, but true criminal slavery. Still, the owner's impulse would be very similar to what a real Dom would feel."

"Possessive." Cooper knew exactly what he was talking about. They all found the possessive instinct at first with Alea. "Any man who would want to buy a virgin is going to be possessive and territorial."

"He wouldn't leave her there for long. He wouldn't leave her training to someone else," Lan added. "I know I wouldn't. And the so-called training they gave her was mostly psychological torture."

"And they got her hooked on drugs," Cooper added. He hated the thought of his Alea strung out and aching. They had used the drugs to keep her calm and quiet and to make her dependent. Alea was strong. He could imagine she'd given the fuckers hell in the beginning. "Do you think they would do that at some buyer's request?"

"No, especially not heroin. That's not cheap," Dominic said. "I don't think they had a buyer lined up for Alea at all. These are not the type of men who allow for installment plans. But they do love a little blackmail. I have a different theory of what happened. I believe the princess was kidnapped and that the men had help from an insider who plotted to draw Alea out, then help to urge the sheikh to pay the ransom as soon as possible."

Tal shook his head. "I never got a ransom."

Dominic leaned forward. "Ah, yes, but from the kidnappers' point of view, why simply take money from the victim's family when they could first blackmail the person who set up the abduction? Once they bled their 'cohort' dry, they could always come to you with an exorbitant ransom request. And by doing it this way, they don't have to give their conspirator any of the promised kickback. They simply could have cut them out altogether or killed them. Either way, they're not sharing the fat ransom. So the longer they kept your cousin, the more likely you would be to pay an outrageous sum to get her back. In the meantime, they were busy getting paid by the same dirtbag who aided them in her kidnapping."

"But the Lennox brothers found her first," Cooper pointed out.

"Yes, and their only job was to rescue the princess and save the girls. They weren't investigating the whys and wherefores because everyone assumed Alea had been caught up in a simple slavery ring. So the question becomes, who hates the princess enough to subject her to hell? And more than that, who needed the money her ransom would have brought?"

Dane held up a hand. "You said this had something to do with that girl on TV, the Hahn woman. Are you trying to tell us she had something to do with this?"

"Not at all," Riley replied. "She really was a victim, and as far as I can tell, she has some very dark emotions toward Alea. You see, we believe that her story is true. Alea really was there during her torture, but maybe she was forced to use drugs as well. If so, her memory is not necessarily accurate. She would have had nightmares and delusions. It would be easy in that situation to see Alea as a villain. She wasn't raped the way Brittany was. Even without the drugs, it's possible that, because Alea's torture was easier than her own, she would be resentful. I've talked to some of the other victims, and most of them see Alea as one of them. A couple of the women asked me to reach out to her. They want to meet and talk because they're the only ones who really know what happened."

"So if she's not the one who helped with Alea's kidnapping, what does she have to do with the person who did?" Cooper was starting to get antsy. His instincts had always been good, and he didn't like the way his spine was prickling now. Something was very wrong.

It was the same feeling he'd had when he and Dane had been in the Korengal Valley just before everything went to hell. It was a combination of adrenaline and pure doom.

"Someone sent her money to buy a new wardrobe before her TV appearances."

"Someone put her up to this? Someone wants to ruin Alea's image?" Lan asked.

"Yes, the same someone who wanted to use her to make money. It would have been easy to hire someone to simply kidnap the princess. She was vulnerable in the States. She didn't have the same type of security. The flip side was not a lot of people knew her connections to the royal family. There were some people in the embassy, but almost no regular New Yorkers knew who she was."

Dominic Anthony seemed to deeply love the sound of his own voice. He was dragging this thing out like Sherlock Holmes reporting to the damn queen. "Who? Just give us a damn name please."

Law seemed to be the only one who wasn't into theatrics. "It's one of the Thurston-Hughes people, most likely the chick, Yasmin. She was working for Reaching Across Cultures, the charity fund Alea had originally set up and planned to head once she got her master's degree. The money that went to Brittany Hahn came from an account directly accessed by the charity fund director. I also confirmed that the Thurston-Hughes family has several offshore accounts, several in the Caymans."

Talib had turned a dull red. Cooper briefly wondered if they still chopped off heads in Bezakistan. "Yasmin offered to head the charity in Alea's stead. She was also the first one to call and to beg me to pay whatever ransom they asked for."

"She was a jealous child," Rafe said, running a hand through his hair. "She had everything given to her, but she couldn't stand the fact that Alea lived in the palace. That Alea was called princess. Her mother and father were incredibly wealthy. Our parents were close to them. After Alea's mother and father died, Yasmin's parents offered to take her in, but my mother wouldn't have it. She told me she was afraid Yasmin would make Alea's life difficult. I would have thought she'd have grown up and gotten over it."

"I don't believe she has. She only married Oliver because she thought Alea wanted him. I overheard her talking to some friends at her engagement party," Kade said.

"And you never bothered to mention this?" Talib asked.

"I thought she was just a jealous bitch. I didn't realize she was crazy enough to have Alea kidnapped," Kade shot back. "Do we know where Yasmin is in the palace?"

Cooper felt his blood run cold. "She's in the palace? Why the fuck is she here?"

Dominic answered that one. "I thought it was best to bring her here. I wanted to be able to keep an eye on her. I suspected either she or her husband was involved about a week ago. I had Talib invite them here to discuss the further search for Alea. We told her that she could be critical to the effort. I knew she couldn't resist being the center of attention."

"So this time she just intended to kill Alea?" Lan asked.

"Oh, no. That plane was insured heavily, plus she managed to bilk her brother-in-law into opening up his accounts so she could upgrade security. I had someone tailing her and listening in on her cell phone conversations for a couple of days. She pocketed the cash. I'm a little worried though because she recently took out a twenty million dollar life insurance policy on her husband. I think once she decided Alea was dead, she no longer needed Oliver Thurston–Hughes. Since she signed a prenup, eliminating him would be her only way of taking as much of his family's wealth as she could. I intend to have a discussion with Oliver as soon as this meeting is over."

Tal reached for the phone on the conference table in front of him. He pressed a single button. "I need you to put Yasmin Thurston-Hughes under lockdown. Yes, that's right. She does not have freedom to roam the palace. Cut her phone lines and her Internet access. Do not allow her to leave under any circumstances. And find her husband. Bring him to me in the conference room."

Dane stood, placing both hands on the table. "Do you want to explain why you chose to cover this up until now?"

Dominic went positively arctic. "I didn't cover up anything, Mitchell. We just got confirmation today. At any point in time, she could have bolted and she has the resources to disappear. I wanted her brought here so she couldn't escape. Besides, it was rather safe since Alea wasn't in the palace. Now she's under guard, and I suspect you three won't let her out of your sight. She's locked up in her room. She's not allowed visitors."

"I never said she couldn't have visitors," Tal said, picking up that phone again.

Cooper didn't wait for the order. He shoved his chair back and took off running. He prayed Alea was safe and sound and locked away, but his instincts were screaming otherwise.

Even as he shoved through the doors and into the vestibule, he felt Dane and Lan beside him.

Whatever happened, he wouldn't be alone.

* * * *

Alea looked down at the floor and wondered how long Oliver had. He was bleeding badly, curled on his side. She couldn't see exactly where he was hit, but it had been somewhere in the torso, perhaps his stomach or right at the bottom of his rib cage.

Oliver probably didn't have long, but then she wasn't sure she had much time, either.

"You're home for just a few hours but you're already all over my husband." Yasmin stared down at the man she'd promised to love and cherish, a disgusted look on her face.

"I have never touched Oliver. Not ever." Alea tried to

keep her voice calm. Where was the guard? How had Yasmin gotten in? She looked over to the door.

Yasmin's lips curled into a wicked smile. She was dressed to kill in all black, from her tight slacks to the shirt that clung to her. It had a plunging V-neckline that showed off her nearly skeletal chest. Yasmin had always been obsessed with being thin, but she was gaunt now. She sported a pair of leather gloves on her hands. She'd obviously been concerned about leaving fingerprints. "The guard isn't going to help you, cousin. He was a little too trusting of females. He let me get really close, so I shot him. Do you like the silencer? It really helps. And of course you never touched Oliver. He never wanted you, you stupid cow. Who would want you when they had me? God, Lea, you were even in a brothel and no one wanted you."

Panic got shoved down in the place of anger. "You were behind all this?"

"Of course. Look, all of our lives, you've always gotten everything. Poor little Alea. Her mommy and daddy died so she gets to be the princess. You were ugly and fat and everyone felt sorry for you. But it should have been me. I'm princess material. I should have been the one who lived in the palace."

Alea seriously wanted to slap the bitch. Yas was seriously screwed in the head if she thought that losing her parents and being an orphan had all been made better because she had Her Royal Highness in front of her freaking name. But she couldn't do what she wanted because that gun would take out more than just Alea. It would take out her baby. Her baby with Cooper, Dane, and Landon. She had to stay calm and give herself time until she could find a way out or her men came for her. Someone *would* come for her. As soon as that meeting was over, they would be beating down her door.

Unless they were still furious at her for what she'd done and wouldn't talk to her tonight. They might go back to their rooms and let her stew. She wouldn't blame them. She'd basically told Dane that she didn't love them. She'd put him in a horrible position.

Oh, god, she couldn't die like this. She couldn't die when they thought she didn't love them.

Everything she'd suffered before seemed to fade away. She'd spent so much time holding her pain close to her that she hadn't embraced the love they gave her. Tears blurred her eyes.

She had to keep Yasmin talking. The balcony doors were open to her left. Her bedroom was to her right. If she got the chance, she could bolt one way or the other. Yasmin loved to talk about herself. "Why didn't you just have them kill me? Why have them take me to a brothel?"

She glanced back at the door, but then turned back, the gun held casually in her manicured hand. "I didn't care where they took you, but I laughed my ass off when I found out it was a brothel. I had a blast thinking about you taking it up the ass from anyone with a couple of pesos." She frowned. "They were supposed to ransom you. I was going to get a twenty percent cut as a finder's fee and for working Talib on this end. The assholes decided to squeeze me. If you hadn't been found when you were, I was going to be in serious trouble. They were going to turn me over to Talib."

"And you don't think Tal is going to be mad that you killed me now?"

She shrugged a little. "I've set everything up so it looks like you killed yourself and poor dumb Oliver. You couldn't handle the truth. Everyone knows you helped your kidnappers torture those girls. No one will be surprised you couldn't handle the guilt. And Oliver was having an affair with you. I'll tearfully testify to that. His brother already thinks very little of him. When he hears about this, he'll think even less. He'll open the checkbook to me."

"Is this about money?"

"It's about everything, Alea. I'm not about to just accept my place in the world. I fight for more, unlike you."

Her heart was racing, pounding in her chest like a barreling freight train. She was so mad, but that anger had to come second to survival. Which safe haven was closer? The balcony. But the doors to the balcony were made of glass. She would have to climb down the trellis. The bedroom was the safer bet, but it was much farther away and lacked cover. If Yasmin was any kind of shot, she would hit Alea in a second. What should she do? She had to make the right decision. Her baby was counting on her. And she wasn't the only one with a baby.

"What about your baby, Yasmin? How could you kill the father of your baby?" Keep her talking. She could still see the faint movement of Oliver's chest. He was still alive. She had to hope that he stayed that way.

A nasty laugh came out of Yasmin's mouth. "Are you kidding? I'm not pregnant. I'm not some dumb animal who's going to allow a parasite to suck me dry and make me fat. I pretend to be pregnant every so often and then I tragically lose the baby. To soothe me, he'll buy me whatever I want for a while. I'm not wrecking my body for some disgusting infant."

So pleading to her maternal side wasn't going to work. Alea drew a deep breath. Her cousin was lost, truly without any redemption. She wasn't sure how it had happened, but there was something missing in Yasmin that had allowed her to become a true sociopath. Nothing Alea could do would save her. The childhood they had shared had been a lie. The face Yasmin showed the world had been a mask.

Yasmin sighed as though the whole exercise bored her to tears. She reached into the pocket of her pants and pulled out a second pair of gloves. "I need you to put these on."

Yasmin tossed them her way, but Alea allowed them to hit the sofa that came between her and Yasmin. The black gloves hit the cushions and fell to the floor.

"Why?" It was obvious, but Alea would do just about anything to put off that time when she had to make the decision. Her men just needed a little more time. They would be here. She just knew it. She let her eyes roam the room for anything she could use as a weapon.

"Because if you don't, I'll shoot you here and now."

Out of the corner of her eye, she saw Oliver move slightly, his head coming up. He was trying to change positions, turning very slowly.

"It's not going to work," Alea said quietly.

"It is. Men in this country can't believe a woman would do anything terrible. I used to get away with a lot when we were kids. I'm just moving on to murder. And after this, I'll be set. The truth of the matter is, I got lucky when those mercenaries found you because they killed anyone who could have identified me as the person who set you up. I really owe them a lot. And now I'll get an even bigger slice of the pie because I'll get Oliver's insurance money, since you're going to go crazy and kill him."

"I'm not going to cooperate."

Oliver got to one elbow. She could see blood on his hands as he pushed himself up. He was behind Yasmin, his stare finding her back and his fists clenched, red dripping from his palms. How much had he heard? Did he know she wasn't carrying their child? Did he know she'd never loved him, wasn't capable of love?

Yasmin frowned. "Yes, you are because I'll shoot you otherwise."

Another thing Yasmin rarely did was to really think something through. All throughout their childhood, Yas had come up with outrageous plans only to run up against a wall of logic anyone with half a brain could have seen a mile away. She needed Alea to cooperate, but there was no real incentive to, beyond making Yasmin's job of getting away with double homicide easier, and Alea just wasn't in a giving mood.

"You'll shoot me anyway, so I don't see why I should help you out." Besides, if she moved, she left the relative safety of the sofa. It was an antique with a high back that reached the middle of Alea's chest. It had been a piece from her mother's childhood, handed down from generation to generation from the seventeenth century. It would survive a bullet better than she would.

Yasmin huffed a breath from her mouth in a frustrated sigh, but a grim light hit her eyes, and she leveled that gun again. "Fine. I'll put them on you afterwards."

Oliver was still fighting, now almost to his knees. "Am I supposed to have shot myself in the head from ten feet away? You know the rest of the world watches TV. Everyone knows that the police can figure out the distance a gun was fired from. You need to be closer. You need to make this look like I shot myself in the head and my arms aren't that long, Yas. You always sucked at math."

If there was one thing Yasmin loved more than her clothes and shoes and money, it was complaining about how terrible things had been for her.

Yasmin's face went a dull red. "Well, how could I compete with the egghead? I just went to school. I didn't have an army of tutors to do my work for me."

Yasmin had gone to the world's most expensive private schools, but that had never been enough for her. There was something deeply empty inside her cousin, something no amount of money or fame or possessions could ever fill. Even if Yasmin succeeded, she wouldn't be happy. She would find all the flaws in life and hold them tight to her because she believed the world to be against her. She saw herself as a victim. It was how she excused everything she did. It was how she managed to live with herself. What a miserable existence. But it was all Yasmin understood.

Alea realized that she could have become just like Yasmin if she'd kept trekking down the path to empty bitterness. She would have shut out anyone who could have loved her, and resentment would have ruled her life. Her men had saved her from that. The island had saved her, and now she wanted life and love in the real world, too. It wouldn't be easy, but nothing worthwhile was. That simple truth was what Yasmin had never understood.

"This isn't going to work, Yasmin. No one is going to save you from your short sightedness this time. Put the gun down, and I'll talk to Talib about sending you to a place where you can get some help." A psychiatric hospital would be a good place for Yasmin. They could figure out if she was a complete sociopath.

For the first time, Yas looked a little uncertain. "I can't. I'm not going down for this."

"I disagree, bitch," Oliver's words were guttural as though forced through sheer willpower from his chest.

Yasmin screamed and turned, her gun firing wildly, hitting the balcony doors and sending glass flying out. The sound filled the room and her ears, making her heart pound again. Now she had to decide which way to run toward safety.

Oliver shoved at Yasmin, toppling her and sending her to the floor. His dress shirt had turned a horrible muddy red and she could see the gray cast to his skin. His hands shook as he reached for his wife's throat. Yasmin scrambled, the gun still in her hand. She kicked out and got to her knees.

The bedroom was too far away, and Yas had a direct line of sight. If she could get a shot off, it would likely hit Alea in the back.

Another little ping zipped through the air as Yasmin fired wildly.

Alea dashed to the doorway, sprinting as she looked back, trying to see what was happening with Oliver and Yasmin. Yasmin kicked out, catching Oliver's chin and sending him flying. Alea heard his body fall, then another little ping.

She made it to the balcony before Yasmin turned. Alea forced herself to not breathe as she moved around the glass at her feet.

"Where did you go, bitch? Do you think I won't find you? I don't care about anything now. I just want to kill you! You wrecked everything! Everything!"

Alea clung to the marbled walls, inching away from the door. She had to get to the trellis and hope that she could still make it to one of the trees that were planted close. When she'd been a child, she'd been able to make it to the ground by jumping from the railing to the tree and shimmying down. Her aunt and uncles had been horrified. Talib had called her a little monkey. Who knew the skill might come in handy now. God, would the branches even hold her?

She heard a door slamming open. No doubt Yasmin was searching for her in the bedroom.

This was her one chance. She stepped across the glass, crunching it under her shoes and stepped up on the terrace railing. Shit. It was a long way down.

"Lea! Lea!"

"Lan?"

Landon stood on the ground beneath her, a gun in his hand. He quickly shoved it into his holster and held his arms up. "Jump, Lea. Jump and I'll catch you. I swear I will. Jump, darlin'."

"Got you," Yasmin snarled as she came through the doors.

Alea jumped. No question about it. She would rather die trying to get to Lan than face down a bullet. She heard herself scream as she made the short trip from the second story.

Her breath huffed from her chest as she landed in strong, warm arms.

"I can kill you both." Yasmin stood on the balcony, her gun in her hand.

Lan moved fast, turning so his back was to the gun, and he pressed Alea to the ground.

A loud report filled the air. That hadn't been Yasmin's gun with its silencer. Then whose?

273

"Thank god," Lan whispered and pulled Alea upright.

Yasmin's gun fell to the ground, her body slumping over the balcony railing. She hung there for a moment, eyes wide, as Dane and Cooper charged through, both with a semiautomatic in their hands.

Alea gasped in horror as Yasmin teetered, her body unbalanced, then tipped over the railing. She fell through the air, her blonde hair flipping with her body before she hit the ground with a sickening thud. A glance told Alea that Yas's neck hung at an unnatural angle. She was dead.

Dane looked over the railing. "Is Alea okay?"

"I've got her," Lan yelled. He scooped her up, holding her to his chest.

Alea stared at Yasmin's dead body as he carried her away, brutally aware of just how close she'd come to a very similar end. She clung to Lan and cried.

Chapter Fifteen

"How is Oliver?" Piper asked as she poured out the tea and waited for the servant to step back. "Thank you so much. That will be all for now. We should be finished in an hour or so. Until then, I'd like to be alone with my cousin, please."

The servant frowned, but nodded and bowed as he left the room.

They were finally alone. It seemed like Alea was never alone these days. "He's recovering but very slowly. His brothers arrived a couple of days ago. When the doctors say he's stable, they want to move him back to England."

She'd met Callum and Rory at the airport and escorted them to their brother's side. She'd felt a horrible pressing guilt the whole time. Oliver had been a target because of her. She'd apologized, but the brothers had hugged her and assured her they placed no blame on anyone but Yasmin. Callum had mentioned that if Oliver had followed his initial instincts and pursued Alea instead, none of it would have happened.

Yasmin had already been cremated, her urn placed in the family crypt by her grieving mother. Alea had felt so badly for her aunt. Though Yasmin had been horrible, her aunt had loved her only daughter. Her grief was complicated. She'd been horrified by what Yasmin had done.

So much sadness. And there had been so much rage in Oliver's eyes. Even through the pain of his surgeries, she could see the hatred there that burned for the woman he'd once called his wife.

"I'm glad to hear he's going to make it," Piper said, putting her tea down and looking at the door as it closed.

Landon was standing outside the door, his silent figure a monument to his protectiveness.

Unfortunately, she wanted his figure to be a monument to sexiness and love, but that hadn't happened. Despite the fact that she'd tried to talk to them about why she'd refused the marriage in the beginning, they didn't seem to be listening. Oh, the wedding plans were going through. They were scheduled to be married in the garden next week, but Dane and Landon seemed to be going through the motions with grim determination.

"Are you all right?" Piper asked.

She nodded. "I'm fine. No morning sickness at all. I feel great physically."

In fact, the doctor had said she was healthy and that sex wouldn't be a problem at all, even sex with all her fiancés as long as they were careful.

But Cooper and Landon were the only ones who had slept beside her in the four days that had passed since she'd leapt from the balcony and into Landon's arms. She'd tried to explain, and Dane said he understood, but he'd been remote.

They were circling each other like wary sharks, and she needed to break the stalemate. She wanted her wedding to be a joyous occasion, not something they all went through for the sake of the baby.

"I wasn't talking about your health physically. How are you emotionally?" Piper asked. "I saw that two of the other women from the brothel called you. How did that go?"

Jennifer and Lisa. She barely remembered them, but they had given her so much strength. She'd been terrified at first, but they had drawn her out, getting her to really talk about what had happened. They had cried, all three of them. They had cried for each other, for themselves, and for the girls who hadn't made it.

"I'm starting a new foundation. I'm bringing Lisa and Jen into it with me. It's going to fight international slavery and push the United Nations and other countries to advance women's rights."

Tears formed in Piper's eyes, and she put down her teacup and reached for Alea's hand. "A long time ago, Dane told me that how we handle the pain we've been given is the way we're measured in life. A strong person can take the horror and pain and use it to make the world a better place. Lea, I think that's a wonderful idea."

She was excited about it, and especially excited about the fact that Jen and Lisa were going to get some of the others together for a visit at the palace so they could meet and talk and help each other heal.

Alea was going to reach out to Brittany, too. She was letting go of her anger because it had no place in her life. It solved nothing, but forgiveness and understanding…those could solve everything.

She was done with anger and bitterness. She was ready to move on, but she had no intention of moving on without Dane Mitchell.

There was the sound of a door opening, and Landon walked in. His blue eyes found hers, and she was shocked at how her heart pounded in her chest at the very sight of him. He nodded toward Piper. "Your Highness."

"It's Piper, Lan. In a couple of days we'll be family, and no one in my family calls me Your Highness. Well, except for my sister, but it sounds more like Your High Ass. She's a classy one, my little sis."

Lan's smile made him beam. "I'm excited to meet her. I'm also excited that Coop's family is going to descend on the palace tomorrow morning. I think it might be the first time that monstrosity Tal calls a plane gets completely filled."

Alea couldn't wait to meet Cooper's family. She just hoped she could remember all their names. There were six brothers and five of them were married with eleven kids between them. But first, she had a job to do. "Are you going to help me?"

Lan put a hand on her hair, smoothing it back. "Always, Lea. You're sure the doc said it was all right?"

He was killing her, treating her like she was made of glass. "Lan, have you ever heard of pregnancy hormones?"

Piper shook her head. "Oh, honey. I have a load of those." She also proved she had Alea's back. "But it's okay because your men are taking care of you, right?"

She was so glad Piper was on her side. She shook her head. "No. They're not taking care of me. They're very gently making love to me, but only once since we got back and only Cooper."

Lan went a stark red. "Lea, baby, should we be talking about this?"

Piper stood up and wagged a finger at him. "How could you? Pregnant women need sex. Crazy, dirty, nasty sex. So, you liked having sex with her so much that she got pregnant, but now that she's expecting, you've lost interest. Is that the way it is?"

"No. God... N-no, not at all. I'm so horny...." He shut his mouth and started to laugh. "This is one of those times when you two are having fun with me, isn't it? Well, fine. I can deal. If you're going to make it a royal decree that I get down and nasty with the love of my life and share her with my best friends, then I have no choice. I have to follow a royal order. Do you have the key to the dungeon, Piper? Cooper is going to get Dane down there in twenty minutes."

Piper smiled and handed over a key. "You guys have fun. The bed is in the back if you decide to stay down there. There's also a phone that goes directly to the kitchen. We had that installed a few months back because Kade gets hungry when he's playing. Y'all have fun. I'll keep Tal busy elsewhere."

Lan took her hand and started to lead her down the hall. She threaded her fingers through his, but worry still swamped her. "Are you sure you want to do this with me?"

Lan looked down at her. "Do I want to play bondage

games with the most beautiful woman in the world? Uh, yeah."

"You haven't seemed to want me lately." He'd been perfectly polite and he'd said all the right things, but he hadn't made love to her. "I said some terrible things when we first arrived at the palace. I was reeling and I didn't mean them. And—"

"Stop. Lea, I love you. The last few days have been rough. You almost died, baby. You're pregnant. I'm so worried that I'll do the wrong thing."

"I'm not fragile, Lan."

"You sure felt that way when you jumped off the balcony and into my arms. If I had been off, if I'd tripped or stumbled, I would have lost both you and the baby."

She hugged him close. "Oh, you never would have done that. You wouldn't have dropped me. Why do you think I just jumped? I realize now that no matter what way I would have gone, someone would have saved me. Cooper came in through the back rooms of the suite so he would have found me in the bedroom. Dane came in through the front. And you were going to climb right up to the balcony. I was protected on all sides. She didn't have a chance."

"She had a chance to take a shot at you."

"Don't, Lan. I want this afternoon to be perfect. I'm alive. Our baby is alive. The doctor said I can have sex just about any way we want. We only have a few more days to have crazy single sex before we move on to crazy married sex." She sighed and rested her head on his chest, listening to the sound of his heart. "Please, Lan. I need to know if I've lost Dane."

"You haven't lost any of us, baby. Dane just feels the weight of what happened. And I'm a little worried that he thinks he needs to change. That's why Coop came up with this insane plan." He leaned over and kissed her, his lips brushing against hers. "You have to prove to Dane you can handle the whole Dom thing. I know he thinks he can live without it, but there will be a huge hole in his life."

And in hers as well because she craved the kind of dominance only Dane could give her. "I want him to be happy, Lan. And I want this part of him. I trust you and Dane and Cooper. I love you all so much. I want to try everything. I don't want any walls between us."

"All right. Let's get this ball rolling then. You're wrong about the single sex though, baby. I haven't been single since the minute I saw you. I think I married you in my heart a long time ago."

God, he always said the right things. He thought he was inept, but he always knew how to calm her. She smiled at him, and they started down the hall, to the dungeon, where their lives together were going to begin again.

* * * *

"It's down here," Cooper said, practically pulling Dane along.

What was up with that? Dane pulled back.

"Coop, the only thing that way is the dungeon." And he didn't want to be there. God, he hated the fact that there was a dungeon right here and he would never step into it with Alea. He would never lovingly bind her and torture her for their mutual pleasure. He would never hear her call him Master.

Husband. He had to be satisfied with being her husband. She couldn't handle the missionary position, so he definitely couldn't expect her to climb onto a St. Andrews Cross and count it out for him.

"Yeah, what I need you to see is in the dungeon," Cooper insisted. "Come on, man. It's a surprise for Alea. It's for our wedding night."

"In the dungeon?"

Cooper shrugged. "It's the one place I don't expect her to look. Come on, Dane. Don't tell me you're still having doubts."

About loving Alea? Not a chance. About being the right man for her? Yeah. He was having all kind of doubts about that. He could still remember the minute he'd seen the guard dead in front of her room, his body lying there like a message to Dane. *You'll lose her. You can't keep her, you fucking pervert. You ruin everything you touch.*

He could still hear his ex-wife and his father. He'd lost one family over his needs. Was he ready to lose another one? Did he even deserve another one?

"I love Alea, but the last couple of days have been rough. I had to kill her cousin. I think I should give her some space."

"Her cousin was a jealous whack job who was trying to kill her. I think she's going to be fine with you pulling that particular trigger. The al Mussads are wonderful, but I have to say that the extended family leaves something to be desired. First Khalil and then Yasmin. I think we should take a look at the old family tree and prune it proactively of any other cousins who don't live in the palace. Really, it'll save us so much time and crap in the future," Cooper said.

Dane turned to him. They were getting closer to the dungeon, and he really didn't get Coop's good mood. Well, he did. Coop had been making love to Alea. Coop had been wrapping himself in her sweetness. Lan was too worried. And Dane just kept his distance. She hadn't wanted him since their time on the island, and he couldn't shove his needs on her. Alea was pregnant, and he'd forced her to marry the three of them. Oh, she'd said all the right things lately, but she'd only said them after she'd learned about the baby.

"This isn't something to joke about," Dane growled.

Cooper sighed. "Buddy, you have to get out of this mood."

"She almost died."

"But she didn't. She's alive and needs to know that we

still love her. She needs to know that her men will always be here for her."

Probably. But did she love them? If he could shove his darker desires down, maybe after a while she would.

"I'm not going anywhere, Coop." He would be right there standing beside them when they married Alea, and then he would prove he could handle being vanilla. He would prove he could find a place in this family. And not entering the dungeon would only prove now that he was a pussy. Tal was a Dom. If Dane was going to live in this palace, he had to get used to being around all the things he couldn't have.

"I know, but you're not really here either. You're just existing, and it shouldn't be that way. We're getting married. We're having a baby. This is the time of our lives, and you're stuck in the past. It's time to get you unstuck." Cooper put a hand on the door.

"Man, you need a key to that." Tal didn't just leave the dungeon door open.

"Not today, I don't." Cooper turned the knob and pushed open the heavy door.

"Holy shit." Dane stood there for a moment because the dungeon wasn't empty. Not at all. Two occupants waited for them, one gloriously naked.

Alea. His beautiful Alea was bare and standing next to Landon, as they looked over a tray of jewelry. Not jewelry. Toys. Clamps and beautiful chains. All lovely things to decorate a submissive with. He felt his cock go stiff and long, pressing against his slacks as though trying to punch its way out.

"What the hell is this?" Dane croaked hoarsely.

"Baby, you're on," Cooper said. He was obviously in on whatever this was. He shrugged out of his shoulder holster and put it within reach, and started to pull off his shirt. "Just like we practiced, Lea. Dane, lock that door. Piper knows we're in here, but I wouldn't want the staff to walk in."

Running on autopilot, Dane shut the door, his whole

body on the edge. He locked it because they apparently had something to say, and Coop was right. They didn't want anyone walking in.

He stared at the dark wood of the door, unwilling to turn around and see her again. "Alea, what is this about?"

"It's about you, Dane." Her voice sounded slightly unsteady. "I love you. I want to play with you now and for the rest of our lives. I want to give you what you need. Cooper and Landon want to play, too."

"I don't need this, Lea." He forced himself to swallow down a long breath. "We're fine the way we are." He would never force her to do something she didn't want. "I won't treat you like your captors."

The last few days had been about far more than just the fact that Yasmin had tried to kill his woman. He'd read every article that had been written about the crash and all the crap those reporters had dug up. Tal had done a good job of keeping it quiet the first time, but the press had gone insane when Alea's plane crashed. Every sordid truth had been detailed. From her kidnapping to the nastiness of the brothel, to ways she'd been tortured and the fact that she'd been force-fed heroin.

He couldn't take her control again.

A soft hand cupped his shoulder. "You don't ever, *ever* compare yourself to them. I won't have it."

He turned and was surprised at the anger in her dark eyes. Tears shimmered there, too, but her mouth was a flat angry line. "Lea…"

"Not ever, Dane. They were evil, and you're so good. You've spent your life protecting people. You gave up your career to save lives. You are a hero, and I will not allow anyone to make you think less of yourself. I am so sorry I forced you into a terrible position in front of Talib. I really do want to marry you. I want *you*. Can you forgive me?"

Something deep inside him softened. She was standing here, naked in front of him, her fierce soul finally on display.

Yet she was trying to protect his nasty ass. Though he outweighed her by a hundred pounds, she looked ready to take on anything that might be a threat. For him. Cooper had been right. This wasn't a woman who gave a shit about how much money he had or his social status. She'd been trying to spare him, but he didn't want to be spared. He only wanted her and he wanted her happy and safe and whole. After years of living the lifestyle, he finally understood. It wasn't just about putting her needs before his. It was about putting her first always. She was the center of their universe. Alea and their babies were everything to him. They were his future.

"I forgive you. Alea, baby, I love you. I don't need this. I know I've been a little aloof, but you just answered every question I had. We're okay. Let's get you dressed and go back to our room, and I'll make love to you properly."

With all the gentleness she deserved. He would let her make the pace and only take what she was willing to give. He could handle it.

"Properly?" She frowned his way. "That sounds boring, Dane. I want you, especially that dirty, nasty side you've been trying to pretend doesn't exist."

Dane sighed. She seemed determined to not make this easy on him. He felt his whole body tighten. "Lea, you don't understand what you're asking for."

She took a step back, and he missed the heat of her body. "Yes, I do. I was on that island. I know what you want. I can handle it, Dane. I can more than handle it. I want it. I crave it."

She was so fucking gorgeous. Her whole body was a fucking temple, and he worshipped it. From the pitch black of her hair to her round breasts to the sweet curve of her belly and the flare of her hips. He loved her fucking feet. He usually didn't give a shit about feet, but hers were so sweet. He always had the craziest impulse to rub them and kiss them because they held her up and moved her along beside him.

"Lea, after everything you've been through, you don't

need my damage."

"It's not damage, Dane. It's part of you, and I damn well do need it. I wouldn't be where I am if you hadn't pushed me."

Tal had said that Alea needed him most of all, especially his Dom side. Maybe…the sheikh had been right.

"Do you know what I did today?"

His heart was aching because she was everything he wanted in life. "What?"

"I set up an international agency to fight for women's rights across the globe. I made plans to meet with women who were taken at the same time I was so we can talk and make plans so that what happened to us stops happening to other young women. I became more than a victim. I became a force that those who took me and everyone like them will have to deal with."

Damn, those tears were starting again. He'd looked at her so long ago and he'd known what she could be. This warrior in front of him was the woman that girl had become. She could change the world if she set her mind to it.

"Lea, baby, sometimes bad shit happens to the right people. It sucks and it's horrible but those people can fix things for everyone else. You're that person. You can stand up for everyone else. This is why it happened to you." He hated that she'd gone through so much pain, but she had an opportunity to make the world better. He'd spent years fighting in wars, but Alea was the one who would truly fight the good fight. And he would be right there, protecting her.

She stared up at him, her eyes so passionate. "And this is why everything that happened in your childhood, with the Navy, and with your wife happened to you. Dane, can't you see that? These roads we've traveled, they were hard and rough and they made us the people we are. They brought us here—together. I couldn't have become this person without you, Landon, and Cooper. And this damage you're talking about…you endured and grew because of it. It's your strength. Damn it, Dane, it's *our* strength."

She took a step back and sank to her knees in a perfectly graceful move down to slave position, her knees splayed wide and her palms up. The black waterfall of her hair reached to her breasts, the ends almost tickling her nipples. She squared her shoulders. The deeply submissive position left her pussy and her breasts on glorious display. Her nipples were erect, pointing his way, as though trying to tempt him to lick them and suck them into his mouth. And her pussy was a jewel, gold and pink, with just a hint of the arousal he wanted to flow from her.

Landon walked up to her left side, and Cooper to her right. They had both shucked their clothes and each one only had eyes for Alea. They were staring down at her, longing plain on their faces. They were ready for some playtime with their fiancée, their woman, the center of their goddamn whole world.

"We all want this," Lan said.

He hadn't counted on the fact that he wasn't the only one who needed this.

"None of us would be here without you, buddy," Cooper said. "It's time to claim our sub."

Their submissive. Such a misnomer. Submissive. Dominant. They were just words to describe a truth. In the end, they were just men in love with a woman. It was just another way to express the fact that he was crazy about her and he'd do anything to show her.

"Do you need this, Alea?" This had to be about her. At some point, his world had shifted and his own needs had taken a backseat.

Her eyes came up, and he saw only truth in them. "I crave this, Dane. I need you. I want to explore what we found on that island. I want to make it real."

It had always been real. He'd just been afraid to trust in it. Fuck. It was everything he'd ever wanted. More than he deserved, and only a stupid man would turn it down.

Dane Mitchell wasn't stupid.

"Eyes down, Alea. And spread your knees wider. Spine straight. For tonight, the only safe word you need is 'no.' Later we'll come up with a fun word so we can play all sorts of nasty games, but for now, a simple 'no' will suffice." Relief flowed through his body. He felt like a prisoner who had just been granted parole. Or a man who had received full forgiveness and learned that he'd never really sinned at all.

This was his woman. This was his family.

"Landon, I think we should warm our little sub up. She's been quite a brat lately. Actually I think she was born a brat, but we can handle that, can't we?" Dane heard his voice go deep, and it felt so fucking good. He pulled his shoulder holster off. His eyes strayed back, thinking about the door.

"We absolutely can handle her. And relax. We're perfectly safe here," Cooper said as though he could read Dane's thoughts. "The whole palace is in lockdown for the rest of the day. I believe Piper and the al Mussad boys are having a private meeting up in her rooms. Talib doesn't like to be interrupted. We have nothing to worry about."

Dane would always worry about her. He would always need to keep her safe, but there was a time to let that worry go and to revel in the love they made. He pulled his shirt off. "I need to order new leathers."

He wanted to take her to a club. He would take such pride in showing the world the woman he shared with the best men he knew. He imagined how beautiful she would be on a St. Andrews Cross, her trust for her men plain for the world to see.

"I think we all need to order some leathers because the thought of really topping her is doing something for me," Lan said. "I think the dungeon might be the only place where I can be in charge with her."

Alea frowned prettily. "Oh, it hasn't felt that way, Landon. You're always bossy with me. 'No, Alea. You can't have a moment to yourself. No, Alea, you're not going to the marketplace.'"

Dane stared down at her. "Every word that comes out of your mouth makes the orgasm trail that much longer."

She grinned, obviously misunderstanding.

Cooper snorted a little. "Honey, he means your orgasm is at the very end of a long trail, not that the trail is littered with orgasms."

The sweetest pout hit her lips. "I don't like the sound of that."

Still, she put her head down again, regaining her submissive pose.

"I think we all agree that in the real world, we'll let Alea have her say." Dane fixed his gaze on the most beautiful sight he'd ever seen. "But here, we're the Doms. We're her princes and she's our princess."

She kept her head down, but there was no way to miss her slow smile. "You three are always my princes. And I'm ready to do your bidding."

Only one thing was holding him back. "Alea, what about our baby?"

He didn't want to wait nine months to claim his sub, but he would. He would wait forever because there was no other woman for him. He'd gone into his first marriage because it had seemed like it was time to marry. This was something different. This was worth waiting for. He'd made a mistake before because there was only one marriage that counted, and that was the one he fought for, bled for, and lived for. Their Alea. Their family.

"We've talked to the doctor, and he understands what is involved with a Bezakistani marriage," Alea explained. "Piper is farther along than I am, and her activities haven't been curtailed yet. So we're in the clear for now. Let's not waste any time. Love me. I want you all to love me. I need my men to come to me as the Dominants you are."

His cock twitched, begging him to jump at the offer. She was a smart woman. She knew her mind, and she damn well knew what she wanted. He dishonored her to think she didn't. She was his and she was ready. "Hands and knees, Alea. Did you think you could refuse to marry us and there wouldn't be some punishment?"

She moved, but not before he caught her smile. "I should have thought about that, Sir."

"Master," he corrected. God, he loved the way that word sounded. He'd never been anyone's Master. He'd only ever been a Sir. A Master was committed, devoted, forever. "You're about to marry me. I'm your Master. I won't ever have another submissive. You are the end-all, be-all of my existence as a Dom, so give me my due."

She shifted on the floor, moving forward and finding her position on her hands and knees, her hair hanging down around her.

"Yes, my Master," she breathed, emotion choking her voice. "And I deserve some discipline for the other day. It was never about not loving you all. I love you so much. I ached the whole time we fought. I should have trusted you to be strong enough to stand with me. I should have trusted us."

"Why? What have you learned?" He wanted to hear it. He wouldn't believe it until it came from her lips.

"I should have turned to you because families face hard times together. Because my problems are your problems. We share everything. The good and the bad. I promise you, I will never push you away again. I will cling to this relationship because it's my life."

A well of peace opened inside Dane's heart. He'd waited his whole life for those words with these people in this one place where he belonged. He let go of the leash he'd kept himself on forever. "Never again, Lea. You will never place me in that position again because I will do the same thing. I will fight back and I will fight dirty because you belong with us."

"This is where we all belong," Cooper said, running his hand across her back, worshipping her skin with his own.

"Do you know how beautiful you are?"

"You're so gorgeous." Landon touched her hair, skimming it with his fingers. "I love you like this. You're pretty in those gowns and stuff, but I always think of you naked and kneeling."

Dane walked around to her back, enjoying every inch of the view. Her spine was straight, her knees splayed wide so he could just start to see her pussy. It pouted between her legs, glistening with a light coating of her juice. That peach would be even riper and more ready after he was finished. "Gentlemen, let's get started. We all need to know how to spank this ass. Landon, you start us out. For now, it's a count of twenty."

Landon didn't hesitate. He moved to her backside, getting on his knees and bringing his hand back. He proved he'd been listening on the island. He used the flat of his hand on the fleshiest part of her ass. A loud smack reverberated through the room. He loved that sound and the way Alea gasped, her whole body flushing beautifully. She held herself still. Her hair moved, and he could see the way her shoulders shook as the erotic torture continued. Lan smacked her ass again and again. Dane walked over so he could watch. He loved the way her flesh moved under Lan's hand, the color turning a pretty pink.

"Hold your hand on her ass. Let the heat sink in." He needed to teach his partners so they would always know how to discipline their sweet sub. "Let me show you."

Lan immediately stepped back, allowing Dane to move into place. They moved almost fluidly, and it sent a wave of calm through Dane. They could do this. The Dom in him was possessive, but it was easy now, because Alea needed Cooper and Lan. And he needed them, too. This life he was embracing would be extraordinary because he got to share it with his friends.

"Make it a quick smack, then a slow burn." After five quick smacks to that round ass, he let his hand grip her, feeling the shudder go through her. And he could smell what getting naked and kneeling before her Masters had done to her. The musky spice of Alea's arousal tightened his cock and made him crazy. He wanted to mount her and shove his cock deep, taking her over and over until he'd imprinted himself on her, but that wouldn't serve his purpose. Patience was required. Patience would make the pleasure so much more stronger, would bond them all together. "Are you all right, baby?"

"I'm getting my ass smacked, Dane. All right is a weak description."

He loved her bratty mouth because it just made it all the easier to discipline her. "That's another ten."

"Dane," she pleaded, her head turning back. "Dane, I'm already dying here."

It was time to really begin her training. She needed to learn patience as well. "You keep your eyes to the front unless I tell you otherwise."

Smack. Smack. Smack. Smack. Smack.

He held his hand tight to her flesh. She was turning a glorious shade of pink, and he could feel the heat radiating from her flesh.

Cooper got to his knees on the other side of Alea. "Let me help."

And Landon could start getting things ready. It seemed to have been his role in this plot. Dane couldn't be angry about it. It had been a huge gift his partners and their woman had given him.

"Landon, find a proper pair of clamps. I think we should dress our little sex toy before putting her to good use."

Alea's little moan let him know she was okay. There were still so many things that could trigger bad memories for her, but they wouldn't know how far they could go without pushing her boundaries. He nodded at Cooper, and they took turns smacking her ass, finding a rhythm. Alea swayed slightly and the throaty sounds that came from her mouth went straight to his dick.

When he finally counted thirty, her head had dropped, shoulders relaxed, and she simply swayed with every slap to her ass. She wasn't fighting or struggling. She was floating on pure sensation. She was right where he wanted her.

"Such a good sub," Dane muttered, allowing his hand to stroke her hip. He leaned over and placed a kiss on the small of her back. He wondered how pregnancy would change her. She would be so beautiful, all round and soft and filled with their child. He would coddle her and spend his days rubbing her feet and her belly. Yeah, he was looking forward to that. "I think a good submissive should get a treat."

His fingers trailed down and found the soft flesh of her pussy. It was engorged with blood, a flower in bloom. His fingers slid easily around her labia and around her clit.

"Dane, Dane. It feels so good. I'm so aware. I can feel everything," she said on a moan.

That was the whole purpose of the spanking. He'd forced her out of her own head and left her no choice but to be in the moment with them. A woman as smart as Alea could sometimes get lost in her thoughts and worries and be unable to connect with the intimacy of sex. Especially given what she'd been through, Dane wanted her wholly in the moment. In this dungeon, there was no room for anything but them. There was only pleasure and erotic pain and the deep connection between lovers.

She whimpered a little as he brushed against her core.

"Do you want a cock up this pussy?" He loved dirty talk, but he'd hesitated until now, worried it would send her back to a bad place.

Not this time. She thrust her backside toward him, trying to lure his fingers deeper. He immediately pulled back and smacked her ass again.

"Dane, please."

He loved hearing her plead. It showed him just how far they would come that she felt safe enough to play this way. It gave him so much peace and made him feel powerful. "No, Alea. You're not in control here. I believe I mentioned there would be a point when I took the power back. Well, tonight is the night, my love. You're going to be sweet and obedient. Only then will you have pleasure like you've never known. But not until we've had our fun. Now, on your knees. I believe Landon has found some pretty clamps to decorate your nipples."

Landon walked up carrying two pretty ruby clamps. He approved of the choice. He could control just how tight they got, making them bite into her nipples but not so tightly she would be in danger of real damage. Lan turned them over and he held them up as Cooper helped Alea get to her knees, her lovely body flushed with frustrated arousal. That was just how he wanted her. He moved to the front and showed her the dangling clamps.

"They look like earrings, but I know what they're for," she said with a soft smile. "Do you want me to hold my breasts up for you, Master?"

God, she knew what she was doing. He dropped down beside her. "I think I'll deal with that in a moment. First, I forgot to do something. I want to set up a few rituals and traditions. Rituals are very important in BDSM, but each relationship can have different ones. I want to talk about how you greet your Master, even when we're in the vanilla world."

She ran her tongue along her lower lip. "I'm listening."

"You always kiss me. When I walk in a room, you are to find me and greet me with a kiss."

"I can do that, Master." She tilted her head up, offering her lips.

He took her head in his hands and kissed her. He didn't waste time with nibbling and playing. He devoured her like the starving man he was. Days had gone by without a single taste of her, and he couldn't do it again. He needed her. He would kiss her and love her every day. Even on days when they couldn't make love, he would get a taste of her like this so she was always on his tongue, a reminder of why it was so good to be alive. He forced her mouth open and slid his tongue against hers in a silky dance. Over and over, he thrust in and dragged out in a perfect imitation of what he wanted to do to her.

When he was breathless and aching, he brought his head up and broke the kiss. He stared down into the brown eyes that kicked him in the gut every time he saw them. "That's what I want from you."

Her eyes were warm as she looked up at him. "I want it, too, Dane. I want it from all my men."

"Then you'll have it." He got up and allowed Cooper to take his place.

Cooper kissed her, pulling her against his body and rubbing himself all over her. The minute he moved, Landon was all over her. None of them wanted to wait. They all wanted their kisses. And they were about to get a whole lot more.

"Landon, I know how much you love our sub's breasts. Why don't you get them ready for her clamps?" Dane asked.

"Absolutely," Landon agreed. He wrapped her in his arms and forced her chest up so his mouth was level with her breasts. He sucked a nipple into his mouth, pulling hard on it.

Alea's breath hitched, her whole body wrapping around Landon as he began to suckle her breasts. Landon lavished them with affection, biting and sucking and rubbing his face against her. He made sure her nipples were hard little nubs, ready for the kiss of the clamp.

Landon pulled back, and Cooper had already moved into position. They were already a well-oiled machine. Cooper got behind her, his big hands cupping the breasts Lan had made ready. He held them up like the ripest of fruit, offering them to Dane.

Dane held the clamps up, allowing them to dangle so she could see them. "The rubies will look beautiful against your skin. Well, this pretty red glass will."

Alea shook her head. "You're kidding, right? Tal doesn't do anything halfway. Those are two carats apiece, and I assure you they're natural and not lab created. Welcome to your new world, gentlemen."

Fuck. He was about to clamp his sub with a hundred thousand dollars' worth of jewels. Before it would have made him nervous, but now he was happy they were real. She deserved real. Alea didn't need money from him. She had millions in her trust funds. But he did have something she needed, something only he could give her. He had his love, and she'd made him realize that his love was worth something. "I assume the actual clamp is real gold. All the better to bite you with, my dear."

He took the left peak in one hand and twisted it with a nasty little nip before sliding the clamp on and tightening it. She would definitely feel that. He gave the right nipple the same attention before he clamped it and sat back to look at his handiwork.

Her breasts were gorgeous, the nipples a dark red. He'd been right. The rubies shone against the gold of her skin, making her look like a work of art. They would bounce with her breasts when they finally fucked her.

Dane got to his feet and made quick work of his boots and slacks, tossing them aside and setting his cock free. He was harder than he could imagine. The damn thing was nearly pulsing in his palm.

"Lea, it's time to serve your Masters." He stepped in front of her, placing his hand on her hair. "I love you, you know that, right? You can stop this at any time, and we'll take it slower. We can take all night." His dick protested, but his dick wasn't as important as she was.

She smiled up at him. "I'm fine, Dane. This is nothing like what happened to me. This is warm and loving. I'm not going to let what happened then hold me back now. Yes, I'm ready to serve my Masters because they serve me so well. I want to return the favor."

A savage joy raced through him. She was fine. And it was time to push some boundaries. "Gentlemen, why don't you join me? It's time to see just how sweet our submissive's mouth is."

Dane held his cock out and everything in him tightened as he gripped her hair and let his Dominant nature flow.

* * * *

Alea looked at the cock in front of her and felt her eyes widen because Dane's big, beautiful cock wasn't alone for long. Cooper came to his left side and Landon to his right. Both had their cocks in hand, looking down at her with hot eyes.

Her whole body felt like it was on fire. Dane was a damn fine erotic torturer. She'd hoped that they would just fall on her and start the evening right, but no. That wasn't Dom Dane's way. Her Master wanted to make her crazy for him, Lan, and Coop before he was going to give her what she needed so badly.

But it didn't matter. All that counted was that all three of her men were here and there were no more problems between them. The shadows of the past had been exposed to the light, and she didn't need to cling to them anymore. She could be with these men and figure out who she was becoming. She couldn't go back to the girl she'd been, but she could move forward and be a woman they would all be proud of. A woman who was strong enough to survive. A woman who could love the way she needed to love, without apologies and with a heart full of passion.

If Dane Mitchell thought this was torture, well, two could play that game.

She leaned forward and licked at the head of the thick purple cock in front of her. Dane didn't say a word, but she could see how every muscle of his body tightened, and he was forced to change his stance so he wasn't off balance. A little pearl of silky fluid pulsed from the slit of his dick. Yeah, he wasn't as calm as he wanted her to believe. He was right here with her, desperate to connect in the way they only could through play.

Alea moaned a little as she swept the salty fluid up with her tongue and sucked the head of Dane's cock into her mouth. She lightly scraped him with her teeth, then rolled her tongue around the head. She'd thought she wouldn't love this, serving her lover in this way, but she'd been wrong. She loved sucking their cocks and feeling them in her mouth. So much power and so much trust between them.

She sucked Dane in long passes, forcing her jaw open a little more each time.

"God, baby, you give the best head. Do you have any idea what your mouth does to me?" Dane growled the words.

Alea let her eyes drift up to see Dane was watching his cock disappear between her lips. His face was a hard mask of desire. His hands tightened in her hair, pulling her hard onto his cock.

"Take more. Let me feel the back of your throat."

He was huge, but she worked at getting him all the way in her mouth, until he filled every inch and she couldn't move her tongue, could only move her mouth over and over his cock.

She pulled away finally, turning slightly toward Cooper. She had more than one Master. A long sexy huff came from Cooper's chest as he pulled her toward him.

"Take my dick, baby," Cooper said, his voice a harsh grind of words. "I want to feel you."

"You suck their cocks, Lea," Dane commanded. "You don't stop until I tell you to."

He moved away, and she got the feeling that he was going to play some more. He liked to challenge her, and he had a pervertedly devious mind.

She sucked on Cooper's cock as she heard Dane moving

around in the background, opening doors and pulling out drawers. What was he planning?

It didn't matter because she was caught in the moment. She loved the way Cooper tasted. Of all three of her almost-husbands, he was the one who loved to talk during sex.

"I love how hot your mouth is. It's so fucking tight, Lea. Cup my balls." The hand in her hair became demanding, pulling and pushing her.

She reached a hand up and cupped his testicles. Landon hovered close, his hand on her shoulder as he watched her suck his best friend's cock. She loved the way he didn't blink, just stared. There was no jealousy between them, just lust and love. She reached up and gripped Landon's cock, running her hand across the velvety flesh.

"Tighter, harder," he commanded. "Be rough with me, Lea. I can handle it."

She moved between the two of them, sucking each and running her tongue from tip to balls where she drew them into her mouth and reveled in the way her men shook.

She felt Dane move in behind her. "Keep it up, Lea. You're handling them beautifully."

And then she gasped because Dane spread the cheeks of her ass and chilly lube dribbled between them.

So much sensation. She felt alive from her scalp to her nipples, to her pussy and ass now clenching in anticipation.

"Don't stop sucking, Lea, or we'll have to start all over again. Right from the beginning." She could hear the sadistic chuckle in Dane's words.

He was going to kill her. She couldn't go back. She was dying now. She sucked Landon's cock in her mouth while she stroked Cooper's.

Dane's fingers, warm and insistent, played at the ring of her ass, pressing in and circling. She shivered, but she didn't stop running her tongue over Lan. She wasn't going to let Dane win. This was play, but she was going to win.

She switched to Cooper as Dane breached her ass, his

finger rimming her before going deep.

"You can't keep me out," Dane murmured. "In a minute, you're going to wonder why you ever wanted to. Let me show you a little trick. Keep pleasing Cooper and Lan, and I'll give you a treat."

She really wanted a treat. She wanted her men's cocks but Dane seemed determined to make this last hours.

A second finger joined the first, but not in her ass. This clever finger found her pussy and drove deep.

It wasn't nearly enough, but it felt so good. She pressed back.

Cooper groaned. "Whatever you're doing, man, keep it up. Every time she moans, I feel it on my cock. I don't know how long I'll last."

Dane was moving again, both fingers fucking into her. His free hand was around her waist, holding her still. "Don't you come. Tonight we come together inside her. But she deserves to come more than once. After all, she has three men. She deserves all the orgasms we can wring out of her."

Cooper pulled away. She looked to Lan, but he shook his head. "I'm close too, baby. That mouth of yours feels so damn good. Go on and get on your hands and knees. If Dane is doing what I think he's doing, it's going to be easier for you."

He helped her ease to the floor, and she felt Dane's thumb slip over her clit.

Oh, holy hell. Her whole body felt like it was going to light up. He had fingers in her pussy and her ass and he was rubbing her clit. Lan slipped a hand under her and played with the clamps, making her breasts flare. The sensation went straight to her pussy. She'd thought she was wet before, but now she felt her arousal peak, making her warm and wet. She felt Cooper's hands on her, stroking down her back.

"Give it to us, darlin'. I want to watch you come," he said. "Do you like having something hard and warm in your pussy and your ass?"

She nodded. Dane had found a rhythm, his fingers fucking into her before he finished with a long slow glide over her clit, only to start the whole process over again.

A loud *smack* cracked through the air, and Alea yelped.

"I asked you a question, Lea," Cooper said, his hand touching where he'd just smacked. He seemed to be finding his inner Dom.

"Yes, Master," she replied.

"Yes, what?"

He wasn't going to let her get away with anything. Dane's fingers were moving faster, making her blood pump and taking her breath away, but if she didn't give Cooper what he wanted, Dane might stop. "Yes, I like his fingers in my pussy and my ass."

"That's my sub," Cooper said.

Lan twisted the right clamp, and Alea gasped. Dane found some magic place, and suddenly she went off like a rocket, the orgasm detonating deep in her body.

As she came down from the high, Dane pulled his hand free. "That was beautiful, Lea. I'm going to clean up while Lan and Cooper get you on the bed. I don't want to wait another second to get inside you."

She sagged in Lan's arms. He moved her so he could get an arm under her legs. He picked her up as he stood, his strong body never showing a bit of strain. She loved it when they carried her around. It made her feel delicate and feminine and so beloved.

Lan looked down at her, a smile tilting up the corner of his lips. His blue eyes were shining. "I love you, Lea."

Her Landon. He was so sweet under that badass exterior. He was her protector, the silent one who had always been there, waiting to step in front of whatever came her way. "I love you, too. So much."

He took her to the big bed in the back of the room. Cooper was already there, lying on his back, his arms open. His muscular body was spread out for her pleasure. Her

Cooper. He was the one who always made her laugh, who kept the peace between them all when her stubborn nature surfaced.

"Come here, baby. I want you to ride my cock."

Lan set her on the bed, helping her to mount Cooper. Her body was already coming to life again.

"I need to get the clamps off first," Dane said, joining them on the bed. "I can't leave them on too long."

Her Dane. He was the one who held them together, the immovable object who wouldn't allow them to drift apart. He'd been willing to fight everyone, even her, to make a place in her life. They were here because of him.

Her men. Her loves.

Cooper moved between her legs and she felt the head of his cock probing. He rolled his hips up and filled her with one hard thrust. "That's where I've wanted to be all day. Now hold still and let them do what they need to do."

It was hard to do when she could feel Cooper so deep inside her. All she wanted to do was ride that cock, but his hands were tight on her hips, holding her in place.

"This is going to hurt, but only for a second." Dane was to her right, his hand moving for her breast.

"I'll make the pain go away," Lan promised.

They moved almost as one, both men removing the clamps from her nipples, while Cooper held her, his hips moving just a little, keeping them connected.

The blood rushed back into her nipples and she screamed, but her men were ready. Dane and Lan lowered their heads, each taking a tortured nipple into his mouth and soothing it with their tongues.

The pain that had flooded her sent a jolt of adrenaline through her system, rousing her from the drugged feeling the last orgasm had left her with. She came back to vibrant life as they suckled her nipples and Cooper filled her pussy.

Dane came off her nipple and kissed her roughly. His cock was straining and there was a tube of lubricant in his hand. "I love you, Lea. Are you ready?"

Was she ready to have all three of her men at the same time? Hell yes. She wasn't afraid of being held down by them. Dane would cover her body with his, but she wouldn't be caged. She was never more free than when she was with her men. "Yes."

Dane kissed her again and disappeared from the bed. Lan got up on his knees, offering her his cock. She couldn't help but admire those perfect abs and his cut chest. He was beautiful from his sandy hair to his strong legs to his thick cock.

"Suck me, Lea. I want to come in your mouth."

She felt the bed dip as Dane moved in behind her. Cooper in her pussy, Lan in her mouth, and Dane taking her ass. With a smile, she leaned over and licked at Lan's cock.

"Take a deep breath, then let it out, baby. You're ready for this." Dane rubbed more lube on her empty, clenching hole before lining up his cock. She could feel him, his hands gripping her waist as his cock probed.

He was so much bigger than the plug, and Cooper was enormous in her pussy.

"It's all right, baby." Lan smoothed her hair back. "He'll fit. It's just going to feel like he's splitting you in two for a minute. Then you'll stretch, and it'll feel so good."

"Done this much, Lan?" Alea was panting. The pressure was making her crazy.

"Don't make me spank you, Lea," Dane warned.

Lan winked down at her. "Yeah, baby, don't make us stop and spank you."

She had to watch her mouth. "You don't have to spank me. I'll be good."

Maybe it was best that he just shoved something in her mouth so she couldn't say anything sarcastic. A light joy overtook her. She wasn't worried about anything now. She was fully here with them. The past could never go away, but now she could see that it had brought her to this glorious future.

She sucked Landon into her mouth as Dane breached her ass. God, she was full, so full. They took up all the space inside her, clear to her heart, and Dane was ruthless. He wouldn't stop, gave her no moment to pause, simply fed his never-ending cock into her in one slow thrust. Dane and Cooper held on, forcing her to be still as they invaded, heating her from the inside out. She was full to bursting and they held themselves inside her.

"You ready, Cooper?" Dane asked, his voice a low rasp.

"She's so fucking tight. I won't last long." Cooper's hands were restless on her skin.

"I know I won't last long either." Lan winked down at her as he thrust into her mouth, filling her with his clean, masculine taste.

Her core was already humming, her skin sizzling with anticipation. She worked Lan's cock, trying to concentrate. She ran her tongue over him and sucked hard, trying to draw him out. His pleasure was her goal.

"None of us is going to last, but the good news is we've got about fifty or sixty years to perfect it. I'll take that. Let's give this a shot." Dane started to pull out of her ass, and she couldn't help the gasp that erupted from her. Every nerve ending in her backside screamed with pleasure.

Dane pulled out while Cooper thrust up, his pelvis grinding at her clit.

Pure sensation wracked her. She sucked at Landon, trying to stave off the moment when she exploded. It felt so good, so sweet as she was rocked between them. She never wanted it to end. She was completely surrounded, utterly taken by them.

They found a pounding rhythm. In and out. Out and in. Someone was always deep inside her, filling her and bringing her closer and closer to the edge.

All the while she sucked at Landon. He fucked her mouth hard, thrusting until his cock hit the back of her throat.

She swallowed hard and felt him pulse as warm come coated her tongue.

"That's right, baby. That's what I need." Landon moaned, falling back as he popped out of her mouth.

As though they had been waiting, Dane and Cooper tightened, holding her close as they picked up the pace. She felt a hand slip between her and Cooper. Lan was on his knees beside her, helping his partners out.

"Give it to us, baby," Landon said.

Alea rocked between them, her whole body on the edge, every sense engaged with them. They were her whole world, her sight and smell and feel. Her future.

Dane thrust in, his cock going deep, lighting her up. She rode the wave, rolling her hips, riding them as hard as they were riding her. She belonged here, with her men around her, worshipping her and allowing her to love them back.

Lan's fingers pinched her clit and the orgasm was on her, more powerful than anything she'd felt before. She screamed with the pleasure, her whole body going nuclear. She felt Dane come, his big body shuddering as he spilled hot jets inside her.

And then Cooper thrust up, his cock surging and spilling, heating her.

She collapsed onto Cooper, Dane at her back. There wasn't any room for fear now. She laid her head on Cooper's chest as Dane rolled off, sliding to her side and wrapping an arm around her. Lan smiled down at her.

Dane's hand found her belly, his palm resting over the spot where their baby lay. "Get used to this. No more sleeping alone for you."

Tears filled her eyes even as her body still pulsed with the love they'd made.

She wouldn't be alone again. Not ever.

Epilogue

Eleven months later

The palace was filled with cries. They seemed to ring down the hallways at all hours of the night. The babies, born so close together, seemed to know when the other was awake, and they would yell out in chorus as though they were linked.

Alea heard Matin start to cry and wondered how long it would be before Piper's son howled in sympathy. Sabir, the future sheikh of Bezakistan, was a few months older than Alea's baby, but he was already turning over and trying to watch out for his cousin.

Alea picked up her sweet Mat and cuddled him, hoping to settle him down before the whole palace was up.

"Hey, baby, just bring him into bed." Lan stood in the doorway yawning.

She glanced at the rocker. "I can nurse him in here and then the three of you can get some sleep."

Coop strode up, looking over Lan's shoulder. His face lit up when he saw Mat. "We don't sleep when you're not around. Come on. Bring Matty to bed. You know he'll be up for an hour. Besides, it's close to dawn and we have to prepare for the trip to New York. The plane leaves in four hours. We can sleep on the plane."

She heard Dane's laugh as he joined them. "Sleep on the plane? With two babies? You are an eternal optimist, man. Besides, I just turned on the news and you're never going to believe what I saw."

She still wasn't in love with reporters, but she followed her men into their bedroom to hear the latest. The nursery was a new addition to their wing in the palace. It made nursing her very hungry little guy so much easier. She settled on to the bed and saw that Dane had paused one of the morning shows. She'd barely uncapped her nursing bra before Mat had latched on and was enthusiastically sucking. He was a world champion nurser. She smiled down at his tuft of dark hair. He was the most beautiful thing in the world. "Are they covering the speech at the UN?"

She was due to talk about human trafficking in front of the United Nations Council as a part of her organization's push to raise awareness. All during her pregnancy she'd worked hard. She'd grown the charity with her new friends and she'd seen a counselor who helped her break through the chains she'd been in since that terrible day. And she'd basked in the love of her husbands.

Sometimes bad things happened to the right people. Dane had told her that. Sometimes terrible things happened, but when the right person pushed through and found the other side, she could be a hand to lead others. She could be a voice for those who had none.

"They won't cover your speech until Wednesday, baby. I have a whole lineup of interviews for you. Don't give me that look. You have to do them." Dane had taken over a position with the charity, organizing and planning her appearances. He was a whiz at getting her the best spots. "No, this is about our old friends at Anthony Anders Investigations."

He clicked the remote and the broadcast began.

Dominic Anthony and the Anders brothers, Lawson and Riley. She hadn't talked to them in a couple of months. They had sent Mat a lovely baby gift, but from what she understood, they were involved in a big case.

A picture of a beautiful blonde in a designer wedding gown filled the screen.

"Heiress Kinley Kohl was kidnapped yesterday afternoon from her hotel room in New York City. She was preparing for her five o'clock wedding to the controversial tycoon Greg Jansen. FBI sources have been quietly investigating Jansen for possible criminal activity, but no charges have been filed. At first Miss Kohl was considered a runaway bride, but security camera footage shows the bride in a laundry bin, being hauled out of the hotel by two men dressed as employees."

The grainy security footage flashed on. It was of two men rolling a large laundry cart down a hallway. The top of the cart opened and a woman's head popped out, complete with a veil. She shook a fist and tried to climb out, but one of the men stuffed a rag over her face, and she relaxed in his arms. He was deeply tender as he placed her back in the bin, smoothing the veil down so it didn't cover her face. The men seemed to argue for a moment, and then the camera caught a face.

"Holy shit, that's Law," Cooper said, staring at the TV.

"It could be Riley. They look so alike." Lan looked closer. "Nah, you're right. Only Law can look that mean. Damn. I figured they were serious about finding a woman to share, but I didn't think they would kidnap one."

The report went on, naming the Anders brothers and their boss, Dominic Anthony, as the men responsible for the heiress's abduction.

"Something's up with them. Damn, but I would like to know what," Dane said with a wolfish grin. "I'll have to see if I can get in touch when we get to the States. Well, if they haven't already been arrested, that is."

"Maybe we can offer them asylum in Bezakistan," Cooper offered.

Alea frowned. "They just kidnapped a woman."

But she didn't buy it. She'd gotten to know those men. They were rough but very gentle around women. Dominic had offered his services to her organization, and all three had put in hours of work to shut down trafficking and bring girls home to their families. If they'd taken Kinley Kohl, it was for a good reason.

Alea smiled at Dane. "Give him a call. See if we can help."

It was what she did now. She helped and she opened her heart. She was so much richer for it.

The baby in her arms wriggled, and she settled in. She had a few hours to be warm and peaceful with her guys. Lan cuddled up beside her as Dane started talking about all their plans. Cooper got under the covers, his hand cupping Mat's little head.

Dane stopped at the end of the bed, staring at them. "Hey, have I told you you're beautiful today?"

Tears filled her eyes. He said it every single day, and every day she held the words to her heart and believed them just a little more. She nodded and blew him a kiss.

She was a princess by title, but her men had turned her into a queen.

Read on for excerpts from Shayla Black, Lexi Blake, and Jayne Rylon.

Ours To Love – A Wicked Lovers Novel
by Shayla Black

Coming May 7

Between two brothers…

Xander Santiago spent years living it up as a billionaire playboy. Never given a chance to lead his family business in the boardroom, he became a Master in the bedroom instead. His older brother inherited the company and worked tirelessly to make it an empire. But while the cutthroat corporate espionage took its toll on Javier, nothing was as devastating as the seemingly senseless murder of his wife. It propelled him into a year of punishing rage and guilt…until Xander came to his rescue.

Comes an irresistible woman …

Eager to rejuvenate Javier's life, Xander shanghais him to Louisiana where they meet the beautiful London McLane. After surviving a decade of tragedy and struggle, London is determined to make a fresh start—and these sexy billionaire brothers are more than willing to help. In every way. And London is stunned to find herself open to every heated suggestion…and desperately hoping that her love will heal them.

And inescapable danger …

But a killer with a hidden motive is watching, on a single-minded mission to destroy everything the Santiago brothers hold dear, especially London. And as fear and desire collide, every passionate beat of her heart could be her last.

For more information, pre-order links, and a preview of the first chapter visit shaylablack.com.

Wicked All The Way – A Wicked Lovers Novella

by Shayla Black
Available now!

Retired military colonel Caleb Edgington has spent two long years trying to achieve the most important mission objective of his life—but not behind enemy lines. He's trying to capture a woman with a broken heart. Having lost at love once, he understands being gun shy. The residual fears from Carlotta Buckley's nasty divorce have stood between them, but he's done with that. And he's got the perfect strategy to lure her in…

Carlotta never thought she'd fall in love again. Once bitten, she's now more than twice shy. And Caleb is everything she can't handle—fierce, relentless, uncompromising…sexual. She's managed to mostly avoid him, but now his son and her daughter need their help. Can Caleb and the spirit of the season convince her that she's ready to take a chance on love again?

Excerpt:

"You deserve to be protected and pampered, Lottie. You deserve someone who will be happy to indulge your whims every now and then just for the pleasure of seeing you smile. And you need someone willing to make sure you take care of yourself properly."

Carlotta seemed to hold her breath. She blinked at him. "I am too old now for matters of the heart. I have two beautiful grandsons and—"

"And if you finish that sentence, you won't like what comes next. You are not old." He gritted his teeth, his palm itching to meet her backside. Hell, he hadn't felt an urge to punish a woman this way in years… None of them had mattered enough to try. "Do you hear me, Lottie?"

"Caleb, stop. I know that I am no longer young. Once I

was pretty, like my Kata."

"You're still so goddamn beautiful it makes me hurt to hear that you think otherwise. If you'd give me half a chance, I'd exhaust myself proving over and over how incredibly lovely I think you are."

A pretty rosy flush crept up her cheeks. "I am far too old for sex."

Caleb snorted. Is that what she thought? "Wanna bet? I guarantee you that I could make you think otherwise."

For more information, pre-order links, and a preview of the first chapter visit shaylablack.com.

A Dom Is Forever

by Lexi Blake
Available now!

A Man with a Past...

Liam O'Donnell fled his native Ireland years ago after one of his missions ended in tragedy and he was accused of killing several of his fellow agents. Shrouded in mystery, Liam can't remember that fateful night. He came to the United States in disgrace, seeking redemption for crimes he may or may not have committed. But the hunt for an international terrorist leads him to London and right back into the world he left behind.

A Woman Looking for a Future...

Avery Charles followed her boss to London, eager to help the philanthropist with his many charities. When she meets a mysterious man who promises to show her London's fetish scene, she can't help but indulge in her darkest fantasies. Liam becomes her Dom, her protector, her lover. She opens her heart and her home to him, only to discover he's a man on a mission and she's just a means to an end.

When Avery's boss leads them to the traitorous Mr. Black, Liam must put together the puzzle of his past or Avery might not have a future...

Excerpt:
"I want you." She wanted him so badly. She just didn't trust that he could possibly want her.

"No, you don't, but you will." He stepped back and tucked his shirt in. "We're going to do this my way. We tried yours and it didn't work, so I'm taking control. I should have done it in the first place. If I thought you had some, I would tell you to change into fet wear, but you don't happen to have a corset and some PVC hiding in that closet, do you?"

"I don't know what PVC is," she admitted, her heart aching a little. "I don't think this is a good idea, Lee. I don't think I can be what you need. I'm not experienced, and what experience I have wasn't very good. Don't get me wrong. I loved my husband, but the sex wasn't spectacular. I think I'm just one of those women who can't be sexy. I was trying to please you, but I couldn't."

Even in the dim light, she could see him staring, assessing. "And I think you're one of those women who can't stop thinking long enough to let her body take over. Look, Avery, the sex you've had happened with a kid. Was your husband older than you? More experienced?"

She shook her head. They had both been virgins.

"Then you have no idea what it can be like. I look at sex differently than most people. It's an exchange, and it should be good for both parties. I don't want you to spread your legs and let me have you because you want someone to hold you. If you want me to hold you, ask me. I want you to spread your legs because you can't wait another single second for my cock. I want that pussy ripe and ready and weeping for a big dick to split it wide and have its way. I want your nipples to peak because I walk into a room and you remember every dirty thing I can do to them. I want you to want me. I can make you crave me. I don't want some drive-by fucking that gets me off and I forget it five minutes later. I want to fuck all night long. I want to feel it all the next day because my cock got so used to being deep inside your body. If that's what you want, then get dressed in the sexiest thing you own and agree that I'm the boss when it comes to sex." He turned and walked out. "I'll give you five minutes to decide. I'll be waiting in your living room. If you really want me, you'll dress exactly how I've told you to dress and you'll present yourself to me for inspection. And Avery, no bra and no underwear. You won't need them."

The door closed behind him, and she had to remember how to breathe.

She wasn't sexy. She wasn't orgasmic.

But what if she could be? Lee hadn't been right about everything, but he had a few points. He'd told her he wanted to be in control and then she'd tried to make all the decisions. He had more experience, but she'd decided she knew best. She hadn't listened to him.

He wanted control. He wanted her to really want him. She didn't understand, but if she ever wanted to understand, she had to try.

She'd taught herself how to walk again. That had been an enormous mountain to climb. Why was she so scared of this? She'd faced worse, but she was cowering in her boots over not wearing underwear and a bra? She'd lost so much. Was she willing to lose this, too?

What was she really risking? She might look dumb. She could end up with her heart broken, but at least she would have proven it still worked.

She'd come across the ocean to change her life—to have a life. What was life without a few risks?

She got her phone out and sent a quick text to Adam letting him know she was home and who she was with so if she was serially murdered, at least they would have a starting place for where to find her body.

But she was going to do this because she felt safe with Lee. And because she wanted to finally understand what it really meant to want someone.

For more information, visit www.LexiBlake.net.

Pick Your Pleasure

By Jayne Rylon
Available now!

Ever read a book and wish the heroine hadn't done that, gone there, or slept with that guy? Well, now you're in charge. The reader decides what happens here.

Tailor your perfect short story or be adventurous and read through all the different paths to see where life can take you…if you choose.

Go ahead, pick your pleasure.

Linley Lane, CEO of Lane Technologies, has had enough of blah dates. When she decides to shake things up with a visit to an underground sex club she's heard rumors about, she realizes she's way out of her league. This is no usual hookup spot.

Presented with two potential guides for the night—men who turn her on more in a matter of minutes than a year of lame dating in her high-class circles did—she's got some tough decisions to make about how she wants to spend the rest of her evening and just how dirty she intends to get.

Will she choose to be romanced by a sexy gentleman? Or will she indulge the rare anonymity Underground affords to revel in wild excess with a like-minded rebel? And where will they go from there?

Excerpt:

"You'll require a guide for your adventure tonight." her greeter said as if he could sense the uncertainty swirling around her brain. "New members are always paired with a veteran on their first go around to ensure their enjoyment."

"I thought that was your job?" She tipped her head as she examined his expression.

"I wish I were so lucky." He gave her a tiny bow.

"Chase and Ryder have both offered their company this evening. We'll leave the choice to you. Play nice, boys."

The greeter winked at her before retreating, perhaps to collect another very willing guest from the garage.

"So long as I don't have to fight fair." The bump on scruffy guy's nose attested to his experience with brawling. She felt bad for prince charming across the table if things came to blows.

"Wouldn't expect you to, Ryder." The burnished blond shook his head though he smiled as he said it.

Dashing, dangerous, and devilish, Ryder scooted closer and laid his palm high on her thigh. Entirely too close to the hem of her dress for someone she hadn't even officially been introduced to yet.

Denying the electricity his skin conducted would have been pure insanity. Hot and firm, his touch did things to her she'd never imagined possible with a single contact. He didn't wait for her approval or shrink from her—Linley Lane, CEO.

Was it like this for other women? Or was this man something special?

A tiny connection and he did more for her than the parade of perfect men who'd come before him. She blew out a sigh that ruffled her bangs, washing her cheeks with a cool breeze.

"Hands off my lady, please." Chase didn't seem disturbed by the zero-to-a-million-and-sixty approach Ryder adopted with her. His quiet confidence made her do a double take at his model good looks. Hell, he had most of Hollywood beat in her book.

Piercing blue eyes met her curious stare. He didn't flinch from her inspection. Patient yet persistent, he waited for her to look her fill. With thick lashes and a couple of laugh lines that hinted at a good nature, she hoped she wasn't drooling.

What were the odds? Two men. Both of whom she had compelling—if completely opposite—chemistry with.

317

Hot damn.

Linley licked her lips.

"Would you care for a drink?" Chase's smooth baritone made her blink twice before she deciphered his offer.

"Yes, please." She studied his expert handling of the bottle, impressed with how he poured the crisp liquid without spilling a single bubbly drop. When she reached for the stemware he proffered, he surprised her by clasping her fingers in a gentle yet sure hold then dusting the back of her hand with his lips.

A tantalizing appetizer.

Before she could dig in, he slipped the glass into her hand and wrapped her fingers around the delicate crystal.

"What century are you from?" Ryder growled as he ignored his rival to focus on her. "Either way, you'll be ancient before you get to the good shit with him."

The rebel's fingers hadn't moved from her leg. Well, maybe they had. Higher.

Instead of creeping her out, his deft massage encouraged Linley to sink into the tufted velvet, allowing her thighs to relax and part. Just a bit.

"You didn't come here tonight to be bored, did you?" Ryder reached across her to cup her cheek in his broad, slightly callused hand while the other continued to mesmerize her with his intuitive knowledge of her erogenous zones. Nudging her chin up, he forced her to meet his gaze. His fingers curled around her nape, and he leaned forward until his lips nearly collided with hers. "Pick me. I'll make sure you never forget the night you decided to be a bad girl."

When she nearly succumbed to the promise of his slightly rough cheek to steal a kiss, he retreated, though his skilled fingers continued their insidious assault.

"I hardly call romance dull." Chase sipped from his glass, reminding her of the treat fizzing away before her.

Linley downed a swallow or two. Moisture gathered at the corner of her mouth. Before she could reach for her napkin, Chase swiped a droplet from her lips with his thumb then sampled the mingled flavor of the alcohol and her skin.

"Delicious." He savored the taste and looked like he might go for another.

She wished he would. Instead he withheld the pleasure, making her yearn for more.

A glint from Ryder's direction had her glancing away in time to see him chug his drink then pour another round. The powerful flex of his throat—primal and strong—inspired her. In her mind, she could picture nibbling the cords there as he rode her. With him, she wouldn't have to beg for what she wanted.

He wouldn't make her take.

So many times, she had to be the aggressor. In meetings. In dating. Handing over the reins would be a welcome relief. This man would afford her that luxury.

When he was down to the last sip of the second round, he held it in his mouth and set his glass on the table with a clunk. This time he didn't stop when he swooped in. His lips landed on hers without apology.

Ryder proved that though he might lack stealth, he had finesse in abundance. His mouth turned hers pliant as he shared the rich drink and a taste of what a night with him would be like. He sucked on her tongue, using the slightest edge of his teeth to awaken nerves gone drowsy with an intoxicating blend of allures.

When he withdrew, he bit her lip lightly, letting the subtle sting remind her of the things he'd done to her body without effort. Her nipples rubbed against the padding of her bra. She attempted to cross her legs to appease the part of her that screamed for pressure right where she needed it most.

To her surprise, it was Chase who prevented her from trapping Ryder's palm between her thighs. "No, love. Don't hide. You didn't come here tonight for that."

"And what if I've changed my mind?" Having two men bracketing her, promising her their own brand of sexy fun, overwhelmed her. For a moment, she wondered if she could handle it. Or would she disappoint them? It wasn't like she had a ton of experience.

"Then let me take you home." Chase's solution seemed genuine. "That's not code for anything, by the way. I'll drop you at your door, safe and sound, if you'd prefer."

"No one's forcing her." Ryder seemed offended. "But I won't let you lie to yourself, wildcat. You came hunting for this. You're soaked. My finger isn't sliding around on its own down there. I'll make it easy for you, give you things you never dreamed you needed."

Linley's head thunked against the seat as she dropped it backward. "Too bad I can't have you both."

Ryder laughed. The easy, boisterous sound made it clear he did it often. With gusto. "In my world, that's an option. Here we're Underground. The next level below us is called Downstairs. I hang out a bit deeper. The Basement of the club offers the possibility of ménage, among other more daring pursuits. Chase doesn't sink that low, though."

She peeked up in time to catch the other man's tiny frown.

"That's true," Chase confirmed. "I prefer to stick to Downstairs. And I fly solo. I assure you, you won't need other men when you have my full attention. For dipping your toe in, I recommend the first level of the club. Perfect for wading."

"Screw that. Jump into the deep end." Ryder lifted his palm from her saturated thigh, licked his finger, and then held out his hand. "I won't let you drown."

"Neither will I." Chase extended one of his as well.

"So, who will it be, Linley?" She didn't have time to wonder how they knew her name.

Instead she searched inside and uttered her preference for tonight.

If Linley said Chase click here or search for Linley picked Chase

If Linley said Ryder click here or search for Linley picked Ryder

For more information, visit http://jaynerylon.com/

About the Authors

Shayla Black (aka Shelley Bradley) is the New York Times and USA Today bestselling author of over 30 sizzling contemporary, erotic, paranormal, and historical romances for multiple print, electronic, and audio publishers. She lives in Texas with her husband, munchkin, and one very spoiled cat. In her "free" time, she enjoys reality TV, reading and listening to an eclectic blend of music.

Shayla's work has been translated in about a dozen languages. She has also received or been nominated for The Passionate Plume, The Holt Medallion, Colorado Romance Writers Award of Excellence, and the National Reader's Choice Awards. RT Bookclub has twice nominated her for Best Erotic Romance of the year, as well as awarded her several Top Picks, and a KISS Hero Award.

A writing risk-taker, Shayla enjoys tackling writing challenges with every book. Find Shayla at www.ShaylaBlack.com or visit her on her Shayla Black Author Facebook page.

Connect with Shayla online:

Facebook: www.facebook.com/ShaylaBlackAuthor
Twitter: www.twitter.com/@shayla_black
Smashwords:
www.smashwords.com/profile/view/ShaylaBlack
Website: www.shaylablack.com

Lexi Blake lives in North Texas with her husband, three kids, and the laziest rescue dog in the world. She began writing at a young age, concentrating on plays and journalism. It wasn't until she started writing romance that she found success. She likes to find humor in the strangest places. Lexi believes in happy endings no matter how odd the couple, threesome or foursome may seem. She also writes contemporary western ménage as Sophie Oak.

Connect with Lexi online:

Facebook: Lexi Blake
Twitter: www.twitter.com/@authorlexiblake
Smashwords: www.smashwords.com/profile/view/LexiBlake
Website: www.LexiBlake.net

Also from Shayla Black/Shelley Bradley:
EROTIC ROMANCE
THE WICKED LOVERS
Wicked Ties
Decadent
Delicious
Surrender To Me
Belong To Me
"Wicked to Love" (e-novella)
Mine To Hold
"Wicked All The Way" (e-novella)
Coming Soon:
Ours To Love
"Wicked All Night" - Wicked And Dangerous Anthology
Theirs To Cherish

SEXY CAPERS
Bound And Determined
Strip Search
"Arresting Desire" – Hot In Handcuffs Anthology

MASTERS OF MÉNAGE (by Shayla Black and Lexi Blake)
Their Virgin Captive
Their Virgin's Secret
Their Virgin Concubine
Their Virgin Princess
Coming Soon:
Their Virgin Hostage

DOMS OF HER LIFE (by Shayla Black, Jenna Jacob, and
Isabella LaPearl)
One Dom To Love
Coming Soon:
The Young And The Submissive

Stand Alone Titles

Naughty Little Secret (as Shelley Bradley)
"Watch Me" – Sneak Peek Anthology (as Shelley Bradley)
Dangerous Boys And Their Toy
"Her Fantasy Men" – Four Play Anthology

PARANORMAL ROMANCE
THE DOOMSDAY BRETHREN
Tempt Me With Darkness
"Fated" (e-novella)
Seduce Me In Shadow
Possess Me At Midnight
"Mated" – Haunted By Your Touch Anthology
Entice Me At Twilight
Embrace Me At Dawn

HISTORICAL ROMANCE (as Shelley Bradley)
The Lady And The Dragon
One Wicked Night
Strictly Seduction
Strictly Forbidden
Coming Soon:
His Lady Bride, Brothers in Arms (Book 1)
His Stolen Bride, Brothers in Arms (Book 2)
His Rebel Bride, Brothers in Arms (Book 3)

CONTEMPORARY ROMANCE (as Shelley Bradley)
A Perfect Match

Also from Lexi Blake:

MASTERS AND MERCENARIES
The Dom Who Loved Me
The Men With The Golden Cuffs
A Dom Is Forever
Coming in 2013:
On Her Master's Secret Service
Love and Let Die

MASTERS OF MÉNAGE (by Shayla Black and Lexi Blake)
Their Virgin Captive
Their Virgin's Secret
Their Virgin Concubine
Their Virgin Princess
Coming Soon:
Their Virgin Hostage